THE CLUB

... AND PEACE THE WORLD OVER

About the Author

After a long career in the public sector, James Barrett retired to Suffolk with his wife, Gillian. He has been a Rotarian for a number of years, presently with the Diss & District Club, and before that at Framlingham, where he served as President and Secretary, and High Suffolk, where he was Secretary. Aside from Rotary, he has been Chairman of the Management Commitee of a Community Transport Company, and Secretary to four local charities. Some years ago, he ran the London Marathon and now keeps fit running the footpaths near where he lives.

THE CLUB

... AND PEACE THE WORLD OVER

JAMES BARRETT

Matador
Unit E2 Airfield Business Park,
Harrison Road, Market Harborough,
Leicestershire. LE16 7UL
Tel: 0116 2792299
Email: books@troubador.co.uk
Web: www.troubador.co.uk/matador
Twitter: @matadorbooks

ISBN 978 1803135 106

British Library Cataloguing in Publication Data.
A catalogue record for this book is available from the British Library.

Printed and bound in Great Britain by CMP UK
Typeset in 11pt Minion Pro by Troubador Publishing Ltd, Leicester, UK

Matador is an imprint of Troubador Publishing Ltd

To Gillian

PROLOGUE

He drained his whisky glass and set it down beside the lead crystal decanter, now half-empty. He could feel his heart pounding inexorably as he opened the gun cabinet and carefully lifted out his old Beretta 12-bore shotgun. There was a tremor in his fingers as he fumbled for some cartridges and loaded it.

'What are you doing?' she said. 'This isn't the Wild West.'

'It's just a precaution.'

'But you wouldn't actually use it, would you?'

'If I see headlights outside and a large figure carrying a shotgun gets out of the car… I might just have to.'

A tension now gripped both of them. He said, 'The brute is a fearsome sight at any time, but worsted by drink and bearing a shotgun, who knows what he might do?'

The old film was still flickering on the television screen and Cary Grant threw himself to the ground to avoid a low-flying biplane. They waited. At half past two, she went into the kitchen to make coffee. He raised himself slowly from his comfortable armchair and stretched. He shivered; the fire was dying. He picked up another log and dropped it onto the glowing embers. Yellow flames licked up the side of the log, as the fire crackled back to life.

The dog became restless and growled. 'What is it, old chap?' he said, as the warm glow of whisky gave way to a pain in the pit of his stomach and his bowels turned to water. This was it; the moment he dreaded. He turned off the lights and scrabbled for his shotgun in the dim luminosity from the fire. He heard a door open and close. 'What are you doing?'

Before she could answer, the dog ran out through the kitchen door, around onto the drive and activated a security light. There was a brilliant flash and a loud report. The dog fell. It cried piteously as it tried desperately to stand, but its hind quarters had been shattered. Another shot; the dog jerked and collapsed into a pool of blood. It lay still and silent in the blackness, as the security light turned off. The wind gusted and howled, and the rain lashed down relentlessly in an endeavour to wash away the stain of the barbarity that had just taken place.

'What have they done to Humphrey?' She was now in a blind panic. He was unable to answer. His eyes filled with tears and his throat tightened with tension at the savage destruction of his faithful old dog; rage overcame his fear. Something or someone activated a security light again. He stood away from the window and pulled her with him. He heard a blast from a gunshot and a crash. An upstairs window shattered. A second shot rang out and another window shattered. He calculated that the shooter was now reloading. He parted the curtains, opened the window and raised his own shotgun. There was a binding flash: the window exploded with a massive bang. The whole house shook and he fell to the ground. She was at his side in an instant. She cradled his head and looked into the bloody mess that was his face. He was unconscious and losing blood rapidly; one ear had been partially severed. 'Speak to me,' she said. There was no response. 'Please don't die.'

She searched desperately for the phone amidst the dust and disorder. A dark red puddle formed on the light-coloured carpet and the tick of the grandfather clock grew louder as it marked the inexorable passing of time. He lay quiet and still, his life slowly ebbing away.

ONE

Five years ago: a fateful encounter

There was a bump and a scraping of metal, but the early morning shoppers in the small Suffolk market town paid little heed. A strongly built man got out of a car, his face contorted with rage, his dark tousled hair dancing in the gusty wind. He glowered at the man in the other vehicle. Then his facial muscles relaxed into a half smile. 'George Woodgate.'

The other man was of more modest proportions and awkward of movement. 'Alec, Alec Barton. I haven't seen you in a long time.' He looked ruefully at the damage to his car.

'Don't worry about that,' said Alec Barton. 'It's just a scratch, nothing much. I know someone who'll sort it out. He owes me a favour.' Alec Barton looked as though he was capable of calling in a favour when the need arose. The

I

two men fell into conversation and soon found themselves by a coffee shop. Alec pushed open the door, and they inhaled the inviting aroma of freshly ground coffee as they stepped into the warm, steamy fug. The Saturday morning shoppers were too busy sipping coffee and chattering to notice the two men who had just walked in. The two men found a vacant table and ordered coffee.

'I really can't remember how long it is since we ran into each other,' said George. 'I've only seen you a dozen or so times since we left school and that's a very long time ago.' George had come into contact with many people in life, through the world of finance, Rotary and other areas of activity, some of whom he regarded as friends, others as mere acquaintances, but he knew that there was something special about the bond that had developed between the two scabby-kneed boys in short trousers, all those years ago. Although George Woodgate could not have known it at the time, this chance encounter would eventually have a devastating effect on his life and the lives of everyone at his Rotary club in the nearby village of Debenham.

'It's been a long time,' Alec said. 'You may remember that I started working in the building industry. Well, I worked hard, and eventually I set up on my own. I'm doing OK.' He spoke with a sense of achievement, but not boastfully. He had been a promising pupil at the village school, almost as bright as George, but he could never commit himself to academic work.

'You went into accountancy, didn't you?' said Alec.

'Yes, but I'm more or less retired now.'

'You went away to that posh school.'

'It wasn't really posh,' said George.

'I could never have gone there.'

'There were fees.'

'Like Eton,' said Alec.

'Nothing like Eton.'

'Nothing like the village school.'

'It was a very long time ago,' said George.

'You lived there,' said Alec.

'Boarded.'

'I hardly saw you after that.'

'I came home for the holidays,' said George.

'You did well,' said Alec. 'I left in disgrace.'

'I heard.'

'You went to Cambridge, didn't you?' said Alec.

'Did you really kick in the side of old Braithwaite's car?'

'I was a bit crazy at that age,' said Alec. 'You knew him?'

'Of him,' said George.

'We all had a good laugh,' Alec gave a rare smile. 'He threw me out of his class. I just happened to be passing by his car at the time.'

'But you didn't just pass it,' said George.

'No, I gave it a good kicking.'

'You were crazy,' said George.

'I didn't go to public school.'

'Independent,' said George.

'Same thing,' said Alec.

'We did a few crazy things at school,' said George.

'Such as?'

'We pretended to hang a junior.'

'That's crazy.'

'Put a rope around his neck and over a pipe in the classroom,' said George.

'Did anyone notice?'

'It was a weekend,' said George. 'The duty master, old Bertram, saw us from the playing fields.'

'He would've had to do a lot of explaining to the Head.'

'He came tearing in and stopped us,' said George.

'You were really going to do it?' said Alec.

'Of course not. Saturdays were rather boring.'

'What did he do?' said Alec.

'Told us not to do it.'

'Hang a junior?'

'Against school rules,' said George.

There was a brief silence and Alec said, 'I got married last year to Karen. She's a hairdresser.'

'I thought you were married.'

'We divorced and then I met Karen.'

'Apart from work, what do you do with yourself these days?' said George.

'Nothing much,' said Alec. 'The business takes up most of my time. I do a bit of gardening at the weekends, the occasional concert, I read the odd book. We went to Glastonbury last year. That was good fun. What about you?'

'I've been in Rotary for many years,' said George. 'I'm also chairman of a local charity. That's quite separate from Rotary, of course.'

'Rotary's all about eating dinners, isn't it?'

'People always say that,' said George. 'We have dinner every Wednesday at our meeting, but we do some useful things as well, such as fundraising for deserving causes.'

'I'd like to join Rotary,' said Alec.

'I wouldn't have thought that it was your thing,' said George.

'What about the charity?' said Alec. 'What do they do?'

'There're three separate charities that together are known as the Morton Charities.'

'Sounds like the Holy Trinity,' said Alec.

'The Morton General Charity pays small eleemosynary pensions to poor and deserving people in the village, from the interest on its endowments,' said George.

'It pays what?'

'It's got income from various endowments,' said George.

'It pays pensions?'

'Eleemosynary pensions.'

'What are they?'

'A pension paid by a charity,' said George. 'And at the end of each year, it divides its surplus cash between the ecclesiastical and civil purposes of the parish.'

'What, half to the church and half to the village; the pious and the impious equally rewarded?'

'The pious live in the village as well,' said George, who felt compelled to correct his friend.

'Yes, I suppose so.'

'There's also income from another endowment from the sale of land that is available to the incumbent of the parish,' said George.

'Who?' said Alec.

'The Rector.'

'What about the other charities?' said Alec.

'And there's the Sick and Poor Fund,' said George.

'Social Security does that, doesn't it?'

'Not when the Sick and Poor Fund was set up,' said George.

'So, it's a top-up?'

George said, 'If someone from the village goes into hospital, for example, we can help out with taxi fares and refreshment in the hospital cafeteria.'

'So, it's three charities?' said Alec.

'Three, under one umbrella charity.'

'Back to the Holy Trinity.'

'There's also the Rufford Trust,' said George.

'What's that?'

'Set up by Brigadier Rufford.'

'They're usually better at killing people,' said Alec.

'Who?'

'The military.'

'He used to live in Rose Cottage,' said George.

'The Brigadier?'

'Years ago.'

The two sat silently for a moment. 'He left it in his will,' said George.

'Where is Rose Cottage?'

'Castle Rudham, just out of the village.'

'In what way is that a charity?'

'It's for the benefit of an elderly and deserving couple of the parish.'

'How did you choose them?'

'His gardener's son is still alive,' said George. 'He's very elderly now.'

'What happens when he dies?' said Alec.

'There's a stipulation in the trust set up by the will.'

'It goes to someone else?'

'We've never actually let Rose Cottage,' said George.

'What about the elderly gardener?' said Alec.

'He's the son of the gardener.'

'The gardener's dead?'

'Years ago.'

'The gardener and his son were granted life tenancies under the will,' said George. 'The son lives there with his wife.'

'I suppose she's elderly too.'

'Rose Cottage is a listed building, sixteenth-century, thatched roof, low beams,' said George. 'We charge them rent, of course, and maintain the property.'

'Rent?'

'Yes, of course.'

'You're supposed to be a charity,' said Alec.

'It's subject to rent control.'

'You'd charge them more if you could?'

'They pay a modest rent.'

'How much?'

'It's young people who need the help these days,' said George, 'with education, getting somewhere to live and so on.'

'I haven't got any children,' said Alec.

'My son lives in Australia,' said George.

'Do you see him often?'

George said, 'Most of the older people I know are pretty well-off. Take Rotary. Most of them have generous private pensions, as well as their state pensions.'

'That sounds like you, George.'

'Many have a fair bit of cash, invested and paying dividends every month.'

'I don't think I'll ever be like that,' said Alec.

They chatted for a little longer and ordered more coffee. 'We should keep in touch,' said George. 'Our families were friends.'

'My mum was your mother's cleaner,' said Alec.

'You saved me from a few run-ins with the bigger boys when we were at school,' said George.

'I fought a few of your battles.'

'No one was eager to take you on,' said George. 'Not after the pasting you gave Billy Jones.'

'Did you know he was killed?' said Alec.

'What happened?'

'Years ago. He used to work on the farms around here and he had an accident.'

'What kind of accident?' said George.

'No one knows. He was ploughing at the time.'

'But he died?'

'Dead by the time they got him to hospital,' said Alec.

'He was probably doing something crazy at the time,' said George.

'Yes, knowing Billy Jones.'

There was a brief silence, then George said, 'I now know why I managed to get into so many scrapes at school.'

'George, you were always argumentative and stubborn. You used to get involved in heated discussions and you always had a different opinion from everyone else. You would keep on and on arguing until someone decided to punch some sense into you.'

'I always stuck with what was right,' said George. 'I still do.'

'Most people call it pig-headed.'

They sipped their coffee silently for a while, then George said, 'You know, my Rotary colleagues have always commented on my bluntness, and my former business colleagues said much the same. Anyway, Erica made me go for a professional diagnosis a few years ago. She says that there are times when I am rude to people, which is not true. I may be direct, but that's not the same. I suppose I am rather literal and some people speak in a roundabout, convoluted way that I don't always follow, which I find extremely irritating.' George paused for a moment. 'We had a bit of a to-do about it, but in the end, I agreed. Anyway, the woman who made the diagnosis told me that I was on the autistic spectrum.'

'How did you feel about that, being given a label?' said Alec.

'In a way, it was a relief.'

'What do you mean?'

'Well, up to then, I'd spent all my life trying to fit in and the diagnosis meant that I no longer felt that I had to,' said George. 'Now, I can be who I am and not worry about it. I feel a great sense of freedom.'

Alec said, 'My mum could have told you that years ago, except that she wouldn't have said autistic spectrum. No one knew anything about spectrums in those days. She used to say, "That George is such a nice little boy, so polite, but there's something very strange about him".'

George said, 'I'm not strange. My brain is wired up differently, so I think differently; that's all. It can be useful. It gives you a different perspective on an issue.'

They finished their coffee and went their separate ways.

TWO

The present: May, two months before the end of the Rotary year, and the end of Frank Wilder's term of office as president of the Rotary Club of Debenham.

'Did you know that there's a "sold" sign outside The Old Forge?' said George as he peered through the window at the house across the lane.

'It's been there for days,' said Erica.

George and Erica had met when she had started working at his firm's offices. She, the tall nubile secretary, had taken an unlikely interest in the gawky young man with a sharp mind, for whom she had felt inexplicable compassion. His capacity for remembering, understanding and regurgitating figures was extraordinary, even for this newly qualified accountant, but he was socially handicapped by something she could not fathom. George took this curiosity on her part as a serious romantic interest but was unsure what to do about it; no woman had fallen in love with him before. He sent flowers to the office, to her acute embarrassment and the amusement of everyone else, not that he noticed. After some awkward moments which, had it been any young woman other than Erica, could have been disastrous, an understanding between them blossomed into romance. Eventually, they married.

'Well, I haven't seen it before,' said George.

'A chap came along in a van,' said Erica.

There were few houses in the narrow lane where the Woodgates lived, near the pretty Suffolk village of Debenham. The River Deben rises just outside the village and flows along a ford, said to be the longest in England. It continues past Woodbridge with its tide mill, whose wheels and stones still grind grain, as they have over the centuries, and continues into a tidal estuary, to enter the North Sea near Felixstowe. The Old Forge was a large, thatched house, with ample land and several shabby outbuildings with rusting corrugated iron roofs. Cedric Elgin, the previous owner, who had been the churchwarden at St Mary's Church in the village for as long as anyone could remember, had died after a short spell in a residential care home. His passion, aside from Anglicanism and gardening, was cricket. Cedric had been steady through his nineties, and it looked as though he might reach his century and carry his bat. However, the nervous nineties are aptly named and on ninety-nine, he faced a vicious googly. Save for his Christian faith, this delivery would send his leg stump spinning into oblivion, but beckoning, was a brilliant light, an irresistible force and the distant sound of the choral music of Thomas Tallis, which had flowed down through the centuries from the time of Henry, the reformation and the dissolution of the monasteries, moving effortlessly between Catholicism and Anglicanism. The irresistible force bore him upwards, into clouds of white and crimson, leaving far below a cadaver of skin and bone and the bed on which he had lain, as he breathed his last.

*

George's early morning walk with his English pointer, Humphrey, took the same route every day. It afforded certainty and familiarity in his daily life; a change of routine would detract from that sureness and could make him anxious. It was the time of day when he could be at peace with himself in bucolic solitude.

A dreary mist hid the early morning sun, and the distant hedgerow formed a line of shadows across the far edge of the field, like ghostly mounted warriors. They waited upon the order to charge and fill the air with an explosion of cannon, thundering hooves, the battle cries of soldiers and the screams of the wounded. The order never came, and they endured, inert, not to disturb the early morning quietude and George's inner tranquillity. Gradually, the shapes changed form, as the mist began to dissolve and a pale watery disc appeared, hanging in the thin air. The heavy ground was beginning to sap the strength from George's legs, until at last he reached the firmness of the road and he was able to stride out. A familiar sound began to run around in his head:

for he might have been a Russian,
a French, or Turk or Prussian,
Or perhaps an Italian!
Or perhaps an Italian!

He was now putting greater energy into his stride, as he swung his arms, pulled in his stomach and puffed out his chest. He walked tall.

But in spite of all temptations,
To belong to other nations,
He remains an Englishman,
He remains an Englishman.

George could never understand why Erica was so sniffy about the operettas of Gilbert and Sullivan. They were light opera with spoken words rather than recitative, but so what? They had many a good song, the Victorians were in thrall to them, the Empire was at its zenith and in those days, you took pride in it. Nearing home, he beheld the daffodils, a jaunty yellow, standing firmly to attention on the roadside bank, amid clumps of pale-yellow primroses.

He walked on a little farther and spotted a van parked outside the Old Forge. As he got nearer, the words 'R Smith and Son, Painter's and Decorator's' leapt from the side of the vehicle and struck him in the chest with such ferocity that it brought him up short. Is basic punctuation really beyond the capabilities of the average signwriter? The misuse of apostrophes irritated him beyond all measure. It was sloppy, unprofessional and wrong. There was another vehicle, a BMW. The front door of The Old Forge was open, but there was no one in view. He walked a little farther and strolled onto his drive, down the side of the house and opened the gate into the rear garden.

Erica was coming out of the greenhouse carrying two seed trays of spindly plants. 'George, there you are. Do you think I can plant these out yet?'

'Have you seen the punctuation on the side of that van? Can't anyone write the Queen's English anymore?'

'Evidently not,' said Erica.

'You see bad punctuation everywhere, these days. It's inexcusable.'

'Yes, of course, George.' Erica knew better than to challenge him when he had been upset by something that most people would hardly notice.

'It's just ignorance, pure and simple.'

'If you say so. I'm going to plant these out.'

'It's too cold.'

Much activity was to be observed at The Old Forge over many days. The old house went through a slow metamorphosis from the dilapidated domicile of the now deceased Cedric, and his long-dead wife, whose name had been lost to living memory, forgotten even by her closest neighbours, to a home for a young professional couple decamped from metropolitan London to rural Suffolk. As the decorators departed in their ill-apostrophised van, so the new owners arrived in their BMW with their goods and chattels following on.

'A new member, George?' said Erica.

George was always on the lookout for new Rotarians. Like most Rotary clubs, the Rotary Club of Debenham struggled with membership.

George thought of his own experience when he had joined Rotary all those years ago and his anxiety and irascibility melted away. 'I was thinking of Charles Jackson.'

'Charles was a gentleman,' said Erica, 'so well-mannered.'

'It was Charles who invited me to my first Rotary meeting, you know.'

'Yes, I do know that,' said Erica, 'you've told me often enough. Was it an honour to be a Rotarian?' Erica rolled her eyes, which George seemed not to notice, or if he did, attached no meaning to it. He had no understanding of body language.

'He explained what Rotary did and why it would be a privilege for me to join,' said George.

'Not everyone could get in?' Erica's mock incredulity might have seemed harsh to others, but it was harmless between the two of them and it was her way of coping with life with George.

'Membership was strictly by invitation in those days,' said George.

'No oiks?'

'Only the right sorts were admitted, businessmen, professionals, and senior managers, but definitely no oiks,' said George, with a sense of pride.

'You make it sound even more old-fashioned and stuffy, every time I hear that little speech, George.'

'Charles was too fond of whisky and good living, that's what did for him, you know.'

'The club gave him a good send-off,' said Erica.

'St Mary's was rammed full for the memorial service,' said George. 'We were all there and there were lots of Rotarians from other clubs.'

Erica said, 'We got a choir together and we sang "Abide with Me" and "The Lord is My Shepherd". There was a short silence as they reflected on the end of Rotarian Charles Jackson.

'When I was a new Rotarian, he was always ready with good advice if I needed it,' said George. 'He still is.'

'What do you mean?' said Erica, surprised by this revelation.

'I still feel his presence and sense his words,' said George.

'Do you see him?' said Erica.

'Just a shadow.'

'Frank played the organ,' said Erica, steering the conversation away from the spirit of Charles Jackson. 'He's a good organist.'

'I'm going to organise a concert for Rotary charities,' said George, 'in St Mary's.'

'He's really a pianist,' said Erica.

'But he plays the organ as well,' said George.

'He plays it the same as the piano,' said Erica.

'What do you mean?' said George.

'He doesn't use the pedals.'

'Pedals?'

'You get a richer sound on bass by using the pedals,' said Erica.

'I gave a eulogy,' said George.

'It's not really important for playing hymns,' said Erica.

'I was president.'

'It was your year.'

'I told that story about when Charles went to see his doctor,' said George. 'Everyone seemed to like it.'

Erica said, 'Did the doctor tell him to stay off the whisky and take only a small glass of red wine at dinner?' She had heard the story many times before but tried not to roll her eyes again.

'Charles said to the doctor, "My dear chap, I put more than that in a shepherd's pie".' George had not found the story humorous, and he had been surprised when everyone laughed so loudly.

They were silent for a moment, then George said, 'The best time to recruit new members is when they've just retired or moved into the area.'

'Before they get involved in other activities?'

'Yes, of course.'

'What about our new neighbour?' said Erica.

'He'd make a good Rotarian,' said George. 'We need some new blood.'

'Like Dracula?' George did not register the sarcasm in the comment.

'He just doesn't know it yet,' said George, 'but Rotary will be good for him.'

'What about his wife?'

'Pretty little thing.'

'Might she be a new member?'

'Good Lord, no,' said George. 'She wouldn't be right for the club.'

'Rotary is supposed to be diverse these days.'

'We've got some lady members.'

Erica said, 'Just three and they're the only ones with any sense.' George was duly reproached.

George thought that three lady members was exactly right for the club. Any more might overwhelm the rest of the membership. From three, came other words and music:

Three little maids from school are we.
Pert as a schoolgirl well can be.
Filled to the brim with girlish glee.
Three little maids from school.

George could remember them as new Rotarians with girlish glee, but perhaps not quite as little maids. *We were all young then, we had energy and Rotary ruled the world. But we let time slip through our fingers, like sand running through an egg timer, except you can't turn it over and start again. We should have done much more with it, but it didn't seem so precious then. Now, we sit by the fire, making old bones. We look into the dancing flames to see the past, but the future is unreadable, like the smoke that curls upwards and disappears through the chimney.*

'And how many black and gay members?' said Erica.

'What?'

'Are you listening to me at all, George?' said Erica. 'I said, how many black and gay members do you have?'

'None, as you know, perfectly well,' said George.

'Anyway, we do have a diversity, equity, and inclusion statement in Rotary, if that's what you're getting at. All clubs have to sign up to it.'

Erica was about to make a reply when an Audi drove slowly onto the drive, crunching over the gravel. Frank Wilder, the club president, whose term of office was coming to an end, waved. 'Hello, I was just passing, so I thought I'd pop in for a chat.'

'Hello Frank, it's good to see you,' said George.

'Is this likely to be a Rotary chat, Frank?' said Erica.

'Well to tell you the truth, Erica,' said Frank, 'yes, it is.'

'I'll go and make some coffee and you two can go into the conservatory,' said Erica.

They chatted inconsequentially for a while, until Erica arrived with a tray of coffee and biscuits.

'You seem as though you've got something on your mind, Frank.' It was Frank's unexpected visit that prompted George's comment, rather than anything that he recognised in Frank's demeanour.

'How do you see the future of the club, George?'

George had not expected that and pondered as he poured coffee and passed the milk jug to Frank. 'Our main problem is membership. What are we now, just twenty-one members?'

'But we still manage to carry out the fundraising activities that we always have,' said Frank.

'Time was when we had thirty-five plus members from the villages around here and a deal younger than we are now,' said George.

'We were those members,' said Frank.

'We really need some younger people, Frank. People who will drive the club on into the future, the members who will replace us eventually.'

'What is the critical mass, below which we cannot survive?' said Frank.

George thew back his head and rubbed his chin. 'It's fifteen.'

'That's very precise, George, very you.'

'Well, a club needs twenty members to get its charter. Medium-term it could cope with five fewer, but no fewer than that.'

Frank did not pursue the point. 'Membership is not our only worry. We need to think about direction.'

'What direction do you have in mind, Frank? I'm happy with our present direction. It's the right direction and it's right for us.'

'Andrew is going to be our president in the next Rotary year and that's only a matter of weeks away,' said Frank.

'Andrew's a capable chap,' said George.

'That's not the problem.' Frank sipped his coffee. 'The thing is, George, he's been listening too much to our assistant governor and one or two other wrongheaded people. It came up at the assistant governor's meeting last Saturday morning.'

'Assistant governor's meeting?'

Frank said, 'Our assistant governor started them this year. He hosts a meeting every six weeks or so for the club presidents on his patch. It helps him to keep in touch with his clubs and presidents to keep in touch with each other. Every president-elect goes along as well.'

'So, Andrew was there?' said George.

'The latest fad is modernisation, or trashing the club, depending on your point of view,' said Frank. 'And Andrew showed an unhealthy interest.'

'In what way?'

'Doing away with grace, the loyal toast, the Rotary toast, the Rotary bell,' said Frank. 'That sort of thing.'

George could feel anger boil up inside him, mixed with an overwhelming feeling of anxiety at the prospect of change. 'That's outrageous,' said George. 'He'd better come to his senses and pretty soon, too.'

'Well, don't count on it,' said Frank. 'Andrew seemed very keen on the idea and our assistant governor will support him. Andrew is a recent convert to modernisation and there's no one holier than a convert. In a way I'm not surprised. He reads *The Guardian*.'

'Oh, that's where he gets his strange ideas,' said George. He was silent for a moment then continued, 'I will not let Andrew Parker or anyone else trash our club. If we lose those things, we begin to lose our sense of who we are, what we stand for, the values we espouse, the pride we take from being Rotarians. It's not easy to define those things, Frank, but old Rotarians like us understand them. They're correct and proper. I can't abide sloppiness.'

'Phillip comes after Andrew,' said Frank.

'Phillip is pretty sound.'

Frank said, 'He can repair some of the damage that I fear that Andrew is going to cause.'

'Then it's Dominic,' said George.

'Dominic's a bit of an enigma,' said Frank. 'I've no idea where he would stand on modernisation, but as president,

I doubt that he would have the energy or determination to pull things back to where they should be. I also happen to know that he has some serious health issues.'

'What's the matter with him?' said George, bluntly, without feeling.

'I'm not sure,' said Frank. 'All I do know, is that it came out when Carol was in discussion with some of the other Rotary ladies. She told me, of course.'

'Well, you're club president.'

'I'm her husband, George.'

'I didn't know that, about Dominic, I mean.'

Frank said, 'The implications for the club are, that in all probability, he will never serve his term as president. That means that whoever is elected president-nominee at the special general meeting in November, will advance one year and be president in just over a year from then.'

'Are these health concerns serious or is he just making a fuss about nothing?' said George.

'The big question is who will stand for president-nominee at the special general meeting in November?'

'Well...'

'It's got to be you, George.'

George's reply was unequivocal. 'I've already served a term as president and I've decided not to do it again. Everyone has accepted that.'

'I do hope that's not your last word on the matter, George.'

'Frank, from what you are saying, the danger is now,' said George. 'If Andrew Parker trashes the club in the forthcoming Rotary year, it's going to be difficult to get things back to normal, a year on, never mind two years after the event. Besides, he would also need the support of the club to make the major changes you've outlined. He couldn't be sure of that.'

'Yes, quite so,' said Frank, 'but we can't just give up.'

'I'm prepared to stand for club council,' said George, 'but I will not serve another term as president.'

Frank said, 'George, I really do urge you to give it proper consideration. You were a good president and members respect you. I shall still be on club council next year, as immediate past president, so I shall be able to keep an eye on Andrew. But the following year I shall be bumped off. It's a requirement of the club's constitution. I've checked it. No doubt it's designed to ensure a turnover of members on council.'

*

It was later that week that George saw his neighbour in the garden, struggling with years of neglect, following Cedric's slow decline and eventual demise. This new neighbour had kept to himself, but now George had his chance. The new neighbour stopped digging and looked up as George approached.

'Hello there, you must be the new neighbour,' said George in a statement of the blindingly obvious. 'I'm George Woodgate from just over the road.' He extended his hand.

'I'm Oliver Green.' They shook hands.

'Settling in?'

'We wanted a change, some peace and quiet after London.'

'You can't have retired,' said George.

'Perhaps one day.'

'What do you do?'

'I work for a large financial outfit, finance, IT, management consultancy, that sort of thing,' said Oliver.

'Why did you move away from London?'

'I work from home most of the time, at least I shall from now on,' said Oliver, 'and you?'

'Retired, well, more or less. I still have a few old clients.'

'A lot of time to fill?'

'Rotary takes up some of it.'

'How interesting,' said Oliver, with a distinct lack of interest, which George failed to recognise.

'I was a partner in a firm of accountants.'

'Locally?'

'So, why did you leave London?' said George.

'It's good to get away.'

'What part of London?'

'It feels as though you are giving me the third degree,' said Oliver.

'It's not a difficult question, is it?' said George.

'No, not at all.'

'So, what's the answer?'

'North London.'

They chatted for a little longer, then George said, 'I'll bring you along to our Rotary meeting on Wednesday, as my guest. We've got an interesting speaker. You'll meet some of the people who live around here, and you'll enjoy it.'

'I don't think so.'

'What do you mean?' said George. 'Don't you want to come?'

'No.'

'Why on earth not?' said George in exasperation.

London's a big place, thought George, *he doesn't give much away. Who is this new neighbour, a generation younger than me, with a public-school accent, who had lived somewhere in north London and now lives here in Suffolk? The answer is, a new, younger, Rotarian. He's just being difficult; why are some people so irritating?*

Across the lane, Erica watched the two men in conversation. George was determined to befriend this new neighbour and recruit him as a Rotarian, but first he had to get him to attend a club meeting as a guest. Once he had done that he would be hooked, like a trout; well, possibly. Erica hoped that George would not be too blunt in his approach and make an enemy before they had even got to know their new neighbours. Once people knew George, there was never a problem, they accepted him and his bluntness, but you have only one opportunity to make a first impression and, with George, that could be disastrous.

Erica dutifully supported George at Rotary events. She had accompanied him to the club's charter night dinner last month; a celebration of the anniversary of the day the club received its charter as a Rotary club. It was a black-tie event and the guest speaker this year had been the Police and Crime Commissioner, who spoke eloquently about policing in the county over the last year. He was confident of winning the Rotarians' votes in his bid for a further term of office when the time came. There were also speeches from Frank, as president, and the district governor, Ian Johnstone. The bar remained open until carriages at half past eleven and members made good use of it. Erica, who had sipped fruit juice all evening, was on chauffeuring duty, an arrangement of necessity. George had continued to talk and drink to well beyond the point when he would have welcomed a confrontation with an officer of the law bearing a breathalyser, and he had heard earlier in the evening about the increase in police enforcement. Erica had done plenty of talking and laughing but left the drinking to George.

At some point in the evening, they laughed about some of the amusing incidents that had occurred at Rotary events. 'Do you remember when we went to Holland at the invitation of that Dutch club?' said Andrew.

'They arranged a band and, on the Saturday evening, we all processed through the town to the restaurant in our DJs,' said Frank.

'Do you remember when we got on the ferry at Harwich on the way over and we received our cabin keys?' said Kye. 'They had us all mixed up and none of the husbands and wives were together.' They all laughed.

'Andrew was put with Claire,' said Frank.

'Your good lady did manage to negotiate a swap, Andrew,' said Kye, 'but you shouldn't have looked so disappointed. She still blames you for it.'

Andrew's good lady, Susan, did not laugh with the others. Claire smiled demurely. Susan had an innate sense of insecurity, self-doubt, inadequacy, and this seemingly harmless quip exacerbated a tension that endured and bound the three in a triangle, taut, inflexible, stressful. The tension, of which Claire was blissfully unaware, played out in the Parker household and Andrew would soon be president, which meant working closely with club secretary Claire on the arrangements for meetings and other Rotary business. A mixture of anger and anxiety overwhelmed Susan. She felt her face redden; she sensed people looking at her; she had to escape. She rose from her chair and picked up her handbag. 'Excuse me.'

'Are you all right, Susan?' said Claire. 'Shall I come with you?'

'No.'

Claire was slim and elegant, and her naturally fair hair was cut in a simple classy style. She was a divorcee and if she had gentlemen admirers, she was too discreet to say and no one asked. She was the first woman to hold the post of club secretary, and no one doubted she was the most efficient.

When the evening finally came to an end, George and Erica and the other guests walked from the hotel into the cool night air. 'Good night, Andrew.'

'Good night, George. Think about what I said.'

'What was that?'

'I've forgotten.' They both laughed.

George and Erica got into the car and were just about to drive off, when Kye opened the rear nearside door and tossed in some balloons. 'Have some balloons. Good night, George, brilliant evening. Good night, Erica.'

'Good night, Kye, I'm not sure we really need those,' said Erica.

As they drove, the balloons started to bobble around, illuminated by the headlights of the car following behind. 'Kye really is a pain. Those balloons are distracting with headlights shining on them.'

Kye Wilbanks was the son of a pilot of the Mighty Eighth, the United States 8th Airforce, that came to Suffolk in 1942. The roar of the mighty B24 Liberators and B17 Flying Fortresses echoed throughout Suffolk, as they took to the skies in huge formations. There had been 50,000 US military personnel based in Suffolk during the War. They brought with them Coca Cola and chewing gum, and at the end of the War, many took home local girls as brides; others left behind sweethearts and broken promises and went home to their wives. Art Wilbanks was different. He married a local girl and settled in Suffolk. Kye was the elder of their two sons.

'Now we are clear of other traffic, the balloons are not really bothering me,' said Erica.

'I think this stretch of road is restricted,' said George.

'What do you mean?'

'It's thirty along here.'

'That's very observant for someone in your state,' said Erica.

'I could drive us home safely if I had to.'

'George, at this very moment, I wouldn't allow you to operate my hairdryer.'

Erica saw the balloons turn bright Rotary blue and yellow, as the headlights of a police car picked them out. She stopped as directed and a young police officer got out of the police car and walked to the driver's door. Erica wound down the window.

'Do you know why I stopped you, madam?'

'I've no idea. You've probably got nothing better to do.'

'You have just committed a road traffic offence. You were driving at thirty-three miles an hour in a restricted area.'

'Is that it?' said Erica. 'That's pathetic.'

'I can smell alcohol,' said the policeman. 'I have reason to believe you've been drinking. I shall have to ask you to take a breath test.'

'I haven't been drinking,' said Erica.

'We'll soon see, won't we?'

'You have absolutely no reason to breathalyse me.'

'I have reason to believe that you've been drinking,' said the policeman again.

'That's my husband. He's absolutely blotto.'

'But he's not driving. Is he?' The policeman's tone of voice hardened. 'Get out of the car now, please.'

Erica gave George a sharp jab in the ribs with her elbow. 'George, he wants to breathalyse me.'

'Yes, all right.'

'What do you mean all right?' said Erica.

'Out of the car now, please,' said the policeman.

Erica got out. It had started to drizzle with rain and she shivered as the policeman sorted out his breathalyser. He seemed to take a long time and Erica could feel her hair flopping and her dress becoming damp.

'Blow into here and don't stop until I tell you. Keep going, keep going, stop.'

He stared at the instrument. 'You haven't drunk anything stronger tha fruit juice this evening.'

'I could have told you that.'

Erica got back into the car feeling tired, emotional and bedraggled. As she fastened her seat belt, the policeman said, 'Good night, madam. Drive safely.'

Erica wound up the window and was about to drive off, when George opened his eyes. 'Are we home yet?'

'No.'

Perhaps he'll have no interest in Rotary, this new neighbour, Erica thought, as she came out of her reverie. *He might sing. We need more tenors in the choir. Perhaps his wife sings, but getting sopranos and altos was never a problem.* The choir's last challenge had been Mozart's "Requiem" and Erica often joked that she had sung so many requiems over the years that she had become an honorary Catholic.

The first conversation between the neighbour old and the neighbour new came to an end and George trundled up the path.

Erica smiled. 'Have you signed him up, George?'

'No, of course not. I invited him to our next meeting, but he said he didn't want to come. I don't know why.'

'George, I hope you weren't too insistent. You know what you can be like sometimes.'

'I don't know what you mean.'

Erica said, 'If he's from Islington, he probably thinks we still use the village ducking stool to root out witchcraft and scratch a living from the rabbits we manage to snare.'

'Of course not. I told him I was an accountant.'

*

'Why the hell would I want to join Rotary?'

'What's the matter, Ollie?' said Imogen.

'The old chap over the road has just invited me to a meeting of his silly bloody Rotary club. He practically insisted. Do I look like a Rotarian?'

'You shouldn't be rude about them, Ollie. They're our neighbours now.'

'I can't imagine why anyone would want to join Rotary, apart from another old dotard,' said Oliver.

'You don't have to join.'

'It's roll up your trouser leg, noose around the neck...'

'Funny handshakes, as well, I suppose?' said Imogen.

'You'd know,' said Oliver.

'That's not Rotary, Ollie, it's Masons.'

'Stonemasons?'

'Freemasons.'

'Your dad was a Freemason,' said Oliver.

'Not a Rotarian.'

There was a silence between them for a moment as Oliver regained his composure. 'There's something not quite right with him, you know.'

'In what way?'

'There's an awkwardness about him and he seemed to avoid eye contact,' said Oliver, 'and also, the way he talks.'

'What do you mean?'

'He's very blunt and direct. In fact, he was downright rude.'

*

The days were becoming longer now, and George was spending more time in the garden. He had cut the grass and the recent rain had brought everything to life. The peonies had unfurled their leaves, shining green, edged with red. The buds on the rose bushes were bulging, as the petals pushed to escape into the spring air. George glanced towards the Dublin Bay roses; climbers. They too were stirring from their winter slumber, a brilliant red just emerging. He started to think about Rotary and then he remembered the task that Fiona had given him. *I must call in at the Black Lion this evening about the great Easter egg raffle, otherwise Fiona will be most displeased and that's best avoided.* He continued hoeing, taking down the weeds that had emerged since their last encounter. Gardening was like that; it was a battle with nature. You can never quite win, but it's vital to play for a good draw. The two horse chestnut trees were now in blossom, the delicate pink flower, exquisite but ephemeral. In the field beyond, the yellow flower of the rapeseed was beginning to emerge. Very soon there would be a carpet of yellow as far as the eye could see. The sun was warmer now, higher in the sky, and white fluffy cumulus clouds were scattered across an expanse of blue.

The flowers that bloom in the spring
Tra la
Breathe promise of merry sunshine
As we merrily dance and we sing
Tra la
We welcome the hope that they bring

Tra la
Of a summer of roses and wine
Of a summer of roses and wine

The operettas of Gilbert and Sullivan, that George heard in his head when he was relaxed and at peace with the world, gave him moments of intense pleasure. When he was in a busy and stressful environment, they provided a source of warmth and comfort, a place in which to escape from the world, if only fleetingly. In truth, he preferred solitude and order to people and chaos, but Rotary, like most things in life, was about people and a measure of chaos, so he faced down his demons, as he had trained himself to do all his life.

*

'What can I get you on this fine evening?' said the landlord of the Black Lion, a short, red-faced man, with a large belly. It was early evening and George was his only customer.

'I'll have half of Ghost Ship.'

'You're one of those Rotarians, aren't you?' said the landlord, setting down the half pint of beer on the counter.

'I'm a member of the Rotary Club of Debenham.'

'It's all about eating dinners, isn't it?'

'What, Rotary?'

'Rotary,' the landlord confirmed.

'That's why I'm here,' said George.

'Have you booked?'

'No, I don't want dinner. I shall eat at home this evening.'

'It's just as well,' said the landlord of the Black Lion. 'We haven't started serving dinner yet.'

'Anyway, Rotary isn't all about eating dinners,' said George, 'although it's part of what we do.'

'What else do you do?'

'We raise money to support good causes at home and overseas,' said George.

'You're best known for eating dinners,' said the landlord.

'Well, we're gregarious and we enjoy meeting together on our Rotary nights as well as other events and social occasions.' Although George used the word gregarious, he was not sure that he experienced it in the same way as other members of his club. 'It's what we call fellowship.'

'Fellowship?'

'Fellowship is an integral part of Rotary and just as important as raising money and promoting good causes,' said George, but without conviction.

'What sort of good causes?' said the landlord.

'That brings me to the main point of my visit this evening, apart from supping your beer, of course.'

'What's that?'

'I want you to take part in our great Easter egg raffle,' said George.

'What's great about it?'

'Well, it wouldn't do to call it our small and trivial Easter egg raffle, would it?' said George.

'It doesn't sound so great.'

'It's for the benefit of local children's charities,' said George. 'We do it every year.'

'At Easter?'

'That's why it's our great Easter egg raffle,' said George.

'Not particularly,' said the landlord.

'Why not?' said George. 'Your pub took part last year.'

'You probably explained it to my wife.'

'Your wife was most helpful.'

'Just like me then.'

'You're not helpful at all,' said George.

'You meet every Wednesday at the White Horse, eat your Rotary dinners and spend lots of money,' said the landlord of the Black Lion.

'Yes, we meet at the White Horse.'

'A rival pub.'

'We can't meet everywhere.'

'You could meet here. I'll offer you a good deal. What do you pay at the White Horse?'

'You did take part in the raffle last year,' said George.

'My wife agreed.'

'I don't like the Black Lion,' said George.

'What's wrong with it?' said the landlord of said hostelry.

Before George could answer, he heard a voice behind him. 'Hello, you're the Rotary man,' said Gladys, the landlady, who seemed to appear from nowhere.

'Yes, hello again,' said George.

'We'll do the Easter egg raffle again, won't we, Roland?' said Gladys.

Roland with the round face and the round belly, thought George. *It suits him. I'll make a note for next year.*

'We were just talking about it,' said George.

'Have you got the Easter egg?' said Gladys.

'No,' said George.

'And the board?'

'No, I'll bring them in as soon as I can,' said George.

'How much did you raise all together last year with the Easter eggs?' said Gladys.

'We raised more than £500 for children's charities,' said George.

'That's brilliant, isn't it, Rolly?'

'Brilliant.'

'I'll be back in a few days,' said George.

'But not Wednesday evening,' said Roland.

'No, it's Rotary,' said George.

'At the White Horse,' said the landlord of the Black Lion.

'Yes, it's a better pub, with better food and a better landlord,' said George, as he swallowed the last of his beer and walked out.

Later that evening, the phone rang. 'George, about the Easter egg raffle…'

'Hello Fiona, remind me how it works.'

'It's very simple, George. Even a man should be able to understand it.'

'I went into the Black Lion this evening,' said George. 'Roland said he'll do it again this year. At least his wife did.'

'Have you got a board to give them?' said Fiona.

'With the squares?'

'It's a hundred squares,' said Fiona. 'The phone number goes in the square. Don't forget.'

'It's a pound a square?'

'As many as they like.'

'I'm sure I can remember that.'

'I've now got the rest of the Easter eggs,' said Fiona. 'I'll bring them to Rotary on Wednesday.'

THREE

November: it is seven months in the future, and the (very strange) election of the president-nominee.

- *Andrew Parker is president, and he has introduced his modernisation programme, but not without a battle;*
- *Alec Barton has been admitted to the club;*
- *Fiona and Alec are standing for president-nominee (George's refusal to nominate Alec had caused bad blood between the two);*
- *George had refused to stand for president-nominee, so he has no personal interest in the election (or so he thinks!).*

'You're early, Claire,' said Bill, the landlord of the White Horse.

'I'll have a fruit juice, please,' said the secretary of

the Rotary Club of Debenham, as she passed some coins across the bar.

'That's exactly right.'

'It's our special general meeting this evening,' said Claire.

'Is that why you're so early?'

'Bill, what would you say about Alec Barton becoming president?'

'I don't think that's very likely.'

'More likely than you think,' said Claire.

'Your members would have anyone over him,' said Bill. 'Wouldn't they?'

'As I said, it's our special general meeting this evening,' said Claire.

'What's that?'

'We elect our club officials,' said Claire.

'The president?'

'And others.'

'Sounds like an important night for the club.'

'Alec Barton is on the ballot paper for president-nominee,' said Claire.

'President?' said Bill.

'Yes, that's it.'

'He's a surly so and so.'

'Bill, I need your help,' said Claire.

Bill said, 'He turned really nasty when I asked him to pay for his dinner, that time he was absent and hadn't put in an apology.'

'He doesn't like you or your hostelry, Bill.'

'He wouldn't.'

'He wants to move the club to the Black Lion,' said Claire, silently excusing herself a small white lie for the common good.

'Not to Round Roland at the Black Lion?'

'That's what he'd do, if he ever became president.'

'Your members wouldn't let him do that, would they?' said Bill.

'Presidents usually manage to get their way if they're determined enough.'

'What do you want me to do?' said Bill.

'Bill, you and Marlene used to be involved in amateur dramatics, didn't you?'

'That was years ago,' said Bill. 'We had a lot of fun, but we don't have the time nowadays. Why do you ask?'

'Bill, I'd like you to do something for me this evening.'

'Oh yes, what's that?'

Claire said, 'I need to get George out of the room for a few minutes. I'm going to send you a text message at a certain point in our meeting. As soon as I send it, not ten minutes later, but immediately, I want you to burst into the room with a great sense of urgency, and a message for George.'

'What sort of a message?'

'Tell him he's got a very important phone call and he needs to take it immediately.'

'He won't fall for that,' said Bill.

'Well, that's up to you, Bill. You're the old thespian, you've got to be convincing.'

'I could stagger in and collapse on the floor from the stress of bearing this vital message,' said Bill, who was now warming to the task. 'That would get his attention, but what about the phone call?'

Marlene, blonde, buxom and flirtatious, who had been listening to the conversation, came over. 'I'll play the French tart. That should keep his attention. It still works for Bill.'

'Claire doesn't need to know that,' said Bill.

'We've got to do the same with Alec Barton,' said Claire.

Marlene said, 'What sort of plot have you dreamt up, Claire? It's not going to work twice.'

'Alec Barton won't be a problem,' said Claire. 'Just come in and say that his car is blocking in one of your customers. He'll become angry and refuse to move.'

'You can't be sure of that,' said Marlene.

'I know he'll refuse to move,' said Claire. 'He's very predictable in some ways. Tell him that the customer is threatening to damage his car. He'll be out of the room like a shot at the prospect of maiming someone.'

They all laughed. Claire had painted a compelling picture of Alec Barton.

'How do you manage to plot and scheme like that?' said Marlene, with admiration. 'Don't the other members realise that you choreograph everything that happens in the club?'

Claire said, 'The trick is to persuade them that whatever I need them to do, was really their idea in the first place!'

'Anyway, why do you need to get them out of the meeting?' said Marlene.

Claire smiled. 'Information is on a strictly need to know basis.'

Soon other members began to arrive and Bill was busy pulling pints of beer. 'Good evening, George,' said Andrew. 'A pint of Ghost Ship?'

'Thank you, Andrew,' said George.

Fiona came in with Frances, then Mark, who seemed to stoop to get through the door, then Frank, dapper as ever, and Paul, with Phillip and Alec. Eventually all the membership was present, with the sole exception of Roger.

A few minutes later, Bill announced, 'Rotarians, dinner is served.' He had been delighted when the club asked if they could put up a plaque saying 'The Rotary Club of Debenham meets here every Wednesday'. It put him one up on Round Roland at the Black Lion. It was now up to Marlene and him, thespians both, to keep it that way.

Members trooped through to what was their private dining room on Wednesday evenings. Since the introduction of President Andrew's controversial modernisation programme, that a divided membership had narrowly approved, there was no Rotary bell for the president to call members to order and no grace, which seemed very strange to the traditionalists in the club, such as George, Frank, Paul and others.

'It's the sense of ceremony I miss, not just the grace,' said George. 'It's no longer Rotary.'

'It's more like a heathen feast,' said Frank, which made Paul laugh. George did not understand what Frank had meant.

'This is what it's like at the camera club, the gardening club, or any other ordinary club,' said Frank.

'And they probably wouldn't have dinner,' said George, 'or beer.'

Bill started serving steak and mushroom pie, with mashed potato and green beans. It smelled delicious to the hungry Rotarians. After the main course, Bill cleared away the plates and Marlene brought in dishes of spotted dick and custard. 'Who hasn't got a spotted dick, I've got one over?'

'There's no answer to that,' said Kye.

'It's me, Marlene,' said Claire. 'I'm not sure I can manage a heavy pudding this evening.'

After dinner, Andrew said, 'We'll take a short break then crack on with the main business.' He raised his voice to ensure that he was heard above the hubbub as members started to move around, and to go to the bar. The Rotary bell, much missed by George and others, had been declared redundant in Andrew's new Utopia, breaking with years of tradition.

George was walking towards the bar when he felt a sharp shove in the back. He stumbled, then recovered his footing. 'You let me down, you bastard,' said Alec Barton. 'Lucky for you, Kye has nominated me for president-nominee. I'll have you out when I'm president.'

'Are you all right, George?' Claire had seen him stumble, but not what caused it.

'Yes, of course,' said George, 'just tripped over my feet, that's all.'

'Two pints of Ghost Ship, Bill.' George could feel

his hands trembling as he picked up the glasses. He immediately set them down again.

'You don't look quite right, George,' said Frank. 'Let me carry those glasses.'

Back in the Rotarians' room, George began to recover his composure. *I can cross Alec Barton off my Christmas card list. In fact, I'll add him to the Lord High Executioner's little list.*

As someday it may happen that a victim must be found,
I've got a little list – I've got a little list…
He's got 'em on the list – he's got 'em on the list;
And they'll none of 'em be missed – they'll none of 'em be missed…

Not many people would miss Alec Barton. The thought of him languishing in a Titipu prison on Ko-Ko's little list for execution, cheered up George enormously. *I think I might abstain on president-nominee this evening.*

'Are you all right, George?' said Andrew. 'You look a bit distant.'

'I've never felt better,' said George, still holding the thought in his head.

'Right, let's make a start,' said Andrew. 'Apologies for absence.'

'There's an apology from Roger,' said Claire.

'Do I have your agreement to sign the minutes of the last meeting as a correct record?' said Andrew.

There was a chorus of 'agreed' from the assembled Rotarians.

'The next item is the presentation of the examined accounts. Mark, what have you got to report, as honorary treasurer?'

'Mr President, I have the honour to present last year's accounts, which were circulated with the agenda. There are two sets: the club account, which relates to the internal running of the club, and the charity account, which covers all our charitable activities. There's also a brief statement from Cranford and Mann and I shall be pleased to answer any questions.'

'Who are Cranford and Mann?' said Kye.

'They're accountants,' said Mark. 'They examine our accounts.'

'I thought they were audited?' said Kye. 'What's the difference?'

'It's a lighter touch,' said Mark.

'You mean it roots out rampant corruption but not the odd fiddle by the treasurer?' said Kye.

'That's not funny,' said Mark.

'Kye, have you got any serious questions?' said President Andrew.

'There's been a lot of recent spending that's not shown here,' said Kye.

Mark said, 'I would remind members that these are the examined accounts for the last Rotary year that ended on 30th June, nearly five months ago.'

'Why is 30th June the end of the Rotary year?' said Kye.

Mark said, 'It goes back to 1910 and Rotary International's first convention in Chicago. They set the new year as the day after the convention ended in August. At the 1912 meeting—'

'That's really fascinating information, Mark, but it goes a long way beyond the item under discussion,' said Andrew.

'I was really interested in that,' said Kye.

'Has anyone else got any questions for Mark?' said Andrew. There was no response. 'Do I have your agreement to receive last year's examined accounts?'

'Agreed.'

President Andrew said, 'The next item is the election of club officers to serve for the next Rotary year beginning on 1st July, over to Claire.'

Claire said, 'Thank you, Mr President. Under the Rotary constitution, in the next Rotary year, when you step down, Phillip, as president-elect, moves up to become club president, and Dominic, as president-nominee, will move up to president-elect.'

'We are all mindful that Dominic has some health issues,' said Andrew. 'Dominic, are you prepared to carry on for now?'

'Yes, I am,' said Dominic, 'but if things get worse, I might have to reconsider.'

'Thank you, Dominic,' said Andrew.

'Then there's a replacement for Dominic as president-nominee,' said Claire, 'our president some two years hence. We need to elect him or her at this meeting.'

President Andrew said, 'Perhaps we should deal with the other club officers first. We have to elect the treasurer and the secretary. The two current post holders have agreed to carry on and there have been no other nominations. Therefore, Mark will remain as treasurer and Claire will continue as secretary. Is everyone content?'

'Agreed.'

Claire now held her mobile phone under the table and started texting. A moment later, Bill burst into the special general meeting of the Rotary Club of Debenham.

'Urgent phone call for George,' he said in a panicky voice.

'I'm in the middle of a meeting,' said George. 'Can't you take a message and say that I'll ring back?'

'This is urgent.'

'I'll ring back.'

'You've got to take the call.'

'I'm in an important meeting.'

'This call is vitally important, and I don't want to be held responsible for not passing on the message,' said Bill.

'We're about to elect our president-nominee,' said George.

'It's really urgent. You've got to take it.' Bill was now gripped with blind panic. His mouth was dry, his pulse racing and he was having difficulty breathing. He was enunciating his words in a loud clear theatrical voice, as he had done so often in times past. This has got to work. He was really beginning to ham it up now. *All the world's a stage, and all the men and women merely players: they have their exits and entrances. George this is your exit, please, please, just exit stage left and go to the phone. Don't wreck Claire's masterplan and let in Alec Barton.*

The conversation took place across the room, as Bill stood by the door and George sat at the far side. The interruption had brought the meeting to a halt and members looked from one side of the room to the other in bewilderment, as first Bill spoke and then George, back and forth for the whole exchange, like a tennis match. They had never seen Bill in such a state. George was irritated to have this episode played out so prominently in front of the whole club. He was used to a quieter, more civilised discourse.

'Very well,' said George testily, as he stood and followed Bill out of the room.

At least he had no personal interest in the election and the outcome was a foregone conclusion. He had resisted pressure to stand, even though it left the club with a difficult and disagreeable choice. If the members elected Fiona, she would shake up the club. "Difficult" was the description usually ascribed to her, but George thought she was quite mad. The only other candidate, and almost certain winner, was Alec Barton. He was not popular and his experience as a Rotarian was limited, but the mainly male membership would never vote for Fiona. He was troubled about Alec Barton's lack of experience, but Alec would have two years to grow into the role of club president.

'I do hope that it's nothing serious, perhaps we—' said Ernie.

'Bill's just a drama queen,' said Kye.

'Perhaps we should wait for a few minutes to see if he comes back,' said President Andrew, in a weak attempt to distance himself from the deception about to take place.

'No, let's carry on,' said Claire, ignoring Andrew's reticence as she prepared to distribute the ballot papers.

At that moment, Bill came in again. 'Urgent message for Alec Barton, you're blocking in a customer's car.'

'I'm not blocking in anyone,' said Alec, angrily.

'He says you are.'

'Well, I'm not moving.'

'I think you'd better.'

'I am not moving.'

'You've got to.'

'Tell him to go to hell.'

'He said that if you don't move your car, he's going to kick in the door panels and smash your lights,' said Bill.

Alec leapt to his feet, with surprising agility for a man of his bulk, and disappeared through the door, ready to inflict grievous bodily harm on anyone who got in the way.

'I think we should press on,' said Claire. 'We can assume that George and Alec will vote for themselves.'

'I don't know, perhaps we should wait,' said President Andrew, still troubled.

Claire was now distributing the ballot papers and ignored Andrew's exhortation. 'There are three candidates, George, Alec and Fiona, and you have one vote only. If you vote for more than one candidate, I shall disqualify your ballot paper.'

Members scrutinised the ballot papers in front of each of them.

'I thought that George wasn't going to stand,' said Kye.

'Life's full of surprises,' said Claire.

'Has anyone got a pen?' said Andrew.

'Here you are,' said Claire. 'Anyone else need a pen?'

'Yes,' said Kye.

'Come on, hurry up,' said Claire as she handed Kye a pen.

'You're not usually in such a hurry, Claire,' said Kye.

Claire was now aware of time passing. She had to complete the election and get President Andrew to announce the result before George and Alec Barton returned. She grabbed up each ballot paper the instant a member voted. 'You're the last one, Kye. It's not that difficult, is it?'

'I haven't got my reading glasses,' said Kye.

'Whom do you wish to vote for?' said Claire. 'I'll fill it in for you.'

'I thought this was supposed to be a secret ballot,' said Kye.

'Just hurry up,' said Claire.

'I'm surprised that someone's managed to persuade George to stand,' said Kye.

'Hurry up, Kye,' said Claire, 'we're all waiting for you.'

At last, Claire gathered up the ballot papers and passed them to Andrew. They began to count.

Meanwhile, in the bar, George grabbed the phone that Bill thrust at him. *I hope nothing has happened to Erica.* 'Hello, this is George Woodgate.'

A woman's voice answered; sexy, breathy, with the hint of a French accent: 'Georgie, you're a naughty boy.'

'Hello, who's that?'

'It's Gabriel. You remember me, darling.'

'I don't know anyone called Gabriel.'

'I think you do, darling.'

'Stop calling me darling.'

'Shall I remind you what I look like?'

'No.'

'I'm blonde and I'm a big girl, Georgie. I'm wearing black underwear, black stockings and suspenders. You like that, Georgie, don't you?'

'Suspended? You're talking complete drivel.'

'That's what you like, Georgie, big, blonde and sexy.'

'I don't know anyone big, blonde and sexy.' George had raised his voice and other customers were looking in his direction.

'Georgie, don't shout. You don't usually shout at me.'

'I don't know you. What do you want?'

'It's not what I want, it's what you want, darling Georgie.'

'I don't want anything.'

'You can come over to my place or I can visit you.'

'You don't know where I live. You don't know anything about me.'

George was about to slam down the phone, when the voice at the other end said, 'But you told me everything, Georgie; where you live, your lovely wife, Erica...'

'How do you know my wife's name?' said George angrily. 'Keep her out of it, d'you hear?'

'Yes, of course, Georgie. She doesn't need to know a thing.'

'There's nothing to know.'

'But there is, Georgie.'

'Who are you and what do you want from me?'

Another voice came on the phone. 'Hello sir. This is The Big Window Company, double glazing. I do apologise if my secretary was giving you a bit of a come on. She likes to encourage our gentlemen customers.'

George slammed down the phone in exasperation. 'Where's Bill?'

'He's gone into the back,' said a customer. 'He'll be here in a moment.'

A large hand swept back the arras and Bill appeared, serene and composed, in contrast to his demeanour a few minutes earlier. 'All right, George?'

'No, I'm not. Who was that on the phone?'

'Don't you know, you've just been speaking to her?'

'No. I don't know anyone called Gabriel, if that was her real name.'

'Your secret is safe with me, George,' said Bill. 'I don't make judgements about my customers.'

'Then a man, I heard a man's voice,' said George.

'A man's voice?' said Bill.

'Yes, he sounded, well, a bit like you.'

'Well, that's amazing. It's a small world.'

Meanwhile, outside in the car park, chaos was building. Alec walked quickly to his car. He saw another man going towards the car parked next to his. As the man opened the driver's door and lifted his left foot to step inside, the full force of Alec Barton crashed against the door, which he then flung open. The man crumpled in front of him.

'Don't you bloody dare touch my car,' said Alec.

The stunned and crushed man sat on the ground in a daze, with his back resting against the door pillar. He looked up at the menacing figure of Alec Barton standing over him. 'Why did you do that?'

'You've got plenty of room to get out,' said Alec. 'Do you really want me to move?'

'No thank you, but it's kind of you to offer.' The man struggled to his feet.

The activity in the car park had attracted attention and three men came over to see what was going on. 'Are you all right, mate?' said the first man.

'He offered to move his car so that I'd have more room to get out,' said the stunned and crushed man, who was running his fingers gently over his ribs. He seemed to have more than he had before.

'It was a funny way to attract your attention,' said the first man.

'I can't laugh, my ribs hurt,' said the injured man.

'What did you do that for?' said the second man to Alec.

'He expected me to move my car,' said Alec.

'That was uncalled for, mate,' said the third man.

Alec scowled as he tried to push past the three men to return to his expected triumph in the pub, but they pushed back.

Meanwhile, back inside the White Horse, Andrew was about to announce the result of the ballot. 'The votes cast were as follows: George fifteen votes, Fiona two and Alec three. I declare that George is duly elected as our president-nominee for the next Rotary year, and our president in just over two years.' At that moment, George walked in.

'Is everything all right, George?' said Andrew.

'Yes, there was no emergency, nothing important,' said George. 'It was just a stupid phone call.'

'Who was it?' said Claire.

'I've no idea.'

'Oh, good,' said Claire.

'What?'

'Nothing,' said Claire.

'George, I'd like to be the first to congratulate you,' said Andrew.

'Well done, George. I knew it couldn't be me,' said Fiona.

There was applause from all the assembled Rotarians, but George had no idea what he had done to deserve it. 'I don't see the need for that,' he said tetchily, 'I've only taken a stupid phone call.'

Andrew looked at Claire, who gave a barely perceptible shrug of the shoulder, which meant *that's George.*

Before President Andrew brought the evening to a close, there was some more light-hearted business to conclude. 'Let's go to the fiddle,' as the weekly draw was known. 'Over to you, Dominic.'

Dominic took out a money bag and handed it to the president. 'A pound from everyone into the bag, please.' Then he delved into a bag of balls, each of which bore the number allocated to a member. 'It's number 11, which is George.'

'You're really on a roll, George,' said Kye.

'I hardly think so,' said George. 'I haven't won the raffle for as long as I can remember.'

'But you were successful in…' said Kye, who suddenly became aware that Claire was staring at him with a disagreeable intensity and realised that he was about to step on a landmine of some sort.

George also had noticed the puzzling look Claire was giving Kye. *That chap's not right in the head. He spends the whole meeting talking gibberish and guffawing like a lunatic at nothing at all. At least he's shut up for once.*

'And finally, over to our sergeant at arms, Kye,' said Andrew.

'First, Mr President, I'm fining you for starting the meeting late.'

'Well, I'm not sure about that,' said Andrew.

'Mr President, I shouldn't have to remind you that the job of the sergeant at arms is to keep order and issue fines for all misdemeanours, real or imaginary, and entirely at my discretion. That'll be another fifty pence for complaining.' Kye proceeded to work down the list he had made during the meeting. 'George and Frank were late back from the bar after the break. That's fifty pence each. Our three lady members for sitting together and giggling loudly, that's fifty pence each. And Ernie, that joke about the Viagra advert that said it didn't make you James Bond, but it would make you Roger More. That's fifty pence from you.'

Members laughed, George looked puzzled, and Ernie protested, 'But *you* told *me* the joke.'

'Yes, I know, but I'm fining *you* for listening,' said Kye, 'and I'd better fine myself, just in case I've done something wrong.'

'Thank you, Kye. We will now have the final toast.' All the members stood to a scraping of chairs on the old wooden floor of the White Horse, and raised their glasses.

'Rotary and peace the world over,' said the president.

'Rotary and peace the world over.' At least the Rotary toast had survived Andrew's reforms. It was the only nod to the way the club used to be before the cataclysm.

The meeting drew to a close and members left their room in twos and threes. As they went through to the bar of the White Horse, the door from the car park burst open, crashed against the wall, and there remained, quivering on its hinges. Alec Barton staggered in. He was bleeding from the mouth, the nose and his right ear. His jacket was torn, his tie knot was under his left ear and his shirt gaped open to the waist. He had taken a pasting, but he had poleaxed two of the men the moment the fight had got going. Then the Young Farmers, who had been drinking at the White Horse that evening, joined in, although on whose side, it was never established.

A British tar is a soaring soul,

As free as a mountain bird,

His energetic fist should be ready to resist

A dictatorial word.

A British builder, rather than a British tar, thought George, *but his energetic fist was not quite enough tonight.*

FOUR

Back to the present: it is May. Frank remains president until the start of the new Rotary year on 1st July.

- *George is elected to serve on club council;*
- *Rotary traditions and customs continue, for now;*
- *Alec Barton has not yet been admitted to the club.*

It was Wednesday, which meant Rotary in Debenham, a few minutes' drive for George. For Erica it was a welcome evening off from cooking. A quick rummage in the freezer would produce a portion of something to go in the microwave. *I think I'll have a glass of sherry and watch some television.* Meanwhile, George was getting ready. He put on a clean shirt, selected a tie and attached his Rotary pin to the lapel of the jacket he would wear this evening. He drove into Debenham, to the White Horse, in his old Mercedes, at his usual sedate pace. The evening air felt cool on his face as he walked from the car park into the pub.

'George, old chap, let me get you a drink,' said President Frank, now in an end-of-term mood. As June came to a close, his term of office would finish and Andrew would assume the role of president. Frank was slim and dapper in a navy-blue blazer. His dark hair was smoothed down with hair dressing and he sported a pencil moustache. Frank was musical and played the organ for Sunday service in St Mary's Church, Debenham.

'The usual for George, when you're ready, Bill.'

Bill knew every member's "usual". It was his business to know. He was a good old Suffolk boy, who looked after his Rotarians because they were good customers. His lank mousy-coloured hair was too long, his blue and white striped shirt was crumpled, and beer-stained, and the waistband of his trousers slipped over his belly and clung tenaciously to his hips.

'I'll be with you in a moment, Frank,' said Bill, who was serving another customer.

'I'll get those for Frank,' said Marlene. 'It's always a pleasure to serve the president.'

'Not for much longer, Marlene,' said Frank. 'My term of office comes to a stuttering conclusion at the end of June.'

'Then it's Andrew, isn't it?' said Marlene.

'That's right,' said Frank. 'He takes over on 1st July, the beginning of the new Rotary year.'

'Is someone talking about me?' said Andrew, who had just arrived at the bar.

'And one for Andrew,' said Frank.

'Your usual, Andrew?' said Marlene, pulling the two pints of Ghost Ship. 'Frank was telling me that I'll have to call you Mr President soon.'

Members of the Rotary Club of Debenham continued to chat until Bill said, 'Frank, you can go through now.' The Rotarians repaired to their meeting room, carrying a buzz of conversation with them.

President Frank brought members to order with an ear-jangling strike of the ceremonial Rotary bell. He paused momentarily until everyone was silent, still, attentive. 'Good evening, members.'

'Good evening, Mr President.'

Members of the Rotary Club of Debenham had formally greeted their president with these words for the past thirty-five years. The same words began the meetings of most other clubs in the land and beyond. It was an acknowledgement of the authority of the president, as he stood before his fellow members, wearing his chain of office, replete with a bar for each of his most recent predecessors, whose names had been inscribed with care and reverence at the end of each Rotary year. This brief ceremony would soon be under threat when Andrew Parker took office.

President Frank said, 'Kye, I shall be pleased if you will say grace.'

Kye looked around, from the black timber beams of the old pub, hewn by the rough hands of ancient craftsmen, to the large fireplace with its stone surround, and then to his fellow Rotarians, standing stiffly to attention, hands clasped, in a moment of solemnity. He put his hands together, bowed his head and said, 'Good food, good meat, good Lord, let's eat.'

'Amen.'

There was a chuckle and the sound of chairs scraping on the old wooden floor of the White Horse, followed by a resumption of chatter, as the assembled Rotarians sat down to dinner. Bill was serving a delicious beef and mushroom casserole, with mashed potato and green beans. There was apple crumble and custard to follow.

As dinner came to an end, President Frank rang the Rotary bell. It cut through the general hubbub and the room fell silent, apart from the noise of Marlene clearing away the plates.

'Please be upstanding for the loyal toast,' said Frank. He paused until all were quiet and still. 'The Queen.'

'The Queen,' came the response, as members raised their glasses.

'God bless her,' said Kye. Despite the strong ever-present influence of his American father during his childhood, circumstances and geography made him feel English rather than American.

'We will now have a short break and you may recharge your glasses,' said President Frank.

'Mr President, may I buy you a drink?' said George, amid the commotion of everyone moving to the bar or moving around to speak to other members.

'Just a half of Ghost Ship would do nicely, thank you, George.' Frank reckoned that a pint and a half was the limit to keep on the right side of the law when driving, and there was no other way of getting around in country areas.

This evening it was the club's annual general meeting, when the club reviewed its activities during the Rotary year, now coming to a close, and made a number of formal decisions. After ten minutes or so, members drifted back to their seats and the meeting resumed.

'We have no apologies for absence, so let's move on to the minutes,' said Frank. 'May I have your agreement to sign them as a correct record?'

There was a murmur of assent.

'Next item is the annual report of club council and committees. Club council is me, of course. I shall assume that you have all read my report so I shall not go into any great detail, unless you wish me to.'

'I haven't actually read your report,' said Kye. 'It was too boring, but there's no need to go through it.'

One or two members laughed. Frank ignored the interruption. Club council was the club's governing body and, as president, he was its chairman. The membership comprised the club officers and three ordinary members, elected each year at this meeting.

President Frank proceeded to run through the matters council had considered during the course of the year. His delivery was swift and professional.

'That's my report of what we did in club council during the year,' said President Frank. 'Any questions?'

'Mr President, you didn't mention the matter of Alec Barton and charter night.' Kye's voice boomed across the room. There were one or two suppressed sniggers and rather more rolling of eyeballs.

'No, I didn't,' said Frank.

'Was the complaint that he put his hand on the lady's leg or that he didn't?'

'Thank you for that contribution, Kye,' said Frank. 'Let's move on.'

'Is she self-employed?' said Kye.

'Kye, what are you talking about?' said President Frank.

'Sexual harassment at work can't be a problem for the self-employed,' said Kye.

'We really must get on...'

'Sexual harassment is no joking matter,' said Fiona angrily, 'it can ruin women's lives.' Fiona was small and feisty. She had held a senior position in the international branch of a large bank. Although she had grown up in an affluent upper-middle-class family, her father had been violent and abusive towards her mother. She had had a difficult and unhappy childhood. University in the 1960s gave her a great sense of freedom, but in her last year she became pregnant, and her domineering father required her to marry the scoundrel. It was not a good marriage and they soon separated. She married again, but although there were no further children, Fiona's daughter had given her three wonderful grandchildren.

Frank struck the Rotary bell aggressively and spoke in a loud voice, 'Let's move on. The next report is club administration, that's Andrew.'

'There's no need to shout, Mr President,' said Kye, 'we're not mutton.'

'Mutton? What are you talking about, Kye?' said Ernie.

'Mutt and Jeff, deaf,' said Kye. 'It's rhyming slang.'

Andrew Parker was the president-elect and by custom and practice, responsible for club administration, the internal running of the club. 'Thank you, Mr President. As I said in my written report, during the year under review I negotiated an increase of £2 in the cost of meals and I think that members are generally agreed that the standard has gone up.' Andrew moved swiftly over one or two other housekeeping matters and then brought his contribution to an end.

'I think that an increase of £2 is excessive,' said George. 'We're here every week. It's a set meal and we all buy drinks at the bar.' Ostensibly, he and Andrew had always been friends, but a clash of opinions and aspirations for the future of the club would soon test that friendship to breaking point.

'Apart from the money we spend every week, we occasionally pop in for Sunday lunch and bring family and friends,' said Paul.

'Bill does pretty well from Rotary, especially from the president's drinking fund,' said Kye. The president was not amused.

Andrew defended his position. 'Bill has held the old price for several years and in all the circumstances, I think £2 was reasonable. I reported to the club at the time and members approved it.'

'I thought that Bill only wanted another £1,' said Kye. 'Did you negotiate him up rather than down?'

Andrew let the comment pass. 'That's the end of the club administration report.'

Frank said, 'Foundation and international are Paul.' *This could take a long time.*

'I am pleased to remind members that this year, we have donated £1,000 to Foundation and another £500 to the eradication of polio,' said Paul. 'As you know, Foundation is Rotary's own charity of more than one billion dollars, held by Rotary International in America, and we all contribute to it. It's Foundation that enables Rotary International to make global grants to humanitarian projects, at home and overseas, so our support is vital.' Paul paused for a moment then continued, 'In 1988, three significant organisations, the World Health Organisation, UNICEF, and Rotary Foundation, began an effort to eliminate polio around the world.'

'You told us all that last year,' said Kye.

Paul ignored the interruption and continued, 'Others have been involved in this huge effort, including the Bill Gates Foundation. Polio is a dreadful crippling disease that affects mainly children and young people. I am sure that some of our older members can remember when polio was endemic in this country.'

'We've heard all that, too,' said Kye.

Paul continued, 'All of us in Rotary have been at the forefront of this fight and we are winning.'

'There are still some countries where polio exists,' said Fiona. 'There's still some way to go.'

Paul said, 'Yes, polio persists in three countries: Pakistan, Afghanistan, and Nigeria, but India is now polio-free. We are so close to the elimination of this terrible disease. On a personal note, Jackie and I went to India two years ago to help with the vaccinations, and I know that other members have also done so in the past.'

Eventually, Paul brought his report to a conclusion and President Frank said, 'Thank you, Paul, for your very able advocacy and also for the huge personal efforts you have made in fundraising for Foundation. We now turn to Phillip for membership.'

'Mr President, I have to report that there are twenty-one members in the club, plus one honorary member. As I said in my report, our membership evening was not successful in bringing any new people into the club.'

'Any comments or questions for Phillip?' said President Frank.

'I have a new neighbour,' said George. 'I have only just met him, but I'm going to bring him into the club.'

'Well, that's good news, George,' said President Frank.

'Does he know yet?' said Kye.

'Of course, he knows,' said George. 'I've told him.'

And so, the meeting went on with each chairman presenting his report, when called by the president. The next item after the chairmen's reports was the report of the treasurer and the setting of annual subscriptions.

The tall, willowy figure of Mark, the treasurer, rose from his chair. 'I have considered the club's finances and I am pleased to recommend that subscriptions should remain unchanged in the forthcoming year.'

The meeting approved the recommendation. No one wanted to pay any more than necessary, especially as most of it went to support the higher echelons of Rotary.

'We now come to the election of three ordinary members to club council,' said Frank. 'Over to Claire.'

'Mr President,' said Claire, 'two weeks ago, I invited all members to make nominations and I have received four nominations for the three places.' Claire took charge of the election. She passed round a ballot paper to each member. 'The four nominations are for the three existing council members and George. Put a tick against three of the names. If you vote for all four candidates, I shall disqualify your ballot paper.'

Claire gathered up the ballot papers and took them to President Frank. Together they counted the votes for each candidate. Frank announced the result. 'The votes cast are as follows: Ernie 16 votes; Paul 17; Kye 12; George 18. I declare that Ernie, Paul and George are duly elected as the three ordinary members of club council for the next Rotary year.'

Kye was not happy that George had replaced him. For once he had nothing to say.

Frank said, 'Let's go to the fiddle, so it's over to you, Dominic.'

Dominic took out a money bag and handed it to the president. 'A pound from everyone in the bag, please.' Frank put in a pound and handed it around.

Dominic dipped into the bag of balls and pulled one out. 'It's number 15, which is Kye.'

Kye cheered up. 'So you decided to put my ball in this week, did you? It's about time.'

'And finally, our sergeant at arms, Kye,' said Frank.

'First, Mr President, I'm fining you for starting the meeting late.'

'Well, I'm sure I didn't,' said Frank.

'Paul and Mark were late back from the bar. Frank's tie is so loud I can hardly hear myself think. It's as loud as the giggling from our three lady members. That's fifty pence from each of you. And George is looking too serious. I'm fining him as well. It's not difficult to tell the difference between George and a ray of golden sunshine. That's another fifty pence.' Kye worked his way down his list of misdemeanours and then said, 'And I had better fine myself, just in case I've done anything wrong.'

Andrew said, 'Thank you, Kye. We will now have the final toast.' All members stood to a scraping of chairs and a raising of glasses.

'Rotary and peace the world over,' said the president.

'Rotary and peace the world over.'

*

'You remember I said that I needed to go to Ipswich,' said Imogen.

'Ipswich?'

'To do some shopping. I think I'll go today.'

'Today?'

'Today.'

'All right.'

'The weather's good. I need some space.' Imogen was clearing away after breakfast.

'Space?' said Oliver. 'Is there space in Ipswich?'

'I just need to get out of the house.'

'What's wrong with the house?'

'Nothing.'

'That's good,' said Ollie, as he looked up and smiled. 'We've only just moved in.'

'It gets claustrophobic after a while. That's all.'

'I've got a lot to do,' said Ollie.

'I haven't seen a soul for ages, apart from Erica and you, and you're always working.'

'We didn't come to darkest Suffolk to retire.'

'Remind me why we came.'

Ollie said, 'You, well we, decided that we needed to move away from London and the life we were leading, after, well, you know.' The sudden death of their baby had been a devastating blow. After years of waiting and rounds of fertility treatment, the sudden and unexpected death of an otherwise healthy baby boy had shattered their world. Imogen had suffered a bout of depression and a move to the country was a last desperate attempt to salvage her health and their marriage.

'Anyway, I need to do some shopping.'

'I'll be busy,' said Oliver.

'Are you going to spend the whole of the day stuck in front of that computer?'

'Most of it. I'll make some more coffee a bit later and I'll probably go for a short run before lunch.'

Running in the Suffolk countryside was a delight and Oliver had come to prefer it to his old London gym. There were narrow treelined lanes, footpaths over open farmland, big skies with puffed-up clouds and the forever changing scenery. Fields were ploughed and sown and crops grown. The bare brown earth yielded to precocious green shoots; cereals, perhaps wheat, the foundation of civilisation, or barley to produce good Suffolk beer. The yellow carpet of rapeseed stretched to the horizon.

'I shall go as soon as I'm ready,' said Imogen. 'I've left some cold meat and salad in the fridge. You can get it when you're hungry.'

'Yes, all right. I've got a video conference at half past ten with some of the guys.' Imogen did not know any of the guys. They would exist physically elsewhere and manifest in digital form in the study at the due time.

A little while later, Imogen popped into the study. 'Ollie, I'm going now. I've put some washing in the washing machine. It's whites. When you get back from your run, please put all your running gear in and start it. Don't forget.'

'Yes, of course,' said Ollie, his mind already on his conference call.

'And Erica said she might leave some of her rhubarb at the back door.'

'I don't like rhubarb.'

Imogen kissed Oliver a quick goodbye and she was gone. Through the open window he could hear her footsteps crunching on the gravel, as he was busy on the computer. Before his conference call, he went out into the kitchen, put some coffee beans into the grinder and began to make some strong black coffee. Coffee was essential to focus mind and body, and this conference call was not going to be easy.

Oliver's video conference had been more difficult and stressful than he had expected. It was after midday and time for his run. He got up from his chair and stretched. He went upstairs to the bedroom and changed into his running kit, white shorts, a crisp white tee-shirt and white socks with blue bands. He went out through the back door, which he locked and put the key under a flowerpot. Anyone could have found it, had anyone ever looked, but this was rural Suffolk, not lawless London. He did a few stretches and then jogged the length of the garden and back to warm up. He started his stopwatch as he ran out of the gate and along the lane. After a few hundred yards he turned left onto a footpath that led into open farmland. To his left a field of wheat, long, luscious and a dazzling green, waving in the breeze. It was a long time until harvest. Immediately to his right was a ditch, with another field of wheat beyond. The footpath was uneven and he looked down as he ran to avoid disappearing into a rabbit hole, like Alice in Wonderland. Oliver reached the gap in the hedgerow at the bottom of the field and ran over the flimsy wooden bridge into the next field. As he did so, there was a squawk, squawk, squawk and a furious flapping of wings. A flash of red wattle and brightly coloured plumage rose up into the sky. He had startled a pheasant. Oliver took the path to his right and saw a crow a few yards in front of him. It nonchalantly flapped its wings and moved farther along the path and, as Oliver got closer, it did the same again. The third time the crow flew off the path into the field and Oliver ran past it. *What did old Arthur, our postman, say? If you see a crow and there are lots of them, it's a rook, and if you see a rook and it's alone, it must be a crow. These country folk are a strange lot.*

It was a glorious day. The sun was hot, but there was a welcoming cool breeze. He was lean, fit and athletic in build and he felt a great sense of exhilaration and freedom, as the ground moved swiftly under his feet. Soon he reached the farthest point of his circuit as he ran along the bottom of the field and began the return journey, up a gentle incline. He reached the lane and turned right, increasing his pace on the firm surface. At his gate, he clicked his stopwatch. It showed 24 minutes and 56.9 seconds. Under 25 minutes, his quickest ever over that route. He felt endorphins coursing around his body. The stress and frustrations of his morning video conference were gone. He was euphoric.

Oliver was sweating profusely as he let himself in through the back door. He took a carton of orange juice from the fridge, then put it down. He had spotted a bottle of Adnams Broadside. Oliver was not a great beer drinker, but he had taken to Broadside, partly because of its story. Adnams had begun brewing Broadside in 1972 to commemorate the Battle of Sole Bay, which had taken place four hundred years ago, off the coast of Southwold, the home of the Suffolk brewery. During the Anglo-Dutch wars over trade routes, in the seventeenth and eighteenth centuries, a fleet of seventy-five ships of the Dutch navy surprised ninety-three ships of the Royal Navy, at anchor in Sole Bay. The outcome of the battle was inconclusive, but both sides claimed victory.

Ollie opened the bottle. He slowly poured the silky, strong, dark beer and took a long draught and then another. Soon, he had drained the glass. He took his lunch from the fridge, put it on the kitchen table and turned on the radio. As he started to cool down, his tee-shirt began to feel cold, wet and uncomfortable against his skin, so he decided to shower before lunch. He was just about to leave the kitchen, when he remembered what Imogen had asked him to do; the washing machine. He took off his tee-shirt, opened the door of the washing machine and bowled the wet garment underarm into the machine. His socks were next. First, he took off his right sock, pulling from the toe; he lifted up his right leg and bowled it underarm towards the machine. It hit the rim and fell to the floor. He became aware of the music coming from the radio: the stripper. He did the same with his left sock.

Meanwhile, Erica was preparing to walk across the lane with the rhubarb she had promised Imogen. She walked out of the house onto the drive and across the lane. In The Old Forge, the Broadside Oliver had drunk on an empty stomach and the endorphins raging around his body made a heady mix. He was reaching the climax of his act. Off came his pants and he swung them around his head and let go at the wrong moment with his arm in an upwards flourish and they landed on the lamp shade. With both hands punching the air and his feet apart, he thrust his groin out in time with the music. At that moment Erica arrived at the door with the freshly cut sticks of rhubarb, long and red, and glanced through the window.

'Oliver Green!' she shrieked in horror.

*

The Woodgate household was just finishing lunch. 'I must try to have another word with Oliver over the road,' said George.

As Erica cleared away, George looked down the road from the kitchen window. Oliver was out in the garden.

George walked over the road. 'Hello Oliver, I've been looking out for you.'

'I've been busy indoors, but I really do need to do something about the garden.'

The garden had suffered many years of neglect. There had been a time when it had been a joy to poor old Cedric and his wife. George could not recall her name. She had passed away many years ago and now Cedric had joined her. Maybe Oliver would transform it to its former glory, but somehow Oliver did not seem a natural gardener.

'You've got quite a job on your hands,' said George. 'Cedric was pretty keen on his garden when he could do it, but it's hardly been touched these past years.'

'You said that you'd been looking out for me?'

'Just to see how you were getting on and to invite you to a Rotary meeting.'

'About the same as when you waved to me two days ago.' Oliver ignored the reference to Rotary.

'Yes, quite so. Last time I asked you to come along to a meeting of my club you were busy.'

'I can't remember.'

'We've got an interesting talk next Wednesday. One of our members knows a retired chief superintendent and he's going to give us a talk on some aspect of policing, not too sure of the details.'

'How interesting.'

'He's got a projector and some slides.' Chief Superintendent John Howell had a computer and a PowerPoint presentation and was a very accomplished speaker.

'I'm not sure that I'm ready for Rotary.'

'Next Wednesday.'

'I don't think so.'

'You really should.'

'We're going to a concert, a local choir, they're doing *The Messiah.*'

'Oh! You're keen on music? Do you sing?' *If he's being rather slippery about Rotary, he might be of some use to Erica for her choir*, thought George.

'No, not at all. I'm interested in music, but I can't sing. A friend of Imogen's is playing in the orchestra, the string section.'

'A fiddler?' said George, a term he had heard Erica use often enough.

'No, she's perfectly honest,' said Oliver and laughed at his own joke. George stood stony-faced, silently questioning the sanity of his new neighbour. *He's laughing like a lunatic. What's the matter with him?*

'Perhaps another time.'

'Ask me in twenty years.'

'Twenty years?'

'Rotary.'

FIVE

Trouble at Rose Cottage

The following Saturday afternoon, George's phone rang. Erica answered. 'Hello, Luke, yes, he's here. Just a moment.' Luke Chadwick was the part-time secretary to the Morton Charities and their only employee.

'George, I think that you ought to know that I had a call from Mrs Preston earlier on.'

'Who?'

'The tenant of Rose Cottage. The daughter-in-law of Brigadier Rufford's gardener. She's very old now.'

'I know who she is; didn't recognise the name.'

'She's got no electricity,' said Luke. 'It just went off all of a sudden.'

'Is there a power cut?' said George.

'No, it's a problem at the house,' said Luke. 'Putting off a rewiring at the house wasn't the best decision the trustees have ever taken, if you don't mind me saying so.'

'Yes, I do. As trustees we have to have regard to costs as well as the welfare of our tenants. Have you spoken to the electrician chap we usually have? The advice you gave us was that the electrician said that it was not essential for the time being.'

Luke ignored that. 'I've been ringing Mr Jenkins' landline without success and I haven't got a mobile number for him. He must be away for the weekend.'

'Have you tried anyone else?'

'I've rung several other electricians, but no one is answering the phone.'

'Keep trying,' said George.

'Do you actually know the Prestons?' said Luke.

'No, should I?'

'They're delightful old country folk.'

'Apart from when they have a problem,' said George.

'Mr Preston has worked on the land all his working life.'

'So did most people around these parts at one time,' said George.

'He suffers from arthritis.'

'It's old age.'

'He used to be fit.'

'Just keep trying,' said George.

'What, to get an electrician?'

'Yes.'

'There's not much light in that old house during the day and it'll be dark in a few hours,' said Luke.

'I can tell the time.'

'They've got plenty of candles,' said Luke. 'Enough to burn the house down.'

'That can't happen, can it?'

'Old timber, thatched roof, what do you think?' said Luke.

'Tell them not to carry a candle up those stairs,' said George.

'Yes, all right.'

'Have they got a torch?'

'Yes.'

'Tell them to use the torch and stop messing about with candles,' said George.

'The battery's dead.'

'They must have a spare battery.'

'Mrs Preston's old cooker gave up about a year ago,' said Luke.

'So what?'

'The trustees bought her a new one.'

'We can be generous,' said George.

'It's electric.'

'Of course, it's electric. There isn't any gas around here,' said George.

'Exactly,' said Luke. 'They can't even boil a kettle.'

'Luke, can't you sort it out?' said George, irritated by this intrusion into his weekend. 'What do you expect me to do?'

'I thought you ought to know, as chairman of the trustees.'

'Actually, there is someone I could try,' said George. 'I'll get back to you.'

George picked up the phone and dialled. 'Hello, is that Karen? It's George Woodgate. I'm a friend of Alec's. Is he there?'

'No, he went out about an hour ago. He said that he wouldn't be long.'

'Will you say I rang and ask him to ring me back?'

'Yes of course, but you might get him on his mobile.'

Alec's mobile rang and rang. *Just pick up the phone, will you?* thought George, as he was directed again to leave a message. The afternoon was now coalescing into evening, but there was still daylight for some time yet.

'Come on, George, you need to get ready,' said Erica. 'Please don't spoil my birthday.'

'Yes, I'm just coming.' He rang the number one more time, not expecting a reply. He didn't get one. As he put down the phone, it rang. 'Alec?'

'Any progress with the electrician?' said Luke. 'I've had Mrs Preston on the phone again. She's beginning to get very agitated. We've got to do something.'

'Luke, I'm trying to contact a friend of mine who might be able to help, but I can't get hold of him.'

'I'm really worried for Mr and Mrs Preston. They've had no power for hours, no hot food, not even a cup of tea.'

'Can't they get a Chinese takeaway?'

'People of that generation don't eat "foreign muck".'

'I'll ring you as soon as I can.' George put the phone down. He did not want the problem that Luke Chadwick had dumped on him, not today. He felt agitated, stressed; he started rubbing his hands together in a handwashing motion.

George and Erica drove to the Queen's Head, an old country pub, where generations of ploughmen had drunk pints of beer, chatted and played darts or skittles and still managed to duck under the low beams, no matter how many pints they had downed.

'Not many rabbits around this year,' one might have said.

His drinking partner would probably have replied, 'No, you're right there.'

These days the Queen's Head was a gastropub that served good quality food and wines. The chatter now was more likely to be of house prices or the state of the economy. They still served plenty of beer, but the good old Suffolk boys had all gone.

A waitress showed George and Erica to their table and gave them menus. 'May I get you something to drink?'

'Two gin and slimline tonics, ice and lemon,' said George.

'Don't drink any more this evening, George. I'm not driving on my birthday.'

George's mobile phone rang as the smoked salmon starters arrived. 'George, Mrs Preston is most distressed,' said Luke. 'Any progress? They haven't had any hot food or a cup of tea since this morning.'

'It's Erica's birthday and we have gone out to dinner. I'm doing my best to contact some help. Tell her that.'

'I don't think she'll want to know that you're having a nice dinner.'

'Just tell her that I'm trying my best to get some help. What more does she expect?' George raised his voice and a woman at the next table glanced round.

'George, do you really have to do this when it's my birthday dinner?' said Erica.

Before he could reply his mobile phone rang again. 'Alec, where are you?' He got up to move away from the other diners, as the waitress brought the main course. The slow-roasted Blythburgh belly of pork, reared on the sandy soil of Suffolk's heritage coastline, had been carefully arranged alongside dauphinoise potato and glazed carrots, and served with a tarragon sauce.

'Would you be so good as to take the plates back to the kitchen and keep them warm, and I'll have another gin and slimline tonic,' said Erica. 'I'm sure my husband won't be long.'

George was now in frantic conversation with Alec. 'You really must be joking, George. It's Saturday night and most builders, electricians and everyone else, will be down the pub.'

'All of them?'

'Yes, of course. The electrician I use is here with me now.'

'Can you persuade him to sort out Mrs Preston's electrics?' said George, who could hear Alec speaking to someone.

'George, I've just asked him if he'll do an urgent job now and his reply, well, it ended in "off".' George could hear laughter. 'To tell you the truth, I wouldn't trust him to change a fuse at the moment. Mind you, he's a good sparky when he's sober.'

'Alec, I'm being irritated by endless calls from the secretary to the trustees,' said George.

'Who?'

'He keeps telling me that the old couple who live in Rose Cottage are desperate and they've got no light and no cooking facilities,' said George. 'However, more to the point, it's Erica's birthday dinner tonight and I don't want to spoil it for her.'

'I tell you what, George, as a favour to you, I'll pop over and have a look. If it's something I can fix, I'll fix it. If I can't, I can't.'

'Alec, thank you so much,' said George, who felt a huge sense of relief, as his anxiety and irritability began to ease.

'I shall be charging your charity weekend rates and double time,' said Alec, 'and you can buy me a pint next time you see me.'

'Yes, of course, Alec.'

When George arrived back at the table, Erica was on her third gin and slimline tonic and she had mellowed. The waitress arrived with their plates and they settled down to an enjoyable birthday dinner.

The phone rang early the next morning.

Luke's voice came down the line. 'I'm sorry to ring you on a Sunday morning, George. I've just had Mrs Preston on the phone. According to her, the man you sent around to fix the problem at Rose Cottage turned up drunk. He spent half an hour messing around and then said he couldn't fix it. She is now at the end of her tether.'

'Well, what do you expect me to do?'

A moment later, George was on the phone speaking to Alec. 'I thought you were going to fix the problem. Instead, you've made it worse.'

'Hold on a minute,' said Alec. 'I was doing you a favour. Unfortunately, I couldn't fix it.'

'Why not?'

'It was a bit more than mending a fuse,' said Alec.

'Is it serious?'

'Probably, I'll ring my sparky. At least he'll be more or less sober now, and with a bit of luck, he won't be going to church this Sunday morning.'

It had been a tense phone conversation and the seriousness of the situation was all too stark. George had two frail and elderly tenants without power and no means to get a hot drink. He was the chairman of the charity that owned the house and it was his responsibility to do something. It was Sunday morning, and everything depended on Alec's electrician friend being willing and sober enough to solve the problem.

The phone rang again. It was a woman's voice. 'Hello, Mr Woodgate, chairman of the Rufford Trust? And a former president of the Rotary Club of Debenham?'

The voice on the phone sounded very young and George's spirits rose. Was this help from an unexpected source? 'Yes, George Woodgate speaking.'

'I'm Georgina Archer. I'm a reporter with the *Daily Mail*.'

George took a deep breath. 'The *Daily Mail*?' His mind was racing. *What does she want, this Miss Georgina whatnot from the Daily Mail?*

'We're running a story about Mr and Mrs Preston, your tenants at Rose Cottage. You have left them over the weekend without power. They can't cook or even make a cup of tea. Can you confirm that?'

George said, 'Well, yes, they've got a problem with the electrics.'

'Isn't it your problem? Your charity owns the property and it's your responsibility to maintain it, isn't it?'

'Well, yes, technically.'

'What do you mean, technically?'

'Well, yes.'

'The Rufford Trust is responsible for maintenance. That's correct, isn't it?'

'Yes.'

'Can you confirm that while Mr and Mrs Preston were sitting shivering in Rose Cottage, without even a hot drink, you were out celebrating last night, with champagne and lobster thermidor?'

'No, that's not true,' said George.

'So, you deny that you were out celebrating?'

'It was my wife's birthday.'

'So, you went out to celebrate with champagne and lobster thermidor,' said Georgina.

'We didn't have champagne and lobster thermidor.'

'So, you're quibbling about the menu?'

'No, the menu was fine,' said George.

'While you were out eating a celebration dinner,' said Georgina, 'you did nothing to help Mr and Mrs Preston. That's true, isn't it?'

'That's not true,' said George. 'I arranged for someone to go round and fix the problem.'

'Was that the man who was too drunk to do anything?'

'He wasn't drunk.'

'How do you know?'

'He told me he wasn't drunk.'

'So, Mr Woodgate, you took the word of a man who had been drinking that he wasn't drunk, is that correct?'

'But he wasn't drunk.'

'But he had been drinking?'

'He'd been in the pub.'

'So, he had been drinking, hadn't he?'

'Yes, I suppose so.' By now George was sweating. His mouth was dry and his hand was trembling so much that he had difficulty holding the phone. He was in a state of acute anxiety.

Georgina said, 'You send a man who had been drinking to the house to tamper with the electrics? But you deny that he was drunk?'

'Our usual electrician is away for the weekend, and we couldn't get anyone else.'

'What about your backup electrician?' said Georgina.

'Who?'

'You haven't got any backup for weekend emergencies, have you, Mr Woodgate.'

'No,' said George, 'but Alec Barton, the man who went to the house, is a builder and he did try to get an electrician friend of his to go.'

'But the electrician friend was drunk?'

'How did you know?'

'You've just confirmed it,' said Georgina. 'I put it to you that this electrician was drunk and you've just confirmed that he was. Do you know any electricians who aren't drunk?'

George's head was in a spin. This loud and demanding woman was creating chaos in his world. 'No.'

'So that's it, is it?' said Georgina. 'You're not going to provide the help they need?'

'I can tell you that I have things in motion as we speak,' said George, in a weak attempt to gain the initiative. 'My friend is arranging for his electrician to go round immediately.'

'Is that your friend who had been drinking, but was not drunk, and his electrician who was drunk?'

'Where did you get all this stuff from?' said George. He felt overwhelmed by sensory overload and the incessant questions from this woman.

'I'm afraid that we can't reveal our sources, Mr Woodgate, but I can tell you that I have just been to see Mr and Mrs Preston,' said Georgina.

'How are they?'

'You have no idea how they are? You have not even contacted them by phone. I shall add that to our piece, *that Mr Woodgate had to ask our reporter how these frail old people were, because he had no idea.* It doesn't look good, does it?'

'Are they all right?' said George. He did not understand how they might be feeling, but he knew that he ought to enquire.

Georgina said, 'Shall I tell you what our newspaper has done, because of the hopelessness of the position you've left them in?'

'What?'

'We have contacted social services and they are trying to find a residential care home to admit them for respite care, for a week,' said Georgina. 'We'll send you the bill.'

'You can't get social services at the weekend,' said George.

'Mr Woodgate, my paper can get the president of the United States at the weekend, if we need to. We'll be publishing our story in tomorrow's paper.'

'You're not going to put the blame on me, are you?' said George.

'You are chairman of the charity, aren't you?'

'Yes, but I'm a non-executive chairman, I don't actually do anything.' George thought that he had made a telling point.

'I think we have established that, Mr Woodgate.'

'Well, I shall sue; I shall ring my solicitor in the morning,' said George, with desperation in his voice. 'He'll be on to your editor like a flash.'

'If we think that we might be at risk, we'll clear the story with our libel lawyers, but I don't think that'll be necessary because you have confirmed everything.'

'No, I haven't,' said George. 'I deny everything.' George's head was spinning. This Georgina woman had bombarded him with questions, one after another, interminably, like a pyroclastic flow.

'You have been most helpful, Mr Woodgate,' said Georgina. 'You can't sue a paper for telling the truth.'

'It's a pack of lies,' said George weakly.

Georgina said, 'Goodbye, Mr Woodgate, and thank you for your co-operation. Just one thing before I go. One of our photographers is on his way to get some pictures of Rose Cottage and we'd like a nice picture of you too. He'll catch up with you later today.'

'Are you trying to be funny? I don't want my picture taken and I forbid you to take any pictures of Rose Cottage, the tenants or anything to do with the Rufford Trust. Do you hear me?' Miss Archer supressed a giggle.

Before George could draw breath, the phone rang again. 'I've been trying to get you,' said Alec. 'I've spoken to Wayne.'

'Can he help?'

Alec said, 'Wayne went round and had a look. He said he wouldn't touch it. The electrics are in a right state. The house could have burnt down at any time. It's serious, George. Fubar is how Wayne described it.'

'What?'

'Mucked up beyond all recognition,' said Alec.

'Well, it must be mubar, then,' said George, with a snort of indignation.

'It's a technical term, George. There's no need to get too hung up on it.'

'Why did you say fubar if it's mubar?'

'George, that place needs a complete rewire and it'll take at least a week, probably longer, and a few thousand quid.'

'How many thousands?'

'Wayne's doing a full estimate. He'll ring you later.'

'Wait a minute,' said George, 'the other trustees will want to get at least two other quotes for the work.'

Alec said, 'How long's that going to take? Wayne was there when the reporter went round, so he knows that Mr and Mrs Preston will be going into a home for a week, which might be just about enough time for Wayne to do the work, but he'll have to start first thing tomorrow morning.'

'I'm not sure I'm able to agree to that.'

'George, I thought that you were chairman of this bloody charity. Don't they let you decide anything?'

The comment stung George. 'I can take executive decisions in an emergency.'

'Isn't this an emergency?'

'Of course, it is.'

'Well, there you are then,' said Alec. 'Wayne will be round there first thing. Mrs Preston gave him a key. He knows that Mr and Mrs Preston will be gone by then.'

'All right.'

Alec said, 'If you're really worried about quotes, Wayne would usually ask the client to get two other quotes first. If Wayne knows what the lowest quote is, he'll come in a shade lower. Of course, that could be a tad difficult if he has already started the work.'

'I don't want to hear this. I shall have to get two more quotes and do it properly.'

'George, I'll tell you what we'll do. Wayne can get them. He knows lots of people who owe him a favour.'

'Wayne can get what?'

'Two more quotes. Wayne's got lots of mates who'll write him out a quote.'

'I don't want anything to do with that sort of business.'

'You worry too much, George.'

'Alec, don't tell me that Wayne spoke to the reporter, Miss Georgina Whatnot.'

'Of course, he did,' said Alec. 'She was very tasty, according to Wayne. She asked him about Saturday night and did he go drinking every night.'

'Oh no.'

'Wayne was really chatting her up. He told her he got pissed every Saturday night and he told her about some of the jobs he's done. Like when he rewired this large house and when he'd done the job there was—'

'She's going to write about all this, is she?'

'Of course, she is. She even asked Wayne how to spell his surname to make sure she got it right in the paper. She was really making up to Wayne.'

'I bet she bloody was.'

'She asked him his professional opinion on the state of the electrics. He told her they were a disgrace, poor old Mr and Mrs Preston were in grave danger. Then this photographer turned up and started taking pictures, the house, the tenants and Wayne.'

'Oh no, this is getting worse.'

'Wayne will be round there first thing tomorrow. He may have a drink on a Saturday night, but he works hard all week and he's a bloody good electrician.'

'I haven't even got an estimate from Wayne, let alone three estimates for the job,' said George.

'You won't want Mr and Mrs Preston to come home and find the house in the same state, because you're messing about getting quotes,' said George. 'Georgina won't be very impressed either.'

'What about Wayne's quote?' said George.

'He'll let you have that as soon as he can,' said Alec.

JAMES BARRETT

'He's a busy man. He doesn't want to spend all his time messing around with paperwork.'

'I'll ring one or two of the trustees, the ones most likely to make a fuss. Alec, you'd better not let me down on this.'

The call ended and George rang the Revd. Anthony Masters, an ex officio trustee, to explain the present predicament. 'It's urgent. We've got to act immediately.'

'Are you mad?' said the Revd. Masters. 'The man's taking you for a fool.'

'There's no alternative.'

'You've got yourself into this mess,' said the Revd. Masters. 'You can get yourself out of it.'

'Perhaps I'll ring some of the other trustees,' said George.

'Don't bother ringing Lucas or William, because they will agree with me.'

'How do you know?'

'They're my churchwardens,' said the Revd. Masters.

'They can make up their own minds.'

'They'll do as I say.'

The conversation ended on a sour note and George had omitted to mention the catastrophic story that was going to appear in the *Daily Mail* the next day.

'George, what on earth is going on?' Erica had heard one side of some these conversations and was becoming increasingly alarmed.

'It's nothing really, just a bit of charity work.'

'There's not much charity in leaving poor old defenceless people to burn to death in your house.'

'It's not like that.'

'Yes, it is, George, and you should be ashamed of yourself. We'll never be able to hold our heads up again when all this comes out in the paper tomorrow. What are the Women's Institute going to say at our next meeting?'

'I don't give a damn about the Women's bloody Institute.' George stormed out of the room, leaving a dumbfounded Erica in his wake. At that moment, a car drew up and out got a man with an expensive looking camera with a zoom lens.

*

It was Monday morning. George had spent a torrid night in a sixteenth-century house, thatched roof ablaze. He had heard the crackling of the straw as the flames reached upwards. Acrid smoke entered his nostrils and penetrated deep into his lungs. An evil woman in a white dress torments him with a red-hot iron, as she shouts questions, to which he has no answers. To his horror, he realises he is shackled, unable to move, she astride him with her long dark hair tumbling over her face. She rips open his shirt and looks into his eyes, as she touches the hot iron on his bare chest. His flesh burns and sizzles, the pain excruciating. He screams out in agony, to her palpable satisfaction. The pain eases as a blackness overcomes him. He drifts into unconsciousness, aware only of a white dress riding up over the strong thighs that grip his torso.

Daylight began to creep through the windows, around the curtains and into the house, bringing with it a new day. George touched his chest, gingerly moving his fingers towards the wound he expected to find. He felt no pain, but his movement was constricted; he tried to open his eyes, but they were seared onto his face like two burnt raisins atop a fruit loaf. A voice said, 'Stop making that noise, George; what's the matter with you?' but there was no response. George was somewhere between this world and another, hovering between consciousness and catalepsy.

*

His urgent need to buy a copy of the *Daily Mail* pushed all thought of the night out of his head. Perhaps the editor would be more understanding of the situation and the difficulty he was in at the weekend when no one was available. He might take one look at Miss Georgina Whatnot's invective and tone it down, so as not to misrepresent matters and mislead his readers. He must contact Alec to see if Wayne was getting on with the rewiring of Rose Cottage. Then there was the problem of the trustees, which he would have to resolve, and not to mention Erica and the Women's *bloody* Institute. And what would his fellow Rotarians think? They would surely be more understanding, well the men anyway, but not Fiona, and Fiona could create big waves for someone so small. George was in a state of acute anxiety. The world was conspiring against him, as he struggled to see a way through all his problems.

It was a cold crisp sunny morning, with fluffy clouds floating in a bright blue sky, as he entered the newsagents.

'Good morning, George,' said Fred, with his customary cheerfulness.

'I'll take the *Daily Mail*, Fred.'

'You don't read the *Mail*,' said Fred.

'I want the *Mail* this morning,' said George, 'if you don't mind.'

'I'm afraid you're out of luck,' said Fred. 'The *Mail* had some sort of printing problem last night, so they've had to reduce the numbers for all the newsagents. Luckily, I've got enough for all my usual customers, but the few extras I had have all gone.'

'I've got to have one,' said George. 'Can't you let me have one of those under the counter?'

'I don't have anything under the counter,' said Fred. 'All the copies I have in the shop are to satisfy those customers who have the *Mail* on a regular order. I can't let them down. What do you want to know?' Fred pulled out a copy of the *Daily Mail*. 'I haven't had time to see the *Mail* this morning.'

'Hurry up,' said George.

'Let's see, the front page has got a picture of an old, thatched cottage,' said Fred, studying the paper carefully. 'The headline says DEATH TRAP. Under that it says—'

'Let me see that,' said George, as he glared at Fred.

Fred continued, 'Underneath that, it says ROTARIAN CHARITY CHAIRMAN LEFT ELDERLY TENANTS WITHOUT POWER IN DEATH HOUSE. Is that you, George?' Fred had moved nearer to the counter and George leant forward and grabbed the paper, but Fred hung on to it. They wrestled for a moment, and then the paper tore and George was left holding most of the first few pages.

'Hey, come back. Look what you've done to this paper,' said Fred. He was furious with George for such an outrage.

Then old Mrs Smith tottered in and he immediately calmed down. 'What's going on? Have you got my *Daily Mail*?'

Mrs Smith's intervention allowed George to get into his car and zoom off. He drove home with a great sense of foreboding. First, he would have to face Erica, to whom he had said something about not caring a damn about the Women's bloody Institute.

Erica was waiting, with her arms folded. She was standing by the kitchen table, on top of which was a copy of the *Daily Mail*. She stared at him in silence.

'Where did you get that?' said George.

'Mrs Thompson kindly lent it to me. She said she was just passing. What have you got there?'

'I went out to buy a copy of the *Mail*.'

'Why didn't you buy a whole one?' said Erica.

'I tried to but...' His words dried up in his anxiety.

Erica said, 'I've read the whole sorry story. How could you do it? How could you be so stupid and say all those things?'

'It was an ambush.'

'You've seen politicians being interviewed on television, haven't you?' said Erica.

'Yes, of course.'

'Do they ever answer the questions they're asked?'

'They've had special training,' said George.

'They just talk about something else.'

'Can we talk about something else?' said George.

'No, we can't.'

'It's not so easy to change the subject, then, is it?' said George.

The doorbell rang. Neither of them had heard Mrs Thompson's footsteps. 'I've come to collect my paper, dear.'

'Mr Woodgate, this dreadful story in the paper isn't true, is it? You can tell me what really happened.'

At that moment the phone rang and Erica answered. Without saying a word, she thrust the phone at George. George put it to his ear. 'Hello, yes, who? No, I don't want to give an interview, with pictures, to the *Daily Mirror*.' He slammed down the phone.

The phone rang again. 'Excuse me,' said George. He picked up his car keys and charged out of the house, propelled by his anxiety. Erica answered; it was a reporter from *The Sun*. 'He's not here.' She put down the phone and it rang again.

George drove to Rose Cottage, not knowing what he was going to say to Wayne. It was just a short drive from home, but a long way from Erica, Mrs Thompson and the *Daily Mirror*. He parked and got out of the car. It had been quite some time since he had last viewed Rose Cottage. It appeared tired and unkempt. He looked up and, to his dismay, the thatch was in need of attention in places. The front door was open, so he tapped tentatively and listened. There was activity inside. 'Hello, anyone there?'

A large figure in overalls appeared. 'You can't come in 'ere, mate, it's too dangerous.'

'I'm George Woodgate, I'm chairman of the Morton Charities. You must be Alec's friend, Wayne.'

'Oh, Georgie, Alec mentioned your name.'

'No, I'm… never mind. Have you started the work?' said George.

Wayne said, 'Have you seen the *Daily Mail*? Great story, with my quotes, "from a professional electrician", she said. Loads of pictures, as well. Especially that one of me pointing to what she called a death trap. There's a good one of you, looking out of your window from under the curtain. You look like a frightened rabbit.' Wayne could hardly stop laughing. 'Great girl, that Georgina. You should have seen her.'

'What about the electrics in the house?'

'Georgie, it's bad and it's going to cost you. You can almost double my previous estimate.'

'You haven't given me a previous estimate.'

'No, don't worry, Georgie, I'll do you one before I finish here.'

George felt that he had completely lost control of events and he was feeling more and more anxious. 'You'll be finished by the end of the week?'

'It's a big job.'

'The tenants are due back at the end of the week,' said George.

'I won't be finished by then.'

'They've only got a week in that old people's home.'

'It's going to take me ten days to two weeks,' said Wayne. 'There's so much to be done.'

'Can't you hurry up?' said George.

'This is going to cost you a packet, Georgie.'

'Double your original estimate that you never gave me, I suppose?'

'You'll just have to pay for another week at the old people's home,' said Wayne. 'Your charity's got loads of money.'

'I think Alec must have given you the wrong impression.'

'Loads of money. Set up by a rich old general years ago,' said Wayne.

'Brigadier.'

'Pots of money?'

'No.'

'I'll get it done as soon as I can, Georgie, but it'll take at least ten days.'

'I've got nowhere else for them to stay,' said George.

'It's too dangerous here.'

'Ten days?'

'More like two weeks, it depends on what else I find,' said Wayne. 'I was supposed to be on another job this morning, but I've had to let them down because this is so urgent.'

'I'll speak to Luke,' said George.

'You must have saved a fortune on maintenance over the years,' said Wayne. 'Just look at the place, it's a death trap for those poor old people.'

'It's really that bad?'

'Have you seen the state of the thatch?'

'On the roof?' said George.

'Well, it would be, wouldn't it?' said Wayne. 'Old Mrs Preston could slam the front door and get a ton of thatch on top of 'er 'ead. You'd better get that seen to, Georgie.'

'Yes, all right. And by the way, I was christened George, not Georgie.'

'No problem, Georgie, George.'

'You're called Wayne because that's what you were christened.'

'Well, you're wrong there,' said Wayne. 'I was christened Miles. When I first started work, I was a shy sixteen-year-old, wouldn't say boo to a goose and my boss said, "What's yer name, son?"

'I said, "Miles" and he said, "Miles? That's a bit la de dah. I can't call out Miles on a building site. I tell you what, I'll call you Wayne." The name stuck. I haven't even told Alec that story.' Wayne laughed at his story.

George looked stony-faced. He was not interested in silly stories. He went outside and took out his mobile phone to ring Luke Chadwick.

George related the conversation he had just had with Wayne and refused to discuss the *Daily Mail*'s story. He said, 'Luke, will you get on to the home and get an extension of Mr and Mrs Preston's stay, with an option for up to two weeks.'

'You'll need the approval of the other trustees for that and all the work.'

'There's not time.'

'You haven't got the authority.'

'Just do it. We can't leave them on the street. I'll worry about the trustees later.'

George's mobile phone rang. The Revd. Anthony Masters said, 'I was most distressed to read the terrible story in the *Daily Mail*. I've spoken to the churchwardens, and we are of the opinion that you must call a meeting of the trustees immediately.'

The Reverend Anthony Masters was the incumbent of St Bartholomew's Church in the parish of Castle Rudham. He and the two churchwardens were ex officio trustees of the Morton Charities, permanent and immovable, not mere appointees for three years, like the other trustees. At that moment, George realised that he stood completely alone. The church had formed an unofficial alliance against him. Not even God was on his side. His stomach churned and his head ached.

SIX

Club assembly: Andrew sets out his plans for his year as president

The Rotary year was moving forward relentlessly. The wheat in the fields was turning a Norwich blend of colours, with yellowing beards and green stems. Harvest was still a long way off. The weather was warmer, the Easter eggs had been won and consumed by greedy children, and a local children's charity had received a donation of nearly £600.

'It must be a first for the club,' said George.

'What is?' said Erica.

'No one's going to the RIBI Conference.'

'I can never remember what RIBI stands for.'

'Rotary in Britain and Ireland,' said George.

'Why aren't we going?'

'No one else from the club is.'

'We went last year.'

'We went to Harrogate one year.'

'We've been since then.'

'Very nice hotel.'

'There was some good entertainment.'

'It's district assembly on Saturday, at Bury St Edmunds,' said George.

'What's that?'

'The incoming district governor sets out his plans for the new Rotary year, which starts next month,' said George.

'The district governor?'

'Ian Major.'

'Who's he?' said Erica.

'The new DG.'

'Do you know him?'

'He takes over on 1st July.'

'Do his plans matter?'

'The idea is that what the clubs in the district do, fit in with what district is doing,' said George.

'You always say that district don't do anything,' said Erica.

'They don't.'

'District assembly won't take long, then,' said Erica.

'The bar should be open at lunchtime.'

'When does Andrew take over from Frank?'

'1st July,' said George.

'He's been waiting for ages.'

'He's been president-elect all this Rotary year and president-nominee the year before,' said George.

'Good succession planning?'

'It's club assembly next week,' said George.

'How interesting.'

'Andrew will outline his plans for next year.'

'So, everything's going to change?' said Erica.

'We do the same every year.'

'The same?'

'More or less.'

Erica said, 'So, district sets out its plans for next year, but it doesn't actually do anything, and the club's new president sets out his plans for next year, but they're the same as the year before. What's the point of that?'

'Continuity. That's it, continuity.' George did not like this assault on Rotary and its ways. Erica simply didn't understand the subtleties of Rotary.

'Continuity?' said Erica.

'District does do *some* things, but it's in the clubs that the real Rotary happens.'

*

Andrew's first task as incoming president was to present his plans for his year of office to the club assembly. Information had trickled down from the President of Rotary International in America, to Rotary Districts, then individual clubs. The new Rotary International President always had a neat little aphorism to encapsulate his year in office. Was it *Rotary Serving Humanity?* Or was that from a previous year? Andrew could not quite recall, but no matter. Rotary International was a million miles away and the club was where Rotary was really carried out.

'You can go through now,' said Bill in a loud voice that brought Andrew out of his quiet moment of contemplation, during which his half-empty beer glass had adopted a perilous attitude. He corrected it and processed through to the meeting room, with the other members.

When all was quiet, Frank opened his last meeting as president. 'Good evening, members.'

'Good evening, Mr President.'

'Roger, will you say grace, please?'

'Lord, thank you for this food, for rest and home and all things good. For the wind and rain and sun above. But most of all those we love. Amen.'

'Wind, rain and sun above?' said Kye. 'We didn't want the weather forecast.'

Members chuckled and sat down. Bill was serving venison sausages and onion gravy, with mashed potato and green beans, a favourite with most Rotarians, followed by ice-cream, and coffee.

'Venison bangers?' said Kye. 'Oh dear.'

Frank said, 'We're honoured this evening to have Peter Wright, our assistant governor, who has come to see how we do things in Debenham and particularly what we will be doing next year.'

'Thank you, President Frank. It's always a pleasure to come to Debenham.'

'You say that to all your clubs, Peter,' said Kye.

'As assistant governor, I look after seven clubs and Debenham is my favourite,' Peter said with a laugh. It was better to go along with the banter.

'Claire has completed and returned the form you sent us,' said Frank. 'I hope you have all the information you asked for.'

'I'm concerned about your membership,' said Assistant Governor Peter. 'It's very low. I shall look forward to hearing your plans to get your membership back up. You should consider the image you present to the world beyond Rotary. Why aren't new members joining? Are you becoming too stuck in the past? Is the way you do Rotary here in Debenham too old-fashioned?'

Frank said, 'I'm not sure that I would agree with that analysis, Peter. I shall now hand over to Andrew, our incoming president, who is going to outline his programme for the new Rotary year, with the help of his committee chairmen. Over to you, Andrew.'

'Thank you, Mr President.' Andrew paused to ensure that all members were attentive. 'This is a time to look forward. It's an occasion when I, as your new president, must set out a vision for the year ahead and it's a time when chairmen set out their own goals. It's also a time when we think about our own future as a thriving Rotary club. Will we be stronger in a year's time? Or could we quietly fade away? Membership is the key to survival. We've already heard this from Peter this evening. I have some ideas on modernising the club.'

Andrew paused for a moment to ensure that he still had everyone's attention. 'So, what are the challenges that lie ahead? Where will the next international disaster arise? I can tell you this. Next year, there will be a disaster somewhere in the world. It might be a hurricane or an earthquake or something else, but it will devastate a community of people and render them homeless. The forces of nature are unpredictable and unrelenting. And what will our response be?'

'ShelterBox,' said Kye.

Andrew was raising his voice at this point. 'Thank you, Kye. Yes, we will continue to support ShelterBox. We'll be outside the Co-op on a Saturday morning rattling our collection tins.'

Andrew continued, 'ShelterBox has had a long association with Rotary. It was a Rotarian who founded the charity in the small Cornish town of Helston in 2000. It's now one of the world's leading disaster relief organisations, with the support of Rotary International and Rotary clubs around the world.'

'Its headquarters are now in Truro,' said Kye.

'Yes, thank you, Kye. I really find your interruptions most irritating. A ShelterBox—'

'That's in Cornwall too,' said Kye.

'Yes, quite so,' said Andrew. He continued, 'A ShelterBox contains a tent, cooking equipment, blankets, mats, water filters, solar lights and, where necessary, mosquito nets. What could be more important to a family whose home has been devastated? So, ShelterBox will remain a high priority for next year.'

'Mr President-elect, you don't even like camping,' said Kye.

Andrew had finally run out of steam. 'I shall now call upon each chairman to summarise their own personal goals for the year.'

Phillip had little new to offer on membership. 'We've tried holding membership evenings, but they don't seem to bring us any new members. Last time, a few people drifted in to a barrage of Rotary information, but no one showed any real interest; I'm ever hopeful that next year will be different.'

'Perhaps we should try the strippagram approach,' said Kye. 'She could pretend to be the new lady president wearing only her chain of office. That should bring them in. She could position the president's chain of office so that—'

'Thank you, Kye,' said Andrew in a loud irascible tone.

There was an embarrassed chuckle from the men.

'Kye, are you a complete lunatic?' said Fiona. She was angry; he really had overstepped the mark this time.

'Only on my father's side,' said Kye. 'He used to fly Liberators and Flying Fortresses over Germany during the war when they were trying to blast him out of the sky. You need to be mad to do that. That's what he used to say.'

It's the personal touch, thought George. *Personal introduction is the best way to bring people into the club. Why is Oliver being so difficult?*

Phillip was well aware that he had given a lacklustre performance but the membership chair was an impossible role; it was Rotary's poisoned chalice. Perhaps George's Oliver, whoever he was, would come good. The remainder of Andrew's incoming team, which was largely the same as the outgoing team, spoke briefly about their aspirations for the next Rotary year and then Andrew handed back to President Frank, now back in the chair for the last time, as his year of office came to an end.

'Please be upstanding for the Rotary toast.' He waited until everyone was still and quiet. 'Rotary and peace the world over.'

'Rotary and peace the world over.'

SEVEN

July and the beginning of the new Rotary year: Andrew is president, George is in hot water

The phone rang. 'George, it's Andrew,' now president of the Rotary Club of Debenham. 'I thought I'd have a word before this evening's meeting.'

'What about this evening's meeting?'

'Well to put it bluntly, I've had one or two of our illustrious members on the phone,' said Andrew. 'They may not be natural *Daily Mail* readers, but they've all seen your splash and so have I. It's not a pretty story, is it? This sort of thing reflects badly on the club, and it reflects badly on Rotary. Frank should have dealt with it. Your escapade took place before the end of his year as president. Anyway, members want to debate it now.'

'That's all very well, Andrew,' said George, 'but the facts as reported are misleading.'

George really did not wish to be lectured by Andrew Parker, president or not.

'Are they?' said Andrew.

'If people knew what really happened, they would understand,' said George.

'I haven't heard much understanding from one or two of our members.'

'All I'm saying is, remember where you read it. It wasn't in *The Times*.'

President Andrew said, 'I'm putting you on notice that I'm going to allow a debate this evening, so you had better have some answers.'

'Of course, I've got answers.'

'Fiona will be asking the questions.'

'That's no great surprise,' said George.

'I shouldn't be surprised if they want you to resign,' said Erica. She had heard half of the conversation and could guess the other half. The atmosphere had been a little frosty at home, as of late.

George thought about resigning from Rotary, to escape from this constant anxiety, but that would amount to an admission of guilt. No, he would tough it out, with Rotary and also the trustees of the Morton Charities. He rang Luke Chadwick. 'Have you booked the additional respite care for Mr and Mrs Preston?'

'It's not that simple,' said Luke. 'The manager says that the room isn't available for a second week.'

'Why didn't you tell me?' said George. 'What are you going to do now?'

'The manager did give me the names of some other

homes, but she said that she thought that they would be fully booked.'

'But you did manage to find a place?' said George.

'No, they're all fully booked.'

'So, what now?' said George.

Luke said, 'I had another word with the electrician, and he said that the work is definitely going to take two weeks.'

'So, in a few days' time we'll have an elderly couple who are going to be homeless, brilliant.'

'I can find the names of old people's homes further afield,' said Luke.

'Just find an answer, Luke. I'm going to visit them to explain that they can't go back home.'

George got into his car and drove to Framlingham and the Orchard House Residential Care Home. He parked and went to the door and waited until a carer let him in.

'Hello, I'm Joan. Can I help?'

'I want to see Mr and Mrs Preston. They came in for a week's stay,' said George.

'We call it respite care.'

'Yes, that's it, respite care,' said George. 'May I see them?'

'Are you a relative?'

'No, I'm George Woodgate. I'm the chairman of the Morton Charities. We own the house in which Mr and Mrs Preston live.'

'Are you the man who left them to burn to death in that death trap of a house?' said Joan.

'That's not what happened.'

'Oh, you're a different Mr Woodgate?'

'No, I'm the same Mr Woodgate, but what you might have read isn't necessarily what happened,' said George. 'May I see them?'

'I don't know if they'll want to see you,' said Joan. 'What a dreadful business, those poor old people. You ought to be ashamed of yourself.'

'Will you let me see Mr and Mrs Preston?'

Joan turned and walked off, leaving George standing awkwardly, not knowing what to do. A few minutes later, there appeared a formidable-looking woman, short and chunky.

'Mr Woodgate? I'm Mrs Boston, I'm the manager of Orchard House.'

'I need to see Mr and Mrs Preston,' said George. 'The work on their house won't be finished for another week and I understand that they can't stay here for an additional week. Are you absolutely sure you can't squeeze them in somewhere?'

'Mr Woodgate, we don't squeeze in old people. They would need a room and next week we won't have a room for them. I explained all this to your Mr Chadwick.'

'I don't see why not,' said George.

'I can't understand why he didn't pass it on,' said Mrs Boston. 'I can give you the addresses of some other residential homes in Suffolk, but I really don't know whether they will be able to help.'

'May I see Mr and Mrs Preston?'

'I'll go and see if they want to see you,' said Mrs Boston. 'Wait here.'

As he waited, George glanced around him. The only old people's home he had ever been in had been a dark and dingy place with peeling paint and a lingering odour; a sour mix of boiled cabbage and stale urine. Orchard House was light and airy. Natural light was streaming in from the large windows and the glass door at the front of the building, through which he had just entered. Some distance ahead, beyond a large well-furnished sitting area, there were windows and a glass door leading to gardens. George could make out some activity, although he could not determine exactly what. The décor was bright and modern and there was a sense of space and tranquillity. *This could be a new and expensive hotel*, thought George. He did not dare think how much a week's stay for Mr and Mrs Preston was going to cost the charity. George's thoughts were interrupted by Mrs Boston returning with Mr and Mrs Preston.

'You can sit in the sitting area here,' said Mrs Boston, 'and we can keep an eye on you.'

'I don't know this gentleman,' said Mrs Preston. 'I thought you said it was the man from the Morton Charities, Mr Chadwick.'

'I'm George Woodgate. I'm the chairman of the Morton Charities.' Whether George intended to impress them was not clear, but Mrs Preston was far from impressed.

'We only know Mr Chadwick,' said Mrs Preston. 'He comes and collects the rent and has a chat with us. I thought Mr Chadwick was the chairman.'

'No, he's not the chairman,' said George. 'I'm the chairman.'

'What's Mr Chadwick, then?' said Mr Preston, not wishing to be left out of the conversation.

'Mr Chadwick is the secretary to the Morton Charities. He does all the administrative work.'

'The secretary? That's a girl's job,' said Mr Preston.

'Have you got any identification?' said Mrs Boston.

'I've got a driving licence.' George started to dive into his pockets. He found it and handed it over to Mrs Boston.

'And a utility bill addressed to you at your home address, or your passport.'

'I don't carry around loads of personal documents just in case someone wants to check my ID,' said George.

'In that case, I shall have to ask you to leave,' said Mrs Boston.

'Leave?'

'Leave.'

'I haven't done what I came for,' protested George.

'You're upsetting my residents.'

'I only need five minutes with Mr and Mrs Preston.'

'I'm calling the police,' said Mrs Boston.

'Look, I'll ring Mr Chadwick and if he recognises me, will that meet your identification threshold?' George fished out his mobile phone.

Luke's home phone was ringing. *Answer the phone, will you?*

'No answer?' said Mrs Boston. 'That's an old trick, pretending to call someone.'

'He's not answering,' said George.

'Leave now, Mr Woodgate or whoever you really are,' said Mrs Boston in a loud and severe voice.

'Let me try once more,' said George, as his anxiety began welling up.

'Out you go,' said a determined Mrs Boston.

George was frogmarched to the door, still dialling. 'Hello, Luke. That's not Luke.'

'This is Jennifer, Luke's wife.'

'I need to speak to Luke,' said George.

'He's in the shower,' said Jennifer.

'This time of day?'

'It's not against the law.'

'I need to speak to him, now, immediately, urgently,' said George.

'He's wet and naked,' said Jennifer.

'Well, I only want to speak to him,' said George. 'I don't have to look at him, do I?'

'I'll ask him to ring you when he's out,' said Jennifer.

'How long's that going to be?'

'He usually takes about twenty minutes.'

'I haven't got twenty minutes to stand here.'

'Where are you?' said Jennifer.

'I'm at Orchard House,' said George.

'Never heard of it,' said Jennifer.

'It's… never mind.'

'He's been about fifteen minutes.'

'Tell him not to rush on my account,' said George. 'It's raining now.'

'Well, wait inside,' said Jennifer.

'They threw me out,' said George.

'I don't think Luke will want to speak to anyone who gets thrown out of places. Goodbye.'

George rang again. 'Hello, Luke.'

'Jennifer said someone had rung my mobile.'

'I need to get back into Orchard House. You'll have to vouch for me.'

George rang the bell. Mrs Boston opened the door. 'I thought you'd gone.'

'Please speak to Mr Chadwick on my mobile.' George handed his mobile phone to Mrs Boston.

'Are you sure he's the person you think he is?' said Mrs Boston into George's mobile.

'Yes,' said Luke on the other end of the mobile.

'Can you describe him?' said Mrs Boston.

'He's tallish, but not as tall as me,' said Luke.

'I don't know how tall you are,' said Mrs Boston, to whom most people seemed tall.

'I'll try something else,' said Luke. 'He's a Rotarian.'

'That's him,' said Mrs Boston.

'Are you satisfied?' said Luke.

'Mr Boston was a Rotarian,' said Mrs Boston. 'I'd know one anywhere.'

'Really?'

'He's gone now,' said Mrs Boston.

'You mean Mr Woodgate?' said Luke.

'No, my husband.'

'I'm so sorry.'

'No, he's not dead,' said Mrs Boston. 'More's the pity.'

'But he's not around anymore?' said Luke.

'No, he's up in Newcastle,' said Mrs Boston. 'Not *up there*.'

'You're trying my patience and wasting my battery,' said George. 'Are you satisfied now?'

'Not entirely,' said Mrs Boston, 'but you may see Mr and Mrs Preston. I'll go and get them.'

'We thought you'd gone,' said Mrs Preston.

George was becoming more and more exasperated. Time was moving on and he wanted to be able to tell the club that evening that he had sorted out all the difficulties, and that the scandalous story in the *Daily Mail* had been a dreadful misrepresentation. He was aware that he was wringing his hands, but he could not stop.

'Why don't we all sit down and perhaps we can sort it out,' said Mrs Boston, who had no intention of leaving Mr and Mrs Preston with the dubious Mr Woodgate. They walked into the sitting area and sat in some comfortable chairs.

'Mr and Mrs Preston, are you happy to talk to Mr Woodgate?' said Mrs Boston. 'I'm going to stay here with you, so there's nothing to worry about.'

'Yes, all right,' said Mrs Preston and Mr Preston nodded.

At last, George could get down to the business he had come for. 'I've enquired about the work at your house and the electrician—'

'You mean Wayne, he's a laugh,' said Mrs Preston. 'He really liked that nice girl from the paper, and I think she liked him too. Do you know, Wayne's real name isn't Wayne at all? His real name is Miles.'

'For God's sake.' George did not want to hear a second-hand version of the story, which he had not understood the first time around.

'There's no need to blaspheme,' said Mrs Preston, 'what with you being the chairman of the Morton Charities and all.'

'Shall we ask Mr Woodgate what he needs to talk to you about?' said Mrs Boston.

'I've asked Mr Chadwick to try to find another old people's home for next week because Wayne needs another week to complete the work on the house,' said George.

'There's no need, we'll stay here,' said Mrs Preston.

'I'm afraid you can't stay here, dear, because your room won't be available next week.' Mrs Boston was trying to be kind, but there was clearly no room for negotiation.

'Mr Woodgate is trying to find another home for next week, aren't you, Mr Woodgate?' said Mrs Boston.

'What's she saying?' said Mr Preston.

Mrs Preston explained, 'Mr Woodgate is trying to find another old people's home for us for next week.'

'Well, I'm not going into an old people's home,' said Mr Preston. 'I want to stay here.'

'This is an old people's home, you daft old bugger,' said Mrs Preston.

'Have you got any children?' said Mrs Boston.

'We've got one son, and two grandsons,' said Mrs Preston.

'Does your son have enough room for you to stay with him for a week?' said Mrs Boston.

'What's she saying?' said Mr Preston.

'She said, has Thomas got enough room to put us up for a week,' explained Mrs Preston.

'Of course, he has,' said Mr Preston. 'They've got a very big house.'

George was beginning to feel almost cheerful. 'Shall I ring him, Mr Preston?'

'Not now,' said Mr Preston, 'he'll be abed.'

'Is he ill?' said George.

'No, it's dark,' said Mr Preston.

'Dark?' said George.

'He lives in Australia,' said Mr Preston.

'Well, why didn't you say?' said George irritably.

'Are you all right, Mr Woodgate?' said Mrs Boston.

'No, I'm not,' said George. He was now in a state of high anxiety and wringing his hands relentlessly. 'I just need a swift resolution to a pressing problem.'

'The only other thing that I can think of is a hotel,' said Mrs Boston.

'And a large gin and tonic,' said George.

'We don't mind going to a hotel,' said Mrs Preston.

'That's most helpful,' said George.

'No need to thank us, Mr Woodgate,' said Mrs Preston.

'We'll get it all sorted out,' said Mrs Boston.

'Tommy thinks he's already in a hotel,' said Mrs Preston.

'We take pride in this home,' said Mrs Boston.

'We'd like to go to the coast, there's a nice hotel in that posh town where all those yuppies go, according to Mrs Gregory.'

'You don't mean Aldeburgh?' said George. He was thinking of a modest bed and breakfast.

'It's very posh, but we don't mind,' said Mrs Preston.

'I think we have found you a solution, Mr Woodgate.'

'Bed and breakfast costs a fortune there,' said George.

'That's no good,' said Mrs Preston.

'What?' said George.

'Bed and breakfast.'

'You eat breakfast, don't you?' said George.

'We eat all our meals,' said Mrs Preston. 'That's three meals a day.'

'Can't you buy a sandwich at lunchtime?' said George.

'No, of course not,' said Mrs Preston. 'Tommy likes a proper hot meal.'

'He would,' said George.

Mrs Preston said, 'I tell you what, Mr Woodgate. We'll have all our meals at the hotel. It's called full board; makes it easier.'

'And expensive,' said George.

'There's the answer to your little difficulty, Mr Woodgate,' said Mrs Boston, 'but I think it's going to cost your charity a lot of money.'

'The other trustees are not going to like this,' said George.

'Mind you, at Orchard House we have to charge a lot,' said Mrs Boston.

'So, how much has this week cost?' said George.

'Don't worry, Mr Woodgate, we'll send you the bill when we've totted up all the extras.'

'They've got a nice hairdresser here,' said Mrs Preston. 'Such a pretty girl. I've had a lovely perm and highlights and even old Tommy had a haircut. Not that he's got much hair to cut.'

'You look lovely, dear,' said Mrs Boston.

'Old Tommy's a laugh,' said Mrs Preston. 'He asked if she did massages.'

'We don't do massages,' said Mrs Boston, crossly.

'A pretty girl like that's no good for Tommy,' said Mrs Preston. 'He can barely raise a smile these days.'

Outside in the car park, George rang Luke and gave an abridged version of events and asked him to make the arrangement for Mr and Mrs Preston for next week.

'You haven't got the authority to spend so much money without the agreement of the trustees,' said Luke.

'Make sure that we don't pay for hairdressing and beauty treatments,' said George. He felt irritable, anxious and utterly defeated. *I've just been completely outmanoeuvred by an old woman of eighty-something and a daft old bugger.*

*

Members of the Rotary Club of Debenham gathered in the White Horse for their customary drinks before dinner. Andrew, pint in hand, was talking to Claire, who was sipping fruit juice.

Roger was talking to Jeremy and Freddie about farming. 'When I was a boy,' said Roger, 'my old grandad used to say a peck of March dust is worth a king's ransom.'

'Why is that?' said Ernie.

'You need the cold March winds to produce good malting barley and it blows up a lot of dust.'

Frank, Paul and Dominic were listening to Kye, who as far as one could tell from the grin on his face, was telling a risqué joke. He was laughing so much that he had difficulty delivering the punchline.

'I've got another one for you,' said Kye. 'A polar bear walks into a pub and the barmaid says, "What are you going to have?" The polar bear replies, "I'll have a gin…" then, after a pause, he said, "and tonic." The barmaid said, "Why the big pause?" and the polar bear said, "I don't know, I was born with them."' Kye's audience laughed with him. The door opened and George came in with Frank. One or two members greeted them cordially, others carried on with their conversations. George ordered two pints of Ghost Ship. A moment later, Bill called, 'Rotarians, dinner is served.'

When members were standing in their places, Andrew rang the Rotary bell to bring everyone to order. 'Good evening, members.'

'Good evening, Mr President.'

Andrew said, 'Roger, will you say grace, please?'

'Mr President, on behalf of all members,' said Roger, 'I'd like to welcome you to your first meeting as president.'

'Hear, hear.'

'Thank you,' said President Andrew, 'it's a great honour to be president of this great club.'

Roger continued, 'Lord, may the roof above never fall in, and friends below never fall out.'

'Amen.'

As soon as the members were seated, Bill came in with plates of spaghetti bolognaise and a mouth-watering aroma filled the air. The hungry Rotarians could already taste the delicious combination of beef and tomato, with garlic, herbs, and pasta.

After dinner, Andrew said, 'Please stand for the loyal toast.' There was a scraping of chairs and when all were still and silent, 'The Queen.'

'The Queen.'

'God bless her,' said Kye.

After the customary break to refresh glasses, Andrew said, 'As you know, Paul, our Foundation and international chairman, has been talking to Robert Chapman of our neighbouring club about the water and sanitation project in Uganda that we've been considering. I'd like to call upon Paul to introduce our guest. There is also another matter that we need to discuss, after Robert has left us. We wouldn't wish to burden our guest with our internal business.'

Paul said, 'Thank you, Mr President. Some weeks ago, the club authorised me, as Foundation and international chairman, to enter into discussions with Robert to see if we could join with his club in this project. He has come here this evening to talk in more detail about the project. We can then take a final decision and make the necessary application to Rotary International for a global grant. I would now like to bring in Robert.'

Robert rose to his feet. 'President Andrew, I bring greetings from President Sebastian.'

'Please take my greetings back to President Sebastian,' said President Andrew.

'It's good to be here this evening,' said Robert. 'Please feel free to shout out questions as we go along.'

'We will,' said Kye.

'As you know,' said Robert, 'the objective of this project

is to provide a clean water supply from a new borehole to a storage tank and reservoir.'

'How will it be pumped?' said Kye.

'There'll be a solar pump,' said Robert.

'Well, they've got plenty of sunshine,' said Kye.

'From there, water will be distributed to households for domestic use, as well as providing basic toilets for the households,' said Robert.

'What about irrigation?' said Ernie.

'Water from the reservoir will be available for the irrigation of smallholdings,' said Robert.

'Who's going to benefit from the project?' said Fiona.

'More than 500 people in a small community in this District of Uganda. At present, they have no borehole and collect water from a neighbouring community.'

'I believe the local Rotary club is involved,' said Paul.

'Yes, the local Rotary club identified the needs of this community and made it known through Rotary,' said Robert.

'Is labour available locally?' said Ernie.

'We can get local labour to carry out the basic construction work and each household will provide the housing for their own toilet,' said Robert.

'What are the arrangements for maintaining the equipment in the future?' said Claire.

'The local Rotary club asked the local community if they are prepared to own and manage it, when the equipment has been installed,' said Robert.

'And are they?' said Claire.

'Yes,' said Robert. 'We're planning to set up a water users' committee, nominated by the community, which must include at least one woman.'

'Will they need training?' said Claire.

'The members of the committee will be trained in basic repairs and maintenance of the borehole.'

'Why only one woman?' said Fiona.

'At least one woman,' said Robert.

'But no more than one woman?' said Fiona.

'It depends who the local community nominate,' said Robert.

'I suppose only the men can nominate?' said Fiona.

'We must respect local culture,' said Robert.

Fiona said, 'In the African countryside, it's the women who do all the work in the fields, while the men sit in the shade drinking beer.'

'I can't agree with that,' said Robert.

'I can't agree one woman,' said Fiona.

'The local Rotary club thought that a woman representative was acceptable,' said Robert.

'Well, it's certainly not acceptable to me or to this club,' said Fiona.

The murmur from around the table suggested that Fiona did not speak for the whole of the membership, but protocol did not permit rancour in front of visitors.

'The committee will also be responsible for collecting a small fee from the users and ensuring that the project is sustainable,' said Robert.

'How can we judge the benefits of the project?' said Claire.

'The local health centres have confirmed the presence of water-borne diseases such as typhoid, cholera and bilharzia, as well as dysentery and scabies,' said Robert.

'That sounds dreadful to us in the first world,' said George.

Robert said, 'The availability of a proper water supply will improve health and hygiene. Also, the construction of a reservoir would provide irrigation to improve subsistence farming. The community might even have a surplus to sell.' Eventually, Robert came to the end of his talk and members clapped politely.

'Are there any more questions for Robert?'

A number of hands went up, but Fiona got in first. 'Why will there be only one woman on the water user committee?'

'There could be more than one,' said Robert.

'But it's not a requirement?'

Robert was beginning to feel uncomfortable. 'I don't think I can add anything else on that particular point, Mr President.'

'I find this totally unacceptable, Mr President,' said Fiona. 'We should have an equal number of men and women on the committee and unless we do, this club should refuse to provide any financial contribution to this otherwise splendid project.'

'Are there any more questions for Robert?' said President Andrew.

'I will not be ignored, Mr President,' said Fiona. 'I formally move that we do not support this project, unless there's an equal number of men and women on the water users' committee.'

'This is not a business meeting and we have already given approval to the project,' said President Andrew.

'Approval in principle only, I believe,' said Fiona.

'Approval in principle, subject to a presentation, which we have received this evening,' said Andrew.

Fiona said, 'That may be so, but now we've seen the details, we don't like them. There is nothing in the Rotary constitution that says we can only take decisions at a business meeting, as you well know.'

'Yes, quite so, Fiona,' said Andrew.

'The Rotary constitution doesn't even mention business meetings,' said Fiona, pressing home the point.

'I'm not going to accept your proposal, because the club has already decided the matter, subject to a condition that has now been met this evening,' said Andrew.

'In that case, Mr President, I move that the previous decision on this matter be rescinded and that we do not support this project, unless there are equal numbers of men and women on the water users' committee,' said Fiona.

'I'll second the proposal,' said Frances.

Andrew looked to Claire for help. Claire gave a shrug of the shoulders. 'Fiona, I'm disappointed that you are pressing for a vote on this, but I shall allow it if you insist.'

'I do insist,' said Fiona.

'Does anyone want to speak on the motion before I put it to the vote?' Andrew willed everyone to keep quiet. 'All in favour of the motion that the previous decision on this matter be rescinded and that we do not support this project, unless there's an equal number of men and women on the water user committee.'

Fiona and Frances put up their hands. 'That's two in favour. Those against, please show.' All hands went up except Fiona's and Frances's. 'The motion is lost,' said Andrew.

'So where does that leave us now, Mr President?' said Frank.

'I wasn't intending to put this to the vote this evening. But let me state the position, so that there's no doubt. Club council has signed off on the project and the club has approved it in principle, subject only to receiving the presentation that Robert has given us this evening. So, the position is that we have approved the project and the contribution we were asked for.'

'Mr President, as always, I accept the views of the majority, and I can't say that I'm surprised at the club's decision,' said Fiona. 'However, I always reserve the right to speak out on issues that I consider important, such as the rights of women, and I will never be silenced.'

'Thank you, Fiona,' said Andrew. 'We would expect nothing less of you.'

Fiona ignored the sarcasm in the president's comment. She had made her point and discomfited some of her fellow Rotarians. She thought of herself as a free spirit and a force for good in an unjust world.

'I would like to thank Robert for coming here to talk about the project this evening,' said President Andrew. Members clapped politely as Robert took his leave.

Andrew paused for a moment until Robert had left the room. 'It's perhaps rather late in the evening to go on to something else, but one or two members have asked me to allow some time this evening for a particular matter. It concerns George and some rather unsavoury reporting in the *Daily Mail*. George, do you wish to say something about it before I let other members come in?'

George wondered how Charles would have handled this wretched business. *What would you have done? Sackcloth and ashes, an admission of culpability and a plea for forgiveness? Or more likely, a full-blooded charge at his detractors?* The question remained unanswered, hanging in George's thoughts; the ghosts of old Rotarians seldom spoke. George paused and centred himself like a Shakespearian actor. He looked out at his audience and when he was ready, spoke in a clear steady voice, free of hesitancy or penitence. 'Thank you, Mr President, I certainly do. As members will know, I am the chairman of the Morton Charities in a personal capacity. That is to say that the Morton Charities are not in any way connected to Rotary in general, or this club in particular. On the weekend in question, a great misfortune befell the elderly tenants of a house the charity owns, that is the Rufford Trust, one of three charities that comprise the Morton Charities. The electricity failed and the couple were left without power.'

'We read it in the paper,' said Fiona.

'This meant that they had no light and no cooking facilities and, of particular significance to the stories that appeared in the press, it was the weekend, so summoning help was difficult,' said George.

'You didn't do much to help,' said Fiona.

George said, 'The secretary to the trustees tried to contact the electrician, but he was away for the weekend and that's where the difficulties began.'

'Sounds like Fred Karno's army,' said Kye.

'Through no fault of mine, the trustees, or the secretary to the trustees, we could not get an immediate response from any competent person to carry out an emergency repair.'

George went through the events of that fateful weekend. He mentioned everything that he perceived to be in his favour and glossed over all that was not.

'For the first week, the elderly couple went into respite care in Orchard House, an excellent residential home for the elderly, but the home did not have any vacancies for the second week. The Trust eventually arranged to place them in an expensive hotel for the second week of the work. That's all I need to say at this point, Mr President, but I reserve the right of reply to anything that members may raise.'

'Thank you, George,' said Andrew. 'Yes, Ernie.'

Ernie was a retired civil servant, a bureaucrat, a panjandrum. He was a small man, meticulous in both habit and appearance; he was punctilious about procedure and precedent, and he had been horrified by what he had read.

'I am very concerned about the lack of attention to the rules and procedures of the charity. If you are required to get three quotations for the procurement of work or goods, then you should act accordingly. George abrogated himself to a position to which he had no legitimate right.'

'The Civil Service is good at rules and procedures,' said Fiona.

Ernie continued, 'Then there's all the dreadful publicity. You should never tell the press anything except what they could find out anyway. You can be very free with the kind of information that's out there somewhere in the public domain that they haven't yet stumbled upon.' He paused for a moment to allow his insight into the workings of bureaucracy to sink in. 'If you tell them enough, it sometimes puts them off the scent entirely. Also, in the Civil Service, when we made a cock-up and put some wrong information in the minister's brief, we always found a way of blaming someone who'd just retired. We'd tell the minister that we'd stopped his pension, as a punishment. That would make the minister feel better. Mistakes happen from time to time and it doesn't really matter very much. What does matter is getting found out and the dreadful publicity that usually follows. That's when heads roll.'

'Perhaps they should stop your pension, Ernie,' said Kye.

Ernie continued, 'The great advantage of the whole system is that the minister always has to take responsibility for what goes on in his department.'

Members had listened carefully to Ernie's revelations of the workings of the great departments of state and pondered on whether they had any relevance to George's situation. 'The position of the minister would be more relevant to my position in the charity, as a non-executive chairman, than to an official in his department,' said George.

'Paul, you've indicated that you wish to speak,' said Andrew.

'Thank you, Mr President. At first sight what goes on in any organisation with which a member of this club is associated is not a matter for the club. However, there are two points that worry me. First, I have been chairman of Foundation for some years and I have a great concern for anyone who is made homeless by a natural disaster. Therefore, the plight of these elderly tenants much closer to home was a matter of great concern to me. We in this club take pride in alleviating homelessness arising through natural disasters in far-off places and not causing it closer to home. However, I am relieved that George has taken decisive action to put them in a hotel where they will be well looked after. I remain concerned about the publicity that George has brought to our door. It reflects badly on Rotary and this club. I think that George should seriously consider his position.'

Thanks a lot, Paul, thought George. *You were doing all right until the last comment*, but he said nothing.

Frank felt compelled to come to the defence of his friend. 'George was caught up in a set of circumstances that were not of his own making. As soon as he was aware of the problem, he acted. He did everything he could to help the tenants. It wasn't his fault that it was the weekend and it was difficult to contact anyone. Then he put the tenant up in a luxury hotel. What more could he have done in the circumstances? It seems to me that the secretary to the trustees has some questions to answer. Surely, he could have foreseen the need for weekend cover; also, why on earth didn't he have the electrician's mobile phone number? If he'd been a bit more on the ball, he might have quizzed the charity's electrician about the need for rewiring and the whole sorry affair would never have happened.'

'Mr President, may I make a small contribution to the debate?' said Fiona. This was the moment that George had been dreading.

'Yes, of course, Fiona,' said Andrew.

'Mr President, Frank asks what more could George have done? Well, let me see if I can answer that question for him. These elderly tenants live in a sixteenth-century thatched house in a picturesque setting. It sounds idyllic, but the reality is rather different. The stairs are difficult to negotiate. There's a sharp bend to the left halfway up. The kitchen is small and difficult to work in. The walls are crumbling and there are patches of mildew, caused by damp. The thatch on the roof is in a parlous state. The real problem, and I don't know whether the present work has been completed yet, is the electrical system in the house. A house so badly in need of rewiring is a death trap. Just imagine how it would have gone up in flames, if there had been a fire. These people wouldn't have stood a chance. Why did the charity neglect to do anything until they absolutely had to? An electrician took one look at that house, the house for which George, as chairman of the charity, was responsible, and said that he wouldn't touch it because it needed to be completely rewired. The inaction of the charity was negligent and George was the chairman of that charity. Let's consider another matter. Why didn't the charity have any contingency arrangements to cover emergencies at weekends and holidays? The charity didn't even have contact details for the electrician who usually did work for the charity. Not that it would have helped a lot, because he was in the Yorkshire Dales for a long weekend. And what sort of an electrician was he anyway to keep the charity happy by bodging up any problems and ignoring the need for rewiring? The charity has a duty of care to its elderly tenants, and it has failed miserably. The question is this. How far are the failings of an organisation to which a member is connected and the bad publicity it has engendered, a matter for us? Did George recklessly bring the club into disrepute by his actions or inactions and what is his future as a member of this club? I can see that other members wish to speak, so I shall give way.'

Several more members spoke, but brought nothing new to the debate. They were all, to a greater or lesser extent, cross about the publicity that had fallen upon the club and things were not looking good for George.

Claire had listened carefully to the debate and decided to speak. 'I am not going to go over the arguments that have already been made. It seems to me that George's actions or inactions in regard to an organisation to which he is connected are of no concern to us, except to the extent of the bad publicity it has visited upon us. Is the failing of the charity George's responsibility? As chairman, it probably is. Ernie referred to ministerial responsibility and it's a bit like that. In Government, of course, ministerial responsibility is a constitutional convention, part of the set of informal rules that operate in this country because we don't have a written constitution. It doesn't apply in the same way in other organisations. So, where does the blame lie? George must take his share, but the only person connected with the charity who has any executive responsibility is the secretary. As I understand it, he is responsible for not only the meetings of the trustees and other administrative tasks, but he is also responsible for all financial matters, including the charity's investments and on top of that, the maintenance of its properties. Perhaps the charity should review these responsibilities.' Claire paused for a moment before continuing, 'George and the other trustees can only take decisions based on the information that the executive secretary of the charity presents to them. How satisfactory were his relations with the usual electrician? What really passed between them? Did that electrician give adequate warning of the dangers? Maybe he did and the secretary ignored them. Maybe he didn't. We have no way of knowing. Maybe the charity did not receive proper advice. We just don't know. Should the trustees have asked more questions about the state of the property? Should they have been more curious? Should there have been some sort of cover at the weekend? My own view of it is this: whatever George's responsibility, the events of that weekend, and the bad publicity, were to a greater or lesser extent, bad luck and a lack of foresight, so far as he was concerned. The charge against George is that he brought bad publicity upon the club through his decisions. However, in making those decisions, whether they were good or bad, he was not motivated by unscrupulous or base intentions and there is no suggestion of any sort of dishonesty. In fact, he was reacting to a difficult and developing situation. The accusations against George, in my view, do not stand up. There is no question of wrongdoing of that kind, by George, as a Rotarian and a member of this club. The problem arose through a series of actions and non-actions within the internal workings of the charity and not as a result of what George did or did not do on the particular weekend, and the publicity to which it gave rise. George and his charity may not have resolved the problem quickly but they did all they could in the circumstances. The problem that arose was to do with sins of the past, sins of omission.'

The last word went to Fiona. 'Claire gave a very eloquent defence of George. It was a lawyer's argument about who knew what and when and the concept of innocent until proven guilty, which is laudable in other circumstances. As far as I'm concerned, the buck had to stop with George, even if someone else had failed to advise him properly. However, that's not the reason I wanted to speak again. What I would say to bring matters to a conclusion is this. No matter what his failings, George did not intend to bring bad publicity to this club and the publicity was to do with matters that are of no interest or concern to the club. George has not acted dishonestly, which is something we could not condone in any circumstances. The charity's failings of the past were the real cause of the problem and the subsequent publicity. That is something the charity should consider, but it cannot be a matter for this club. In my opinion, there should be no question of the club asking George to consider his position.'

Thank you, Fiona, for once, thought George.

'We have spent a lot of time on this,' said Andrew, 'and I want to draw matters to a close. I don't think that any further action is required. Is everyone happy with that?' It was late and no one had the energy to challenge the president's assertion. George was relieved that the matter had reached a conclusion, so far as the Rotary Club of Debenham was concerned, but he knew there was another battle yet to be fought.

Andrew said, 'As it's late, we'll leave the sergeant at arms and the fiddle. Please stand for the Rotary toast. Rotary and peace the world over.'

'Rotary and peace the world over.'

EIGHT

Andrew's first business meeting: reform or die

Members of the Rotary Club of Debenham were gathering in the White Horse for Andrew's first business meeting as the club's new president. He was determined to carry out a programme of reforms to update and modernise the club and he was confident of the support of many members, in particular, Fiona. However, he was concerned about the reaction he would get from Frank, George and other traditionalists in the club. 'Let me get you a drink, George.'

'Thank you. I'll have a pint of Ghost Ship.'

As Bill pulled a pint of Ghost Ship, Andrew said, 'I've been considering the future of the club, George, and, you know, it really is time we started to modernise our image and widen our appeal.' Andrew knew that George would not welcome the changes that he had in mind, but he hoped George would not be implacably opposed.

George took a long draught of his beer and said, 'I do hope you're not going to take any notice of the nonsense that our assistant governor has put in your head. I will not support you and nor will other members of the club.'

Andrew was a little taken aback by the candour of George's response. He said, 'Well, I'm going to float the idea this evening, under item 4 on "The Future of the Club".'

George said, 'Well, don't expect me to support all that nonsense,' and walked off, leaving Andrew staring into his beer glass.

The Rotarians went in to dinner and President Andrew stood in his new place at the head of the table. Members chatted, but Andrew stood still and silent.

'The bell, Mr President, it's your job now,' said Kye.

A silence had descended and members stood still, uncertain of what was happening. They expected a single strike of the Rotary bell, but it did not come. The president, the sole custodian of said bell, was motionless. It was time for the Rotary bell and the instant silence it brought, followed by grace, then dinner. The bell needed to be struck and only the president had the authority to do so. Bill was waiting to serve dinner: pork chops and crackling, with apple sauce, mashed potato and green beans. There was bread and butter pudding and coffee to follow. An appetising aroma was wafting through the door from dinner without, making for a very hungry assembly of Rotarians. The membership of the Rotary Club of Debenham had been classically conditioned, like Pavlov's dogs.

'I deliberately didn't ring the Rotary bell and, in a minute, I shall explain why. But first, I shall ask George to say grace.'

'Thank you, Mr President. Lord, make us truly thankful for good company, pleasant conversation, and for the patience of an indulgent president. Keep us ever mindful of the watchful eye of the sergeant at arms, and his ever pressing need to fill the bottomless coffers of the Treasury. And let us be granted freedom from the ravages of old age, especially those that leave us weak and limp when we need to be firm and upstanding. Amen.'

'Amen.'

There were a few chuckles, as members scraped their chairs on the floor and sat down. That was a good grace.

Andrew said, 'The reason I didn't ring the bell is because in this day and age it's irrelevant. It's a feature of Rotary that we can do without. And it's not the only thing.' Andrew was aware of George glaring at him and continued, 'Why don't people want to join Rotary anymore? It's because of the silly rituals we have and our fuddy-duddy, boring image. As this is a business meeting, I put it on the agenda.'

'I never saw it,' said Kye.

'Nor did I,' said another voice.

Andrew said, 'Item 4 on the agenda is "The Future of the Club".' There were murmurings of dissent, but President Andrew pressed on. 'Let's discuss it when we get to it on the agenda.'

After dinner, President Andrew said, 'Please be upstanding for the loyal toast.' He paused for a moment, then raised his glass. 'The Queen.'

'The Queen.'

'God bless her,' said Kye.

'We'll take a short break now,' said Andrew.

Some members drifted off to the bar, others remained. When they reassembled, ten minutes or so later, Andrew said, 'We'll make a start on the business meeting. Apologies for absence.'

'There's an apology from Roger,' said Claire.

'The next item is the minutes of the last business meeting,' said Andrew. 'May I sign them as a correct record?'

'Agreed.'

'We now come to "The Future of the Club",' said Andrew. 'The purpose of this item is to consider our direction as a club, which comes down to membership. Phillip reported that we are now down to twenty-one members and that's not because we haven't been trying to recruit new members.'

'How many new members have you introduced, Mr President?' said Kye.

Andrew continued, 'Let's be clear, finding potential members is a task for everyone in the club, not just the membership chairman. In answer to Kye, no, I haven't been successful in finding any new members. I am keenly aware of the reason for that and the club's failure to recruit any new members for quite some time. We need to modernise.'

Fiona said, 'I'm with you on updating the club, Mr President. You don't need to wear a tie to be a good Rotarian.'

'That argument works perfectly well the other way around.' George took a very logical view of this particular point.

'You mean that you don't need to wear a tie to be a bad Rotarian,' said Fiona.

'That's not what I meant at all.'

'It sounded like it to me,' said Fiona.

George said, 'It's us old Rotarians who wear ties and who turn out to Rotary fundraisers, whether it's rattling tins outside the Co-op or anything else.'

'It doesn't mean that we shouldn't modernise,' said Fiona.

'It's up to each of us to take pride in Rotary, put in a bit of effort, not just be a knife and fork, who turn up for Rotary one night a week to eat dinner,' said George.

Andrew said, 'There are a lot of things that we should consider changing. What I have in mind is a package of measures.'

'Let's start with dress code,' said Fiona.

'Dress code, as Fiona mentioned, is one,' said Andrew. 'We've never had a formal dress code, but we, the men that is, have always worn ties and jackets.'

'We need to get rid of all that,' said Fiona.

'In the last year or so, we have taken a more relaxed view of standards in the summer months, and members have left off ties and occasionally jackets in warm weather,' said Andrew.

'These days people don't expect to put on a tie to go to a club, a pub or anything else, so they're not going to join Rotary,' said Fiona.

'That's rubbish, Andrew,' said George and not *Mr President*. 'There are restaurants that won't let you in without a tie. They'll even lend you one, if you've forgotten how to dress properly.'

'Now who's speaking rubbish?' Fiona had raised the matter of informal dress and she was not going to let it go. 'That might have been the case a few years ago, but not anymore. Times are changing and we have to change with them.' Fiona had been a Bob Dylan fan in the sixties and the words ran around in her head – *will still shake your windows and rattle your walls, for the times they are a-changin'.*

'I've already mentioned the bell,' said Andrew. 'We just don't need it.'

'You mean the Rotary bell, that we received as a gift from our neighbouring club, when we chartered over thirty years ago,' said George. 'It symbolises what we are and who we are.'

'Rubbish,' said Fiona. 'It gives a bad impression to guests who are not Rotarians, and not used to Rotary's old-fashioned ways.'

'Mr President, so we are to dress down, how far down I dread to imagine,' said Paul. 'We're to get rid of the Rotary bell. Is there any limit to this madness?'

'Just a few more to consider,' said Andrew. 'We don't need to say grace, nor do we need the loyal toast or the final toast.'

By now, George was apoplectic with rage. 'It would be an insult not to toast the Queen. The loyal toast is a matter of protocol at State and military occasions.'

'We don't need any of it, George,' said Fiona.

'Don't interrupt,' said George. He was now feeling desperately anxious, but his anger helped to overcome it.

'I'll speak when I want to.' Fiona was as irrepressible as ever.

Frank came in to support George. 'The loyal toast is also a display of patriotism at civilian events like Rotary. Are we turning into a bunch of scruffy, left-wing republican heretics and fanatics?'

'I think we've heard enough rubbish from Frank, Mr President,' said Fiona.

'I haven't finished yet,' said Frank. 'And doing away with grace and the final toast? They're part of our tradition as Rotarians. We might as well chuck it all in and just not bother. Is that what you want?'

'What we want is for you to stop talking,' said Fiona.

'No wonder you never learned to swim, Frank,' said Kye, 'you can't keep your mouth shut.' Everyone laughed.

'That's an outrage,' said Frank, who was now looking rattled.

Fiona held up her agenda and started to tear an inch-wide strip from the top downwards. She tore slowly, very slowly, agonisingly slowly.

'Will you stop doing that?' said Frank.

Frank continued, 'With no Rotary bell, how is the president expected to get attention, tap a knife on a glass? That's vulgar, dangerous and totally unnecessary, and you won't be president in a year's time.'

Fiona had started to tear another strip of paper from her agenda. She could see Frank getting more and more agitated.

'Will you stop doing that?' said Frank.

'I don't know what you mean,' said Fiona.

Frank screwed up his agenda in rage and threw it at her.

Fiona said, 'Mr President, I have just been assaulted by one of our members.'

'I didn't see anything, Fiona,' said President Andrew.

'I was assaulted, even if you weren't looking,' said Fiona.

'Is this supposed to be a serious complaint?' said Andrew.

'I'm deadly serious,' said Fiona.

'As I didn't see, perhaps you would kindly enlighten me,' said Andrew. 'Who's the culprit?'

'It was Frank,' said Fiona. 'He tried to hit me.'

'Is this true, Frank?'

'Well, I missed anyway,' said Frank.

'He can't deny that he tried to hit me,' said Fiona.

'It was only a screwed-up agenda, not a lead pipe,' said Frank, who, at that moment, wished he did have a length of lead pipe.

'There're some very weighty matters on this agenda, Mr President,' said Kye, which puzzled George. *He's definitely not right in the head.*

'This is getting us nowhere,' said Andrew. 'Fiona, I really don't think it was a very serious assault. I suggest that Frank apologises to Fiona and Fiona withdraws her allegation.'

'I will not apologise to that woman,' said Frank. 'She's been mocking me and tearing up pieces of paper all evening.'

'I don't see why I should accept Frank's apology. A Rotarian should never assault a woman and not for tearing a small piece of paper.'

Frank was now reaching for that imaginary lead pipe.

'Are you going to apologise, Frank?' said Andrew. 'We must get on.'

Frank was going to refuse, but decided that would be a puerile gesture. 'To resolve the matter and enable us to move on, I will apologise to Fiona.'

'And make him promise not to do it again,' said Fiona.

'For pity's sake,' said Frank.

The debate raged on for a little longer, but most members, shocked by the hostility they had witnessed, declined to express their views, and gradually tempers cooled, and the evening came to an end. George had found the evening most distressing. His stomach was churning and his head ached, but he took some satisfaction from the level of opposition that the modernisation proposals had attracted. However, many members had not spoken and there had been no formal vote.

Andrew had miscalculated the response to his proposal. It was not everyone who had opposed him, but those who had, were the most vocal. He had never intended to push through his ideas this evening, but simply to float them to gauge the club's reaction. It had been interesting, he just needed to let tempers cool and reason emerge. He would bring them back again later in the Rotary year. After that, he would no longer be president and his opportunity would have gone.

*

After President Andrew's first inflammatory business meeting, things quietened down and got back to normal. There was the garden party to organise and the concert. The garden party was an event that the club had been running for a number of years, since Charles Jackson started it in his year as president. The concert was something new. George had made contact with the Lovel Choir, who performed a programme of summer concerts for the benefit of local charities. The club had not shared George's enthusiasm, in fact one or two members were strongly opposed to the idea of a concert. 'It won't work in Debenham,' was Jeremy's assessment. However, George made a persuasive argument and eventually the club agreed.

'I'd like to remind you all that the concert is not far away,' said George. He was addressing the small group of members sitting around the kitchen table. 'Our task, as the concert committee, is to organise and promote the event, so that all the choir has to do is turn up and sing. The larger the audience, the more they will contribute to our charity account.'

'Well, let's hope it's all worth it,' said Fiona, who was not convinced that it would be.

'I met Katrina and Conrad Vaughan, the churchwarden, a few days ago,' said George. 'The concert can go ahead in the church with the kind permission of the Rector and the churchwarden.'

'We assumed that, otherwise we wouldn't be sitting here,' said Kye.

St Mary's was a beautiful mediaeval stone edifice that had stood in Debenham for a thousand years and was the largest building in the village. There was a plaque behind the pulpit in memory of Robert Green, a young lieutenant from a family of the parish, who had fallen at the Battle of Trafalgar in 1805. Debenham, like so many other villages and towns, had sent young men to fight in Nelson's famous victory, which established Britain's supremacy of the sea, that lasted until the Great War. The church and the adjoining cottage were part of village life and used for many village events.

'Who?' said Kye.

'The concert secretary of the Lovel Choir,' said George.

'Katrina?'

'Kye, I'm sure that I've mentioned Katrina before,' said George. 'She's the concert secretary.'

'OK, just checking,' said Kye.

'We've got a lot to get through, so can we just get on?' said George.

'So, what happened?' said Fiona.

'Nothing happened, I am just trying to outline Katrina's requirements,' said George. He paused for a moment, and when there were no further interruptions, he continued. 'The choir want somewhere to sit quietly before the performance, with drinking water, squash and biscuits. They will need this from half past six. They also need a power source.'

'Can't they use the cottage?' said Fiona.

'What cottage?' said Phillip.

'St Mary's has a small building within the curtilage of the church,' said George. 'It's got a kitchen, so it's ideal.'

'You don't live in the village, do you, Phillip?' said Fiona.

'Power to brew up tea?' said Kye.

'You're just a heathen, Phillip,' said Fiona.

'Power in the concert venue,' said George.

'They won't want tea in the church,' said Kye.

'The power is for the keyboard,' said George.

'For the accompanist?' said Kye.

'Although, he'll probably play the piano,' said George.

'That doesn't use power,' said Kye.

'Yes, quite so,' said George.

'What about the church organ?' said Kye.

'The organ would hardly be suitable for the concert,' said George.

'Why not?' said Kye.

'If the accompanist is satisfied with the piano in the church, he'll play that instead of his keyboard,' said George.

'How long will it last?' said Fiona.

'They will arrive at about half past six on the night,' said George, 'and go to the cottage, have a cup of tea and a biscuit and then have a short rehearsal before the concert at half past seven.'

'Why do they need a rehearsal?' said Kye. 'I thought they practised every week.'

'They might not have a rehearsal,' said George.

'But they will have tea and biscuits?' said Kye.

'The running time is about an hour and a half and there will be an interval of twenty minutes,' said George.

'What are they going to sing, George?' said Fiona.

'It'll be a varied programme,' said George.

'I hope this isn't going to be an evening of boring classical music,' said Fiona.

George said, 'The idea of these concerts, apart from the charitable aspect, is to give the choir an opportunity to sing other material. There'll be some folk music and—'

'Don't tell me they're going to murder some Bob Dylan songs,' said Fiona.

'Bob Dylan made a good job of that himself,' said George. 'Will you just listen for once?'

'Not if you're going to shout like that,' said Fiona. She could shout much louder.

'No one is shouting, Fiona. If we all keep calm, perhaps we can get through our business and go home.'

'You are at home, George.' Kye could not let that go.

George said, 'It'll be a programme of music of all genres, some folk, definitely not Bob Dylan, some comedy numbers, a medley of music from the theatre, some pop and even a little classical.'

'I think we should donate £50 for the use of the church,' said George. There was no dissent. 'Tickets will be £10 each.'

'What about children and students?' said Fiona.

'They can come in free,' said George. 'I've printed off some tickets from my computer and Fred has agreed to hold some for sale.'

'Who?' said Kye.

'Fred, the newsagent,' said George.

'Oh, that Fred,' said Kye.

'I've also asked Richard to draft and print some posters,' said George. 'Kye, you and Richard are going to put boards on the roads leading into the village.'

'All right,' said Kye.

'Fiona, will you put some flyers in the Co-op, and also the notice board outside the doctors' surgery, and other shops in and around the village?' said George. 'You know the ones we use? There are also all the surrounding villages. We'll have to split them between us. Phillip, are you all right with the bar?'

'Yes, I've got the glasses, the wine and soft drinks organised and I'll get someone else to help on the night.'

'Is the church going to allow alcohol?' said Phillip.

'St Mary's is Church of England, not Methodist,' said George.

'Are we going to apply for a licence?' said Fiona.

'No, technically we are not selling alcohol,' said George.

'Are we giving it away, George?' said Kye.

'We'll just ask for contributions,' said George.

'Will anyone go to prison if we get caught?' said Kye.

Fiona said, 'Kye, if it comes to that, we'll volunteer you.'

'We'll suggest a minimum contribution for a glass of wine,' said George. 'I shall ask a couple of other members to take money on the door and, Fiona, are you able to arrange a raffle?'

'Of course, I can organise a raffle.'

'Well, will you do so?'

'Yes.'

'What about parking?' said Phillip.

'I've agreed that the choir can drive one vehicle into the small parking area at the church, because they might be bringing a keyboard,' said George.

'I thought they were going to use the piano in the church,' said Kye.

'Katrina has tried out the piano and she is satisfied with it, but she said that the accompanist will decide for himself,' said George.

'What about our promotion at the Co-op on Saturday?' said Fiona.

'I've had a word with someone at the small industrial area off the High Street,' said George. 'We can use their site for parking.'

'On Saturday we're meeting outside the Co-op, at nine o'clock sharp, to hand out leaflets to shoppers and generally promote the concert,' said George.

'We'll be there,' said Kye.

'OK, thank you everybody, that's been really useful,' said George. 'I think we'll leave it there.'

It was ten days to the concert. George's concert committee had done sterling work to make the arrangements and members had carried out their individual tasks. But all was not well. George had been into the newsagent in the village, ostensibly to buy the *East Anglian*, but really to check on ticket sales.

'Your concert tickets aren't going very well,' said Fred.

'Well, I didn't expect you to sell all sixty of the tickets I left with you.'

'I've sold four.'

'What do you mean four? You must have sold more than that. There must be some mistake.' George was gawking with incredulity into the old biscuit tin he had given Fred two weeks earlier to hold the tickets and money. There were four limp £10 notes and a bundle of fifty-six tickets. 'Fred, you are supposed to be selling the tickets, not hiding them away.'

'Well, I have got one of your concert posters in the window,' said Fred, 'there's not much more I can do.'

'You need to try a bit harder,' said George, as he picked up his paper and walked out.

It so happened that a few minutes later, Andrew walked into the newsagents. 'Good morning, Fred, it's a nice sunny day.'

'George didn't think so.' Fred told Andrew about the disappointing ticket sales for the concert and George's reaction.

'Disappointing? I should say. Poor old George, he's invested a lot of his time and effort in the concert and it would be a great shame for the village if we have to cancel.'

'It seems as though the village isn't very interested in the Rotary concert,' said Fred.

Andrew pondered this as he walked to the car. Like all members, he had hoped for a successful event even if it didn't make a lot of money, but he could not help feeling a sense of schadenfreude at George's failure. Perhaps it was the cocksure way that George Woodgate had assumed that the concert would be a successful fundraiser for the club, when many members had misgivings. But it was more than that. He resented the way George Woodgate had managed to win over the membership so easily, with his confident, if slightly gawky, public-school manner. Although ostensibly they were friends, at that moment, President Andrew Parker disliked his Rotary colleague with a passion bordering on odium, even though he could not quite articulate why.

Andrew lived not far from Debenham, in the small village of Ashfield, which did not have a shop or a pub, like so many small villages in Suffolk. By the time Andrew had reached home he had decided to call a special meeting of club council. He couldn't just leave this to George and his concert committee and he would enjoy humiliating George in the process.

Soon, Andrew was talking on the phone to club secretary Claire.

'This sounds disastrous, Andrew, I'll ring round and see if I can arrange a meeting within the next day or so.'

On the evening of the meeting, members drifted in to be greeted by Susan, Andrew's wife. Claire was always first and the others followed soon after. They went into the dining room and sat around an old oak table, which lent the gravitas that the matter before them required.

Andrew said, 'Thank you all for giving up your evening at short notice, but we need to take a decision about the concert.'

'Let's not be too hasty,' said George.

'We've only sold four tickets and this looks like a disaster about to unfold before us,' said Andrew. 'I, for one, had my doubts about the idea of the concert from the start, and I know that many other members felt the same. We can't allow the club to be embarrassed.' He looked from member to member. There was a look of perturbation about them, apart from George, whose conscious thoughts lay elsewhere. Andrew continued, 'Has everyone got a glass of something? There are soft drinks as well as the wine.'

George was anxious but focussed. 'Let's not assume that all is lost. The position is not as hopeless as you are suggesting.'

'Are you completely mad? We've sold four tickets and the concert is on Saturday week,' said Fiona. She was not a member of club council, but she had insisted that she should attend and Andrew had relented.

George sat back on his chair and said with a confident air, 'We can still do it.'

'There is no way that we can sell enough tickets to hold a concert. We'll be a complete laughing stock in the village if only four people turn up,' said Fiona. 'I might be a member of concert committee, but I don't want any responsibility for a fiasco like that.'

Andrew listened to Fiona's vitriolic comments with huge satisfaction. He was content to leave it to Fiona and others to take the attack to George. He would delight in seeing George squirm.

'Yesterday was a bit of a surprise, I'll admit,' said George, 'but I've been thinking about this carefully and I'm confident we can still go ahead.' This was George's alter ego, when he was able to step aside from the anxiety that overwhelmed him so often.

There were some murmurings and Fiona was just about to make another contribution, when the door opened and Susan backed in, carrying bowls of chilli con carne and rice, and a basket of crusty bread. The worried looks turned to smiles as Susan passed bowls of hot food around the assembled Rotarians.

'That looks lovely,' said Claire. Other members agreed, Andrew topped up glasses and members began to eat. The warmth of the chilli and a decent Malbec eased the tension, but there was still a big decision to make.

Susan cleared the bowls. She did not mind supporting her husband in his new role as president, at least she could keep an eye on him with Claire never far away. Susan had her own interests; there was the village gardening club and the Women's Institute, or jam and Jerusalem, as Andrew and everyone else called it.

'Let's get on, shall we?' Andrew brought everyone back to the business in hand. It was time to give George the opportunity to struggle in vain to extricate himself from the large hole into which he had fallen. 'George, what do you have to say, as concert chairman; surely, we'll lose money if we go ahead? Isn't the truth of it that this concert idea is self-assured hubris on your part and doomed to failure?' He lifted his glass and took a sip of wine to hide his smirk. He could barely wait to hear George's pathetic response.

George said, 'It was a bit of a surprise to discover that Fred had sold only four tickets, but let's look at it another way.'

'Four is pathetic,' said Fiona.

'I fear you're correct, Fiona,' said Andrew. 'We should never have agreed to the concert in the first place.'

George said, 'If you'll just listen, I can answer the doubters.' Although he could see that this was becoming a defence of his personal integrity, he knew that he had the answer.

'This really is a mess,' said Andrew. 'You've put the club in a very embarrassing position.'

George said, 'Mr President. Look at it like this. We have twenty-one members, each of whom has a wife or husband. If everyone buys two tickets, that's forty-two tickets sold—'

'What makes you think that I'll buy two tickets?' said Fiona.

'If we all support the concert that's £420,' said George.

'I might be washing my hair that night,' said Fiona.

George pressed on. 'Then there's the ticket money we'll take on the night from people in the village who make a late decision to come along. Add to that the takings from the bar and the raffle and we should have a successful fundraising event.' He paused for a moment to let members absorb that line of thought. 'We should carry on as planned, because we can make a success of it.'

'Fiona has got a point,' said Andrew. 'We can't assume that every member will buy two tickets.'

'Well, they should support the concert,' said George. 'It's a club event.'

'I think I'll give it a miss,' said Fiona.

'What about the raffle?' said George.

'What about it?'

'You said you'd organise it,' said George.

'Did I?'

'I asked you and you said you would,' said George.

'Only if I go.'

'You need to go to the concert,' said George.

'Well, I might,' said Fiona. 'Just don't assume too much.'

George continued, 'Also, we have this Saturday and the following Saturday, to hand out flyers outside the Co-op to promote the event.'

'More assumptions, George?' said Fiona.

'It's an expectation,' said George.

'We can't expect members to be the only ones who put their hands in their pockets,' said Andrew.

'It behoves us as Rotarians to support our own club's events,' said George.

'Why bother with a concert?' said Fiona.

'It's a cultural event for the village,' said George.

'I haven't noticed many grateful villagers,' said Fiona.

'I think there will be,' said George.

'We might just as well all put in £20 and save ourselves the trouble,' said Fiona.

'What trouble?' said George.

'Organising a concert,' said Fiona.

'Come on, Fiona, you're not taking this seriously,' said George.

'I'm very serious,' said Fiona.

'Look this isn't getting us anywhere,' said Andrew.

'We don't do chequebook Rotary,' said Fiona.

'Well surely, we can expect our own members to support our own events?' said George. 'That's hardly chequebook Rotary.'

'You should ask members first,' said Fiona.

'There may be one or two members who genuinely have other commitments, but I would expect most members to come along,' said George.

'Perhaps some members have friends and neighbours who'll come as well,' said Frank.

George said, 'Yes, of course. If members buy forty-two tickets and we have, say, half a dozen friends, we could soon be up to fifty tickets,' said George.

'That would make forty-eight,' said Fiona.

'You're being pedantic,' said George.

'It's mental arithmetic, not pedantry,' said Fiona.

'Just think about it,' said George. 'We've put out quite a bit of publicity, so a lot of people in the village will know about it already.'

'But they don't care about it,' said Fiona.

George said, 'When people from the village go into the newsagents to buy a newspaper or make some other purchase, they don't ask Fred for two tickets for the concert because they don't have a spare £20 with them. And Fred doesn't have a card machine.'

George continued, 'But it's in their minds; they know that there's a concert in the village and if the weather's fine and there's nothing on television, which there never is on a Saturday night, they'll come along.'

'I might come too,' said Fiona.

'I expect it,' said George.

'I'll wash my hair another day.'

'It's a good event,' said George. 'It'll add to the cultural life of the village. People should support it.'

'What's it in aid of?' said Fiona.

'ShelterBox,' said Andrew. 'We agreed that ages ago.'

'That's a worthy cause,' said Fiona.

'George, how many tickets do we need to sell to cover our costs?' said Andrew. 'We need to be clear on that before we can make any decision.'

'Phillip's getting wine for sale or return and a free loan of the glasses,' said George.

'There won't be a problem with the bar,' said Phillip.

'We have printed all our own flyers and the tickets, but we have incurred some printing costs for posters, say £60,' said George.

'The choir costs a bomb,' said Fiona.

'We pay their expenses,' said George. 'We only pay them if the concert goes ahead.'

'They might demand payment,' said Fiona.

'Katrina has always referred to the payment as expenses for the choir and not a fee for performing the concert,' said George. 'If they don't perform the concert, they won't incur any expenses and if we go ahead as planned, we'll have the money to pay them.'

The debate continued a little longer, but in the end, George's determination to carry on prevailed. Andrew said, 'I sense that we are all persuaded that the concert should go ahead. The club will not be at risk financially, and club members will form the backbone of the audience, if we don't get enough support from the village. And, with a little luck, the concert might even be a financial success after all.' Andrew managed to hide his disappointment that George had managed to wriggle out of his difficulty so easily, but he was glad that the concert was going ahead. He was president and he would claim the credit for a successful night and if it was not, he could shuffle the blame onto George.

*

On Saturday morning at nine o'clock sharp, George and his team gathered outside the Co-op, festooned in bright yellow *hi vis* tabards that proudly proclaimed "Rotary Club of Debenham". They were armed with flyers, to urge upon unsuspecting Saturday morning shoppers.

'Hello,' said Kye, to the first likely concertgoer he accosted. 'We're from the Rotary Club of Debenham. Do you know about our concert next Saturday? It's in the church and it's in support of ShelterBox. The Lovel Choir will be singing many types of music, some folk, music from the theatre, some pop music. Would you like to take one of our flyers?'

'I saw your advert in the parish magazine and my husband said that you've put signs on the roads leading into the village,' said the woman.

'Well, I'm delighted to hear you say that,' said Kye, 'but do you think you'll come to the concert? There's nothing on television and it's going to be a fine evening. There'll be a bar, so you can have a glass of wine during the interval. In fact, you can get as drunk as you like!'

The woman laughed. 'I'm not too sure about that, but my husband might. Unfortunately, we're already going out next Saturday evening, but good luck with the concert. I'll take a flyer for my neighbour.'

'Thank you, take a few more to give to anyone you know who might be interested,' said Kye.

Well, at least she knows about the concert, thought George, who had been listening to this exchange. He was beginning to have a good feeling about it and his anxiety had gone. He approached two teenage girls and went through a pitch similar to Kye's, but his delivery was awkward and lacking in humour. The two girls shuffled uncomfortably, but were polite enough to hear him out. As George stopped speaking, they looked at each other and burst out laughing.

'Do you think you might come?' said George.

They looked at each other again and walked off giggling.

'George, there's no point asking a couple of teenage girls if they want to go to the concert,' said Phillip. 'It's best to target women of a certain age, either by themselves or with their husbands.'

'Young mothers with young children are probably going to be too busy,' said Claire, 'and arranging a babysitter is not always easy.'

There was a steady stream of shoppers at the Co-op, as usual on a Saturday morning, and George's team worked hard. By midday the footfall was diminishing and George decided to finish for the day. They had exhausted their supply of flyers and there was no more to be done.

'Thank you everyone,' said George.

'We didn't sell a single ticket,' said Fiona.

'No, I didn't think that we would,' said George.

'Why is that?' said Fiona.

'People in the village do know about the concert and we've done our best to remind them that it's next week. If the weather holds up, I really do believe that we'll get a decent turnout. And how's the raffle coming along?'

'I've bought a book of raffle tickets, if that's what you mean,' said Fiona.

'I think you know what I mean,' said George.

'Yes, George, I've got a promise of a large box of chocolates from Fred at the newsagents, a few bottles of wine and a few other things. The tickets will be £1 or £5 a strip. Most people will buy a strip for a charity.'

'Well done, Fiona, I knew I could rely on you.'

'Of course, you did, George.'

*

The next Saturday was the day of the concert. George and his team had assembled outside the Co-op as they had the previous Saturday morning, but their message had a greater urgency about it.

'Are you going to the concert at the church this evening?' said George in an awkward but engaging manner to an early morning shopper.

'The one this evening?' said the woman to whom he was speaking.

'Yes, this evening, you must have heard about it,' said George.

'We might do,' said the woman.

'The weather's going to stay fine, and it'll be a brilliant concert,' said George.

'We're definitely going,' said another woman.

'Lots of people said that they would be going, as they did last Saturday,' said George. 'If they all come along, we should have a decent audience.'

'Don't be too sure,' said Fiona, 'some of them were just being polite.'

Soon after noon, George said, 'Thank you everyone. I think we can stop now. We'll meet in the church this evening.'

*

George arrived at the church early to make sure that all was well and to bring teabags, milk and biscuits. The choir arrived and took up position in the cottage to make tea and munch their biscuits. Phillip was next to arrive. He had driven his car up to the door and began to lift out boxes of wine, glasses and sundry other items. George went out to help.

'Hello, Phillip. You've got everything, I hope. Who've you got to help you with the bar?'

'Dominic volunteered to help.'

'Andrew and I are on the door,' said George.

'What about an introduction?' said Phillip.

'I've also asked Andrew, as our president, to say a few words of welcome and to say something about ShelterBox,' said George. 'He'll also say a few thankyous at the end.'

They worked quietly together setting up the bar at the back of the church. George said, 'I've asked Katrina to make sure that, as they go into the last number before the interval, their music director makes an announcement that the bar will be opening as soon as they finish.'

'Dominic and I will scamper to the back of the church and get ready for the rush,' said Phillip.

'I do hope there is a rush,' said George.

A Volvo estate car drove through the open gates into the small parking area by the church and parked beside Phillip's car. Two men got out of the car.

'I didn't bring the keyboard, because Katrina assured me that the piano has a good tone, but I'd like to try the piano just to make sure,' said one of the men.

'Yes, of course. I'm George.'

'My name's Felix and this is Sidney.'

One's a cat, and the other's in Australia, thought George, as they walked up the nave towards the piano. *I should remember that.* George left them to examine the piano.

'I can't play that,' said Felix in a loud and angry voice. 'It's completely out of tune.'

'Katrina has tried it and she said that it was all right,' said Sidney.

'Is she tone deaf?' said Felix.

George and Frank, who had just arrived, heard the commotion and went to investigate. 'What's the matter?' said George.

'I was assured that this piano was in good order, but it's hopelessly out of tune,' said Felix.

'Have you brought your keyboard?' said George.

'No, I haven't,' said an angry Felix.

'Let me try,' said Frank, as he sat on the stool and tried to play. 'It didn't sound like that the last time I played it.'

'I'm going home to get the keyboard,' said Felix.

'Where do you live?' said George.

'Framlingham,' said Felix.

'There's no time,' said George. 'You'll have to make do.'

'I'm a serious musician. I'm not throwing away my reputation trying to play that thing.' Felix stormed down the nave followed by Sidney.

'I think we've got a bit of a problem here, Frank,' said George, who had an unpleasant feeling gnawing away in his belly. 'The accompanist has just flounced out and the audience is about to arrive.'

Soon, club members started to arrive with their wives and husbands. George was anxious for them to be seated, but they stood around chatting. Gradually more people started to come in, people from the village, people to whom George had spoken this morning or the previous Saturday morning.

It was hardly a rush, but it was a steady stream of people and the cash box, an old biscuit tin, began to fill with notes.

'It's a pound a ticket or a fiver for a strip,' said Fiona, who was selling raffle tickets.

'I'll take a strip,' said a man who had just bought his concert tickets from Andrew.

As people came in and bought their tickets, so Fiona continued to relieve them of five pounds each for raffle tickets.

'George, how much longer are you going to be?' said Katrina. 'Adrian Kingston, our music director, is getting a bit fractious.'

'It's your accompanist,' said George. 'He's flounced off to get his keyboard.'

'He was going to use the piano,' said Katrina.

'He said it's out of tune,' said George.

'It was all right when I tried it,' said Katrina. 'Has anyone moved it?'

'Moved it?' said George.

'Look at the state of this old floor,' said Katrina. 'All the tiles are uneven. If someone was moving a piano around on this surface, it could easily unsettle it.'

Before George could reply, he saw the large figure of the music director, Adrian Kingston, bearing down on them, with his choir following crocodile fashion.

'What's going on?' said Adrian. 'Where's Felix?'

'He's gone to get his keyboard,' said George.

'I'm here to perform a concert with my choir,' said Adrian. 'Why isn't everything ready?'

'Well…' said Katrina.

'I'm not asking you, Katrina, I'm asking him.' He jabbed a large finger in George's direction.

'It's your choir and your performance,' said George. 'You should make sure that you've got an accompanist. He's just buggered off.'

'I will not have that kind of language in my church,' said the Revd. Alice Jones, the rector, who had just appeared and was looking angrily at George and Adrian. 'I thought this concert was due to start at seven thirty. The villagers of Debenham have paid £10 each for a ticket, plus raffle money and they're getting impatient. And there are a lot of them. What are you going to do about it?'

'Why are we waiting…' They were beginning to sing and then they began to get angry.

'I demand my money back, now,' said a loud voice from the back.

'We've got to do something, Andrew,' said Claire.

'I'll make an announcement,' said Andrew. 'What can I say?'

'I'll do it,' said Claire. 'They might not lynch a woman.'

'No, it's my concert and I'll do it,' said George. He was trying his utmost to overcome his anxiety, as he walked to the front of the church and stood still, waiting for silence.

'Let's hear what he's got to say,' said one angry voice.

'It better be good,' said another.

'Ladies and gentlemen,' said George in an outwardly calm and clear voice. 'I am sorry to tell you that we have a delay.' He had spent his whole life trying to conquer the anxiety he felt at that moment.

'We know that,' said a voice from the back of the church.

'Why the delay?' said another even angrier voice near the front.

George continued, 'It's a technical delay. We have had to send for a keyboard as we are unable to use the piano.'

'What's wrong with the piano?' said the Revd. Alice.

'We're going to open the bar, but before that we are going to hold the raffle,' said George. 'I'm now going to hand over to my colleague for the raffle.'

Meanwhile an unhappy Adrian had marched his choir out of the church to take refuge in the cottage and make more tea.

Fiona went to the front with an old biscuit tin of folded raffle tickets. 'Would you like to pick a ticket, sir?' she said to a particularly belligerent man close to the front. He did so and handed it back to Fiona. 'It's green, number 158. That's green 158.'

'It's me, I'm 158,' said a woman in the front row of the pews, waving her ticket.

'Thank you, madam. Please draw the next ticket and if you go to the back of the church, you may choose your prize.' The woman did what was asked of her and Fiona called, 'Pink, number 49. Pink 49.' Another happy concert goer collected his prize.

Fiona completed the draw and announced, 'The bar is now open, at the back of the church. We've got wine and soft drinks.'

Soon, everyone was drinking and talking. 'I hope Phillip isn't going to run out of wine,' said George.

'No, he told me he's brought plenty,' said Frank. 'It's on sale or return. The red's not bad, let me get you a glass.'

During the next half an hour, the atmosphere in the church changed from angry and unpleasant to warm and convivial. The bar had become very popular indeed. Eventually, Felix and Sidney crashed through the door carrying the keyboard. They fiddled about for an age, but no one paid them any heed. 'It's plugged in and ready to go,' said Felix to Katrina, who had stayed in the church to maintain liaison with the Rotary Club of Debenham.

'I'll go and tell Adrian,' said Katrina.

'Hold on a moment. We need to get people seated,' said Claire.

'Andrew, Dominic, will you get everyone seated?' said George. He felt as though he was beginning to lose control of events; he liked things to be orderly.

'It's all right, George,' said the ever-efficient Claire, who had read the signs of his anxiety and began herding people to their seats. Some were reluctant to go. A few glasses of wine had put the concert out of their minds.

The angry countenance of Adrian marched in the door of the church and up the nave, with his choir following behind like a gaggle of geese. Claire saw him and said in a loud voice, 'Ladies and gentlemen, will you please take your seats. The performance is about to start.'

As the choir took up their positions, Andrew stepped forward to welcome Adrian and the Lovel Choir. He followed on with a few words about the beneficiaries of the concert, conscious that his audience would rather listen to the concert than to him. 'I'm now going to hand over to the music director, Adrian Kingston.'

Adrian was a showman. Gone was the angry

countenance; his face now wore a warm smile. He said, 'It's nice to see so many people here this evening. We're going to start with something that's always popular with audiences. We've put together a medley of songs recorded by a singer songwriter, who was very popular in the 1950s, Charles Hardin Holley; or Buddy Holly, to you and me.'

The accompanist started to play and the choir, more used to Mozart and Handel, sang out to fill the church with a foot-tapping medley of "That'll be the Day", "Peggy Sue", "Every Day", "Not Fade Away" and a few more. The effect was electric, a sudden injection of nostalgia; sounds and songs that the audience remembered from a lifetime ago. This was music that stirred the emotions; it was printed on their souls. George looked around him and saw the reaction from the audience and allowed himself a self-satisfied, but imperceptible smile.

The wine lasted the interval, but only just. When the choir returned, they sang some folk music, a Flanders and Swann comedy piece and other numbers. They finished with Mozart's "Ave Verum Corpus", based on a sacred text. The sublime singing of such exquisite music, mixed with copious quantities of wine, reached out to many in the village who would never have admitted to an interest in classical music.

At the club meeting the following Wednesday, Andrew said, 'Well done George and everyone for the concert. It was a great success as a Rotary event, for the village and I hope for our charity.'

'I would like to thank the concert committee and everyone else who helped on the night,' said George.

'There's no need to make a speech,' said Kye.

George continued, 'I'm pleased to report that the total takings on tickets amounted to over £1,100 and the bar raised another £551. With the raffle money, less expenses, the net income amounted to over £900,' said George. 'The full details are set out in the spreadsheet I sent everyone.'

George was thankful for the contributions from his fellow Rotarians for the printing, the publicity, the Saturday morning promotions and everything they had done on the night. It had been George's project from the beginning. He had believed in it when others were reticent. It was his energy that had driven it forward.

'Well done, George,' said Fiona. 'Delaying the concert to sell more wine was a masterstroke.'

'Thank you, Fiona, great raffle too.'

NINE

The garden party: too much red wine?

The long hot sunny days of August seemed interminable. All around looked parched and tired; the earth, and everything in it, desperate for water. 'We really do need a few days of rain,' said Andrew.

He and Susan were sitting on the patio. Open farmland stretched into the distance. The yellow of the rapeseed flowers in the field before them carried their gaze to the hedgerow at the far side. Through the gap, Andrew could see some shapes and movement in the field beyond. 'Looks like a few deer,' he said.

'Muntjac?'

'I can't make them out, they're too far away,' said Andrew. He and Susan were enjoying gin and tonics before supper. 'I'd like to have the garden party here this year, as I'm president. I know it's a lot of hard work, but at least everyone enjoys it. It's an event for our own members and their friends, rather than a public fundraising event. How do you feel about that, Sue?'

Susan was expecting this request or was it a statement of intent? She knew how much work and anxiety were involved, but she had been determined to support Andrew in his year as president.

'I have asked Claire to help with the organisation. You know, asking members' wives to make up salads and desserts. Coordinating the effort, so that we don't end up with twenty bowls of green salad, that sort of thing.'

Susan was well aware of that sort of thing. 'I'm glad that you thought fit to speak to Claire before you spoke to me.'

'I'm sorry if that's a problem,' said Andrew. 'It never occurred to me that it might be.'

Susan was not surprised to be the last to know. She was slightly irritated, but she had come to expect it where Rotary was concerned. She struggled to understand her deep antipathy towards Claire, and it made her feel ashamed. Claire was hardworking, efficient and popular, and everyone connected with the club liked and respected her; except her, Susan. Did she imagine that Andrew had designs on Claire, or she on him? Susan was uncertain of that, but she was mindful of the attention that Andrew paid her, like a slobbering Labrador pup, with its tongue hanging loose.

Susan had been a social worker until she took early retirement. She valued the work that Rotary did for the benefit of people who needed help, at home and overseas, but she could not help reflecting that she and Andrew, and many of his fellow Rotarians, led privileged lives. The quietude of the open countryside, bird song, the squawking of pheasants, as they stood on tiptoes, flapping their wings furiously, deer nibbling the rosebuds, and the screech of barn owls at night. It was these things that symbolised the sense of privilege, rather than pre-prandial gin and tonic. She thought of her own childhood on a rundown council estate in Colchester and how hard her mother had worked to raise two children without the support of a husband, the father she scarcely knew, so cruelly taken by a disease no one understood. She thought of school, chalkboards, and the cold wind against her bare legs on the hockey field; her determination to scrape through her A levels and into a mediocre, redbrick university; a childless marriage to a moderately successful, if unexciting man; her career as a social worker, the pressure of heavy caseloads; and her former clients, with their drink and drugs problems, little education, limited opportunities in life and poor housing in the back end of Ipswich. At that moment, she felt a profound sense of sadness, which she could not quite understand. Why was life, with its ups and downs, successes and failures, so whimsical, uncertain, capricious? 'Yes, of course, dear.' *I thought you'd never ask.*

*

The speaker at this evening's club meeting was Gerald Prendergast, from the Citizens Advice Bureau. Andrew received him in the bar of the White Horse and introduced him to members as they arrived. 'This is Frank. He was president last year and here's George just coming in. I think you two already know each other.' Andrew got some more drinks and after a while, Bill said, 'We're ready for you, Andrew.' Bill had just stepped into the bar from the kitchen where he had been hard at work preparing dinner for a group of hungry Rotarians and their guest speaker. He took great pride in his country pub fare, and he had cooked steak and mushroom pie this evening, which he would serve with mashed potato and green beans. There was apple pie and custard, and coffee to follow.

Andrew had not pressed ahead with his modernisation for now. Members had already taken to wearing short-sleeved shirts in the warmer weather, so there was nothing to modernise on dress code. He would wait until the weather cooled and members would remember the unofficial club dress code of jackets and ties. He struck the Rotary bell, but not for many more times, he thought. 'Who's saying grace this evening?'

Claire said, 'It's me. Lord, bless this food, then bless it some more. I know it needs blessing; we've eaten here before.'

Members chuckled, and at that moment in walked Bill with the first plates of his steak and mushroom pie. There was a sharp, collective intake of breath.

'Yes, I did hear that.' Plates hit table with an unaccustomed thud and Bill stormed out, leaving piles of mashed potato quivering like jelly.

After dinner, Andrew rose. 'Please be upstanding for the loyal toast.' He paused momentarily. 'The Queen.'

'The Queen.'

'God bless her,' said Kye.

'We'll have a short break,' said Andrew. 'Members you may recharge your glasses.'

Members soon began to drift back from the bar under the watchful eye of the sergeant at arms, who was looking for the opportunity to fine any stragglers.

'I shall now hand over to our guest speaker for the evening, Gerald Prendergast, who's going to tell us about the work of the Citizens Advice Bureau.'

Gerald stood and settled himself. He was used to speaking to groups like this and he proved to be accomplished. 'Thank you for inviting me to your meeting to tell you about the work we do at the Citizens Advice Bureau.' He paused for a moment, then carried on. 'We are a national organisation and we have over 20,000 highly trained volunteers. We offer advice to people who have a wide range of problems...' Gerald gave a comprehensive account of who they were, what they did and for whom. He did not hold back. He was proud of his role and the advice his organisation was able to dispense. Members listened carefully, or at least most of them did. This was the point in the Rotary evening when some eyelids, usually Jeremy's, became so weighty that they had to close, but without the owner missing a single word, of course.

'Gerald, thank you, now has anyone got any questions?' said Andrew. There were questions about the clients, their numerous and varied problems and the volunteers and how they were trained, all of which Gerald answered with aplomb. Eventually, it was decided that they had nothing more to ask and Dominic did the fiddle, which Kye won.

'You decided to put my ball in the bag this week,' said Kye. 'That makes a change.'

'We shall now have the sergeant at arms, Kye, over to you,' said Andrew.

Kye had spotted Jeremy's loss of concentration. 'I'll start with Jeremy. It's not so much that you fell asleep in front of our guest speaker, but you started snoring. We couldn't hear a word and we couldn't wake you up. I was about to send for a bucket of water. That'll be fifty pence.' A slight exaggeration, but the sergeant at arms had to generate some levity as well as fines, or he would be failing in his duty. 'And Fiona and Frances for all that chatter about how women were going to rule the world. I think you do already. That's fifty pence from each of you.'

After Kye had finished, Andrew proposed the Rotary toast. 'Rotary and peace the world over.'

'Rotary and peace the world over.'

*

The next day, Claire rang Susan. Andrew answered. 'I think she's, well somewhere. I'll just go and look for her.'

Susan had heard the phone and heard Andrew's call. She came in and took the phone. 'Hello Claire.'

'Hello, Sue, I hope you don't mind but I've made a bit of a start on the garden party, at least with the thinking.'

'No, of course not.' *Yes, I do mind, Miss super bloody efficiency.*

'I thought perhaps a barbecue would be a good idea, what do you think? I did run it past Andrew. I'm sure he must have mentioned it.'

'Yes, sounds like a good idea.' *I really will kill him this time.*

'I've asked Roger if we can borrow his barbecue. It's pretty big and would be just right for the garden party. He'll bring it over, of course.'

Roger farmed not far away. Like most farmers around, he grew rapeseed, wheat, barley and sugar beet, which he rotated from year to year. He used various vehicles on the farm, so transporting a barbecue would present no difficulty. There would be requests for him to transport gazebos, that several members owned, and sundry other items, for the event.

'I'll order the burgers and the sausages from our butcher and I'll get the buns in the Co-op. Phillip is happy to do the bar, as usual.'

'You've spoken to Phillip?'

'Yes, he said he'd do it.'

Susan drew a deep breath. 'It looks as though you've got things well in hand, Claire. I'll speak to you again soon, goodbye.' With that she was gone. It was useful to have a few energetic and efficient people around, but it would be less irritating if they didn't make such a bloody virtue of it. Susan was not happy.

'Andrew, where are you?'

Andrew had heard enough of the conversation. He sensed danger and decided that his best option was to absquatulate. Susan could see him trying to look busy in the garden, but decided to let matters rest there, at least for the moment.

*

'Not a barbecue,' said Fiona.

'It would make a change,' said Claire.

'So would salmonella,' said Fiona.

The Rotary Club of Debenham were discussing the forthcoming garden party and there was a difference of opinion about what they should eat.

'It's perfectly safe,' said Claire.

'So are quiches and salads,' said Fiona.

Frances said, 'And cold meats.'

'But not barbecued,' said Kye.

'It's going to be too hot,' said Fiona.

'I've agreed it with Susan.'

'Salads?' said Fiona.

'Barbecue,' said Claire.

Andrew decided that he ought to come in here, as the criticism of Claire's choice of food was a criticism of his wife's supposed choice. 'I asked Claire to help Susan with the garden party and that's what they decided. I think we should go along with it.'

The men agreed. They closed their eyes in anticipation of the taste and aroma of sausages and burgers sizzling over hot coals. Yes, it would be a barbecue.

'What about numbers, Claire?' said Andrew. 'Are all club members able to come and bring their wives and husbands and perhaps some friends as well?'

And their cousins and their sisters and their aunts, thought George.

'I've emailed all members, most of whom I've heard from, with the exception of the dilatory ones,' said Claire, 'and I'm not looking at anyone in particular, Peter.'

'Yes, I'm sorry I haven't replied,' said Peter, 'but I am pleased to tell you that we are both going to be there and we're going to bring friends. So that's four of us.'

'Thank you, Peter. On that reckoning, with all members, except Jeremy and his good lady, who'll be on holiday, and a total of ten friends of members, it looks like we'll have a total of fifty people.'

'Excellent, thank you, Claire. What about ticket prices?'

Claire said, 'I've done a quick calculation of our outgoings and I am suggesting £12, which is the same as we charged last year. There will be the cost of the food, that's mainly sausages and burgers, but also the buns and other items. Also, anyone who supplies a salad or dessert can claim back the cost. There'll be a raffle, of course. I know raffles are rather boring, but they do bring in extra money.'

'What about the bar?' said Peter.

'Phillip is running the bar and he'll buy the wine and other drinks and suggest a suitable donation. The first drink will be included in the ticket price.' Claire looked in Phillip's direction.

'It's all in hand,' said Phillip. 'I've got the wine on sale or return.'

This was the way that Rotary arranged events, by setting a price to charge themselves, that was affordable and produced a surplus for charitable purposes. It was more fun than rattling collection tins. It was fellowship.

*

The next day, Roger rang Andrew. 'I was just calling you about the barbecue. I thought I'd bring it over after lunch today. I've spoken to Jeremy and I'll collect him and his gazebo on the way. Three of us should be able to manage everything this afternoon, but if anyone else turns up, so much the better.'

'OK, Roger, I'll see you then. Just one thing before you go.'

'Yes?'

'I've got enough tables here but we'll need some extra chairs,' said Andrew. 'I've got about a couple of dozen garden chairs of various types and condition, but I won't have enough. I'm sure you must have some.'

'Claire has already spoken to me. I'll bring what I have and Claire is asking other members to do the same.'

'And the garden games?' said Andrew.

'I've got croquet, hoopla and one or two others, including the one with the blocks of wood that you throw.'

'I never understood that game,' said Andrew.

'I'll see you this afternoon,' said Roger.

The garden party would take place at lunchtime the next day, which was Sunday. Although the hot sunny weather was likely to continue, there was a hint of menace. Thunderstorms were forecast for Sunday evening.

'Come on, Andrew, get a move on,' said Susan. 'We've got a lot to do today. You do know what day it is?'

'Yes, Susan, I am fully cognisant of the fact that it's Sunday morning, the day of the garden party.' Andrew did not want to be hurried over his breakfast.

Soon they were busy arranging tables under the gazebos, covering them with white tablecloths. There were sets of cutlery to be bound in paper napkins, for guests to pick up when they collected their barbecue lunches.

'It was jolly good that Claire brought these tablecloths and she's going to wash and return them to wherever she got them from,' said Andrew.

'Yes, indeed,' said Susan. *Wasn't it just? Good for Claire.*

At midmorning, Susan made some coffee which they drank on the patio.

'You seem a bit agitated, Sue.'

'Yes, of course I am. We've got fifty people coming for lunch and staying all afternoon and we should be getting on instead of sitting here drinking coffee.' *And if Andrew mentions her name again, well, he'd just better not. And as well as being so efficient and eager to please, she is so bloody nice. No wonder Andrew's in thrall to her.*

A little later, Susan was now fully composed and looking radiant in a pretty summer dress. It was midday and guests would soon be arriving. She would take control of events and all would be well.

Phillip arrived with his wife, Mary, and also the drinks for his bar. 'We can use this table for the bar,' said Phillip and began setting out soft drinks.

'What about this red wine?' said Mary.

'I'll leave the boxes with the bottles of red at the back there.'

'And the white wine and beer?'

'Those large coolers should keep everything cool, despite the heat.' He had bottles of white wine, cans of beer and soft drinks in large coolers, packed with ice. He placed his cash box, an old biscuit tin, on the table in front of him, with a float of a mixture of coins and notes.

'Where are my signs with the donation suggestions?' said Phillip.

'They're here,' said Mary.

Phillip took the signs he had printed at home that morning and placed them by the cash box and at either end of his bar.

By the time Phillip had finished setting up his bar, other guests were beginning to arrive. Frank and Carol were the first. Frank wore a flamboyant blazer, in blue and white stripes, and a straw hat. Carol was resplendent in a pink spotted dress. Andrew and Susan were there to greet them, with handshakes for the men and Rotary kisses for the women. The parking area at the house was now full and guests were beginning to park in the lane, which, although narrow, would just about allow other vehicles to pass.

Guests were now taking their first free drinks at the bar and Phillip and Mary were being overwhelmed, so Ernie joined them.

'I'll give you a hand with the bar, Phillip,' said Ernie.

'Thank you, it's getting rather busy,' said Phillip.

Guests began to break into small groups to take their seats at the tables. Most chose to sit under the gazebos, because the sun was now at its hottest, others braved the heat. The buzz of conversation around the tables was of families and friends and of holidays already taken and others awaited. Rotary business, and especially Rotary politics, were, by some unwritten protocol, strictly forbidden.

'Jeremy and Elizabeth are not here,' said Susan.

'They're on holiday, Lake Garda,' said Claire.

'Really, we went there a couple of years ago,' said Andrew. 'It's so beautiful.'

By now the coals on the barbecue were red-hot. Roger was wielding his tongs with great dexterity, flipping burgers and rotating sausages and occasionally quaffing from a glass of cold beer to the side.

Claire, eager to make sure proceedings went smoothly, got up and walked around the tables, encouraging guests to go and get some lunch. 'Do go up to the barbecue and others will follow.'

Susan saw Claire and immediately got up to do the same, but Frances engaged her in conversation. Roger was soon piling sausages and burgers onto plates and guests were dipping into bowls of salads: green salads, tomato salads, some of rice and others of pasta. The bar continued to do a brisk trade. The white wine and the beer from the coolers were particularly popular, whilst the inexpensive red had soared to the point where it was almost undrinkable.

A man was standing by the bar. He was strongly built, with dark dishevelled hair and he had an intensity about him that many people found intimidating. George had kept in touch with Alec Barton after their chance meeting in

Stowmarket and had invited his old school friend and his wife, Karen, to the garden party. Alec had already consumed several cans of beer to assuage his thirst in the hot sunshine. 'That barbecue smells good,' said Alec. 'I'd better go and get some. Give me a glass of red, Phillip, will you?'

Phillip duly served a glass of red wine, which he pushed towards Alec.

Alec picked up the glass and took a long pull. 'What's this foul-tasting muck?' he shouted angrily and he spat it out in disgust. Several other guests were close by, but Alec ignored them and walked unsteadily towards the barbecue. As he returned with a large plate of food, he spotted Karen, who was already eating and talking, and plonked himself down beside her.

'Oh, there you are, I was wondering where you'd got to.' She could see that Alec had spilled beer down the front of his shirt and there was tomato ketchup on his light-coloured chinos. She felt an inward sense of panic, although she had seen him in a worse state many a time. 'Did someone bump into you?' She was dabbing at his shirt with her handkerchief.

'Yes, clumsy.' Alec readily agreed to that suggestion. Befuddled as he was, he knew that he had behaved badly.

Frank and Carol were sitting next to Karen, and Frank said, 'Are you all right, Alec?'

'Of course, I'm all right, why shouldn't I be?' Alec then gave full attention to his barbecue and said little more for the rest of the afternoon.

Meanwhile, word of Alec's behaviour was being whispered around the other tables. Erica said to George,

'Are you really going to propose him as a member of the club?'

'Well, I didn't actually see what happened at the bar,' said George. 'We'll deal with it all in good time.'

Andrew said, 'We have a procedure for electing new members, not that we've used it much of late.'

'Well, I hope your procedure is sound,' said Susan.

'All Rotary procedures are sound,' said Andrew. He glanced at George and laughed. George did not think that Rotary procedures were funny at all. *What was he laughing at?*

'Well, he's a friend of mine,' said George. 'So, he keeps telling me.'

'People aren't always as they seem,' said Kye.

'Well, I think you are,' said Caroline, Kye's wife.

'We went to school together,' said George.

'He went to that posh school of yours?' said Kye.

'No, it was the village school before I went away to school,' said George.

'I don't think of him as a public-school man,' said Kye.

You could always tell when Kye was positioning himself to tell a humorous story or a risqué joke.

'There's a story of the great days of the British Empire.' Kye did enjoy a good joke, particularly his own. 'A new commanding officer was sent to a jungle outpost to relieve the retiring colonel. After welcoming his replacement, the retiring colonel said, "You must meet my adjutant, Captain Ponsonby, an outstanding young officer."' Kye continued, 'The new CO was surprised to meet a bald, toothless, hunch-backed, wizened old man, of diminutive stature. The retiring colonel said, "Ponsonby, old chap, tell the new CO something about yourself."' Kye was already laughing at his own story. "'Well, sir, I graduated with honours from Sandhurst, joined the regiment and won the Military Cross—" The colonel interrupted: "Yes, yes, never mind all that. Tell him about the day you told the witch doctor to fuck off."'

George looked at Erica, who looked at Caroline, who looked at Andrew, who looked at Susan. After a moment's pause, smirks turned into full-bellied laughter, except George, who found nothing funny in the anecdote and thought that the use of coarse language had been uncalled for.

'Kye, you are the only person in the whole world who could get away with a joke like that in polite company,' said Andrew.

'Anyone for croquet or hoopla?' said Claire, who had heard the raucous laughter but, fortunately, not Kye's joke.

'I was pretty good at croquet last year,' said Frank, who was already playing. He had shed his flamboyant striped blazer, but retained his straw hat. 'Come on, Mary.' A few people stirred themselves out of their languor to take up the challenge of games in the full glare of the sun, but most preferred to sit, drink and chat.

The behaviour of Alec Barton was not going to spoil the occasion, but difficulties lay ahead if George insisted on going ahead with Alec Barton's application for membership.

Meanwhile, after the raffle had concluded, storm clouds of a more literal sort were forming overhead, engulfing the hitherto blue sky.

'I don't like the look of that,' said Frank, as black clouds eclipsed the sun and cast everywhere into darkness. At first there were a few large droplets and then an absolute deluge of hard rain cascaded down, causing pandemonium amongst the guests. Those under the cover of the gazebos took what shelter they could beneath them, but still the rain lashed in, driven by a gusting wind. People knocked into garden furniture, upending tables and chairs and sending drinks and glasses flying. Frank, and others on the croquet lawn, were drenched to the skin in an instant.

Susan looked for Andrew to take the initiative as president, but he was nowhere in sight. She stood self-consciously and shouted at the top of her voice, 'Ladies and gentlemen, run for the house.' The ferocity of the rain bludgeoned her words to the ground, to be swept away in rivulets of rainwater, unheard, unheeded by all. Thunder crashed all around and lightning lit the sky. The absurdity of her action struck her, as she stood with water streaming down her face, clothes saturated, her hair matted and flattened to her skull. Slowly, she raised her head to the sky in defiance, and with arms outstretched and the illumination from the tempest flickering across her face, she laughed like a madwoman.

TEN

The ten-day letter is now a seven-day letter

Fiona and Frances were haranguing George. 'Are you really going to put forward Alec Barton for membership of the club, George?' said Fiona. They were gathering in the White Horse for Wednesday's Rotary meeting.

'You must admit that his behaviour at the garden party was disgraceful,' said Frances.

George was feeling uncomfortable, but was saved from the difficulty of a reply by Bill's voice, calling them into dinner. George feigned to the right, went to the left and took up a place next to Ernie. His rugby days were long over, but he was quick on his feet when he needed to be, if a little awkward. 'I'll sit next to you Ernie. I was getting a bit of an earbashing from Fiona and Frances.'

'I thought you—' Ernie's words were interrupted by the Rotary bell.

Andrew said, 'Good evening, members.'

'Good evening, Mr President.'

'Ernie, you're saying grace this evening, I believe,' said Andrew.

'Lazarus rose, Moses led, Noah built, Jesus fed. Amen.' At least Ernie's grace would not offend Bill.

As soon as they were seated, Bill began serving dinner and the aromatic aroma of chicken curry began to permeate the room. After dinner, Bill cleared away and the evening's proceedings could begin.

It was a business meeting this evening, which was never popular, and members were often tempted to take the night off from Rotary.

Andrew said, 'Apologies for absence?' Amazingly, there was none.

'May I sign the minutes of the last meeting as a correct record?'

'Any matters arising from the minutes, that we haven't got on the agenda?' No one said anything.

Andrew moved swiftly through the item on the president's report, on which no one had anything to say. *Not even Fiona*, thought Andrew. Next, the committee chairmen went through their reports in turn, as Andrew called them.

'Let's move now to the garden party. I would like to thank Claire for her work helping Sue to organise the garden party. Phillip for the bar, Roger at the barbecue and everyone else who helped. It was a most enjoyable occasion.'

'The garden party would've been even more enjoyable

if members had kept their guests in order.' Fiona had started her offensive against Alec Barton.

'Are we really going to let that man into the club?' Frances was determined to back up Fiona.

Andrew said, 'Let's just stick with the garden party for the moment. Claire, did we make any money?'

'Mr President, I can report that we had forty-eight guests at the garden party,' said Claire. 'We were expecting fifty, but two of Roger's friends didn't come in the end. As you will see from the spreadsheet I emailed to everyone, we received £576 in ticket money, the raffle brought in £190, and the bar takings were £255. That's a total income of £1,021, less the expenses as set out of £319, making a net income for the event of £702. The only disappointment was the soaking we all received at the end of the afternoon.' Everyone laughed. They all had their own stories of the storm.

There was some discussion about the garden party, that again came round to Alec Barton. 'We have seen first-hand just how unsuitable Alec Barton would be as a member of this club,' said Fiona, 'and I move that we do not accept an application for him to join this club.'

'I am not prepared to accept that proposal, Fiona,' said Andrew. 'The matter of Alec Barton is not on the agenda. Unless or until we receive a formal application for him to be elected to the club, there is nothing more to be done. I am now going to move on to the next item on the agenda.'

'Well, George must know whether he's going to propose Barton or not.' Fiona was persistent.

'Well, I haven't,' said George, 'but I have asked Claire for a form, which she gave me this evening.'

'I am going to move on.' Andrew was now raising his voice.

The business meeting ground on, and the evening finished as ever with the fiddle and the Rotary toast. Although Fiona had not managed to start a full debate on Alec Barton, she had struck a blow.

The next morning, the matter came up again. Andrew heard the phone ring and Susan's voice, as she answered. 'It's for you.' Susan thrust the phone at him. 'It's the club secretary.'

'Claire?'

'She's still club secretary, isn't she?'

'Yes, of course.' Andrew took the phone.

'Hello Claire.'

'Fiona isn't going to be happy, Andrew. I've now received an application form from George proposing Alec Barton for membership. There's a small query that I need to raise with him, but subject to that, it's all in order.'

*

'Andrew, it's almost two weeks and you've done nothing about Alec's application for membership,' said George. 'That's just not good enough. First Claire raised a query and then nothing. What's going on, Andrew?' Phillip, Andrew, George and Claire were in deep conversation in the bar at the White Horse.

'We're moving on it now, George,' said Andrew. 'Claire tells me that the information subcommittee must meet the candidate and the proposer.'

'Who's on the information subcommittee?' said George.

Andrew said, 'Dominic is chairman, and he will formally meet Alec and you for a chat about the application. He'll be in touch.'

'What does this chat involve?' said George.

'It's to consider the applicant's suitability,' said Andrew.

'Suitability and eligibility,' said Claire.

'He's a local businessman,' said George. 'He's built up his own company, and he's solvent, so far as I'm aware.'

'There shouldn't be a problem then,' said Andrew.

'The information subcommittee makes a report to the membership committee,' said Claire.

*

Dominic had met Alec and George and completed the first step of what was going to be a difficult process, with strong opposition likely to come from some quarters of the club. Phillip was chairman of the membership subcommittee and the other members would be Frank, Dominic and Claire.

'Well, I'll speak to Frank and Dominic and try to get everyone together for Tuesday,' said Claire.

Later that evening Mary said, 'Do you really expect me to have that horrible man in this house, never mind the club?'

'He won't be coming to the meeting of the membership subcommittee, so there's no need to worry about that,' said Phillip.

'But you are going to admit him into the club?' said Mary.

'Not necessarily,' said Phillip. 'We'll treat the matter with the seriousness it deserves and I'm sure we'll make the right decision.' Phillip was not sure whether Mary was more irritated by the prospect of Alec Barton joining the club or the fact that he had just assumed that she would give up her evening to whip up a hot supper for his membership subcommittee. But of course, she would. Mary never let him down.

'There are times when you really do sound pompous, Phillip.'

'Thank you, dear.'

Claire was the first to arrive for the meeting. Phillip's aged Labrador roused himself from his basket to greet her. He wandered over wagging his tail and she patted his head. Dominic and Frank arrived soon after and Phillip opened a bottle of Rioja.

Soon they were sipping wine, apart from Claire, who would never drink anything when she had to drive, and very little on any other occasion. Mary stayed to chat with them for a while. She enjoyed talking to members of the club because she did not see them very often. She particularly liked Claire, whom she thought open, friendly and just nice. She could not understand why Susan had taken against her. Maybe it was the way Claire seemed to control everything that happened in the club. She was always there in the background. In all situations domestic, Phillip needed a little aggravation to galvanise him into action. The men at Rotary were probably the same. It's women who got things done. It couldn't be anything to do with that silly mix-up with the cabins when they went on that trip as guests of the Dutch Club, or could it? 'I'm just going to pop into the kitchen, to fetch out the supper. I hope chilli con carne and rice is all right.'

After they had eaten, Phillip decided that it was time to get down to business. 'Claire, perhaps you will remind us of our task this evening.'

Claire had a firm grasp of the club constitution and by-laws. 'According to the club by-laws, we have to consider the report of the information subcommittee and inquire into all aspects of the suitability and eligibility of the candidate, Alec Barton.'

'As you know, I am the information subcommittee,' said Dominic.

'A committee must be at least two people,' said Phillip.

'I think we'll have to overlook that little technicality,' said Claire.

'Let's not get too bogged down in detail,' said Frank.

'If our findings are favourable, we move to the next step,' said Claire. 'Phillip, you have to consult the classification subcommittee and give Alec a classification.'

'His classification is not going to be an issue,' said Phillip. 'We haven't actually got a classification subcommittee, so I shall assume that role and consult myself.'

'Remind me why we have to worry about classification,' said Frank.

'What is classification?' said Dominic.

'Every Rotarian must have a classification according to his business or profession,' said Claire.

'I should have known that,' said Dominic.

'The classification derives from the activity of the firm, company or institution with which the member is connected,' said Claire. 'There are also limitations on the number of members of a particular classification who may join any one club. The idea is to get a wide range of professional people, so that we are better able to serve the community.'

'How do you know all this stuff, Claire?' said Dominic.

'I'm club secretary. It's my job to know.'

'As chairman of the information subcommittee, I'll start,' said Dominic, 'and Claire can help me with anything I've left out.' Claire was the only one with any papers, not that she ever forgot anything. The only facts she could not recall were those she had never known. 'So, the application form gives us his address and other contact details, including his business premises. His business is building and fencing.'

'Presumably he sells fencing, not stolen property,' said Phillip.

They chuckled. 'He does look a bit like a criminal type,' said Frank, with a smile.

'I don't think we'll put that in our report,' said Phillip.

'He tells us that, although he has never been a Rotarian, he has supported many Rotary events over the last few years,' said Dominic.

'George invites him to Rotary events now and again and we're usually pleased to have him and Karen to boost the numbers,' said Frank.

'If we are going to be scrupulous in our approach, we should consider suitability,' said Phillip.

'We need to inquire into all aspects of his suitability and eligibility,' said Claire. 'The general qualification for membership, is that a member should be of good character and good business, professional or community reputation.'

'Let's start with his business reputation,' said Phillip. 'What do we know about it?'

'If you want some building work done quickly or someone to throw up some fencing to keep people out and your property in, you ask Alec Barton,' said Dominic.

'That would suggest that he's cheap and quick,' said Frank.

'Quick and cheap, isn't the kind of slogan that would appeal to everyone,' said Dominic.

'But it's probably all right for selling fencing,' said Frank.

'Is his business sound?' said Phillip. 'Has he overextended? Does he pay his bills on time? Is he in good stead with his bank? Do we know anything about that sort of thing?'

'He was at pains to say that his business is doing well and he gave satisfactory answers to all of those kinds of questions, and George backed him up.' Dominic wanted to make it clear that as chairman of the information subcommittee, he had done a thorough job.

'Well, I suppose we have to conclude that there is nothing detrimental known against him. Are we all happy with that?'

There was a murmur of assent.

'Now let's turn to the trickier issue of his character,'

said Phillip. 'It seems to me that it's entirely subjective. Who'd like to start with that?'

'There is no avoiding it,' said Claire. 'There are two incidents that most people would probably think are the actions of a man who is not of good character.'

'What incidents?' said Dominic.

'The incident with the woman at charter night and the incident at the garden party. Whether he was drunk or sober, they were examples of bad behaviour,' said Claire.

'As you will remember,' said Dominic, 'George was very eloquent in dealing with these matters, because he knew that they would be held against him by some in the club.'

'What else would you expect?' said Claire.

Dominic said, 'At charter night, they were sitting at the table and, according to George, Alec Barton was picking up his fountain pen, that he had dropped on the floor, and he slipped.'

'He was probably drunk,' said Claire.

'He put out his hand and unfortunately, he touched the woman's leg,' said Dominic. 'She went ballistic, and Alec was mortified.'

'That's hardly surprising,' said Claire.

Dominic said, 'As for the garden party, to be fair, the red wine was almost undrinkable, and Phillip, to whom he expressed his dissatisfaction, took no offence, did you?'

'There wasn't much I could do about the red in that heat,' said Phillip.

'What about the beer on his shirt?' said Claire.

'The explanation for that is simple,' said Dominic. 'Someone bumped into him and spilled his beer. It was an accident.'

'The suggestion seems to be that he drinks too much,' said Phillip, reaching for the Rioja to top up their glasses. 'I wouldn't criticise a chap for what he drinks, so long as he can behave himself.'

The debate swung back and forth for a little longer, but in a relaxed and friendly manner. 'Come on now, we got to decide what to do.' Phillip had decided that it was time to bring matters to a close.

'Otherwise, you'll have to open another bottle of this delicious Rioja,' said Frank.

Phillip said, 'We've had a good discussion and my view is this. George is a good solid, long-standing member of this club, well respected by everyone. He and Alec have been friends for a long time and I for one don't wish to embarrass him by turning down flat someone he's proposing for membership. We should let it go forward and if it falls at a later stage, well so be it.'

'I think you're right,' said Frank, and Dominic readily agreed.

They looked at Claire. 'If that's the majority view, I won't oppose it,' she said.

'Thank you, Claire,' said Phillip. 'I shall consult myself about classification and you may send out the seven-day letters to all members.'

'I'll email them tomorrow,' said Claire. 'Don't be surprised if some members object. It won't take Fiona seven days to get her objection in.'

'Any objections can go to club council, and they will make the final decision,' said Phillip.

*

Fiona was already plotting her next move. There was a speaker from a local charity at the next weekly meeting. Although it was frowned upon to raise matters of contentious Rotary business in front of guests, Fiona felt compelled to enquire about progress of Alec Barton's application for membership.

'Mr President, I shall be pleased to have a report from the chairman of the appointments subcommittee.' Fiona looked at Phillip.

'I have nothing to report at this stage,' said Phillip.

'You've just held a meeting,' said Fiona. 'You must have discussed something.'

'You're well informed,' said Phillip.

'I'm not well informed at all,' said Fiona. 'You won't tell me anything. But I do know that you've just had a meeting.'

'I am not going to allow any further discussion on this, Fiona, so let's move on,' said President Andrew. 'I take it that you've seen the seven-day letter?'

'Yes,' said Fiona.

'So obviously, the subcommittee decided to allow the matter to go forward,' said Andrew.

Fiona said, 'You mean they've agreed that Alec Barton is a good and proper person to join this club?'

'I'm moving on now,' said Andrew.

'You haven't answered my question, Mr President,' said Fiona.

'I'm not here to answer your questions, Fiona,' said Andrew.

'Does the membership subcommittee consider Alec Barton to be a fit and proper person to join this club?' said Fiona.

'That's not a matter for us at this meeting, Fiona,' said Andrew. 'The seven-day notice period hasn't expired yet.'

'Mr President, may I have your assurance that you will bring the matter to the club at the soonest opportunity?' said Fiona.

'Fiona, I'm sorry, but I'm not going to allow any further discussion on this matter this evening,' said Andrew.

'We haven't had any discussion at all this evening, Mr President,' said Fiona.

Andrew was now fighting hard to control his rising temper. 'We're going to move on to the next item.'

The business meeting ran its course. The atmosphere was flat, and everyone was relieved when, eventually, Andrew was able to say, 'Please be upstanding for the Rotary toast. Rotary and peace the world over.'

'Rotary and peace the world over.'

ELEVEN

A meeting of the trustees: the fall and rise of the chairman

The *Daily Mail* had published another piece on the saga of Rose Cottage, but with Mr and Mrs Preston happily ensconced in a very comfortable private care home and a holiday in an expensive hotel on the Suffolk coast in prospect, the story no longer had legs. Other papers had written short pieces, but had now lost interest. George still had to answer to the trustees of the Morton Charities and account for the expenditure he had authorised, albeit unwillingly. He rang Luke. 'Luke, will you ring the trustees and find a date for a meeting?'

'I've already had the Revd. Masters on the phone. He said that he'd spoken to you. He seemed a bit irritated that nothing was happening,' said Luke.

'Well, I'd like you to make it happen now.' The phone went dead.

Luke opened his diary. The meeting had to avoid the weekend. After all, Sunday was the only day that the Reverend Anthony Masters worked. He chuckled at the thought. Friday evening was out. It was the start of the weekend. One of the trustees mentioned in conversation that he would be away on a conference for two days. Luke was convinced that other trustees invented appointments occasionally, not to inconvenience him, but so as not to appear to lead totally uneventful and unfulfilled lives. The easiest thing to do would be to email four or five dates to the trustees and ask them to reply tomorrow stating all the dates they could manage. In practice, no one would reply within that time frame, some would ask for further dates to consider and two of the trustees did not have computers. The two elderly trustees in question believed that the instantaneous transportation of text from one person to another was some form of voodoo. He sent the email with little expectation of swift or indeed any responses and picked up the phone. He knew this would be a long and tedious task.

Luke's phone rang. He hoped that would be one of the three trustees on whom he was waiting. 'Hello.'

'Have you fixed up that meeting yet?' said George. 'I asked you to ring me as soon as you had it arranged.'

'I'm hoping to arrange it for Thursday,' said Luke, 'but I'm waiting for three of the trustees to reply. I've emailed and rung everyone and I've left messages for those I haven't been able to contact.'

'Whom are you waiting for?' said George. 'Never mind. Just let me know when you've done it. Just one thing, I want to make a small amendment to the draft minutes of the Rufford Trust before you send them out to the trustees. I'll get back to you on that.'

Luke's persistence paid off. Eventually, he made contact with everyone and they all agreed to meet at seven o'clock on Thursday evening, in the church. He drew up an agenda for the meeting and emailed it, together with the minutes of the previous meeting, with George's further amendment, to all but the two of the trustees who did not own computers. He would have to deliver their papers by hand.

The first trustee to arrive on Thursday evening was William Dunn, one of the churchwardens. William had been a member of the disestablished, but still Anglican, Church of Wales, as a young man, and before that, a member of a small Methodist chapel somewhere in the Welsh valleys, where he had grown up. He had later moved to Suffolk to take up a teaching post and eventually became a churchwarden in the parish of Castle Rudham. He unlocked the heavy eleventh-century door of the church. It creaked on its huge iron hinges, before yielding to William's solid shove. He switched on the lights at the back of the church, where the meeting would take place. George arrived soon after. He glanced along the nave towards the altar, which he could just make out in the gloom. The sound of his footsteps on the old tiled floor echoed around the empty space. The churchwarden looked up. 'Good evening, William,' said George. 'You're always first.'

'I have to be, otherwise no one would get in. Unless Lucas was here, of course.' Lucas Cockrill was the other churchwarden. 'Occasionally, one or two parishioners pop into the church for a moment of quiet contemplation. That's before I lock up, of course.'

Next to arrive was Luke, carrying three large leather-bound minute books and other meeting papers. 'Good evening,' he said. He put down his documents on the table next to the large iron key and busied himself with the layout of the meeting area. He arranged six chairs in an arc in front of the table, a chair behind the table for the chairman, and another on the end of the table for himself. He needed a proper surface on which to write. Earlier minute books went back more than a hundred years, each written in a clear steady hand by Luke's predecessors. The family names of earlier trustees appeared time and time again as the burden of office passed from one generation to the next. Luke would make notes of the proceedings from which to write the formal minutes. The minutes would describe only the matters under consideration and the formal decisions the trustees had taken. Lost forever, would be the mood of the meeting and the rhetoric of the trustees, whether bold and statesmanlike or mean and carping; they were capable of both. The dynamics of the meeting would live on only in the memories of those who were there and the cold stone walls of the edifice in which the meeting took place.

Soon, all the trustees were present and George, as chairman, called the meeting to order. The Morton Charities brought together three separate charities: The Rufford Trust, the Sick and Poor Fund and the Morton General Charity. The membership was common to all and it was their custom and practice to run the meetings of all three charities concurrently. There would be one agenda which would have some items for decision by all three charities, and items relevant to only one or other of the charities. To the casual observer, had there been one, the proceedings would be of one homogenous meeting. It was the task of the secretary, Luke Chadwick, to produce three sets of minutes, making sure that each item appeared in the minutes of the correct charity.

Soon, all the trustees had gathered, and George said, 'Good evening, everyone, shall we make a start? Apologies for absence. I can see that we are all here. The next item is the minutes of the last meeting of each of the three charities, which you have all seen. May I sign them as correct records?'

'Agreed.'

George paused to sign three sets of minutes, in a slow, deliberate hand. 'The next item is the reappointment of two of our trustees for a further three-year term,' said George.

'I move that Noah Alderton and Jacob Akerman be reappointed,' said Steven Acton.

'I second that,' said William.

'Are we all agreed?' said George.

'Agreed.'

'That's carried unanimously,' said George. 'The next item is eleemosynary pensions.' This was an item for the Morton General Charity.

'We are paying only five at the moment,' said Noah Alderton, 'and I know we've kept to five for some time now, but I'm very concerned about Mrs Stubbins, who lives at Strawberry Cottage. She lost her husband recently and I think she's struggling.'

'Well, I won't argue about Mrs Stubbins,' said William. 'I know that she is in difficulty, because I was talking to her only a few days ago, but I would be concerned if we added too many eleemosynary pensioners.'

'I move that Mrs Stubbins be awarded an eleemosynary pension,' said Noah.

'I second that,' said William.

George said, 'All in favour?' All hands went up.

'That's approved unanimously,' said George. 'Next it's the annual review of the amount of the eleemosynary pension.'

'I move no change,' said Noah Alderton.

'I second that,' said William Dunn.

'All in favour?' said George. Again, all hands went up. 'That's unanimous.'

'Now it's Rose Cottage and a report on urgent action,' said George.

Before he could say any more, the Revd. Masters interrupted to say, 'Mr Chairman, as this item concerns you and actions you have taken without proper authority, you should vacate the chair for this item, and I so propose.'

'I second that,' said Lucas. Everyone voted in favour, except George and Jacob Akerman, who abstained. George was taken completely by surprise. He had been ambushed in a move that had been swift and ruthless.

'I move that the Revd. Masters be elected chairman to deal with the item now before us,' said William.

'I second that,' said Lucas. The voting was the same.

George knew that he was in trouble. This church alliance, God's gang of three, were out to get him, or was he just being paranoid? Even if he were not being paranoid, it didn't mean that they were not out to get him. He felt a mixture of anxiety and anger, but the anger overcame the anxiety. He rose slowly from his aged wooden chair, that had seated trustees of an earlier time, as well as many an ardent parishioner. The Revd. Masters stood at the same time and the two walked towards each other to change seats, as though they were about to duel with pistols. As they passed, George looked directly at the Revd. Masters, who stared straight ahead. George turned and, arm straight, squinted down the barrel of his duelling pistol. The Revd. Masters did the same. George squeezed the trigger. There was a loud report, a cloud of burnt powder and the Revd. Masters dropped. He had sat down on the chair and the imagined firearms had disappeared.

Whether chairman or secretary, there is one inalienable rule that you ignore at your peril: preparation. George had prepared himself well enough for the agenda items and had answers to all the questions that any trustee could possibly ask, but there is always the unexpected. What if there is a fire? Or a trustee has a heart attack? What if your car breaks down as you are about to leave home, or a thief sneaks into the church and runs off with the poor box? What if you need your duelling pistols? You have to be prepared and maintain control of the situation, however challenging. George reproached himself. *I should have expected something like this. If only I had spoken to some of the other trustees before the meeting, this might have been avoided.*

The Revd. Masters said, 'It's difficult to know where to begin in all this. Everything went wrong on the weekend in question and all the problems and difficulties stem from that.'

'We received some very distressing publicity in the *Daily Mail* and other papers,' said William.

'There was even a piece in the *Church Times*,' said the Revd. Masters, 'although I must say that I dealt with their enquiry more professionally than George dealt with the *Daily Mail*.'

'I don't know why he told the *Daily Mail* that he only knew drunk electricians,' said Lucas.

'Quite so,' said the Revd. Masters. 'One can always say, "no comment", but to volunteer that sort of information was folly of the highest order.'

The highest order, thought George, *the Revd. Masters was always looking on high.*

'The question is whether you, George, can retain our confidence to remain as chairman. Before I ask you to give an account of yourself, I'd like to hear whether any of the trustees have any initial comments.'

'Yes, I'd like to say something, Mr Chairman,' said Lucas.

Mr Chairman, thought George. *They really are going to oust me.*

'Yes, Lucas,' said the Revd. Masters.

'This charity has suffered a grave injustice at the hands of the press and George has only made things worse,' said Lucas. 'He's incurred huge amounts of expenditure without proper authority, I'm sure Luke can tell us exactly how much.' He glanced in Luke's direction, but Luke thought it wise to keep his head down.

William said, 'He got drunk electricians to go to Rose Cottage, two of them, mind you, and he told the press that he only knew drunk electricians. As you said yourself, Mr Chairman, that wasn't very wise, they pick up on that sort of thing, they do. And poor old Mr and Mrs Preston were left without power for days. You could at least have said a prayer for them, Mr Chairman. I know you wouldn't have let them down like George did.'

'That's bloody outrageous,' shouted George as he leaped from his chair.

'George Woodgate, how dare you shout such profanities in this church, the house of God?' said the Revd. Masters, in a loud voice. 'Sit down before you are struck down.'

By whom, George was unsure, but the rebuke stung him. As he returned to his seat, he glanced down the nave towards the altar and for a moment, he thought he saw a light; small, white, shining brightly through the gloom. It shocked and shamed him deeply, then he saw a shadowy figure in the distance; a parishioner had lit a candle and knelt to pray.

'Anyone else?' said the Revd. Masters, but no one had anything else to say. 'George, would you care to explain yourself and in particular to address the matter of the unauthorised spending.'

George had calmed down, although the experience

with the light had shaken him. 'Thank you.' He refused to address the Revd. Masters as "Mr Chairman".

George looked directly at the Revd. Masters and said, 'The first I knew about the problems at Rose Cottage was when our secretary, Luke, rang me. By then he'd already tried and failed to make contact with Mr Jenkins, our usual electrician. I did my best to find someone else. I contacted a friend, who's a builder, who might have been able to help. He tried to resolve the problem, but he couldn't. Through my friend, I managed to get a qualified electrician to visit Rose Cottage. He advised that the house needed to be rewired and that it was dangerous for our tenants to remain there until the rewiring had been carried out.' George had set out his narrative of the facts.

'The real issue is this.' George paused for a moment and looked at his fellow trustees. They were still, silent and focussed. 'When did Rose Cottage become so dangerous that it was unsafe for our tenants? And when did I, and the rest of the trustees, become aware of that fact? Clearly, a house that is safe one day, does not become unsafe the next. The process is gradual.' The trustees nodded slowly in agreement with the sagacity of their erstwhile chairman.

George continued, 'Our usual electrician, Mr Jenkins, had been to the house to fix a problem six months earlier. He reported back to Luke that the wiring was in need of attention. Luke questioned him and this is where the story becomes rather blurred. According to Luke, Mr Jenkins did not say that the house was unsafe and required the imminent evacuation of the tenants, but he did say that the house needed to be rewired and it would be unwise to leave it much longer. That was just before our last meeting. You have the minutes before you and you have just approved them as a correct record. Their accuracy is now beyond question.' There was more nodding of heads.

'May I refer you to Minute 9 of the minutes of the Rufford Trust under the heading "Rose Cottage – General Maintenance"? It says:

'The trustees considered a report from the secretary, that Mr E L Jenkins, electrician, had visited Rose Cottage to advise on a matter to which the tenants had drawn attention, and recommended that the property be rewired within the near future. It was proposed by the Revd. A T Masters, seconded by Mr L F Cockrill and RESOLVED – that the matter of rewiring Rose Cottage be deferred until the committee considers its maintenance budget for the next financial year.'

George felt that he was now in the ascendancy in this tussle. 'I would emphasise two things: the first of which is, that I was neither a proposer nor a seconder of the motion to defer the rewiring of Rose Cottage. The second thing is that the matter was *resolved* not *resolved unanimously*.' The trustees leant forward in their chairs, careful not to miss a word. 'I would draw your attention to the wording of every other individual minute. Each records that the resolution was passed *unanimously*. It follows, therefore, that, as the minute on Rose Cottage did not record that the decision was *unanimous*, at least one trustee either voted against or abstained.'

The Revd. Masters glowered at George. George ignored him and continued, 'I was the only trustee who did *not* vote for that resolution to defer the rewiring. Therefore, I can reasonably claim to be the only trustee who is *not* culpable in everything that followed. I distinctly recall voicing my concern about deferring this matter, but you decided to overrule me.'

'Well, just hold on a moment,' said William. 'That's just a quirk in the drafting. The secretary left out the word *unanimously*, in error. You can't attach any importance to that. I certainly don't remember you speaking against deferring the rewiring.'

George said, 'William, would you care to look at the minutes of the last meeting, the very minutes that everyone here has agreed, unanimously, to be a correct record of that meeting. Go to the list of those present. Do you see your name?'

'It's not there,' said a bewildered William.

'And just under that, do you see under "Apologies for Absence", that your name, William Dunn, appears in splendid isolation?'

A puzzled look came over William's face. 'I thought I was there.'

George could scarcely believe his own cleverness. 'William, you cannot possibly remember what happened at the meeting, because you were not there.'

The Revd. Masters could see that the church alliance's coup was beginning to crumble. He sat up very straight on his chair and said, 'I was at our last meeting, and I don't recall George expressing his reservations about deferring the rewiring, at least not any more than anyone else. As I recall it, we did struggle with this matter. We all recognised that we had to do the rewiring, but we were mindful of the Trust's parlous financial position and our overall responsibility as trustees. In the end we voted to defer the matter. We *all* voted to defer.' He gave great emphasis to the word "all".

'That's exactly what happened, Mr Chairman,' said William. 'I remember that you told me about it the following Sunday.'

'Yes, we talked about it just before morning service,' said Lucas.

George said, 'It seems that William, who wasn't present, remembers what he was told *after* the meeting, and Lucas' strongest memory is of that same conversation that took place after the meeting.'

George pressed on. 'The fact remains, that I abstained. That is supported by the minutes and those minutes have been confirmed and signed as a correct record of the meeting. They would stand up in any court of law in the land.' George was not entirely sure of his assertion, but it sounded authoritative and would support his narrative.

George continued, 'There's another very important point. Under a resolution of this committee some years ago, the chairman has authority to incur any expenditure necessary in an emergency. It follows, therefore, that the action I took was in accordance with the authority that the trustees formally delegated to me, and this is a report for information only and not one for decision.'

'I thought you'd mention that,' said the Revd. Masters. 'That resolution must be ten years or more old and we've never used it before, as far as I remember. Besides, emergency is not defined in the resolution. This committee delegated authority to the chairman, but in effect, reserved to itself the right to define what is an emergency in any particular case.'

'I disagree,' said George. 'You are misdirecting yourself. The clear purpose of that resolution is to ensure that when something needs to be done immediately to prevent a calamity, the chairman has authority to act. It is for the chairman to decide what is an emergency. How could it be otherwise? We, the trustees, could have attempted to define "emergency", but wisely decided not to do so. Implicitly, we left it to the chairman to decide on a case-by-case basis. If this were otherwise, the chairman would have to call a meeting so that the trustees could determine whether the matter at hand amounted to an emergency. That would be an absurdity.'

'My ruling as chairman is that we will take a formal vote on the matter,' said the Revd. Masters.

'I'd like to say something,' said Steven Acton, a dairy farmer. A little earlier, Steven had been up to his ankles in manure and he exuded a tell-tale pong, more prevalent in Devon than Suffolk, a county of primarily arable farming. 'George did express greater concern than the rest of us. I do remember that. Whether he voted or not, we just have to go by the minutes.'

'That's all we can do,' said Noah Alderton.

'I agree,' said Jacob Akerman.

The debate petered out at that point. The trustees had had their say and the church alliance, God's gang of three, stood against the other trustees, who had aligned themselves with George. 'It's time we brought this item to a conclusion,' said the Revd. Masters. 'Would anyone care to move that:

'The trustees –

1. approve reluctantly, the action of the then chairman to incur the unauthorised expenditure under discussion; and
2. place on record that he be advised to consider his position.'

He looked directly at William as he spoke.

'I so move,' said William.

'Is there a seconder?' The Revd. Masters stared at Lucas.

Lucas felt uncomfortable under this gaze but, as required of him, said, 'I second the proposal.'

The Revd. Masters said, 'All in favour of the proposal, please raise your hand.'

Just as hands were about to rise, George said, 'I wish to move an amendment.' He had quickly scribbled down the original motion on the back of his agenda, using his knee as a table. His pen had gone through the paper in several places in his haste, but it was readable. 'My amendment is to delete the words "reluctantly, then" and "unauthorised" and the whole of the second part of the motion. The amended motion would read: "that the trustees approve the actions of the chairman to incur the expenditure under discussion".'

The Revd. Masters said, 'I now put the motion to the committee, all—'

George interrupted. 'The procedure in any forum is to put the amendment first, so that if it's approved it becomes the motion on which other amendments may be moved.' He spoke with the authority of the rightful chairman of this committee of trustees and a veteran of many fractious Rotary meetings.

'Very well,' said the Revd. Masters. 'I now put the amendment. Those in favour, please raise your hand.' He sat still and stared at his two churchwardens. They did not move. George's hand shot up immediately and he looked at the remaining trustees. Steven Acton put up his hand, followed by Noah Alderton. Still Jacob did not move.

Jacob was mesmerised. He had not understood the discussions and did not know what to do. He was an elderly man; his white hair was sparse, his face taut and lined with worry, exaggerated by the dim light and high emotion of all that had gone before. Now his vote was crucial.

The Revd. Masters said, 'Jacob is abstaining…'

'I think Jacob is raising his hand,' said George, but old Jacob had not moved. 'He definitely is.' Slowly Jacob lifted his hand off his knee and with all the strength he could muster, but failed to raise it. It was three votes for the amendment.

'Those against the amendment.' The Revd. Masters and the two churchwardens, Lucas and William, voted against the amendment. The Revd. Masters said, 'That's three votes for the amendment and three against. I shall use my casting vote, as chairman, against the amendment. The amendment is lost.'

'I now put the original motion. All in favour, please show.' The Revd. Masters put up his hand and the two churchwardens did the same. 'And against the original motion.' George raised his hand and Steven and Noah voted against. Again, Jacob abstained.

'There were three votes in favour of the original motion and three votes against. I shall use my casting vote as chairman in favour of the original motion, which is carried. That concludes this item. We now move on to—'

'Mr Chairman *pro tempore*,' said George with exaggerated emphasis on the words *pro tempore*. 'You were voted into the chair for the item on Rose Cottage. We have now concluded that item. I shall now resume in the chair.'

'We voted to advise you to consider your position. That means we expect you to resign,' said the Revd. Masters.

'I don't care what you expected. I have considered my position, and I've decided not to resign. I have, therefore, done all the trustees' resolution asked of me, so remove yourself from the chair, *now*.' George stood up and walked towards the chair. He stood over the Revd. Masters, who remained motionless. The chairman *pro tempore* saw the determination on George's face and, reluctantly, vacated the chair. Duelling pistols were not required.

Safely back in the chair, George took the trustees through the remainder of the agenda. 'There was some uncertainty on the vote we took on Rose Cottage, so I'm going to take it again.'

'You can't do that,' said the Revd. Masters. 'Once the vote has been taken, that's it.'

George said, 'Not necessarily; the meeting is still in progress, because I haven't closed it.' He continued, 'There are circumstances where the chairman takes the vote, and he is not sure whether he has counted all the hands that went up. Sometimes members put up their hand to vote, but because counting takes too long, some hands start to go down before they have been counted. What's the chairman to do? If he's uncertain on any matter, he takes the vote again, of course. As I said, this meeting is still in progress. It's not over until I declare it to be over.'

'But I was voted into the chair, so I should take the vote, not you,' protested the Revd. Masters.

'You're not in the chair now, I am, and I shall deal with the item,' said George.

'On a point of order—' said the Revd. Masters.

George did not let him finish. 'There is no point of order.'

'You haven't given me chance to put my point of order,' said the Revd. Masters.

'I'm not going to waste time on frippery,' said George. 'I'm chairman, and I shall now retake the vote on Rose Cottage.'

'I move that the chairman vacates the chair for the continuation of the item on Rose Cottage,' said the Revd. Masters.

'I second that,' said Lucas.

'Very well,' said George, 'all in favour, please raise your hand.'

God's trio raised their hands. 'And against.' George put up his hand. Steven and Noah did the same. Jacob was oblivious to what was going on. 'That's three votes for and three against,' said George. 'I shall use my casting vote against, so the motion that the chairman vacates the chair for the continuation of the item on Rose Cottage, is lost.'

George said, 'Now to the vote on the real issues. Let me recap. The original motion was – first, to approve reluctantly, the actions of the then chairman to incur the unauthorised expenditure under discussion, and second, place on record that he be advised to consider his position.' He paused for a moment and looked at his fellow trustees. As soon as the Revd. Masters made eye contact, George felt uncomfortable and shifted his gaze. He continued, 'I moved an amendment to delete the words *reluctantly, then* and *unauthorised* and the whole of the second part. The amendment on which you are now going to vote, reads, "that the trustees approve the actions of the chairman to incur the expenditure under discussion". All in favour of the amendment please raise your hand.'

George, Steven and Noah raised their hands. 'That's three for the amendment. Those against.' The Holy Alliance raised their hands. 'That's three against. I shall use my casting vote for the amendment, which is now carried. I shall now put the amended motion, as a substantive motion. All in favour, please raise your hand.'

George, Steven and Noah raised their hands followed reluctantly by Lucas and William. Then Jacob, who had no idea what was happening, decided to do the same as almost everyone else, and raised his hand. 'Those against.' The Revd. Masters did not move, so the final vote was six votes for the substantive motion, none against, with one abstention. The church alliance had been broken, the coup crushed, and George was jubilant.

Luke had kept his head down during this discussion, in case anyone questioned his role in events as they unfolded. He was thinking of the task that lay ahead of him and the golden rule of any committee secretary. Whatever pickle the members get themselves into, however convoluted the debate or the procedural shenanigans, everything comes right in the minutes. And so, it did.

TWELVE

Will club council uphold the objections?

Susan had heard the phone ring, but Andrew had already answered it. She listened for a moment to see if she could determine who had rung. It was Miss Smarty Pants. She walked off in a huff.

'Yes, we can have our usual meeting room at the White Horse, as you had suggested. I've had to bring it forward to five o'clock to accommodate Mark,' said Claire.

'I wanted everyone to be present because it's going to be contentious and difficult.'

'They'll all be here, except George. He's recused himself, because he is the proposer,' said Claire.

'Yes, quite right, but I don't want anyone else ducking the issue,' said Andrew.

'There's a problem,' said Claire. 'I've had a call from Fiona.'
'Fiona?'

'She wants to come to club council.'

'Well, she can't and that's final,' said Andrew.

'It's not as simple as that.'

'Why not?'

Claire said, 'You've often said that anyone can ask to attend council and she attended once before.'

'I don't remember,' said Andrew.

'Fiona does.'

'I suppose we'll have to let her come then,' said Andrew.

'Bill is going to provide sandwiches and coffee.'

'We'll just have the Alec Barton matter on the agenda. Any other business can wait until our next meeting,' said Andrew.

'Yes, I'll send out the agenda tomorrow.'

'Thank you, Claire.'

*

Council members began to arrive at the White Horse. Claire was first as always, sipping a glass of fruit juice.

'May we go through, Bill?'

'Yes Andrew, it's all ready.'

'I don't like this setup. Will you help me to move these tables?' said Andrew.

They spent a few minutes moving the tables around until they were satisfied that they had a formation to suit them. The door opened and in walked Fiona. Everyone looked in her direction, but she ignored their stares. No one spoke.

223

'Let's make a start on those sandwiches, they look very appetising,' said Andrew, 'and then we can get down to business.'

They all agreed on one thing: sandwiches of fresh white bread and thick slices of dark, sweet, cured Suffolk ham, with a smidgeon of English mustard, were delicious. The next matter would give them more difficulty.

'Do you want a few more minutes or shall we get on?' said Andrew.

'Let's make a start, Andrew,' said Frank.

'We're all here, except George,' said Andrew. 'However, we do have Fiona, by special request.'

'Whose request?' said Frank.

'My request,' said Fiona.

'Is this usual?' said Frank.

'Fiona asked to attend to present her objection,' said Andrew. 'She will not be able to vote. So, welcome Fiona.'

'Why isn't George here?' said Paul.

'He's recused himself,' said Andrew.

'Recused, what do you mean?' said Frank.

'George has a direct interest in the matter, as the proposer, and therefore he is not going to take part,' said Claire.

'Hasn't Fiona got a direct interest in the matter?' said Paul.

'I've got an objection, if that's what you mean,' said Fiona.

'Let's get on with it,' said Ernie, 'otherwise we'll be here all night.'

Andrew said, 'As you all know, George has put forward Alec Barton for membership of this club. The application has been made on the official Rotary form—'

'I'm not objecting to the form, Andrew. I couldn't care less about that.' It was always likely to be first blood to Fiona.

'Quite so,' said Andrew, 'but I'm sure you would have objected if he'd used the wrong form.'

'Probably,' said Fiona.

Andrew said, 'Anyway, it is the correct form, it's been filled in correctly, and signed correctly by Alec Barton, the applicant for membership of this club, and George, as proposer.'

'I'll have to take your word that it's correct,' said Fiona. 'I haven't seen it.'

Claire took a single sheet of paper from her file and laid it before Fiona. 'It's all in order.'

Andrew said, 'Claire has written to all members to give them notice of the proposal to admit a new member to the club, the so-called seven-day letter.'

'The seven-day letter gives seven days for written objections,' said Claire.

'You make it sound like a revelation,' said Fiona.

'At one time it was ten days,' said Claire.

'A seven-day letter gave ten days for objections?' said Fiona. 'That's ridiculous.'

'It was known as a ten-day letter then,' said Claire.

'There are some brilliant minds in the higher echelons of Rotary,' said Fiona.

'I'm now going to ask Claire to bring us up to date,' said Andrew.

'Thank you, Andrew. I've received two objections. One is from Fiona, and I'll come back to that in a moment, and the other is from Frances. Frances has stated that the reasons for her objection are the same as Fiona's. Fiona states that the reasons for her objection are—'

'I can give my own reasons, if I'm allowed,' said Fiona.

'Yes, all right,' said Andrew. 'Have you anything further to add, Claire?'

'No,' said Claire, 'I'm sure it's better if Fiona explains her reasons.'

'Before Fiona speaks,' said Andrew, 'there are just two objections, Claire? You didn't object yourself?'

'There are two objections,' said Claire.

Fiona was keen to get on. 'Why did we object, Frances and I? The answer to that is pretty simple: Alec Barton is not a fit person to be a Rotarian. He's slimy, greasy, lecherous, self-opinionated and objectionable. He's a drunkard; he's unprincipled; he's coldblooded; he's filthy and disgusting. He's got no respect for women, and he's got no respect for Rotary or Rotary ideals.'

'Well, hold on a moment,' said Phillip. 'That's no more than a string of gratuitous insults. What's slimy supposed to mean? Slimy like a snake? Greasy like a workmen's café? If you claim that he's a drunkard and a lecher and all the other insults you have made, you need to say why and to give examples. You need to make a proper argument.'

'I never have trouble making an argument,' said Fiona.

'That's true,' said Frank.

'Phillip has got a point,' said Andrew. 'We can't make a decision based on insults.'

'You want examples?' said Fiona. 'I'll give you examples. What about charter night and that poor woman, Angela?

And the garden party? He was filthy and disgusting, and objectionable on both those occasions.'

Andrew said, 'Let's consider the two occasions that Fiona referred to. The more serious matter was the incident on charter night. Do we really know about what happened?'

Fiona wanted to get in first. 'He got disgustingly drunk and put his hand up Angela's skirt. No wonder she was so upset. Her husband would've punched him if people hadn't intervened.'

'It might have been a mistake to pick a fight with Alec Barton,' said Phillip.

'Does anyone actually know what happened?' said Andrew. 'Someone must have seen the incident. Didn't the woman's husband write a letter of complaint?'

'I was president at the time,' said Frank.

'You didn't do much to help,' said Fiona.

'As Fiona said, the woman's name is Angela, Angela Williams, and her husband is Don,' said Frank. 'Don and Angela are friends of Freddie and Georgina. Freddie invited them to charter night. He was embarrassed about the whole thing. He wanted to support Don and his wife, but he didn't want to cause trouble for the club.'

'What a weed,' said Fiona.

Frank continued, 'Freddie told me that he suggested to Don that he should write to me, as I was president. What he thought I could do, I don't know.'

'You didn't disappoint him then,' said Fiona.

'The problem was between two guests, Angela and Alec,' said Frank. 'It just happened to be at a Rotary event.

Also, I have to say, that Angela is known to be rather highly strung.'

'So, it was all her fault?' said Fiona. 'That's just a typical gutless reaction from a man.'

Frank said, 'In his letter, Don Williams said that Alec Barton was drunk and that he dropped his pen, which he tried to pick up. Don claimed that Alec Barton then lurched over his wife and put his hand on her thigh. She screamed.'

'You made enquiries at the time, didn't you?' said Andrew.

'Yes, of course I did.' Frank did not expect his actions to be brought into question. 'I spoke to a number of members and guests, but no one really saw anything.'

'Everyone heard Angela scream,' said Fiona.

'I would agree with Fiona's contribution for once,' said Frank.

'You should agree more often,' said Fiona.

'Some people may have seen Alec bending down close to her,' said Frank. 'She might have screamed loudly, but the room was very noisy, it was the end of the evening, and to be perfectly honest, we'd all had a few drinks. So, most people didn't think anything of it at the time.'

'What did you say in your reply, Frank?' said Andrew.

'I was as diplomatic as I could be,' said Frank. 'I said that I was sorry about the matter, but couldn't find anyone who had seen Alec Barton put his hand on Angela's leg.'

'Very diplomatic, Frank,' said Claire.

'Pathetic,' said Fiona.

'Even Don has admitted to Freddie that he hadn't seen the hand on the leg,' said Frank. 'He had just said in his letter what Angela had told him. Don readily admits that Angela is highly strung, as he put it.'

'Even Don's putting the blame on his own wife,' said Fiona. 'What a guy.'

'So far as I could determine, the real matter for complaint was the fact that Alec Barton had drunk too much,' said Claire.

'The hand on the leg, if that's where it went, which seems at best, to be unproven, was obviously an accident,' said Phillip. 'I think we can safely disregard that as an objection against Alec.'

'Oh no, you can't dismiss it just like that,' said Fiona. 'Did Frank actually speak to Angela? Did you?'

'No, it was…' said Frank.

'It was too much trouble?' said Fiona.

'I didn't think it would help,' said Frank.

'I spoke to her,' said Fiona, 'and she was terribly upset.'

'I'm not sure it was your place to get involved,' said Frank.

'I made it my business to get involved,' said Fiona. 'I went to see her the next day and I spent a long time talking to her. There was something in her past, but she wouldn't tell me what it was. The last thing she needed was a slob like Alec Barton putting his hands all over her in a drunken stupor.'

'I'd like to bring in other members to get their views. What do you make of it, Dominic?'

'I was nowhere near the incident. I saw Alec and Karen earlier in the evening. We exchanged a few words and that was it.'

Mark said, 'My experience was much the same as Dominic's. Alec was perfectly all right when I spoke to him at some time during the evening. I didn't see anything at all of the incident with Angela.'

Ernie and Paul said much the same. They noticed that something had happened, but had no idea what, at the time.

'Claire, you haven't given us your opinion,' said Andrew.

'I didn't see much to tell,' said Claire. 'But that's not quite the point. We are not making a decision based on what we, as individuals, witnessed on the night. We need to make a judgement on Alec Barton's character and his suitability to be admitted as a member of this club. If Alec Barton did put his hand on Angela's leg, he probably didn't mean to, because he was inebriated at the time. But being drunk is not a defence against such an accusation. And being drunk in public is not conducive to being a Rotarian,' said Claire.

'That's absolutely right,' said Fiona.

'Leaving aside the hand on leg allegation, there is still the question of whether he drinks too much,' said Andrew.

'I don't think that we can really make a judgement about that,' said Phillip. 'How much should a Rotarian drink? There's no answer.'

'You're posing the wrong question,' said Claire. 'It's not about what he drinks, it's about how he behaves in public, because of what he drinks. He's an embarrassment.'

'Hear, hear,' said Fiona, 'and what about the garden party?'

'Well, let's just consider that briefly,' said Andrew. 'We've had a full discussion on the other matter this evening and I don't think another couple of hours would leave us any better informed.'

'I readily admit that the red wine was virtually undrinkable because it had become too warm,' said Phillip. 'And although someone else might have reacted differently, Alec did make his feeling known. And as to the beer stains on his shirt…'

'So, he didn't do anything wrong?' said Fiona.

'All I'm saying is that he had an explanation…' said Phillip.

'That's just a pathetic excuse,' said Fiona, in exasperation.

Andrew looked at his watch very deliberately and then shook it. 'We've been talking for more than two hours. It's time to draw this to a conclusion. Spending another two hours talking about the garden party isn't going to help us. We've considered the objections of two members and the reasons for the objections. Do we accept them or do we admit Alec Barton to the club?'

'I move that we uphold the objections,' said Fiona.

'Hold on a moment,' said Frank. 'Fiona is not a member of club council. She's here on sufferance.'

'She's made us suffer,' said Phillip.

'Fiona, we're pleased that you were able to attend this meeting to explain your objection in this matter so eloquently,' said Andrew.

'Speak for yourself,' said Frank.

Andrew continued, 'However, you are not a member of council, as you know very well. You're here as an observer and to help us to understand your objection, which you have done admirably.'

'A bit too well, if you ask me,' said Frank.

'Therefore, I cannot accept your proposal,' said Andrew.

'In the circumstances, I shall move that we uphold the objections,' said Claire.

'Is there a seconder?' said Andrew.

'I'm not sure that I'm entirely comfortable with the idea of Alec Barton as a member of this club,' said Dominic, 'so I shall second the proposal.'

'Those in favour of Claire's proposition,' said Andrew.

Claire raised her hand and Dominic did the same. No one else moved.

'And those against, please raise your hand.'

Frank raised his hand. No one else moved. 'Are the rest of you going to abstain?' said Andrew. Still, no one moved. In truth, no one really felt comfortable voting to support Alec Barton's application for membership of the Rotary Club of Debenham.

'They don't have to vote if they don't want to,' said Fiona.

Andrew pondered for a moment. He had not expected to be in this position. 'I shall vote against the motion, which means that there are two votes for, and two against. And I shall also use my casting vote as chairman, to vote against. The motion is therefore lost and the objection to Alec Barton's membership falls.'

*

The following day, Claire sent out emails to all members to tell them that the objection had not been upheld and that Alec would be inducted at the next meeting. Some members were disappointed to hear the news, but most members accepted it stoically. Alec Barton was a local businessman and he would be an additional member at a time when membership in Rotary was in decline. That was certainly Phillip's view, as membership chairman. It was a club council decision, and he could justifiably claim that he had not voted against the objection to admit him. The days when only local worthies aspired to membership of Rotary were long since gone.

It was also George's view. He read the email and said to Erica, 'I'm sure you will be disappointed to learn that council didn't uphold the objections to Alec joining the club.'

'Well, I think it's a mistake,' said Erica. 'That man is trouble and you all know it. You just didn't have the courage to turn him down.'

'It was a council decision and I wasn't there.'

'You're on club council.'

'I recused myself.'

'Why?'

'I had an interest because I proposed Alec for membership.'

'I really do question how you can befriend the man.'

'We were at school together.'

'Alec Barton's wife is a sweet little thing and a lot younger than him, I'd say.'

'Probably.'

'What on earth can she see in him I do not know,' said Erica.

George did not feel qualified to comment.

'Why don't you have another go at trying to persuade Oliver to join?' said Erica. 'At least he's good-mannered.'

'I haven't entirely given up on him, but don't hold your breath.'

'You said that you were inducting Alec Barton at the next meeting, what does that mean exactly?' said Erica.

'Andrew, as president, will perform a small ceremony and give him a Rotary badge and a Rotary handbook.'

'What does the Rotary handbook say about drinking and bad behaviour?'

'Drink as much as you like but don't get drunk in public,' said George.

'I don't think so, George.'

'That's the unwritten rule.'

'You might catch Ollie when he goes for his lunchtime run.' Erica felt her face redden, but George did not notice.

'He runs past the house and up to his gate, then walks back for a brief chat,' said George.

'Why does he do that?' said Erica.

'He clicks his stopwatch at his gate.'

'He times himself?' said Erica.

'Yes.'

'How odd.'

George said, 'I saw him go out a little while ago. I might go and see if I can catch him on his return.'

'Don't take too much of his time,' said Erica. 'He's not retired like you.'

Erica watched as George walked down the garden to catch a word with Oliver. *I think I'll make a rhubarb crumble for this evening. It's about time we had a proper pudding.*

'Oliver,' said George.

'Catch you in a minute.' He ran on to his gate, then jogged back.

'Good run?'

'Not bad, not bad at all. Nearly beat my best time on that route. I'll check when I get back.'

'You write it all down?' said George.

'I have a document on the computer and I record every run, date, time, weather conditions, that sort of thing.'

'Good Lord.'

'Do you want anything in particular?' said Ollie. 'I'm getting cold.'

'You're sweating,' said George.

'I am at the moment, but you soon get cold after a hard run if you stand around.'

'Enjoy the rhubarb?'

'Yes, very good,' said Ollie. 'What did Erica say?'

'What do you mean?' said George.

'Actually, I don't like rhubarb,' said Ollie.

'What about Imogen? Does she like rhubarb?'

'I thought you were going to invite me to a Rotary meeting again,' said Ollie.

'Would you like to come?'

'In twenty years, remember?'

George said, 'Did you know, Rotary was founded as a business networking group?'

'Really.'

'Oh yes, and it still plays a part today,' said George. 'You get to know other members in business.'

'I do all my business in London, New York, and Hong Kong.'

'Rotary is international,' said George.

'There's a branch in Calais, is there?' George never seemed to notice when Oliver was being sarcastic.

'There're one and a quarter million Rotarians worldwide, give or take.'

'That many?'

'About 35,000 clubs in 200 countries.'

'Including London, New York, and Hong Kong?' said Ollie.

'There are clubs everywhere,' said George. 'If you're abroad and you're in trouble, you could contact the nearest club and someone would help you.'

'Has that happened to you?'

'Not actually.'

'You mean no.'

'Well, no, but it could have done.'

*

As the evening arrived for Alec Barton's induction, members gathered in the bar in the White Horse. Andrew was in conversation with Kate from Age Concern, the speaker that evening. The door opened and in came George, followed by Alec. Andrew shook hands with George and then welcomed Alec. 'It's good to see you again, Alec, welcome to the club.'

'Thank you,' said Alec.

Andrew said, 'I think you've probably met most of the members, although you probably won't know Kate, who's our speaker this evening.' Kate and Alec shook hands. 'Let me get you a drink. What will you have?'

'Thank you, Andrew, I'll have a pint of Ghost Ship, please.' Alec was on his best behaviour.

Other members came over and shook hands with Alec and George relaxed now that members seemed to have accepted his friend into the club. Earlier in the day, he had checked the attendance for this evening's meeting with Bill and had been relieved to learn that Fiona and Frances had booked themselves out for the evening.

'We're ready for you to go through, Andrew,' said Bill.

As they processed through to their room, the door burst open and in came Fiona, followed by Frances.

They went to the bar. 'Two gin and tonics, please, Bill,' said Fiona.

'Slimline tonics,' said Frances.

'Good evening, members and guests,' said Andrew.

'Good evening, Mr President.'

'Frank is going to say grace, I believe.'

Frank put his hands together. 'Lord, for good food we give thanks, for good fellowship we give ourselves, to good service, we give our all. Amen.'

'Amen.'

As soon as Frank had said grace, the members took their seats and Marlene came in with plates of lasagne, bowls of green salad and garlic bread. When dinner was over, Andrew said, 'Please be upstanding for the loyal toast.' Members rose with a scraping of chairs and when they were all still and silent, Andrew said, 'The Queen.'

'The Queen.'

'God bless her,' said Kye.

'We'll take a short break and then we'll carry on with the evening's business,' said Andrew. After ten minutes or so, members started to drift back to their seats, Kye, as sergeant at arms, taking note of any stragglers.

Andrew said, 'I'd like to introduce Kate from Age Concern, who is our speaker this evening. But before I hand the floor to Kate, I'm going to induct a new member, Alec Barton. It's not very often that I am able to do that. I now ask Alec, and George, as proposer, to come forward.' Andrew felt a frisson of excitement at the prospect of a new member, a feeling that others shared with him; but not everyone.

Andrew, Alec and George were now standing at the front and all eyes were on them. Andrew began, 'George, you have proposed Alec Barton as a member of this club. Do you wish to say anything in support of your proposal?'

George replied, 'I am delighted to propose Alec as a member. He's a local businessman of good standing. He has attended several Rotary events, so most members will know him already. I believe Alec to be worthy of membership of this club and I am sure that he will prove to be a good Rotarian.'

Andrew turned to Alec. 'Alec, you have been elected a member of this club, because we believe you to be a worthy representative of your vocation, in sympathy with Rotary ideals, and that you're prepared to make those ideals effective in your community, and internationally. I am now going to ask Kye to read the Object of Rotary.'

Kye unfurled a sheet of paper and started to read. 'The Object of Rotary is to encourage and foster the ideal of service as a basis of worthy enterprise, and in particular to encourage and foster...' Kye stumbled occasionally. He was less fluent reading than he was with his off the cuff comments and quick wit. He read to the end, '... and the advancement of international understanding, good will and peace through a world of fellowship of business and professional persons, united in the ideal of service.'

'Thank you, Kye,' said Andrew. He now turned to face Alec. 'As Rotarians, we have certain responsibilities. First, the basis of all Rotary, is fellowship. Therefore, regular attendance is essential. For without regular contact, acquaintances cannot be turned into friends. Second, service above self represents an attitude to life, which we should all practise in our different ways, according to our abilities and circumstances.' Andrew was now coming to the final act, which was to present the Rotary badge. 'Alec, I charge you to wear the Rotary badge at all times.'

As Andrew reached the climax of the induction ceremony, Fiona leapt to her feet. 'Alec Barton is a rebarbative drunkard and an abuser of women. He's not fit to wear that badge and he's not fit to be a Rotarian.'

The atmosphere was electric. No one moved. Alec Barton stared straight ahead, motionless, his face devoid of expression. A vein pulsing in his neck was the only clue to his inner emotions. George's face reddened and contorted, he opened his mouth to say something, but no sound emerged. He began to feel anxious, his stomach knotted and he started wringing his hands.

Fiona continued her tirade. 'I object to that man becoming a member of this club. You just haven't got the moral courage to turn him down for what he is. And George, you are a disgrace for bringing him to the club in the first place and for proposing him for membership.'

Andrew managed to control his anger. 'Fiona, I shall be pleased if you will leave this meeting and not return until you can behave properly.'

Fiona was already walking defiantly towards the door. In another moment she was gone. Frances did not know what to do and, in her indecision, remained in her seat. Andrew looked at Alec, who maintained his posture, and then Kate, who was horrified by what she had heard. 'Alec, Kate, I am so embarrassed and ashamed that you have witnessed such a scene and I wish to apologise sincerely to you both on behalf of the club.'

Andrew decided that he had no choice but to conclude the induction ceremony as quickly as possible. 'Fellow Rotarians, I commend to you, Rotarian Alec, and I charge him, not to fail us.' He then turned to face his fellow Rotarians. 'I charge all of you not to fail in your duty to Rotarian Alec, as a new member of this club. Rotarian Alec, welcome to the Rotary Club of Debenham.'

*

The next morning, Andrew was in the garden, well wrapped up in his gardening clothes against a fresh breeze, his thoughts on the meeting the previous evening. An old Mercedes drove onto the drive.

'Hello, George.'

'I have to say that Fiona's performance last night was an absolute disgrace,' said George angrily. 'She has embarrassed both Alec and me and I expect you to do something about it. Her behaviour was absolutely beyond the pale.'

Andrew said nothing to interrupt George's invective.

'It really does bring into question her continued membership of this club. She's got to go and it's up to you to act and to act now. It's no good putting it off and waiting for another incident, and there will be other incidents, as you well know, so what are you going to do? You have to act, as president of this club. That's what presidents have to do. That's what you're there for. We need action and we need it now. If you don't get rid of her, I will take matters into my own hands.'

'I don't need you to tell me what I, as president, should do about Fiona,' said Andrew, who was taken aback by George's verbal assault. 'Last night's events were rather unsettling, I would agree with you on that, but not everyone in the club would. Fiona is prickly, but she contributes a great deal to the life of the club. The Easter egg raffle in local pubs was her idea and she organised it and it was her energy that raised more than £500 for children's charities—'

George said, 'I'm not in the mood to listen to a catalogue of Fiona's achievements as a Rotarian and a member of this club. Nothing entitles her to behave in the way she did at the meeting last night, and in a way that, had it been Alec Barton, she would be the first to complain of. Are you going to act or not?'

Andrew said, 'I'll tell you plainly that I'm not going to be pushed into taking action until I have had time to think things through, speak to one or two other members and weigh up what's best for the club.'

'I've already spoken to Frank, and he supports me on this,' said George. With that, he got into the car and drove off.

Susan came out of the house. 'What's the matter with George? I was going to make coffee.'

'Just a bit of Rotary business,' said Andrew.

There was no doubt in Andrew's mind that Fiona needed to be reined in, but he would be reluctant to see her leave the club. She had supported him in his modernisation programme that he was determined to carry through in his year as president; she was a counter weight to the traditionalists in the club. No doubt he would hear the views of other members in good time. His mobile phone rang. 'Hello Peter.'

'That was a very unfortunate episode last night,' said Peter. 'I thought that you handled it very well in all the circumstances.'

'Do you really?'

'Will Fiona resign?' said Peter.

'Who knows?' said Andrew. 'Some members might feel that she ought. What do you think, Peter?'

'Well, perhaps she should think about it,' said Peter.

'Do you think she'd be a loss to the club?'

'Well, yes, I suppose she would be in a way,' said Peter.

'You don't think we should force her to resign?'

'We wouldn't do that, would we?' said Peter.

'What do you think?' said Andrew.

'I don't know.'

'Why did you ring me?'

'I'm not sure,' said Peter.

'I thought you might offer some helpful advice,' said Andrew.

'You know best, Andrew,' said Peter. 'You're the president.'

They chatted for a while. As they finished the call, Andrew reflected on what Peter had said and what he had left out. Peter had no appetite for excluding Fiona from the club, nor much else. He had not been a success as chairman of public relations last year, nor much else in his years as a Rotarian.

Susan said, 'Andrew, are you coming in for coffee?'

'I'm coming.' He would rather sit in the warmth of the kitchen for coffee, but he would not want to say much to Susan of what was happening.

'What's going on?' said Susan.

'Nothing,' said Andrew.

'How extraordinary,' said Susan.

'What?'

'Nothing going on,' said Susan. 'It's not what I heard.'

'What have you heard?' said Andrew.

'Erica rang me,' said Susan.

'George's wife?' said Andrew.

'Is that a question?' said Susan.

'It was George's wife?' said Andrew.

'How many other Ericas do we know?' said Susan.

'I can't think of any others.'

'You're all being beastly to Fiona,' said Susan.

'No, that's not true,' said Andrew.

'So, Erica is telling porkies?'

'What?'

'Porkies; pork pies, lies,' said Susan.

'Do you have to learn that sort of language to be a social worker?' said Andrew.

'Are you?' said Susan.

'What?' said Andrew.

'Being beastly to Fiona?'

'No, of course not.'

'She's a woman. The only one with any sense in your club,' said Susan.

'There's also—'

'If you're about to mention Miss Smarty Pants to me... just don't,' said Susan.

'I don't know who you mean,' said Andrew.

'Whatever you're doing, just don't,' said Susan.

'I'm not doing anything,' said Andrew.

'Just keep it that way.'

'It's just that Fiona...'

'Fiona is so small and you men are a lot of bullies,' said Susan.

'That's not true,' said Andrew. 'She bullies us.'

'Don't be ridiculous.'

'She can be difficult.'

'You want to throw her out of the club for being difficult?' said Susan.

'No decision has been taken.'

'Don't be so pompous,' said Susan.

'The club have to discuss it.'

'You're president, Andrew. Don't you even dare think about it.'

She really is going to kill me this time, thought Andrew.

'Your coffee is getting cold.'

Ugh, cold coffee. Andrew finished his coffee and repaired to the greenhouse, prepared to take phone calls out of Susan's hearing. You had to be a Rotarian to understand these things. Susan would only make all sorts of comments and suggestions, that wouldn't help a jot. He decided that he would take some soundings from other members and he would pay particular attention to what Phillip had to say, as membership chairman.

Over the next few days there was a flurry of emails. Members' opinions flowed back and forth, as they whipped up into a froth that overflowed onto all other matters. There were also phone conversations; one to one, in-depth conversations that would shape events. Andrew and Phillip conversed, and it is highly likely that Andrew consulted the efficient, unflappable and wise, Claire.

'Her behaviour was outrageous, of course,' said Phillip. 'But you're the president, as George told you.' Phillip had listened patiently to Andrew's account of his conversation with George earlier in the day.

'Yes, he did,' said Andrew.

'If you decide that the matter is too egregious to let lie, you'll have to take it to club council,' said Phillip.

'Is that wise?' said Andrew.

Phillip said, 'Council could suspend her from the club for a period of time and encourage her to resign.'

'I'm not sure I want to do that,' said Andrew.

'But if you want my opinion…' said Phillip.

'Yes, I do.'

Phillip said, 'I'd have a word with her. She's an intelligent woman.'

'She held a senior position in one of the big banks,' said Andrew.

'International department,' said Phillip.

'She might not have the right temperament for customer care,' said Andrew.

'These days, banks put the likes of Fiona in customer care to sort out us whinging customers,' said Phillip.

'They don't care about customers anymore,' said Andrew.

'Actually, Fiona cares a lot,' said Phillip. 'Why not see how she views her membership of the club now that the argument about Alec Barton has been settled?'

'You mean whether she can accept the reality that he is now a member?' said Andrew.

'If she can't,' said Phillip, 'she'll probably resign anyway.'

'That would be logical,' said Andrew.

'But remember, we are talking about Fiona,' said Phillip. 'She's probably thinking one step ahead already. But if you are going to move against her, you'll have to act before next week's business meeting.'

'Yes, I suppose so,' said Andrew.

Phillip said, 'Remember Macbeth's soliloquy, "if it were done when 'tis done, then it were done quickly."'

'Yes,' said Andrew. 'But Macbeth was only worried about assassinating the King of Scotland.' They both laughed. 'Fiona would leave a bit of a hole in the club, you know, what with the Easter egg raffle and the other things she does.'

'She's just hot-headed, a loose cannon,' said Phillip.

'You think that I should do nothing?'

'Speak to her first, Andrew.'

THIRTEEN

The real George?

It was Thursday evening and Erica was busy getting ready to go out to choir practice.

'George, I've left you the rest of the ham and I've put some frozen chips on a tray to go into the oven. You will find some peas in the freezer. They'll need three or four minutes in the microwave. Do you think you can manage that?'

'Is it three minutes or is it four?' said George. 'Four minutes might be only one more than three, but in percentage terms it's thirty-three percent more, or for the pedantic, thirty-three point three recurring.'

'Depends how many you use,' said Erica.

'How will I know?' said George.

'Just tip some in a basin and cook them for three minutes. If they are cooked eat them, if not give them another minute.'

'All right,' said George.

'I'm sorry it's a cold supper this evening, George.'

George thought he could manage. 'Just get on or you'll be late.' George did not venture into the kitchen very often, but he would not go hungry. There was beer in the fridge, and he had recently taken delivery of some Argentinian Malbec. If there was nothing to watch on television, he would read his book.

'I'm picking up Cynthia this evening,' said Erica.

'Be careful.'

'She drove last week.' It was a forty-minute drive to the school where they would be rehearsing this evening. 'I probably won't be back until sometime after half past ten.' It would be nearer to eleven o'clock, by the time they had finished rehearsing and chatting. Erica was not sure why she should be so reticent about going out to choir practice and leaving George to fend for himself for one evening in the week. He always said that he did not mind her going to choir practice, but she was never quite sure whether he meant it.

When Erica arrived in Debenham, Cynthia was ready, as usual. 'Sorry if I'm a few minutes late,' said Erica, as Cynthia got into the car.

'Hasn't it been a gloomy day with all those dark clouds and drizzle?' said Cynthia.

'The days are definitely shortening,' said Erica. 'I really do not like driving in the dark and the wet.'

As they drove along a narrow winding lane lined with trees, Erica said, 'Look, there's a barn owl.' The owl was in their sight for a moment, its wings beating silently, gracefully; then it swooped down to a spot close to the road onto a small unsuspecting mammal, unnoticed by all but the owl. What Erica had not seen at that moment, were three roe deer gliding like ghosts through the undergrowth, into their path. As the deer reached the road, she saw them and jammed her foot on the brake as hard as she could and hit the horn. The deer panicked and ran in different directions. The car skidded to a halt and Erica saw a flash of reddish grey-brown fur and there was a sickening thud. She composed herself for a moment and opened the car door. Cynthia was in a state of shock and quite unable to move. Erica got out. The mangled animal lay before her. 'It's still alive,' she said in horror. The stricken animal was moving and making a pitiful sound. Erica took out her mobile phone.

'Police,' she screamed down the phone.

'You're through to the police. Please give me your name and address.'

'I've just run over a deer and it's still alive.'

'First, give me your name and address, please.'

'Erica Woodgate.'

'And where do you live?'

Erica managed to give the information demanded of her and her location. 'I've run over a deer. It's badly injured but it's still alive.'

The call handler fired a number of questions.

'It's just me and a friend of mine, we were going to choir practice when it happened. There are no other cars involved. No one has been hurt.'

'I'll get some help to you as quickly as possible.'

'What about the deer?' said Erica. 'The poor creature's suffering.'

'We have someone who deals with this kind of incident. I'm trying to contact him now.'

The call ended. Erica tried not to look at the deer; a wretched sight. She got back into the car and burst into tears.

The next week, Erica was still unsettled by the incident with the deer. She had often encountered deer when driving at dusk, but she had never hit one before. She had run over a rabbit, which happened often enough in the country, but a deer was different.

'There's no sense in upsetting yourself,' said George. 'Think of all the venison pies we've eaten at various hostelries around here. Quite possibly shot by the same chap who dispatched your deer the other day.'

'That's not very comforting, George.'

'Just keep things in perspective, old thing.'

'Julia has kindly offered to take Cynthia and me to choir this evening.'

'That's good,' said George.

Erica said, 'After that there are just two more rehearsals and then it's the concert.'

'I shall look forward to that,' said George.

'I said that it wasn't necessary, but she insisted.'

*

George had finished his boiled eggs and he was helping himself to toast and marmalade and more coffee. *The Times* lay on the table beside him.

"Did you have a good meeting last night, George?'

'What?'

'I said, did you have a good meeting last night?'

George looked up from his paper. 'Yes, we had a speaker from a charity that I'd never heard of. It was about a rare form of cancer. They have difficulty raising funds because most people have never heard of it.'

'What's it called?' said Erica.

'What?' said George.

'What's it called, this rare form of cancer?'

'I can't remember, but I did pick up a leaflet. I put it down somewhere.' George felt that this action absolved him from the obligation to remember the name of the rare form of cancer.

'Did you say that you intended to go to Stowmarket today?' said Erica.

'I need to pop into the bank at some time,' said George, 'so I might go today.'

'I need you to do something for me,' said Erica. 'Well two things, actually. You know I was having a bit of a clear out yesterday.'

'I did notice lots of activity.'

'Well, I've got a bag of old clothes that I want to get rid of,' said Erica. 'Would you take them to the charity shop for me, please?'

'Yes, of course.'

'Also, we're wearing black for the concert, as usual, and my black dress, the one I usually wear for concerts, needs cleaning.'

'Cleaning?' said George. 'Can't it go in the washing machine?'

'I wasn't going to bother, but I've noticed some marks

on it, so I'd like to have it cleaned. Will you take it into the cleaners for me, please?'

'Which one?'

'There's only one.'

'They ruined a suit of mine.'

'George, that suit was more than twenty years old.'

'I didn't send it to be ruined,' said George.

'And make sure that they can do it by Saturday morning.'

'Saturday morning?'

'You'll have to go over again on Saturday morning to pick it up.'

'Yes, of course.' George thought he could manage all of that.

The sky was covered by an unbroken layer of grey cloud and the air felt cold and damp, as George stepped out of the house. He was carrying Erica's black dress in a Tesco carrier bag and a dustbin liner half filled with the old clothes for the charity shop. They were heavier and more awkward to carry than he had expected. He put down both items so that he could open the garage door and unlock the car. He placed the bags in the boot, got in the car and reversed out of the garage. In Stowmarket, George drove along the High Street looking out for the premises he needed and a place to stop. The dry cleaners and the charity shop were separated by a newsagent. He sat in the car for a moment, wondering how often traffic wardens patrolled these streets to seek out errant parkers. He got out of the car and noted that he was parked in an area reserved for delivery lorries. He opened the boot of the car and took out the two bags and went into the cleaners. 'Good morning. I've got something for cleaning. I want it by Saturday morning at the latest.'

The woman behind the counter smiled as you would at a small child. 'Yes, we can do that for you, dear. Let's see what we've got in here,' and she began to open the bag.

George had already turned to leave.

'Just a moment, dear,' said the woman behind the counter, 'I need to see what items you have for cleaning.'

'I just need to pop to the charity shop. I'll be back in a moment.' The door of the charity shop stuck momentarily, then the bell above it rang, as he pushed it open. There was a woman behind the counter sorting out some newly arrived items: clothes, old books and other items. Through a door leading to the back of the shop, a woman was ironing a shirt to be displayed for sale.

'Good morning,' said George. 'I've got some old clothes here, no idea what.'

'Thank you, dear, just leave them on the counter.'

George walked out into the street and looked up and down. *That's a traffic warden*, thought George. He got into the car, drove to the car park and then walked the short distance to the bank to conduct his business. That concluded, he was soon in his car again driving home and thinking of lunch. Then it struck him. He had not returned to the cleaners. Slightly irritated at this epiphany moment, he retraced his steps. 'I'm sorry that took me so long.'

'You're back,' said the woman behind the counter.

'Yes, of course I'm back,' said George.

'Your dry cleaning is going to cost you £78,' said the woman.

'How much?' said George. 'For one dress?'

'There were a number of items, but no dress,' said the woman.

George felt as though he had been thumped hard in the chest. It knocked the wind out of him.

'Are you all right?' said the woman. She could see that he was shaken.

A dread now consumed George and his anxiety level became acute. He left the premises at speed, the door rattling behind him. He crashed through the door of the charity shop, causing consternation to those inside. 'That bag I left here half an hour ago. It had my wife's black dress in it.'

'Yes, it was a lovely dress, dear,' said the woman in the charity shop. 'We get some really good quality stuff sometimes.'

'I want it back,' said George. 'I'll buy it.'

'We sponged off a couple of small marks and put it straight into the window.' She went to the window and looked. There was no black dress that had once belonged to George's wife. 'Doreen, have you sold that nice black dress that came in this morning?'

'A lady came in and bought it a short while ago.' Doreen's voice came from the back of the shop. 'She was very pleased with it for £15.'

'I need it, my wife needs it for a concert,' said George. 'What am I supposed to do?'

'I don't quite understand why you brought it in here, dear.'

'Because of the marks on it,' said George.

'You should have taken it to the cleaners, next door but one.'

'Well, I didn't mean to,' said George. 'How can I get it back?'

'We can't really help, dear. We don't keep records of sales. I expect the lady paid cash.'

'Yes, she paid cash,' Doreen helpfully confirmed from the back of the shop.

'What did she look like? The lady who bought the dress.'

'She was medium height, medium build and her hair was…' said the woman behind the counter.

'Let me guess, it was medium.' *What a pickle she's put me in.* George was being disingenuous. He knew he was at fault and if he were in any doubt, Erica would helpfully explain, when he got home.

'How did you guess?' said the lady behind the counter.

'That's not going to help me,' said George and walked out. As he drove home, he felt utterly defeated. There was no possibility that he could locate this medium woman and what if he did? She would not just give up her bargain purchase. He would just have to face the music. Music, concert, very droll.

He heard Erica's voice, as he came into the house. She was in full flow talking on the phone. He heard a reference to the concert and his blood ran cold. At least Humphrey was pleased to see him. He could see two plates of salad covered with cling film on the kitchen table. There was nothing else for it. He would explain what had happened and any rational person would understand, apart from a woman and especially his wife, whose concert was imminent. The conversation seemed to be about to end, but then picked up and continued for several more minutes. The moment arrived, as Erica put down the phone.

'Hello George, I'm sorry I was so long on the phone,' said Erica.

'Hello.'

'It was Cynthia,' said Erica. 'She is coming to the concert after all. You know how upset she was after that dreadful business with the deer.'

'Why's she so upset?' said George. 'She wasn't driving, was she?'

'And you'll never guess what,' said Erica.

'No, I doubt it.'

'She was in Stowmarket this morning,' said Erica. 'I told her that you'd been there, but she didn't see you.'

'A lucky escape.'

'What do you mean by that?'

'Nothing.'

'She was going past the charity shop and she saw this lovely black dress, that would be just right for her for the concert. So, you know what she did?'

'I couldn't imagine.' *Yes, I probably could.*

'She went in and bought it.'

'Really.'

'She got it for £15,' said Erica.

'A bargain.'

'She's absolutely thrilled.'

'Some lunch would be nice.'

'Would you like lunch, George?'

'That's a good idea.'

'I'm glad that she's found something for the concert,' said Erica.

'Yes.' *Has my dear wife forgotten?* thought George.

After lunch, George wandered down the garden and took out his mobile phone. *Please let me have Cynthia's number.* He had. 'Cynthia, it's George, Erica's husband.'

'Yes, I know who you are, George,' said the voice on the phone. 'Erica and I were just talking about you.'

'I'm just ringing…' He was not quite sure what to say.

'Yes, you were in Stowmarket this morning,' said Cynthia. 'So was I.'

'Yes, I know.'

'I never saw you.'

'You bought a black dress.'

'How on earth did you know that, George?'

'I was in the charity shop…'

'In the charity shop?' said Cynthia. 'Are you sure? I never saw you.'

'You bought a black dress,' said George.

'Yes, I thought it was a bargain at £15,' said Cynthia.

'Yes…'

'It's such a pity, but it's too long on me,' said Cynthia.

'I'll buy it from you.'

'George, why do you need a black dress? It would look more like a nineteen-sixties mini skirt on you.' Cynthia started laughing at the mental image of George wearing a very short black dress.

'It's for Erica, for the concert.'

'Are you sure, George?' Cynthia could not stop laughing. 'Erica's already got a black dress for the concert.'

'Well, it's a long story.'

'George, you're not one of thosetransvestites, are you? They dress up...' Cynthia started laughing again.

'I know how they dress.'

'Well, I never.'

'I'm not a transvestite' said George.

'It's perfectly all right, George, I won't tell anyone.'

'I'm not a transvestite.'

'Why do you wear women's clothes?'

'I don't wear women's clothes.'

'George, why are you ringing me?' said Cynthia. 'None of my dresses would fit you.'

'I'm not a transvestite,' said George. 'I don't wear women's clothes and I don't want any of your dresses.'

'Are you sure, George?'

'Erica's black dress needed cleaning.'

'You should have taken it to the cleaners, silly.'

'I meant to.'

'You haven't told Erica?'

'Not yet.'

'Erica's taller than me,' said Cynthia.

'I'll give you £20 for it.'

'Don't be silly, George, you can give me the £15 I paid. And if you come over on Saturday morning, you can collect it.'

'That's brilliant.'

'What you say to Erica is up to you, but I shall just tell her the truth, which is that the dress was too long for me.'

When Cynthia had finished her phone conversation with George she called out to her husband. 'Des, you know George?'

'Who?'

'Erica's husband. We go to choir together.'

'Yes.'

'I've had a strange conversation with him.'

'How strange?' said Des.

'He was interested in that black dress.'

'Oh.' Des could not think of a suitable response.

'I think he's a transvestite, you know,' said Cynthia. 'They dress in women's clothes.'

'But he isn't, is he?' said Des.

'Isn't he?'

'I'm not sure that I quite understand what you're saying,' said Des.

'Well, it was about my dress.'

'You mean he wears dresses?'

'He denied it.'

'Well, he would, wouldn't he?' said Des. 'Come to think about it though, he is a bit odd.'

*

Snape Maltings is a well-known music venue in Suffolk and the home of the Aldeburgh Festival of Music, which the Suffolk-born composer, Benjamin Britten, founded in 1948. Erica's concert had attracted a good audience, mostly older people, but with a scattering of youthful dark heads to add a contrast to the sea of grey. As soon as George and Erica arrived, Erica began to look out for other choir members. She saw a group of three talking loudly and laughing nervously; this evening was the culmination of weeks of rehearsal, of good performances and bad. Cynthia was with them. They saw Erica and waved, then all four disappeared to join the rest of their choral colleagues, leaving George to wander around and mingle with the throng of people until it was time for him to take his seat. He bought a programme and looked down the list of performers to find Erica listed under the sopranos. He had enough time for a drink, so went upstairs to the bar. He took his seat just in time, as the choir and orchestra assembled onstage. The orchestra was at the front of the stage, with the choir to the rear. Erica sat with the sopranos, to George's left, with the tenors behind. The altos and the basses were on the other side of the stage.

The strangled sounds of musicians busily tuning their instruments rang around the old Maltings and then a silence fell, as the leader of the orchestra made an entrance. The audience clapped politely. Moments later, the conductor appeared and the audience applauded enthusiastically, as he gave a deep bow. He shook hands with the leader and turned towards the stage entrance and the soloists walked on to more applause. The young soprano wore an elegant long flowing dress in pink, her fair hair swept up off a small, delicate face. The alto was dark and sultry in a tight-fitting black dress. The heavy build of the bass contrasted with the taller, slimmer tenor. As soon as the soloists took their seats at the front of the stage, the lights dimmed and the conductor went straight into the music, as though he had not a moment to lose.

George sat back in his seat and let the sumptuous sound and sensation of the music flow over him. The interval arrived, the stage emptied, and the audience began to move around, some to the bar, others to buy ice-cream. George climbed the stairs to the bar but decided that his disinclination to stand in a long queue far exceeded his desire for a drink. He walked outside onto the wooden decking and looked up at the stars scattered across an inky black sky. It was a calm evening with almost no movement in the mild autumnal air.

'Do you know that a Suffolk woman wrote the words "Twinkle, Twinkle, Little Star"?' said a voice behind George. 'It must have been on an evening like this. Mozart wrote the music, of course. It's George, isn't it?'

George turned towards a large figure in silhouette with the light from the bar behind him. The man spoke with a soft Suffolk intonation. 'Yes, it is you, George.'

'Have we met?'

'It's Des, Cynthia's husband, I saw you at the last concert.'

'I'm afraid I don't remember,' said George. The man had stepped forward and the light played on a bare pate. 'Yes, of course, I can see you better now. You're as bald as a coot.'

'Great concert, George,' said Des.

'Yes, it's been a most enjoyable evening. They've all worked very hard.'

'Shame about that deer your Erica hit. Have you got the damage sorted out?'

'We've had the car repaired, if that's what you mean,' said George, 'and the deer got a bullet in the head from a local marksman.'

Des said, 'Cynthia managed to get a new black dress for this evening, after the disappointment over the one from the charity shop. You know, the one you wanted.'

'It was just a misunderstanding,' said George. *Why has he got that stupid smirk on his face? He must be soft in the head. It's bad enough having to listen to Kye at Rotary every week.*

'Anyway, it's nothing to be ashamed of,' said Des.

'It was just a silly mistake, that's all,' said George. He was irritated by the man's focus on such a trivial matter.

'I know of other men, who, well, you know…'

'No, I don't know, actually.' George had taken an intense dislike to the man. 'You're talking absolute drivel.'

'I used to be in the Navy and there was this stoker, a really big bloke, tattoos all over…'

George had heard one or two stories about stokers. *They must be a strange bunch of chaps.*

'… and do you know what they found him wearing?'

'I couldn't imagine,' said George.

'A frilly black dress,' said Des. 'All I'm saying is, it's nothing to be ashamed of.'

'I really don't care what a chap does in the privacy of his own home,' said George, 'or the Navy.'

A bell sounded, then a voice said, 'Ladies and gentlemen, will you please take your seats? The concert is about to resume.'

George was glad to get away from this irritating man called Des. *I've got a little list – I've got a little list…*

The second half flew by and soon George was applauding with the rest of the audience. The conductor took a deep bow, then invited the soloists, the leader of the orchestra, the orchestra and the choir to stand in turn to receive applause. The conductor walked off the stage while the audience continued to clap and returned to take a final bow. *He really knew how to milk the applause*, thought George.

Shortly after, George met Erica in the bar for coffee. 'Well done, old thing. That was tremendous.'

'Thank you.' Erica was euphoric. 'Was it all right?'

'You were magnificent, all of you, but especially you. There's such beautiful music in Faure's *Requiem*.'

'I really enjoyed singing it, including the rehearsals, well most of them anyway,' said Erica, talking excitedly. 'But none of the requiems quite compare with Mozart's, which is absolutely sublime. If I could sing only one more requiem in my life it would be Mozart's.'

George smiled. 'I'm sure you will sing many more.'

'I find it difficult to reach some of the high notes these days,' said Erica. 'Perhaps I'll have to move to alto.'

They talked for a while. It enabled Erica to wind down after the weeks of rehearsal, the incident with the deer and this evening's concert. It also allowed most of the concert goers to drive out of the car park.

'I met a chap called Des.'

'Cynthia's husband?' said Erica.

'He kept talking about men wearing women's dresses,' said George. 'He's a most irritating man.'

'Des? No, he's all right.'

'I think he must be a transvestite,' said George. 'I couldn't care less, but I don't want to hear about it.'

'I don't think so,' said Erica. 'Anyway, so what if he is?'

Before George could say anything further, he saw Alec and Karen walking towards them through the throng of people.

Alec said, 'George, I thought I saw you earlier.'

'Alec and Karen, fancy seeing you here,' said George.

'Congratulations, Erica, that was superb,' said Alec.

'Yes, it was,' said Karen.

'Thank you.'

'Can I get anyone another drink?' said Alec.

'We'll be off soon,' said George. 'The car park should be clear by now.'

'So, you're surprised to see me here, George?' said Alec.

'Well, no, only that we haven't seen anyone else we know this evening, apart from Des, the husband of one of the choir members. He's a—'

Erica gave George a sharp nudge under the table. A severe look would never have worked.

'I'm particularly fond of choral music,' said Alec.

'Yes, I really like it, too,' said Karen.

'Erica, the "Pie Jesu" was magnificent,' said Alec.

'Thank you,' said Erica.

'The prayer for everlasting rest,' said Alec.

'I'm glad you enjoyed it,' said George. There was an awkwardness between them that he could not quite understand. It was different when they met at Rotary each week without their wives.

'We go to concerts from time to time,' said Karen.

'You probably thought that Radio Suffolk was the height of my musical interests,' said Alec.

'No, not at all. I've never given it a thought,' said George.

Alec said, 'I played the flute at school.'

'Really?' said Erica.

'Passed grade three,' said Alec.

'Grade three?' said Erica. 'That's good.'

Alec said, 'I used an instrument from the Suffolk music department, but eventually they called it in.'

'That was a disappointment,' said Erica.

'My mum couldn't afford to buy me one of my own,' said Alec.

'They're expensive items,' said Erica.

'I played the piano, not that I was much good at it though,' said George.

'I didn't go to a posh school like you, George.'

'It wasn't that posh,' said George.

'You had a piano at home, didn't you?' said Alec.

'My mother played,' said George.

'So, you took it up as well?' said Alec.

George said, 'It was the second movement of Beethoven's "Moonlight Sonata" that did for me. Set in C sharp minor it has four sharps.'

'Karen and I are going to make a move,' said Alec.

'Never did quite manage it,' said George.

As Alec and Karen walked out of the emptying bar, George looked at Erica. 'What did you make of that?'

'He looks more heavy metal,' said Erica.

FOURTEEN

Rotary tradition v modernisation – round 2

Members were enjoying a drink in the White Horse before their meeting. Kye was telling a story about an expectant father who was shouting frantically down the phone to the doctor that the contractions were only two minutes apart. Kye continued, 'And the doctor asked the caller, "Is this her first child?" Do you know what the father said?'

'No,' said the listening Rotarians.

'The father said,' Kye was laughing loudly at his joke, 'the father said, "No, this is her husband speaking."'

There was some laughter, mainly for Kye's enthusiasm for his own joke. Alec, broody, his dark hair tousled, was one of those listening; he gave a rare smile. He then turned towards George and they resumed their conversation. He was keeping a low profile after recent events.

'You can go through now, Andrew,' said Bill. 'We're ready for you.'

As members stood by their chairs, Andrew said, 'Good evening, members.'

'Good evening, Mr President.'

It was Ernie's turn to say grace. 'For what we are about to receive may the Lord make us truly thankful.'

'Amen.'

'Ernie, will you email me a copy of that grace, so I don't forget it?' said Kye.

Dinner tonight was roast beef and Yorkshire pudding from the carvery. The beef had a hint of pink and the Yorkshire puddings were a golden brown. As Bill was serving, the door opened and in walked Fiona, with Frances trailing behind. 'Sorry we're late, Mr President, we were delayed.' They looked around for empty places at the table and there were two together, one of which was next to Alec Barton. Fiona walked very deliberately towards the seat next to Alec and sat down. Frances sat beside her. The conversation had stopped and all eyes were on Fiona. She turned towards Alec and said, 'Good evening, Alec,' and then turned away and started a conversation with Frances. Most members were too stunned to say anything and gave full attention to their dinners.

Alec offered a slightly flustered, 'Good evening.'

Andrew said, 'I'm glad you two were able to make it, but I did see the sergeant at arms making a note.' When dinner was over and Bill and Marlene had cleared away, Andrew said, 'Please be upstanding for the loyal toast.' Chairs scraped on the floor and Andrew waited until everyone was still and quiet. He raised his glass and said, 'The Queen.'

'The Queen.'

'God bless her,' said Kye.

'We'll take a short break and then we'll get on with this evening's business.' It was a business meeting, which was not universally popular.

As they walked to the bar, Frank looked at Andrew. 'Bloody hell,' was all he could say.

Andrew just smiled to himself.

After a few minutes, members reassembled and the meeting began. Andrew went through the preliminary items swiftly.

'There are no apologies for absence. Minutes of the last meeting; do I have your agreement to sign them as a correct record?'

'Agreed.'

In a firm and challenging tone of voice, Andrew said, 'The next item on the agenda is modernisation.' The tension in the room was palpable. The debate earlier in the year had been just a brief skirmish. This was the real thing. If the modernisers won the day, the club could change for ever. Andrew decided to put his full authority as president behind his proposed changes. He had taken some soundings within the membership, and he knew that it was going to be a close-run thing.

'I know that modernisation will not be universally popular, but in my opinion, it's necessary to keep us in tune with the modern world,' said Andrew.

'We need to do it, Mr President,' said Fiona.

'I'd like to run through the changes I wish to see and then we can debate them. First, dress code…'

'You're not serious about that, surely,' said George. 'We've always worn jackets and ties.'

'Quite right,' said Paul.

'We've had a fine summer and we have dressed down accordingly,' said Andrew. 'I'm suggesting that we should continue in the same way as we move into the colder weather.'

'I've folded up all my summer shirts and shorts and mothballed them for the winter,' said Kye.

'Absolutely, no,' said Frank.

'We all have smart club sweatshirts. What's wrong with wearing them for our meetings?' said Andrew.

'They're a smart navy blue,' said Fiona.

'Sweatshirts are for outside activities; when we're making street collections and the like,' said Frank.

'It gets warm in here when Bill turns up the heating. Sweatshirts are too hot,' said Paul, 'to say nothing of too scruffy by the time they've been through the washing machine fifty times a year.'

'I might manage to go tieless, with a jacket, but that's all I would be prepared to do,' said Paul.

'I think we should be more relaxed in the way we dress and in what we do,' said Fiona. She was wearing jeans, which might have been slashed at the knees, but no one dared to look.

'Good grief,' said Frank.

'I'm fully behind you, Mr President,' said Fiona. 'And the bell's got to go. And grace and the loyal toast and the Rotary toast.'

'Thank you, Fiona,' said Andrew.

'Abolish grace?' said Frank, a man of conviction, of faith, a member of the Parochial Church Council. 'On the most important of Fiona's trio of expendable matters, I would remind the club of this: grace refers to something we receive that we don't deserve, and we say grace to thank the Lord for the food before us.'

'After a hard day trying to be happy and cheerful, I think I deserve my dinner,' said Kye, which diverted the conversation from matters spiritual to a lower plane.

'What about charter night?' said Paul. 'Surely we'll wear dinner jackets, as we always have.'

George said, 'Yes, Paul is right. Charter night is one event in the year when we expect other clubs to come along and support us. Also, we must keep the Rotary toast, otherwise we would be no different from the local camera club, if there is one.'

'Why should we expect a new member to buy a dinner jacket for perhaps one event in the year?' said Fiona. 'That's enough to put anyone off from joining the club.'

'If a chap can't afford a dinner jacket, he should eat at McDonald's,' said George, in a lofty and unworldly way.

'The dress code for charter night could be black tie or lounge suits, to give a choice,' said Claire, seeking to find some common ground.

'That wouldn't be helpful,' said Frank. 'People want to know what the dress code is for any event. They don't want to arrive in a lounge suit and find that everyone else is wearing a dinner jacket, or the other way round.'

'Mr President, is there any Rotary research on the sort of modernisation we are talking about?' said Paul. 'Do we have any reason to believe that new members would come flocking to our doors? I'm not aware of any.'

'It's obvious,' said Fiona. 'People do not wish to dress up to go out any more.'

'Rubbish,' said Frank.

'There have been huge economic and societal changes over the years,' said Fiona. 'We must adapt or die.'

George said, 'And we could trash this club for no good reason and find that anyone with a passing interest in Rotary might be mildly disappointed to find that we don't stand for anything anymore. They'll go and join the gardening club or something like that.' He could feel the stress building inside him, with the noise and chaos of the debate and the prospect of serious and irreparable change in the club.

'Change for its own sake is meaningless,' said Paul. 'It just gives an illusion of action.'

Frank said, 'What do you call a club that has a Rotary bell as a symbol of the authority of its president, a president who wears his chain of office with pride? A club that toasts the Queen, says grace before dinner, where its members know how to dress properly and wear their Rotary badges with pride? A club whose members espouse service above self and high ethical standards? A club that toasts peace over the whole world? Take away all these things and we are but a shadow of ourselves. The gardening club, the camera club and other similar organisations exist to pursue their own particular narrow interests. They are worthy in their own ways, but they do not aspire to anything higher. Rotary is different. We have a higher calling.' Frank paused to draw breath. 'Who's proposing to carry out a project in a small village in rural Uganda that will bring water and sanitation to a small community of people? Rotarians, not just of this club, but the other clubs involved in the project and the wider world of Rotary through Foundation. And what about the cataract project we did in India a few years ago? There are people walking around with their sight fully restored who would be blind if it wasn't for Rotary. We don't know their names and we don't know who they are but we do know that they can see again. Who organised the stroke awareness Saturday, that potentially saved one or two lives in this village? People who had no idea they had high blood pressure. What about polio eradication? And that devastating hurricane and the collection we made for a ShelterBox with the generosity of Saturday shoppers in the village? We did all those things; this club and the wider world of Rotary.' Frank had made a powerful and eloquent contribution. He sat back in his chair, emotionally drained.

'You do talk rubbish, Frank,' said Fiona. 'We could have done all that without dressing up or toasting the Queen.'

This stung Frank and he said, 'You're missing the point. The danger, and it is a very real danger, is that we will lose our direction and our meaning. We won't stand for anything anymore. And once we have trashed the club, failed to gain any more members and finally recognised that it has all been in vain, what then? Could we ever recover?'

'I admire Frank's passionate opposition to the proposed changes, but I am not convinced that he's right,' said Claire. 'We need to move on as a club to keep up with a changing world.'

'Frank told his doctor that he didn't want a lobotomy,' said Kye, 'but the doctor changed Frank's mind.' There was a chuckle from some members that eased the tension.

Fiona said, 'We must embrace change. Much as some enjoy ritual, outside Royal circles, there are few other circumstances where it's justified in the modern world. We need new people, younger people with new ideas. We must be able to offer them a modern outward-looking club, receptive to ideas and new ways of doing things.'

'To attract new members, we have to offer them something more interesting than whatever else is available on a Wednesday evening,' said Ernie.

'As a new member, I would like to say that I agree with these proposals,' said Alec. 'I've always had an interest in Rotary, but it did seem to be a bit stuffy.'

Paul said, 'Over the years we have come to accept a relaxation of standards during very hot weather and that's reasonable and acceptable in the summer, but not in more temperate conditions. As far as I'm concerned, dressing like a lot of hippies is beyond the pale. If a young man presents himself for a job interview in a respectable organisation, he turns up in a smart suit with his shoes well-polished. As for the loyal toast and the other matters, I fully support everything that Frank said so eloquently.'

'No one's talking about hippies, Paul,' said Fiona.

'Those who seek change for its own sake are just following a sad and weary trend. It's everywhere now,' said Paul. 'You see politicians on the television who think they look cool in dark suits and white shirts, just because they take off their ties. What a dreadful fashion statement. If they really have to leave off their ties, they would look better if they wore sports jackets and casual shirts. Mind you, it's happening everywhere. As for Covent Garden, anything goes. The last time I went, I saw people dressed in woolly jumpers that I wouldn't wear to dig the garden. I shudder to think what we will have to wear at our next charter night dinner.'

'The last time you went to London, Paul, you went on a trolleybus,' said Kye.

Several more members spoke, some to oppose the changes, but mostly in support of their president. The sentiment was: it's time for a change. No one had matched Frank's eloquence and passion, or George and Paul's old-fashioned sense of tradition.

Although George hated any sort of change, he recognised that the president and modernisers had won the day. He felt vanquished and stressed with the noise, confusion and chaos, all of which had created an unbearable sensory overload. He realised that he had been wringing his hands, then he escaped for a few moments:

On a tree by a river a little tom-tit
Sang 'Willow, titwillow, titwillow.'
And I said to him, 'Dickie-bird, why do you sit
Singing "Willow, titwillow, titwillow"?
Is it weakness of intellect, birdie?' I cried
'Or a rather tough worm in your little inside?'
With a shake of his poor little head, he replied
'Oh, willow, titwillow, titwillow.'

The measures were agreed, but with the concession that the Rotary toast should remain.

The remainder of the business that evening received scant attention. This had not been the club's finest hour.

*

Alec Barton was determined to overcome his highly controversial induction into the Rotary Club of Debenham and he spoke little at meetings. Most Rotary business was uncontroversial, but sometimes there might be a difference of opinion about how much money the club should donate to this charity or that. Alec always gave his support to any proposal that the president put forward, even if George argued for something slightly different.

In the bar of the White Horse, Andrew said, 'Our new member seems to be doing well, George.'

'Most people have accepted him,' said George.

'With one or two exceptions.'

'At least Fiona isn't rude to him.'

'The choice was simple,' said Andrew. 'Either she got along with him or she left the club.'

'You can never second-guess Fiona,' said George.

'He doesn't seem comfortable with the women in the club,' said Andrew.

Alec came into the bar. 'Hello, George.' They shook hands. 'Good evening, Andrew,' and another handshake.

'Good evening, Alec.' Fiona addressed him in a breezy manner.

Alec gave a nod and a half smile. 'Good evening.' He avoided any physical contact.

'You should have given her a Rotary embrace,' said Kye. Everyone felt an uncomfortable silence.

'I don't need any advice on how to conduct myself, thank you, Kye,' said Fiona. She felt perfectly in control of her interactions with Alec. He squirmed with embarrassment.

This Rotary evening, members talked about the dreadful damage to a small Caribbean island. 'I'm sure that most of us saw the footage on the lunchtime news,' said Andrew.

'It was most distressing,' said Claire. 'The hurricane has devastated those flimsy houses. The television news showed sheets of material that had once been the walls and roofs of people's homes, strewn everywhere. We've got to do something to help.'

'There must be lots of casualties, but no one knows,' said Paul.

'The survivors were just standing or sitting on piles of debris, totally stunned and helpless,' said Frank.

'What are we going to do, Mr President?' said Fiona. 'Paul's International Chairman, what's he going to do? We need action, now.'

'Did you hear the governor of the island?' said Frances. 'His desperate plea for outside help was pitiful. The island's rescue services are completely overwhelmed.'

'We could wait for a coordinated Rotary response,' said Paul.

'Wait? Did you say wait?' said Fiona. 'We need to get on and do something now.'

'We could organise a collection for a ShelterBox outside the Co-op on Saturday morning,' said Paul.

President Andrew raised his voice to address the meeting. 'Quite right, Paul, we need some volunteers to rattle tins outside the Co-op on Saturday morning to raise money for the hurricane relief.'

'I'll volunteer.' It was Alec, keen as ever to play a full role in the life of the club.

'So will I,' said George. Others volunteered.

'Paul, will you make a rota, in say, two time slots, one from nine to eleven and then from eleven to one?' said Andrew. 'Past experience would suggest that shoppers are out and about on Saturday mornings, but we won't collect much in the afternoon.'

'I'll email everyone tomorrow and if everyone can reply quickly indicating their preferred time slot, I'll draft a rota. Who's got the club tabards and the collection tins?'

'I've got them, and I'll bring them on Saturday by nine o'clock,' said Roger, 'and I've still got that demonstration ShelterBox, so I'll bring that as well.'

On Saturday morning at about a quarter to nine, Roger parked his Land Rover outside the Co-op and, with Paul's help, heaved the ShelterBox out of the back of the vehicle and placed it on the ground, just outside the entrance to the Co-op. The day was cool and overcast, with a keen wind. 'I've also brought the Rotary banner, which we can tie on the railings.'

As Roger and Paul were donning their tabards, replete with the words "Rotary Club of Debenham", the other members were arriving, and the small car park was filling up rapidly. Soon, other members were putting on tabards and struggling to fasten the strings, which danced in the wind.

'Good morning,' said George to a young mother with two children, one in a pushchair and the other walking behind. She had just parked next to Paul's car. 'Have you seen our ShelterBox? It contains all the basic necessities for survival after a disaster like the hurricane: a family tent, ground sheet, blankets, cooking stove and so on.'

'I really haven't got time.' She had not welcomed the interruption of her shopping expedition. 'Oh, it's about the hurricane, I saw it on the news last night. It's absolutely dreadful. Those poor people have lost everything. There were small children looking completely lost. I haven't got time to look at the ShelterBox now, but I will give something to the collection.' She opened her purse and took out a five-pound note, which she then stuffed into an otherwise empty collection tin. 'Good luck with the collection.'

'Thank you so much,' said George.

Andrew was talking to an elderly couple, who were looking into the ShelterBox with great interest. 'We didn't see the news on the telly last night. We usually go to bed early, but we did hear about it this morning.'

'How do you get the box all the way out there?' the man asked.

Andrew said, 'The cost of the ShelterBox includes the cost of shipping. We collect money with the generosity of the public and we send a cheque to the ShelterBox charity in Cornwall. They send a ShelterBox out from there

directly to the Caribbean. We don't have to send this one.'
They both laughed.

The woman opened her purse and took out some coins, which she put into Andrew's collection tin. 'Thank you very much,' he said. He noticed that Alec Barton was involved in an animated conversation with a woman, then a man approached him to make a donation. 'Thank you.' When he looked again, the woman had gone.

After about an hour the footfall was increasing, and Rotarians were engaged in conversations with the shoppers, most of whom had something to say about the hurricane. Some shoppers passed by the groups of people milling around the ShelterBox and the collectors spoke to them on the way out. 'I've already put something in one of the other boxes,' said one middle-aged woman to Claire, who had arrived for the second shift.

'I'm so sorry to trouble you again,' said Claire.

'That's all right, I shall put something in your tin, as well,' said the woman. 'I was so upset with what I've seen on television over the last couple of nights.'

'We all were at Rotary,' said Claire. 'That's why we want to help.'

'Claire, will you tell Andrew that I'm going now, but I'll be back by one o'clock to collect everything,' said Roger.

Soon after midday, the weather worsened; it began to drizzle with rain and the cold wind was blowing harder. There were fewer shoppers now. Paul, who had remained all morning, pulled up his collar and said to his fellow Rotarians, 'Roger has just arrived to pick up the ShelterBox, so I think we'll call it a day.'

Roger and Paul lifted the ShelterBox into the Land Rover. The collectors put their tins in a cardboard box in the vehicle and folded their tabards as best they could in the wind.

'Mark, our esteemed honorary treasurer, is coming over to help me count the money and then he'll bank it,' said Roger, as the members headed for their cars.

'The people in the village have been very generous this morning,' said Paul.

'It's the television reporting,' said Claire. 'It really brings it home, the misery and the suffering of people caught up in it all. It's funny how the television crews always get there before anyone else.'

'Well, they've probably doubled our collection this morning,' said Paul. 'By the way, who was that woman that Alec Barton seemed to be having a disagreement with?'

'I don't know, but they obviously knew each other.'

*

'You look tired,' said Karen.

'It's been a long day.' Alec opened the fridge and took out a can of Broadside. He picked up a pint glass and poured. The cool dark beer rose up the side of the glass and formed a white frothy head. As he drank slowly, Karen watched his Adam's apple moving up and down.

'There's some post.'

'All right, I'll have a look at it in a minute,' said Alec, which meant that he would attend to it in his own good time.

'I think you should open this one.' Karen handed him a white envelope with his bank's name printed in corporate colours in the corner.

Alec took it and ripped open the envelope. He pulled out the letter and started to read. 'The bastards.' He spat out the words, as he screwed the letter into a tight ball and threw it in the direction of the kitchen table. It bounced off the tabletop and landed on the floor.

Karen stooped and picked it up. She opened it out and smoothed it as best she could. 'Is it serious?' she said. She knew that it was not wise to say too much, because he seemed to be very edgy these days and reacted angrily to the smallest provocation, but she needed to know what was happening.

'It's just some bloody jobsworth at the bank, just being difficult. I have a slight cash flow difficulty at the moment, if you must know. Money's going out faster than it's coming in.'

Karen understood cash flow. She and the other women at the salon were all self-employed. They each rented a chair and had their own customers. She had to keep money coming in. 'Is it serious?'

'No, it's just a cash flow thing.' Alec was rattled and no amount of bluster could hide his concern. He finished his beer and took another can from the fridge.

'Can I help?' said Karen.

'Not unless you've got a few thousand pounds lying around doing nothing.'

'How many thousand?' Karen wondered whether the money she had in her savings account would be enough.

'I don't want to talk about it.'

'Alec, you can't just get a letter from the bank asking you for whatever it is, and say that you don't want to talk about it.'

'I said I don't want to talk about it.'

'That's the problem. Men won't talk about anything. Why do you think there are so many suicides amongst young men?'

'I'm not a young man and I'm not going to top myself, but I would like to sort out that bloody bank manager and some of his people.'

'Alec, don't talk like that.'

Alec sat brooding. He took another long draught from his glass.

Karen said, 'I know all about the problems of half the people in this village, except you. I'm their hairdresser. They talk to me. It does help, you know.'

'If you want to help, get me another beer.'

Karen did as she was asked and continued preparing supper.

*

Alec said, 'What's Crucial Crew?'

'We need some volunteers,' said President Andrew.

'We help out in October each year,' said Claire.

'It's a national teaching programme to help children to keep safe,' said Andrew. 'It's for Year 6 children, that's the year before they go on to secondary school.'

'Safe from what?' said Alec.

'Claire can probably explain it better than I,' said Andrew.

'The programme teaches them about road safety, crime, substance abuse, fire safety, healthy eating, safety on the internet,' said Claire.

'Where is it carried out?' said Alec.

'The teachers from local schools bring the children to a large community centre and groups of professionals give brief talks,' said Claire. 'There are usually about eight scenarios, as they're called, and the children move from one to another.'

'Where do we come in?' said Alec. No one had given him any help or advice when he was that age.

Andrew was pleased that Alec was taking an interest in Rotary events. 'Another local club is involved with running Crucial Crew. They organise the event, which runs for a week. There are two sessions a day, one in the morning and one in the afternoon. The scenarios are located in different parts of this building and outside. The fire brigade always brings a trailer for their sessions.'

'What's our role?' said Alec.

'We start with the children sitting on the floor in school order,' said Claire. 'We each lead a group of children from one scenario to another, in accordance with a strict timetable. Each scenario lasts thirteen minutes.'

'That's not long,' said Alec.

'You have to listen for the warning whistle at eleven minutes,' said Claire.

'Warning of what?' said Alec.

'At thirteen minutes there's another whistle, which

tells you to move to the next scenario,' said Claire. 'You've got two minutes.'

'What if one of the children wants to go to the toilet?' said Alec.

'The teachers are there.'

'One of the children could be ill,' said Alec.

'It happens,' said Claire.

'Often?'

'The teachers deal with it,' said Claire. 'There's nothing to worry about.'

'How many are there?' said Alec.

'There'll be about 700 children in total over the week,' said Claire, 'and each Rotarian leads a group of about a dozen children.'

'A week?' said Alec.

'You only do one day,' said Andrew.

'You will have your Rotary tabard and be given a board with a letter, that corresponds to the group you are leading,' said Claire, 'and a timetable for the day.'

Alec and several other members put up their hands to volunteer and Claire made a note.

On the first day of Crucial Crew, Rotarians and the leaders of the scenarios began arriving well before nine o'clock. The firefighters were outside the community centre milling around their trailer. Police officers were gathering around their cabin. The drug and alcohol team were in a room off the main hall and others were secreted into the corners of the hall, which had been screened off. Two women were in the kitchen preparing an early lunch for the people running the scenarios and the Rotarians helping. A hot lunch was essential to keep spirits high. The eighty or so children attending the morning sessions would go back to school for lunch and the children coming for the afternoon sessions would have lunch at school.

Soon, the school buses started to drive into the car park and disgorge their cargoes of excited eleven-year-olds, for whom a half day out of school was always welcome. The children followed their teachers into the hall and Rotarian Crispin from the organising club instructed them to sit cross-legged in rows on the floor.

Crispin addressed the children briefly. 'Welcome to Crucial Crew. We haven't got much time so listen carefully. You are in rows in alphabetical order. If you look to the front, you will see someone in a yellow tabard—'

'Please sir, I want to go to the toilet,' said a small boy.

'We haven't got much time,' said Crispin.

'It's Miss Mockett's class,' said a helpful girl.

'Holding a board with a letter. Please follow—'

'Miss Mockett's not here,' said another child.

'I need to go to the toilet,' said the small boy.

'Will someone else take that boy to the toilet?' said Crispin.

'Miss Mockett's the only teacher from that school,' said a teacher from another school.

'She's probably on her mobile phone,' said one of Miss Mockett's class.

'We have no authority for children from other schools,' said the teacher from another school.

'Here's Miss Mockett,' said several children.

Crispin said, 'Will you please take that child to—'

'Please sir, it's too late.' A small girl pointed to a puddle that had appeared in front of the unfortunate boy.

'Please follow the persons with your letter,' said Crispin. 'We have got eight scenarios for you to visit, but you have only got 13 minutes at each. When you are asked to do so, please leave the scenario and follow your guide to the next.'

The Rotarians then led their charges in different directions, with the teachers following behind; each group would start with a different scenario. Alec led group C to road safety. They squeezed into a small room and sat down. The road safety officer had prepared an interactive display for the children. Each had a button to respond to the questions he put to them. He asked them about the age group in which most children were involved in accidents and at what time of year most occurred and a range of other questions. The children were surprised that the answers were not always what they expected.

Then in what seemed like no time at all, the first whistle. Alec said, 'We've got two minutes.' Then the second whistle went. 'It's time to go to the next scenario.'

At the drugs and alcohol abuse scenario, the woman in charge said, 'How many harmful chemicals do you think there are in a cigarette?'

'Three?'

'Higher.'

'Four?'

'Much higher.'

'Six?'

'No, you're all wrong. There are several thousand.'

'I think I'll tell my dad,' said one small girl.

The whistle went twice and they moved on to the next scenario, which was safety online. At this scenario, Alec learned more than the children.

'You should never post any image of yourself online, or send an image to anyone you do not know,' said the woman in charge.

'I don't.'

'Nor do I.'

'Good, because you might just as well put a ten-foot poster of yourself on the wall outside the school gate for everyone to see.'

Then she asked how many children used a particular platform and all hands went up. 'Did you know that you're supposed to be over thirteen?' There was silence. The time seemed to pass in a flash. The first whistle sounded and then the second. Alec cajoled the children to move quickly to the next scenario, which was outside the building, in the fire service trailer.

The children ran up the steps and inside the trailer, where they were confronted with a bedroom scene. 'Can anyone see any fire hazards?' the firefighter asked, and hands started to go up, slowly at first, then all the children were waving their hands excitedly. 'Yes,' she said to one small boy standing at the front of the group.

'Please miss, the towel on top of the television.'

'Very good, anyone else?'

'The football shirt on top of the lamp.'

'Very good, what about this aerosol can on top of the radiator? Is that dangerous?' One or two children agreed that it was. 'Anyone else?'

This went on for some minutes until the children had identified all the hazards. The firefighter moved on to discuss what the children should do if there were a fire at night.

The firefighter said, 'I want you to imagine that it's the middle of the night and you've just woken up and you can hear the sound of burning and you can see smoke coming under the door.'

The lights in the trailer had dimmed and it was almost totally dark. 'You've all got mobile phones, I expect, so dial 999 and ask for the fire brigade. Could you do that?'

'Yes miss.'

'Now test for heat. Touch the back of your hand lightly on the door and the handle. Then open the door slightly. You can see flames, so your exit is probably cut off. Block the gap under the door with a towel or an item of clothing to stop the smoke getting in.'

'Are the fire brigade going to get here in time, miss?' said a rather nervous girl.

The firefighter said, 'I think it's them now, but they don't know where we are. What shall we do?'

'Call out,' said a little girl.

'Perhaps they still can't hear you, what do you do?'

'Shout,' came the answer.

'Yes, we've got to shout. Come on, everyone, let's shout as loud as we can.'

In moments, a dozen excited eleven-year-old children were shouting, 'Help, help, we're in here.' Then they started to stamp their feet as hard as they could. The sound reverberated around the confined space of the trailer, louder and louder, until the ear-shattering noise reached a crescendo. 'It's getting difficult to breathe, let's get down on the floor, there's more oxygen down there,' said the firefighter. The children dropped to the floor. A few moments later, the door opened slowly, admitting a huge cloud of billowing smoke. Through the thick smoke they could make out the shape of a man, a firefighter in full breathing apparatus. He beckoned them to follow, and led them out of the door of the trailer into the sunshine. The children emerged blinking and squinting after the darkness of the trailer. They were talking and laughing loudly, except for one little girl. She was terrified and screamed uncontrollably. She sat down on a chair outside the trailer and refused to move.

'Don't cry,' said Alec weakly, 'we've got to go to the next scenario.' Other groups of children were now jostling them on their way to their next scenarios. 'Where's your bloody teacher? She's supposed to be here to deal with this.'

'She's probably on her mobile,' one boy suggested.

'She's Miss Mockett, and don't swear at us, it's not very nice,' said a girl, who was taller and more mature than the others.

'Yes, I'm sorry,' said Alec.

Crispin, the organiser, appeared. 'You need to be in the healthy eating scenario now.'

'This little girl was frightened by the commotion in the trailer and she won't move,' said Alec. 'Where's her blood… her teacher.' He almost attracted another reprimand from the precocious and bossy child.

For a full minute two grown men looked helplessly at the little girl, not knowing what to do.

'She's coming now,' said Crispin. 'Lead the children into the healthy eating scenario and she can take care of the little girl who's crying.'

Miss Mockett, in a short skirt and tight jumper, sashayed towards them, chatting and laughing into her mobile phone, oblivious to the obvious distress of one small girl and two grown men.

The morning session ended. The children sat in rows again, while Crispin made a few concluding remarks and Rotarians stood by the door to hand goodie bags to the children.

As a queue formed at the serving hatch for lunch, Alec heard a voice behind him. 'Did you enjoy this morning's session, Alec?' said Claire.

'Yes, I did, except that I had a little girl in my group who was terrified by the fire brigade scenario,' said Alec.

'I heard about the commotion, so it was a child in your group?' said Claire. 'Never mind, you can do it all again this afternoon.'

'Hello love, what would you like for lunch?' said a friendly voice the other side of the serving hatch.

Alec looked at the chicken and leek pie, with a golden shortcrust pastry, a rich creamy filling and an irresistible aroma. He had made his choice.

FIFTEEN

Upton village hall committee: refurbish and be damned

'You can go to most of the villages around here and see modern village halls with modern amenities and, what's more, people want to hire them for all kinds of social events that benefit the whole community,' said Mike Haker, chairman of the Upton village hall committee.

The Upton village hall committee were meeting to discuss a pressing issue. Unlike a Rotary club, they did not have pre-prandial drinks, followed by dinner, before they discussed the business at hand. The village hall committee had a problem and there was never quite enough money to deal with problems. Mike was outlining the difficulties. He was a good old Suffolk boy through and through, a stalwart of the village and chairman of the Parish Council, as well as the village hall committee. 'This old village hall was built before the war and it's seen better days. The roof leaks. The kitchen is just not suitable for food preparation for larger functions. I can remember the days when young people in the village would be pleased to have weddings here. They couldn't afford much else in those days. Not anymore. As for the toilets, they are pretty disgusting, especially the ladies', which is a dark and evil place.'

'I can remember when the ladies' toilet was a lot worse,' said Old Mrs Stearns. 'Back in the fifties, before the flush toilets were put in, there was just an old-fashioned bucket. It had to be carried through the hall to be emptied. I was a child at the time, of course.'

Mike started to speak again but Dave, the secretary to the committee, interrupted, 'We know all that, Mike, but are we going to do anything about it?'

Dave Taylor was younger, with a head of dark curly hair, and equally committed to the village and the community. 'I thought we'd agreed that you would get three quotes for doing the work and bring them back to this committee.'

'Yes, I said at the beginning of the meeting, Dave, that I've got the quotes and they are going round the table now.' Old Mrs Stearns, a little hard of hearing, did catch the reference to the papers she had been scrutinising, and slid them across the table to Dave.

'We did talk about a lottery grant,' said Dave.

'The junior football club got one for their new pavilion,' said Old Mrs Stearns.

'Any progress on that?' said Dave.

'I have made some enquiries and I've got the forms,' said Mike.

'If we can get a grant to do the work, all well and good,' said Hugh Ward, the treasurer of the village hall committee, 'but if we don't get a grant, I can't see how we can afford it right now. We'll have to delay it.'

'We've been putting it back as long as I can remember and I've got a very good memory,' said Old Mrs Stearns. Her grey hair was tied in a bun, her countenance stern and unforgiving. She looked at Mike. She said, 'I say, get on with it and stop making excuses. You're supposed to be chairman. If you're not up to it, we'll get someone else to do the job.' Old Mrs Stearns was an outspoken, disagreeable and unreasonable old termagant.

The comment stung Mike. Committee members looked at one another; some stifled smirks, enjoying Mike's discomfiture. Everyone, except Old Mrs Stearns, would readily acknowledge the work he did for the committee and the community. He would tell the committee what he was going to do, tell them that he was doing it and tell them what he had done. Everything that Mike did was inextricably entwined in a candy floss of verbosity and process.

Old Mrs Stearns broke the silence that had descended upon the committee. 'These quotes are outrageous. No wonder we can never get anything done when our chairman gets overblown quotes like these.' She stared at Mike and said, 'What are you going to do about it?'

Austin Stubbs said, 'Mrs Stearns has got a point. These quotes are much higher than we had expected.'

'I agree,' said Seth Gradgrind. 'You'll have to do better than that, Mike.'

Mike said weakly, 'I'll try to get another more favourable quote than the lowest we've got here. I'm not too hopeful, but I'll see what I can do.' He did not wish to lose face after Old Mrs Stearns' onslaught. 'I'll call another meeting of the committee as soon as I've got anything more to report.'

'Just get on with it and no more excuses. We don't want more committee meetings, we want action.'

The meeting broke up and Mike left the village hall and walked along the road past houses on the edge of the village. The evening was damp and cool, which matched his mood as he approached the Spotted Cow. A pint of Adnams would lift his mood. He opened the door and walked over to the bar.

'Good evening, Mike, your usual, is it?' said the landlord.

'I could murder a pint of Southwold.'

An unexpected voice said, 'Mike, I haven't seen you in a while. What are you up to?'

'Alec, you're drinking away from home. What brings you to this parish?'

'A change of scenery.' Alec did not volunteer a clear explanation.

The two men fell into conversation and the beer flowed. They moved away from the bar and sat at a table in the corner.

'I got married again,' said Alec.

'I heard you were divorced.' The mention of his divorce and thoughts of his ex-wife darkened Alec's mood and the beer loosened his tongue. 'My ex took me for all she could get. I nearly lost the business. You have to declare all your finances to the court and she wanted half of the business, the house, everything. It was spite, so far as the business was concerned. She had no interest in it. I built up the business with my own hard work. Twenty-five years of bloody hard graft.'

'So, what happened? You've still got the business, haven't you?'

'Just about; in the end, I had to take out a large bank loan to settle the matter and keep hold of the business.'

'Couldn't you have contested the matter and gone to court?' Mike was beginning to feel the same sense of injustice that Alec felt.

'My solicitor advised me that if I went to court, I'd burn up lawyers' fees and I probably wouldn't be any better off at the end of the day. I know most people think I'm a bit reckless, but I had the sense to take the advice that I'd been given. I've still got the business and it's doing all right, but I have to work hard to stay afloat.'

Mike was beginning to regret that they had strayed into a delicate area and decided to lighten the mood. 'You know what they say about marriage, in the beginning all you need is two hearts and a diamond and at the end you wish you had a club and a spade.'

Alec smiled. It was not very funny, but it moved their conversation away from that delicate area. 'How's your family, Mike?'

'They're well thanks.'

'Are you still running the parish council and the village hall and everything else in Upton?'

'It's the village hall committee that gives me all the difficulties,' said Mike. He began to talk about the meeting earlier in the evening. 'Although Old Mrs Stearns is a pain in the arse, I have to admit that she's right to say that we have deferred the work several times.'

'What work do you need to have done?' said Alec.

Mike outlined what the committee wanted.

Alec was beginning to become very interested in this work at the village hall. 'So, it's basically a new roof, a kitchen refurbishment and sort out the evil toilets. How far have you got?'

'I've got three quotes from builders who live around here. A couple of them have done small jobs for us before. The committee insisted on getting three quotes and they think that they're all too much. They want at least one more. Would you be interested?'

'I'd be interested in doing the work, but I'm rather less interested in spending time working out quotes that don't come to anything.'

'I've just come from a meeting of the village hall committee. I've got some plans and the three quotes.' He rummaged around in an old battered briefcase and retrieved them.

Alec started to look at the plans and the quotations. 'I need to borrow these. Don't worry, I just need them for a couple of days and I promise you a quote that will undercut the lowest one you have here.'

'How can you be so sure of that?'

'As I told you a few minutes ago, I've been a builder for twenty-five years. I know the price that I've got to beat, but you may need to tweak the spec.'

'I can't do that. The committee have agreed it.'

'Mike, you don't have to tell them. All I'm talking about is a few minor changes that no one will ever know about unless you tell them.'

'I'm not sure about this. Perhaps we'd better forget this conversation. Just give me back the papers.'

'Mike, I'm trying to help you out here. Your committee want to do the work for less than the quotes you've got and I can do that. Anyway, you're supposed to be chairman, aren't you? You've got to take some responsibility.'

Mike did not argue. It would certainly take a load off his mind if he were able to report to the next meeting that he had managed to chip a little bit off the lowest quotation. It might even silence Old Mrs Stearns. The next problem would be how to pay for it and that is where the lottery grant would come in.

They parted company. 'I'll ring you in a day or two,' said Alec.

A few days after Mike's chance meeting with Alec in the Spotted Cow, Alec rang. 'Mike, it's Alec. I've looked at the spec for the work at the community hall and I've worked out some figures. I reckon I can knock around £3,000 off the lowest quote.'

'Good.'

'I know him.'

'Who?'

'The chap who put in the lowest quote. His name is Stan King. He's not a bad builder, but he'll take for ever to do the job and he'll argue and quibble about every little thing.'

*

Two days later, Mike pushed open the door of the Spotted Cow and breathed in a mixture of warm beer and the overpowering aroma of last night's curry evening. He ordered a pint of Southwold and sat at the same table he and Alec had occupied on their previous meeting. As soon as he saw Alec enter the pub he got up. 'What are you going to have, Alec?'

'I'll have a pint of Ghost Ship.' Alec watched the beer rise up the glass. He could do with a pint or two after a heavy day.

Soon the two were seated at the corner table and Alec took out the papers Mike had given him and opened them up. 'Here's your quote.'

Mike was relieved. 'For the purposes of committee politics, I've now got four quotes and a small reduction in the price. That might even satisfy Old Mrs Stearns.'

'I've had to tweak the spec to fit the price,' said Alec.

'It should be the other way round.'

'Look, Mike, you've managed to get yourself into a right bugger's muddle,' said Alec. 'I'm trying to do you a favour. There's not much between the highest and the lowest of the quotes. They're not trying to rob you. I've just had to tweak the spec to get my figure down to below the lowest you've got here.' He opened up the specification. 'Look at this, for example. It's really just decorative and—'

'The committee will notice. Can't you just leave it as it is in the spec?'

'The quotes you've already got are not unreasonable. It's your bloody committee that's unreasonable. If I'm going to come below your lowest quote, this is how I've got to do it.'

'Is there anything else you've got to do?'

'Nothing anyone will ever notice.'

'What if you reinstated this decorative item, how much will the price go up?'

'For you, Mike, if I follow the spec on that item, the overall reduction would be about £1,500 on the lowest quote and no one will notice the difference.'

'I'm not sure. It's not right to give you the contract, when everyone else has quoted on a higher spec and, as well as that, you've seen all the other quotes.'

'We made a deal and I've spent a lot of time working on this to help you out. I'm doing you a favour,' said Alec.

'You keep saying that.'

'Well, it's true,' said Alec. 'All you've got to do is go back to that committee of yours and sort it out. I'll get on with the work and you'll be a hero.'

Mike could see that this was the way out of his difficulty with the committee, although he did not feel entirely comfortable with it. The problem was that the committee had come to a collective belief that the three original quotations were too high. That was the problem with committees. Get a group of people together, call them a committee and give them a task, like the refurbishment of the village hall, and they develop a belief system that loses touch with reality. The three original quotations were very close because each represented a fair price for the work, but the committee thought they knew better. The lower quotation Alec had provided would allow the committee to proceed without losing face, although Mike doubted that he would be hailed a hero.

Mike walked home. It was beginning to spot with rain and the wind was picking up. As soon as he arrived, he picked up the phone and rang Dave Taylor, secretary to the village hall committee. 'Dave, it's Mike here. I'm sorry to ring you at this time in the evening, but can you call a meeting of the committee for tomorrow evening? I've managed to get another quote for the work and I want the committee's approval.'

'It's rather short notice for tomorrow evening.'

'Yes, I know it is but it's important and I want to get on with it.'

'I'll see what I can do,' said Dave. 'I'd better ring Old Mrs Stearns first. She is probably already having her cocoa, if she's not actually in bed.'

The following evening, the village hall committee convened, but not without a lot of grumbling about the late notice and lack of consideration. Mike said, 'Good evening, members. I've called an urgent meeting of the committee because I've got some news about the refurbishment of the village hall. As you all know—'

'Just get on with it, will you?' Old Mrs Stearns was even more irascible than usual. 'I don't expect to receive phone calls at that time of an evening. Not from Dave Taylor or anyone else, not unless someone has died.'

'Well, no one has died,' said Dave.

'How do you know?' said Old Mrs Stearns.

'No one I know,' said Dave.

'I don't want phone calls after six o'clock.'

'What time do you go to bed, Mrs Stearns?' said Mike.

'Don't be impertinent,' said Old Mrs Stearns, 'it's none of your business.'

'I need to know, in case I need to ring you again,' said Dave.

'Not after six o'clock,' said Old Mrs Stearns.

'Six?' said Dave.

'Not unless someone's died?' said Mike.

'How late do you take calls when someone has died?'

'Depends who it is,' said Old Mrs Stearns. 'If it's our useless chairman don't even bother to tell me.'

'Preferably before six o'clock?' said Dave.

'Unless it's summer,' said Old Mrs Stearns. 'I'd stay up a bit later then.'

'I'm sorry I disturbed you, Mrs Stearns,' said Dave. Everyone addressed Old Mrs Stearns formally, because that is what she expected and also because no one was sure of her first name.

Mike said, 'If I can get back to the business in hand.'

'Just get on with it,' said Old Mrs Stearns.

Mike said, 'I've managed to contact another builder about the refurbishment.'

'You told us that there were no more builders around here,' said Old Mrs Stearns.

'I ran into an old friend.'

'What about the builder?' said Old Mrs Stearns.

'He was the builder.'

'Was?'

'Is.'

'I hope you've got a lower quote,' said Old Mrs Stearns.

'Yes, I have,' said Mike.

'Mates' rates?'

'It's lower than the quotes we've got.'

'You got,' said Old Mrs Stearns.

'He's given me a quote that's lower than the three I've already got,' said Mike.

'There you are, I told you that the other quotes were far too high,' said Old Mrs Stearns, 'and you wouldn't have it. How much is the new quote?'

'The new quote is lower,' said Mike. He had been feeling pleased with himself, but now he was not so sure.

'How low?' said Old Mrs Stearns.

'It's about £1,500, more or less,' said Mike.

'Well, is it more or is it less?'

'It's £1,400 exactly, if you wish to be picky,' said Mike.

'It cost a fraction of that to build the village hall in the first place,' said Old Mrs Stearns, 'that's outrageous.'

'That was before the war,' said Mike. He had had enough of Old Mrs Stearns and her incessant complaints.

There was further discussion, that began to move towards accepting the Alec Barton quotation. 'Can I have the committee's agreement to accept this quote?'

'We haven't had a vote yet,' said Old Mrs Stearns.

'I was trying to build a consensus,' said Mike.

'A consensus?' said Old Mrs Stearns. 'You mean you want us all to agree with you.'

'That would be helpful for a change,' said Mike. 'Votes can be divisive, I'm happy to have a formal vote, if that's what members want. Would anyone like to put forward a proposal?' He paused and listened: silence.

'I need a proposition from the floor,' said Mike. 'All right, in that case, I move that we accept the quote for the refurbishment of the village hall, submitted by Alec

Barton. Will someone second the motion?' Again, there was silence. 'I really do need someone to second the motion, anyone.' Mike looked around the table, from face to face. 'Dave, what about you?'

'All right, I'll second it.'

'Don't you dare, David Taylor,' said Old Mrs Stearns.

'Perhaps I'll leave it to someone else,' said Dave.

'It looks as though your motion's been lost,' said Old Mrs Stearns. 'What are you going to do now?'

'I thought you were all anxious to make progress with the village hall refurbishment.' There was desperation in Mike's voice.

'Of course, we are,' said Old Mrs Stearns, 'but you need to get on and do what the committee told you to do.'

'I have,' said Mike.

'We told you to find a builder who'll do this work and won't rob us blind,' said Old Mrs Stearns.

'I think this is a fair and reasonable price for the work, Mrs Stearns. What makes you think these builders are trying to rob us blind?' said Mike.

'Well, it stands to reason,' said Old Mrs Stearns.

'What bloody reason is that, might I ask?' said Mike, in exasperation.

'Don't you dare take that tone of voice with me, young man,' said Old Mrs Stearns, 'and don't blame others for your own incompetence.'

Mike was beginning to feel sorry for himself. After all his hard work getting a lower quotation, albeit that his arrangement with Alec Barton was less than scrupulous, and now the committee had refused to accept it. On top of that, he would be in more trouble with Alec Barton, who was never an easy man to deal with.

'That's the end of the meeting,' said Old Mrs Stearns.

'I declare the meeting closed,' said Mike.

'What a waste of time, ringing me up in the middle of the night for that,' said Old Mrs Stearns.

Mike thought of his meeting with Alec, as he trudged towards the Spotted Cow. He opened the door of the pub nervously. Alec was sitting at the same table looking directly at the door.

'Mike, let me get some more drinks in and you can tell me the good news,' said Alec.

Mike walked over to the table and sat down, while Alec went to the bar to get the drinks.

Alec plonked the drinks on the table. White froth ran down the sides of the glasses. 'Tell me the good news, Mike.' Mike looked at Alec with a mournful face. Alec's Adam's apple was moving furiously up and down as he gulped his beer. He put down his glass and saw Mike's expression. 'What's happened?'

Mike blurted out his words as quickly as he could. 'The committee didn't accept any of the quotes.'

'I know that, but what about mine?' said Alec.

'Including yours.'

'What?' Alec was angry now. 'We had a deal, remember?' Mike thought it wise to remember. 'What went wrong? You won't get anyone to do the work any cheaper. Are the members of your committee completely bloody mad?'

'Probably; one of them certainly is.'

'So, what happens now?' Alec was trying to keep calm. He wanted to keep the pressure on Mike, not terrify him.

'Well, I don't know,' said Mike. Alec was a truly frightening man when he was angry. His eyes bulged, his mouth contorted and he seemed to puff up to twice his normal size. Mike's mind was racing, but logical, coherent thought was beyond him. 'I'll have to talk to them again.'

'This time you need to be more persuasive,' said Alec.

*

'Mr Haker?'

'Yes, who is it?'

'It's Mrs Scoggins, I'm sorry to ring you so early.'

Mike looked at the clock. It was half past seven. 'What's the matter?'

'I'm at the village hall.'

'Yes?'

'It's in a terrible state.'

'What do you mean?'

'There's water everywhere.'

'What's happened?'

'It's the roof.'

'What's the matter with the roof?'

'It's leaking.'

'Badly?'

'There's water everywhere.'

'I'll come down and have a look,' said Mike.

'I came in to clear up after last night's booking.'

'What booking?'

'The beetle drive,' said Mrs Scoggins.

'I'll be there in fifteen minutes.'

'I came to check whether they'd left a mess,' said Mrs Scoggins.

'I'll get there as soon as I can.'

'There's water everywhere.'

Mike put down the phone, put on a coat and left the house for the walk to the village hall. As he got to the door, Mrs Scoggins came out. 'Thank goodness you're here, Mr Haker. There's water everywhere.' They went inside and went into the kitchen. 'It's come in through the roof. We had some wild weather last night.'

'Have you got a bucket to catch the rain if it starts again?' said Mike Haker.

'I'll get my mop and bucket and start getting up some of this water,' said Mrs Scoggins. 'It's everywhere.'

'Is there anyone else who can help clear up?' said Mike.

'Elsie's next on the rota,' said Mrs Scoggins. 'I'll give her a ring.'

'I'll need to arrange an emergency repair to the roof, so I'll leave you to it, Mrs Scoggins.'

Mike began his walk home, deep in thought. The roof needed attention immediately, quite apart from the other problems which beset the village hall. He took out his mobile phone and rang Alec. 'It's Mike Haker.'

'It's Sunday morning, Mike. Early Sunday morning.'

'I need an emergency repair to that roof, Alec. Can you pop over?'

'You have got to be joking,' said Alec. 'I spent a lot of time preparing an estimate for the work you want done on the village hall, got below the figure you thought was too high and your committee turned me down.'

'I know,' said Mike, 'but it wasn't my fault. The committee can be unpredictable.'

'Ungrateful, more like.'

'Alec, please. It needs a temporary repair and perhaps we can talk about the other work.'

'Don't mention the other work, unless you're going to ask me to do it.'

'Alec, just come over, please. You're a Rotarian, you're supposed to help people.'

'Not people like your bloody committee.'

'Alec, please, I'm begging you.'

'What about your other builder chap, Stan King?' said Alec.

'I rang him, but he can't.'

'Or won't?'

'He's not happy with my committee either,' said Mike.

'I'll come over if you can guarantee that I'll get the other job,' said Alec.

'All right,' said Mike.

'So, you'll definitely get your committee to accept my quote?' said Alec.

'If you patch up the roof.'

'I'll see you in an hour, Mike.'

An hour and a half later, Alec arrived at the village hall. 'Is Mike here?'

'Mr Haker?' said Mrs Scoggins.

'Yes.'

'You're the builder, Mr Barton,' said Mrs Scoggins.

'Yes.'

'He said he would ring you when you've had a chance to look at the roof,' said Mrs Scoggins. 'There was water everywhere this morning. It's all that rain.'

'I'll need to go up onto the roof.'

'Have you got a ladder?'

'Yes, I managed to think of that,' said Alec.

Later that day, Mike came back to the village hall to check on progress. Alec was gathering up his equipment. 'All fixed?'

'That's a very temporary repair,' said Alec. 'It'll keep the rain out for a while, but it's not a permanent repair. I need the go ahead on the whole job very soon.'

'I'll have to arrange another meeting of the committee,' said Mike.

'Don't cock it up this time,' said Alec. 'Make sure you get them to agree.'

'I'll get on to Dave, our secretary, right away and ask him to set up a meeting. I'll be in touch.'

As soon as Dave finished his brief conversation with Mike, he picked up the phone and got straight down to the task of arranging a meeting. He prepared an agenda and emailed it to those members of the committee with access to email, which was everyone except Old Mrs Stearns. He would deliver her agenda by hand and retreat quickly.

It was seven o'clock in the evening and all were assembled in the village hall. Mike opened the meeting. 'Good evening, everyone. I'm sorry to have to call this meeting at short notice, but we have to make some urgent decisions.'

'Get on with it, we don't want to be here all night,' said Old Mrs Stearns.

'Any apologies for absence,' said Mike. 'We're all here. Minutes of the last meeting. May I sign them as a correct record?'

'Agreed.'

Mike said, 'The next item is urgent repair to the roof over the kitchen. As you know, on Saturday night, we had some severe weather, with—'

'We know all that. It kept me awake all night,' said Old Mrs Stearns.

'I've had to arrange an urgent repair to the roof to keep out the rain for now, but it won't last very long,' said Mike.

'How long?' said Old Mrs Stearns.

'It's difficult to say, but we do need to press on with a permanent solution to the village hall.'

'How much did it cost?' said Old Mrs Stearns.

'I need to ask the committee to approve the urgent repair,' said Mike.

'I said, how much did it cost?' said Old Mrs Stearns.

'I haven't got the bill yet,' said Mike.

'I didn't ask you that,' said Old Mrs Stearns. 'I asked how much it cost?'

'It was an emergency. I didn't have time to get three quotes…'

'So, you've had work done without asking the committee and you don't know how much it's going to cost?' said Old Mrs Stearns.

Dave said, 'That's a bit unfair, Mrs Stearns. Mike couldn't leave the roof with the rain pouring in.'

'I suppose you got that old crook, Stan King, to bodge it up?' said Old Mrs Stearns.

'No, Alec Barton did the temporary repair and I need the committee to approve the action I've taken.'

'Who?' said Old Mrs Stearns.

'He submitted the lowest quote for doing the refurbishment work,' said Mike.

'We've got no choice and I move that we approve the action of the chairman to arrange for the temporary repair to the roof over the kitchen,' said Dave.

'I'll second that,' said Austin Stubbs. His straggly white hair stood out defiantly as he stared at Old Mrs Stearns.

'Those in favour of the motion, please put up your hands,' said Mike.

Hands went up slowly, until everyone had voted except Old Mrs Stearns. 'That's six in favour, and against?' Old Mrs Stearns did not move. 'That's six votes for the motion and none against, with one abstention. The motion is carried.' *That's a miracle, she's only abstained*, thought Mike.

'The next item is the refurbishment of the village hall,' said Mike.

'We've already turned down all the quotes you got, so what have you got to say?' said Old Mrs Stearns.

Mike looked around the table. The members of the village hall committee sat impassively. Old Mrs Stearns wore the mien of a warrior ready for battle.

'We, as a committee, must face up to the situation we're in,' said Mike. 'We have a responsibility for the village hall as a community resource for everyone in the village to use and enjoy. We must take good care of it so that when, at some future time, we step down as members of this committee—'

'In your case the sooner the better,' said Old Mrs Stearns.

Mike continued, 'When we step down, there is still a sound building to pass on to those who come after us…'

'I'll be after you, if you don't get on with it,' said Old Mrs Stearns.

Mike said, 'We have four quotes for the refurbishment we all know we've got to carry out. I urge you all to put aside any views you might have held about the quote being too high. No one here is a builder; how can you make that judgement?'

'I know when I'm being ripped off by a bunch of crooks and charlatans,' said Old Mrs Stearns.

'Mike is right,' said Dave, 'we must think again.'

'Well, I've thought again and they're still crooks and charlatans,' said Old Mrs Stearns.

'We must have another look at the quotes Mike got,' said Austin. 'I'm worried that it's all going to get worse and cost us even more.'

'Quite right, Austin,' said Dave. 'Mike did manage to get a lower quote than the original three we had, even if it wasn't by much.'

'I'm not so sure,' said Seth Gradgrind. 'We were all of the same view about the amount it was going to cost. Why should we change our minds now?'

'I'll tell you why, Seth,' said Mike in exasperation, 'because this committee has been stupid and pig-headed and you've followed the lead of the wrong person.'

'Are you talking about me, young man?' said Old Mrs Stearns.

'No offence intended, Mrs Stearns,' said Mike.

'I do take offence,' said Old Mrs Stearns.

Mike said, 'I'm going to take a chance here and propose that we accept Alec Barton's quote, which has already been reported to the committee.'

'I second that,' said Dave.

'Does anyone want to debate it further or propose an amendment?' said Mike.

'Well, if you're all going to go against me, I say that we tell him that we'll accept, if he knocks it down a bit more,' said Old Mrs Stearns.

'We can't do that. Either we accept it or we don't,' said Dave.

'Not so,' said Seth, 'we could instruct our chairman to negotiate.'

Mike did a quick calculation of his chances of getting approval of Alec's quotation and decided that his best option was to support the compromise that Mrs Stearns and Seth had suggested between them.

Dave took the initiative. 'With the agreement of the seconder, I withdraw my original proposal and now propose that we accept Alec Barton's quote for the refurbishment of the village hall, subject to further negotiation on the price, and instruct the chairman to proceed accordingly.'

While Old Mrs Stearns was still working out quite what it meant and whether she could be sure of a reduction in the price, Mike put the motion, and enough hands went up for him to declare, 'That's carried.'

'How are we going to pay for it?' said Old Mrs Stearns.

'Have you applied for a lottery grant yet?' said Seth.

'Yes, I've filled in the forms,' said Mike.

'But have you sent them off?' said Old Mrs Stearns.

'Yes,' said Mike. He had remembered to post it in the village letterbox on his way to the meeting.

'When will we get the approval?' said Seth.

'Soon,' said Mike. 'I declare the meeting closed.'

He walked to the Spotted Cow for his prearranged meeting with Alec. A fine drizzly rain was falling, but he hardly noticed. *I think I won that one*, he said to himself, with some satisfaction.

'Well,' said Alec, 'have you managed to talk some sense into your committee?'

'I think so.' Mike gave a detailed account of his meeting and how he outmanoeuvred the indomitable Old Mrs Stearns.

'So, you want to negotiate with me?'

'That's what the committee have instructed me to do.'

'Well, that won't take long.'

'Can you shave a little off your price, Alec?'

'No.'

'I suppose that settles that?' said Mike.

'Yes.'

'The committee would expect me to try a bit harder,' said Mike.

'The answer would be the same,' said Alec.

'When can you do it?'

'I'll probably start at the end of next week or the week after,' said Alec.

SIXTEEN

Club council prepares for the special general meeting and an election

A car drew up and Andrew listened for approaching footsteps. It was club council this evening. He got to the door before the visitor had time to press the bell. 'Hello, Dominic, you're a bit early, but do come in.'

'I wanted a quick word before the meeting,' said Dominic.

'Let me get you a glass of wine.'

'I've got prostate cancer.' He blurted out the words so quickly that Andrew almost missed them.

'When?'

'I had a biopsy.'

'How do you know?'

'I just got back from the hospital.'

'You've just had the biopsy?'

'I got the results today.'

'Prostrate cancer?'

'I'm not horizontal.'

'It's not too serious, then?'

'It's *prostate* cancer,' said Dominic. 'I've had the symptoms for some time.'

'Will you get a second opinion?' said Andrew.

'There's no mistake. I've really got it.'

'Prostate cancer?'

'I think I ought to mention it this evening,' said Dominic.

'Yes, of course.'

Other members began to arrive. Claire, in good time as ever, was surprised to find that she had not been the first to arrive.

'It did say half past seven on the agenda, Dominic.'

'Yes, I know.' He said no more. He was bracing himself to tell the full assembly of members when they arrived.

Soon, Phillip, Mark, Ernie, Paul and George arrived in quick succession. Frank arrived a few minutes later.

'Let's get started, shall we?' said Andrew. 'Apologies; I can see we're all here. Minutes of the last meeting. May I sign them as a correct record?'

'Agreed.'

Andrew said, 'I'd like to take the item on "Preparation for the Special General Meeting" first. Dominic has some important news that will affect not just him, but the smooth running of the club. Dominic, would you like to explain?'

'Thank you, Andrew. The reason I arrived early, and even beat Claire, is that I wanted to have a word with Andrew before the meeting.'

'Spit it out, Dominic,' said George.

'I went to the hospital today to hear some test results.'

'Oh, Dominic, are you all right?' said Claire.

'No, not really, in fact, not at all. I've got prostate cancer.'

'That's dreadful news, old chap,' said Frank.

'I was waiting for the results of a biopsy, and today I learned the worst,' said Dominic.

There was a stunned silence, but it was hardly a surprise that an old Rotarian should get prostate cancer.

'Dominic came early to tell me before the meeting,' said Andrew. 'You now know as much as I do. The obvious question is, how's this going to affect the club going forward?'

'Dominic is president-nominee at the moment, which means that he will be president-elect in July,' said George.

'Exactly,' said Andrew. 'How do you see things, Dominic?'

'It's all been so quick. I haven't had time to think about much at all.'

'I think we are being unfeeling about this,' said Claire. 'Dominic should be thinking about getting better and the holidays he and Martina enjoy so much. He shouldn't be worrying about Rotary.'

'To be perfectly honest,' said Dominic, 'I shall have to ask Martina what the doctor said this afternoon. All I heard was prostate cancer. I didn't take in anything else.'

'The role of president-elect does take quite a bit of time and energy,' said Phillip. He spoke with experience as the current post holder.

'We're all concerned, and we don't want Dominic to take on a Rotary job that he is not going to be fit enough to do,' said Andrew.

'We have a decision to make, even if Dominic is fit enough to move up to president-elect in July,' said Andrew.

'We shall, of course, need to elect a new president-nominee, to replace Dominic,' said Phillip.

'As you all know, I've already sent out invitations to members to make nominations for the club officers,' said Claire. 'In all probability, Mark will be returned unopposed as treasurer and I don't expect a challenge for the post of secretary.'

'We are usually relieved if the current postholders are happy to carry on for another year,' said Andrew. 'The big decision is president-nominee. Whom do we want to be president in just over two years' time?'

'And, come the end of June next year, if Dominic decides that he's not fit enough to move up, we'll need to make an additional appointment,' said Paul.

'We really do need to be sure that we have a candidate for president-nominee,' said Ernie.

Claire said, 'It really is the most important decision we take at the SGM. We'll be electing our future president, even if he won't take office for some two years hence.'

'Do we know of anyone with the ambition to stand?' said Andrew.

'Nominations close seven days before the SGM, so there's not long,' said Claire.

'I expect whoever might be interested is awaiting a tap on the shoulder,' said George.

'On whose shoulder do we wish to tap, is the question,' said Andrew. 'Is anyone in this room interested?'

No one said anything.

'What about you, George?' said Andrew.

'Good Lord, no. I have been president and I really don't want another term.'

'Paul?'

'I prefer to stay with Foundation.'

The other men all declined for various reasons. Andrew said, 'Claire?'

'It's good of you to ask me, Andrew, when you've run out of men,' said Claire. Although she did not betray it, she felt slighted. She knew that she had run the club from the time she became secretary. She just had to manoeuvre all the pieces on the board into position to achieve what had to be done. Having the formal position of president would make the task virtually effortless.

'It's not that, Claire,' said Andrew, 'it's just that I didn't think you would be interested.'

'Much as I would welcome the opportunity to be the first woman president in the history of the club,' said Claire, 'I would prefer to remain club secretary, a post that endures.'

'Yes, of course,' said Andrew.

Claire said, 'If the club would like a woman as president, I could sound out Fiona.'

'No, please don't,' said Andrew.

'I'm not sure that would be a good idea,' said George. Other members agreed.

'How interesting,' said Claire. 'I think I just might. Perhaps that's what this club needs.'

'Claire, seriously, I really don't think that's a good idea,' said Andrew. 'No good could possibly come from it.'

'She wouldn't be right for the club as president,' said Paul.

'The real problem is that you're all scared of her,' said Claire.

'No, of course not. We're just thinking of the best interests of the club,' said Andrew.

'She would only need someone to propose her,' said Claire. 'She doesn't need the approval of club council to stand. It would be up to the membership to decide. She might even make a good president.'

The last comment was met with a mixture of grimaces and groans. Club council concluded its business in a subdued mood, but life would go on and so would Rotary.

'I don't think we can say much more this evening. I'm sure that you, Dominic, will keep us informed about your intentions for the future and we'll keep the matter under review,' said Andrew.

*

George got into his car and drove home. Claire wouldn't really put that idea into Fiona's head, would she?

When he arrived home, Erica greeted him. 'Good meeting?'

George picked up the whisky decanter and poured a generous measure of Talisker.

'You're not going to start drinking whisky at this time of night, are you?'

'Just a small one.'

'You'll be snoring all night.'

'You always say that.'

'What's the answer to my question?'

'No, I won't.'

'Did you have a good meeting?'

'Poor old Dominic.'

'What's happened?'

'Prostate cancer.'

'They were due to go on holiday soon.'

'I can't see him wanting to take on president-elect next July.'

'Where were they going?' said Erica.

'We'll need a president-nominee, and we'll need someone who's prepared to go straight to president-elect.'

'Was it Tenerife?'

'Club council.'

'Alec Barton rang.'

'What did he want?'

'Will you give him a ring?'

'Now?'

'I told him you were at a meeting and might be late.'

'It's almost ten o'clock, I was going to watch *BBC News*.'

'He said whatever time you got in.'

'What did he want?'

'He wants you to ring him.'

'I'm not sure that I want to talk to him tonight. I'm going to watch the news.'

'He sounded as though he'd been drinking.'

'I think I'll watch *Newsnight* as well.'

The phone rang.

'Who's ringing at this time of night?' said George.

'It's probably him again,' said Erica.

'Hello, yes, what can I do for you, Alec?'

'George, we're old friends, aren't we?'

'Yes.' *He's absolutely sozzled.*

'We've been friends for a long time.'

'Yes, we went to school together,' said George.

'I looked out for you, didn't I?'

'Are you all right, Alec?'

'Of course, I am.'

'Why don't you go to bed and we'll talk about it in the morning.'

'Have you got thirty thousand?'

'Pounds?'

'I don't mean bananas.'

'I'm not sure that's a question I want to answer.'

'You haven't got thirty thousand?'

'I don't want to talk about it.'

'Either you have or you haven't.'

'Go to bed, Alec.'

'Don't tell me to go to bed.'

'There's no need to upset yourself.'

'I need thirty thousand pounds.'

'I can't give you thirty thousand pounds.'

'How much can you afford?'

'I don't want to discuss lending you money.'

'We'll talk about it face to face. I'll come over.'

'Alec, you're in no fit state to drive. You'll be a danger to yourself and everyone else.'

'Can you manage five thousand, that would help me out for the moment.'

'We'll talk about it in the morning.'

'Thanks, George. I knew you'd help out an old friend.'

The call ended.

'You're not going to lend him money, are you, George?'

'He thinks I've agreed to give him five thousand pounds.'

'Very generous or extremely stupid,' said Erica.

*

'I suppose your good friend, Alec Barton, will be at Rotary this evening,' said Erica.

'Probably.'

'Are you really going to lend him £5,000?'

'He thinks I'm going to give it to him.'

'You won't do that, will you?'

'What's the difference?'

'If it's a loan, at least he'll have acknowledged that he's got to pay it back,' said Erica.

'As I said, what's the difference?'

'I suppose, either way, you'd never get it back.'

'I haven't got £5,000 in my back pocket to give him this evening.'

'What will you say to him?'

'Something like: Alec you're a drunken fool, not capable of repaying a loan. I don't give a damn about your problems. You can go to hell for all I care.'

'You'd hardly say that.'

'Probably not,' said George, 'but if a couple of Rotarians drop a heavy sack on the doorstep this evening and ring the doorbell, you'll have your answer.'

'George, don't be silly. What are you going to do?'

'He must be desperate.'

George bade goodbye to Erica and left for his Rotary meeting.

It was a cold damp evening and a thin mist hung in the air. He entered the White Horse to be greeted by Alec. 'Let me get you a drink, George.'

'I'll have a pint of Ghost Ship, thank you, Alec.' *He's spending my money already.*

'That conversation we had the other evening,' said George.

'Which conversation was that?' said Alec.

'You were asking for some help,' said George.

'I was?'

'You seemed a bit agitated.'

'I'd run out of beer,' said Alec.

'Bad housekeeping?'

'Karen thought I was blaming her.'

'Were you?'

'She gets anxious, you know,' said Alec.

'She's irrational?' said George.

'No more than most women.'

'I don't know.' *I must mention that to Fiona.*

'Have you thought about it?' said Alec.

'I haven't got it in my back pocket.'

'It's only a piece of paper, George.'

'It's a bit more than that,' said George. 'Is it that important to you?'

'Of course, it is.'

'Would I ever get it back?' said George.

'What?'

The conversation was interrupted by Bill. 'Rotarians, dinner is served,' which sounded faintly ridiculous.

'Thank you, Bill,' said President Andrew, 'very *Downton Abbey.*'

'You're the one with the gong,' said Bill, 'even if you don't use it anymore.'

Andrew said, 'Good evening, members.' Without the Rotary bell, he was having difficulty making himself heard. Members sat down without paying him any heed and Bill began serving dinner. Was this the beginning of the slow decline that Frank, Paul and George had foreseen? Was a merger with the local camera club or the gardening club their future destiny?

At this juncture, Bill began bringing out plates of fish pie; succulent cuts of white cod, smoked haddock, prawns and crabmeat, in a delicious cheese sauce, covered in a layer of mashed potato and topped with a crust of melted cheese.

Andrew continued, 'I'm pleased to welcome our speaker this… May I have your attention please?' Members were not deliberately ignoring their president; they had not heard. George decided to come to the rescue.

He picked up his glass and started to tap with his knife. Still, no one noticed until, with one more tap, applied with marginally more force, the glass shattered, and George unwittingly released a pint of Ghost Ship three feet above table height. Those close by leapt to their feet, grabbing napkins as they rose. Glasses of beer, red wine, white wine and fruit juices went flying, with plates of fish pie close behind. The beer cascaded from table to floor, to form a dark sticky patch, with splatter marks radiating outwards. The white sauce of the fish pie landed on top to make a messy contrast, out of which projected vicious shards of glass. Ernie received a sticky wet patch in the nether regions, Fiona had beer on her white blouse. Frances' light-coloured skirt was now a dappled brown and white; she had taken a hit with fish pie. Members a little farther away were less severely affected.

'What the hell did you do that for?' said Fiona.

'I was just trying to get everyone's attention for the president,' said George, rather sheepishly. He was now overwhelmed by anxiety.

'You accomplished that with great aplomb,' said Fiona.

From the other side of the table, a completely dry Paul said, 'I told you this would happen. We had a Rotary bell, which, as well as its significance as a symbol of Rotary and this club, had a purpose.'

'Mr President, you were warned that this sort of thing might happen,' said Frank. He was trying hard to contain his feeling of schadenfreude that the prophecy had come to pass. 'You cannot mess around with tradition and not receive your comeuppance.'

'Mr President, would you agree that a bell is a more suitable item for striking than a pint glass, which is more useful to drink from?' said Paul.

Bill heard the commotion and came running in. He immediately dashed out to return with a bucket and mop and a selection of beer-stained cloths.

'I'm going to adjourn this meeting to allow Bill to clear up,' said President Andrew.

Those who still had drinks carried them through to the bar and those who had lost theirs went to get more. George was horrified by what he had done and offered to buy replacement drinks. 'I'm so sorry. It was all my fault.'

'Don't worry about your trousers, Ernie,' said Kye, 'if you leave them in the garden tonight, they'll make a good slug trap.'

'You do talk utter rubbish sometimes, Kye,' said Fiona.

'Haven't you ever made a slug trap with a drop of beer in a plastic cup set in the ground, preferably Ghost Ship?'

Fiona replied with an emphatic, 'No.'

'We were talking before the entertainment, George,' said Alec. 'Do you know any more tricks like that?'

'What entertainment?' said George. 'What I did was a complete disaster.'

'Well?' said Alec.

'I'm not sure that I can do it, Alec.'

'Why not?'

'It's a lot of money,' said George.

'What is?'

'What we were talking about.'

'Were we?' said Alec.

'What you asked for,' said George.

'Are you worried about reputational cost?' said Alec.

'It's not a question of reputation,' said George.

'What is it a question of?'

Bill announced in a loud voice, 'Rotarians, you may return to dinner.' The room was clean and presentable. Most of the plates of fish pies had survived and Bill had reheated them in the microwave and brought them back into the room. He provided alternative choices from the main pub menu to replace the fish pies he had scraped off the floor. *Messy bloody lot, these Rotarians*, he thought.

Members sat down to eat and for a moment Andrew had forgotten what he had intended to say. Sitting beside him was Henrietta Heston, of Inner Wheel, the guest speaker. 'I didn't know your meetings were so exciting,' said Henrietta.

'I'm sorry that this should happen when you, of all people, are here,' said Andrew.

'I was happy not to have been any closer to the action, but your man, Bill, is a bit of a wonder in a difficult situation,' said Henrietta.

'I haven't even introduced you to members, apart from the few you met before dinner. The earlier events put it completely out of my mind,' said Andrew.

'The fish pie is very good,' said Henrietta.

After dinner, Bill cleared away for the second time.

Andrew spoke out in a loud, clear voice to make sure that there was no repeat of earlier events. 'We are honoured to have as our guest speaker this evening, Henrietta Heston of Inner Wheel, a veteran of many years.'

Henrietta's expression suggested that she did not care for the second part of the introduction. 'Before I hand over to Henrietta, I must first welcome an old friend, Rotarian Spencer, who's here on a scatter.'

'Thank you, Mr President,' said Spencer. 'It's good to be with old friends again and I'm delighted to bring greetings from President Geoffrey.'

Andrew said, 'Please take my greeting back to President Geoffrey.'

'I thought we'd banned all that nonsense,' said Fiona.

'It's one small detail the procedure police didn't think of,' said Frank sardonically.

'It's not too late,' said Fiona, never lost for a quick riposte.

'Now, now members,' said Andrew. 'I'm now going to hand over to Henrietta.'

'Thank you, President Andrew, for your kind invitation,' said Henrietta. 'I'm delighted to have the opportunity to speak to the Rotary Club of Debenham.' She paused for a moment and centred herself, as an actor might. 'Inner Wheel is an all-women organisation, and we have three objectives: to promote true friendship, to encourage the ideals of personal service and to foster international understanding.' Henrietta gave a detailed account of her organisation and eventually ran out of steam.

'Thank you, Henrietta. Has anyone got any questions?'

'If you don't have to have men in Inner Wheel, why do we have to have women in Rotary?' said Kye.

'It's the law of the land. Rotary cannot discriminate against anyone. These days most Rotary clubs have women members. But I'm sure you know that,' said Henrietta.

'Why doesn't the law make Inner Wheel take in men?' said Kye.

'Well, it's different,' said Henrietta.

'It's discrimination,' said Kye.

'Does Kye want to join Inner Wheel, or does he just want to get rid of the women in Rotary?' said Fiona.

'There was a time when we didn't have women,' said Kye.

'Not any more, you've got me and two other women members,' said Fiona.

'And the club is better for it,' said Kye, with a sarcastic grin.

'I'm glad you said that, Kye, because I'd like to take the opportunity to announce that I have been nominated for the position of president-nominee. I could be your president in a couple of years.'

'Oh, good,' said Kye in disbelief.

'I hope I can count on your vote, Kye,' said Fiona.

There were a few groans and eyes turned towards Frances, the likely proposer.

Andrew recovered his composure. 'Any more questions for Henrietta?'

There were none. After the fiddle and the sergeant at arms, Andrew closed the meeting. 'Rotary and peace the world over.'

'Rotary and peace the world over.'

Members' attention was now firmly fixed on the forthcoming special general meeting and the election of president-nominee, the route to the presidency.

SEVENTEEN

Election of the president-nominee: Close of nominations

The next day saw a good deal of activity; emails were hurtling back and forth, and phone lines were red-hot. The issue under discussion was Fiona's bold claim the previous evening that she had been nominated as president-elect. Much of this revolved around Claire; she would know the truth of it, as it was part of her job to receive the nominations and time was running out. At nine o'clock, Andrew rang Claire. 'Who nominated Fiona as president-nominee?'

'Good morning, Andrew. It's good to hear from you at nine o'clock sharp.'

'You know why I'm ringing you,' said Andrew.

'I'm not a mind reader,' said Claire.

'You don't need to be.'

Claire said, 'Nominations close seven days before the

SGM. As soon as we reach that date, I'll be pleased to make an announcement.'

'Claire, I'm president and I want to know now.'

'As of this moment, there are no nominations for anything.'

'What was Fiona talking about last night?'

'You heard her the same as I did,' said Claire. 'There's nothing I can add.'

'You're holding out. You must know something?'

'I've already told you. I haven't received any nominations.'

'You must have heard something?'

'In a Rotary club there are always whispers,' said Claire.

'What whispers have you heard?' said Andrew.

'Andrew, I really cannot say any more. Why don't you ask Fiona yourself?'

'I don't think so.'

After his fruitless discussion with Claire, Andrew rang George. 'Do you really think she's got someone to nominate her for president-nominee?'

'Well, she said she had,' said George.

'Do you think that Claire might be intending to nominate her, after that little exchange at council?' said Andrew.

George said, 'More likely it's Frances. Claire might have put the idea in her head, but she would have kept out of it herself.'

'That's it. Isn't it?' said Andrew. 'Claire put the idea to her, she thought about it and asked Frances to send in a nomination.'

'That's the best guess until we know any more.'

'George, you've got to stand,' said Andrew. 'If no one else agrees to be nominated, Fiona is on the path to becoming president.' Andrew felt ambivalent about George becoming president again, but the prospect of Fiona was just too awful to contemplate.

'It's a bleak prospect,' said George.

Andrew said, 'But you can change it. Everyone else in the club we might want to be president, has his own reason for not standing. George, you've got to do it. You have the respect of the membership, and you had a good year when you were president the first time.'

Both Frank, and now Andrew, had made desperate representations to George to stand for president-nominee, but for very different reasons. Frank wanted George to overturn Andrew's modernisation programme and Andrew wanted him to thwart Fiona's ambitions.

George said, 'I share your concern about Fiona, but I don't want to do another term as president. Someone else has to step forward.'

As soon as George put down the phone, it rang again. 'Hello, George,' said Alec. 'We've been having a conversation over the last couple of days without coming to a conclusion.'

'Yes.' George was cautious in his reply.

'Well, are you going to do it?'

'I'm not sure.'

'It's not much to ask an old friend, is it?'

'I've never asked an old friend for £5,000,' said George.

'I'm not asking you for £5,000,' said Alec.

333

'It's gone up, has it?'

'George, I don't know what you're talking about.'

'The other evening you rang and asked me to lend you some money,' said George.

'I think you've got that all wrong. I'd had a few beers,' said Alec. 'Perhaps I wasn't being clear.'

'Why did you ring me?'

'You heard Fiona last night?'

'We all did.'

'You don't want her to be president, do you?'

'Fiona does a lot for the club, but she wouldn't be right as president,' said George.

'Well, she's going to be if you don't do something about it,' said Alec.

George said, 'I'm not going to stand as president-nominee and potentially go straight to president-elect, if poor old Dominic decides he can't go on. That would put me just a year away from the presidency.'

'No, not you, George.'

'Who?'

'Me,' said Alec.

'You?'

'I had a chat with Claire about the process,' said Alec. 'She was most helpful.'

'You've only been in Rotary five minutes.'

'A few months.'

'Five minutes in Rotary time.'

'Will you do it?' said Alec.

'Nominate you?'

'Yes.'

'I'll think about it,' said George.

'Just remember, we're old friends and I've always looked out for you.'

George put down the phone. A loan or even a gift of £5,000 would have been far simpler.

George and Andrew were soon in conversation again. 'What will you do, George?'

'I really don't know,' said George.

'You can't nominate him.'

'At least with Fiona it's the devil we know,' said George.

'Would he make life difficult for you?' said Andrew.

'He's never made life easy for himself or anyone else.'

*

That evening Alec arrived home, as usual. 'Hello, good day?'

'Not too bad. You?'

'I'll get some supper.'

'Will you get me a beer, please?'

Karen took a can of Broadside from the fridge, opened it and poured.

Alec took a long draught. 'Thirsty work.'

'Where have you been working?'

'The village hall at Upton.'

'You do work hard, but I wish you wouldn't drink so much,' said Karen.

'I've got a couple of lads helping me. It won't be too much longer now.'

'The salon has been really busy this week.'

'Will you get me another beer?'

'Yes, all right, but don't drink any more.'

'I've been thinking,' said Alec.

'My hairdryer conked out,' said Karen.

'I'm going to stand for president-nominee.'

'Nominee?'

'It's number three in line.'

'You?'

'George is going to nominate me.'

'Has he said so?'

'I'll be president in a couple of years. It has a good deal of prestige attached to it, you know.'

The next morning, Alec was on site at the village hall. He took out his mobile phone and rang George. 'Have you thought about it?'

'I am thinking about it,' said George.

'Claire needs to know before the deadline.'

'I don't think you're right,' said George. 'Not yet.'

'Not ever?'

'I didn't say that.'

'I can learn quite a lot in the next couple of years,' said Alec.

'I'm not going to do it, Alec,' said George.

'You might regret that,' said Alec and ended the call abruptly.

Alec was brooding on the turn of events. *It's the least he could do for an old friend. Now he's let me down.*

At midday, Alec took a lunchbreak. He opened a pack of sandwiches and reached for his battered thermos flask. He had set his mind on a bid for the presidency and would have to find someone else to nominate him. He took out his mobile phone.

'Hello, is that Claire?'

'Yes, Alec.'

'We had a chat the other day.'

'Yes, we did,' said Claire.

'You were helpful.'

'I'm club secretary, I try to be.'

'He won't do it.'

'Do what?'

'George.'

'What's he done?'

'No, he won't.'

'Are we talking about your aspiration?' said Claire.

'What do you mean?'

'President-nominee.'

'I've set my mind on it,' said Alec.

'Good for you.'

'I don't know what to do now.'

'George won't nominate you?' said Claire.

'Bastard.'

'I beg your pardon?' said Claire.

'Sorry, not you,' said Alec.

'I should hope not.'

'He's not being very helpful.'

'If George has decided not to nominate you,' said Claire, 'you'll have to accept it.'

'But we've always been friends.'

'Perhaps he thinks you're not ready,' said Claire.

'But it would be two years away.'

'It's not long in Rotary terms.'

'Would you do it?' said Alec.

'Nominate you?' said Claire.

'Yes, you've been helpful.'

'Not that helpful.'

'You gave an answer quicker than George did,' said Alec.

'Alec, as club secretary, it's my duty to organise the ballot, if there is one.'

'What do you mean, if there is one?'

'If there's only one nomination, there won't be a need for a ballot.'

'How many have you got?'

'Nominations won't close for over a week,' said Claire.

'You haven't got any?'

'I can't tell you.'

'Or won't.'

'Same thing.'

'What should I do?' said Alec.

Claire said, 'You'll need to find another member to nominate you.'

'But not you?'

'I organise the ballot,' said Claire. 'It wouldn't look right if I'd nominated one of the candidates.'

'Who do you think I should ask?'

'That's up to you, but what about Kye?'

*

When Alec arrived home that evening, he found Karen tense and lachrymose.

'What's the matter?'

'I'm so worried,' said Karen.

'You've got nothing to worry about.'

'What about these?' She waved another letter in the bank's corporate colours and other envelopes which she sensed contained bills. 'Can we pay any of these?'

'Of course, we can.'

'There was a phone call from the bank. They want you to go in and see them.'

'I work bloody hard to keep my business going.' He gulped from the glass of Broadside Karen had poured. 'People owe me money, as well you know.'

'All I'm saying is that we can't go on like this,' said Karen.

'Do you think I like it? Letters from that snivelling bank manager.'

'You'd better go and see him, otherwise there could be more trouble.'

'There could be a bloody sight more if I do go.'

'I said you'd ring him in the morning.'

'I'll think about it.'

'Promise me you'll ring him in the morning,' said Karen.

'I'm definitely going to stand for president-nominee,' said Alec.

'That doesn't seem the most important thing at the moment.'

'It is to me. It might even put me in better stead with the bank.'

'Don't forget to ring.'

'Kye's going to nominate me.'

'Who?'

'Kye at Rotary.'

'Do you get paid for it?' said Karen.

'Don't be silly.'

'I thought George was going to do it.'

'He turned me down.'

'You've been friends for years.'

'Ungrateful bastard,' said Alec.

EIGHTEEN

Life is a lottery

Meanwhile, trouble of another kind was brewing. Earlier that morning, Dave, secretary of the village hall committee, had received a letter from the National Lottery, which shattered all hopes of a grant for the refurbishment of the village hall. 'I think you need to call a meeting of the committee, Mike.'

'There's probably a mistake somewhere.'

'I don't think so,' said Dave.

'It happens in all big organisations.'

Dave said, 'We're not going to get any money from the lottery.'

'It must be a cock-up.' Mike could not believe that the National Lottery would reject the grant application for the village hall refurbishment.

'*Refused* sounds pretty clear to me,' said Dave.

'I don't believe it.'

'I'll arrange a meeting of the committee,' said Dave.

'I don't know what to tell them,' said Mike, as a vision of Old Mrs Stearns formed in his head. 'I need a lie down in a darkened room.'

Dave started to ring committee members. He found it difficult to convince members that there was an urgent need for a meeting without saying exactly why.

'It's very important, Mrs Stearns.'

'Why, what's happened?'

'It's about progress on the refurbishment of the village hall. Mike will explain it at the meeting.'

'Is that all you're going to tell me?' said Old Mrs Stearns.

'Mike will explain it all at the meeting.'

The following evening, the members of the village hall committee gathered for their meeting. They were a little disgruntled at the lack of information, apart from Dave's insistence that the matter was urgent.

Mike came in and all eyes turned in his direction. 'Shall we make a start?'

'Get on with it,' said Old Mrs Stearns.

'We are all here, so there are no apologies for absence,' said Mike. 'The next item is the minutes of the last meeting. May I sign them as a correct record?'

'Agreed.'

'I wish to add another item to the agenda,' said Mike.

'You called this meeting to deal with an urgent matter and we still don't know what it is,' said Old Mrs Stearns.

'Now you've got an even more urgent matter, since the agenda came out,' said Seth. 'What's going on?'

'What are we going to deal with first, the urgent matter or the extra urgent matter?' said Old Mrs Stearns.

'Why didn't we have proper notice of the business?' said Seth.

'Why isn't the extra urgent item on the agenda?' said Old Mrs Stearns.

In a low voice, which matched his mood, Mike said, 'The additional item is…'

'What did he say?' said Old Mrs Stearns. 'I didn't catch it.'

'I haven't said anything yet,' said Mike.

'Well get a move on then,' said Old Mrs Stearns.

'The additional item is…'

'You keep saying that,' said Old Mrs Stearns.

Mike said, 'The additional item is resignation of chairman.'

'About time too,' said Old Mrs Stearns, 'we've had enough of your incompetence.'

'Well hold on a moment,' said Hugh. 'What's the urgent item?'

'Are the two matters linked?' said Seth.

'What does it matter as long as he goes?' said Old Mrs Stearns.

'I move that we take the extra urgent item last,' said Seth.

'I second that,' said Hugh.

'Do you really want to vote on that?' said Mike.

'Of course, we do. I wouldn't have moved it otherwise,' said Seth.

'All right, those in favour of the motion, please raise your hand.'

All present raised their hands, except Mike and Dave.

'That's unanimous then,' said Old Mrs Stearns.

'Not quite, I abstained,' said Mike.

'Who cares,' said Old Mrs Stearns.

'We'll deal with the urgent item next,' said Mike.

'We're waiting,' said Old Mrs Stearns.

'The secretary to the village hall committee, Dave—'

'We know who he is,' said Old Mrs Stearns.

'The secretary of the village hall committee…'

'He keeps repeating himself,' said Old Mrs Stearns. 'Just get on with it, will you?'

Mike said, 'The secretary of the village hall committee received a letter this morning from the National Lottery.'

'At last, some good news,' said Seth.

'The letter he received this morning from the National Lottery…'

'He's repeating himself again,' said Old Mrs Stearns. 'Just get on with it, will you?'

'I'll ask Dave to read the letter,' said Mike.

Dave started to rummage around in an old battered briefcase. He pulled out a bundle of papers and sifted through them frantically. He then turned the briefcase upside down and shook the remaining contents onto the table. Out tumbled a miscellaneous mass of dogeared papers: old agendas and draft minutes, electricity bills for the village hall, the specification and plans for the refurbishment and sundry other items. One more shake added an apple core, three old ballpoint pens and a dead spider.

'Hurry up, will you,' said Old Mrs Stearns.

'I can't find it,' said Dave.

'You've called us here to a meeting about a letter, and now you can't find it?' said Seth. 'What are we going to do now?'

'Perhaps Dave can summarise the letter,' said Mike.

'I can't quite remember what it said.'

Mike said, 'You told me what the letter said when you asked me to call this meeting.'

'I had the letter then,' said Dave.

'Mr Chairman, as you discussed it with Dave and between you decided to call the meeting, one of you must remember what's in the letter,' said Seth.

'Well, yes, I suppose I do,' said Mike.

'How much did we get?' said Old Mrs Stearns.

'Nothing,' said Mike.

'Nothing?' said Old Mrs Stearns. 'What do you mean nothing?'

'Nothing,' said Mike.

'The letter must have said more than *nothing*,' said Hugh.

'It was two pages long,' said Dave.

Seth said, 'You remember how long the letter was, but you don't remember what it said. How's that?'

'All I remember is that it said that we're not going to get a grant for the work,' said Dave.

Mike said, 'Members of the village hall committee, we need to consider the position this puts us in.'

'I thought you'd resigned for incompetence,' said Old Mrs Stearns.

'It's probably best if he stays on for the time being,' said Seth.

'You told us we'd get a lottery grant,' said Old Mrs Stearns. 'Now they've turned us down. What are you going to do about it?'

'There's not much I can do,' said Mike.

'You can appeal,' said Seth.

'There's no appeal process,' said Mike.

'They've been throwing grants around left, right and centre in the villages around here, and you can't get one for our village hall?' Old Mrs Stearns was not going to let the matter rest.

'You name them,' said Mike.

'There's the village football club for a start,' said Old Mrs Stearns.

'And?' said Mike.

'You should resign for incompetence, you useless good for nothing,' said Old Mrs Stearns.

'We don't want him to resign just yet,' said Seth.

'He buggered up the application form,' said old Mrs Stearns. 'That's what he's done.'

Dave said, 'You negotiated with the builder and now you'll have to tell him about our difficulties.'

'I don't want to stay on as chairman,' said Mike.

'How much did you negotiate off his first price?' said Old Mrs Stearns.

'It was a difficult negotiation…'

'How much?'

'We had to go through the spec line by line…'

'How much?'

'Nothing.'

'Was it negotiation or capitulation?' said Old Mrs Stearns.

'It doesn't really matter if we can't pay him anyway,' said Seth.

'We'll have to tell him,' said Mike. 'That's a job for the secretary to this committee.'

'Hold on a minute,' said Dave. 'You've dealt with him all along. He's a friend of yours.'

'Aren't we forgetting something?' said Hugh. 'The work is only half done. He's going to walk off the site the moment he hears, and then what?'

'We'll never get anyone else to finish the job, not if we can't pay,' said Seth.

Mike looked towards Hugh, the treasurer to the village hall committee. 'Have we got any money, Hugh?'

'No, Mike. We were well below a working balance. We had to make a stage payment on the work he had completed.'

'How do we know that we didn't pay him more than the value of the work he's done?' said Seth.

'We got Stan King to value it,' said Mike.

'That old crook,' said Old Mrs Stearns. 'He's robbed us blind before.'

'Stan said that what he was asking was reasonable,' said Mike.

'Well, he would, wouldn't he,' said Old Mrs Stearns. 'They're both in it together.'

'Anyway, we've got little more than petty cash in the bank,' said Hugh. 'We're practically skint; boracic.'

'Boracic?' said Mike.

'Lint, boracic lint, skint,' said Hugh, who had spent his formative years in London, and liked to use dated London slang from time to time.

got to decide how we move on from here,' said

'You'll have to tell him,' said Dave.

'Yes, I suppose so,' said Mike.

'Oh no you don't,' said Old Mrs Stearns. 'If you tell him, he'll walk straight off the site, and we'll be left in a proper bugger's muddle. I say we let him finish the job and then we tell him. That way we get the work done.'

'That would be dishonest,' said Mike.

'It's better than letting him walk off the job,' said Old Mrs Stearns. 'If we can't pay him anyway, it makes no difference.'

'I don't think he'd see it like that,' said Mike.

'No good him taking us to court to get his money,' said Old Mrs Stearns, 'we haven't got it.'

'He'll probably kill me,' said Mike.

'Yes, and a good job too,' said Old Mrs Stearns. 'Best to get the work done first.'

'There's sense in what Mrs Stearns is saying,' said Seth.

'We could say that the National Lottery are taking a long time to give us our money,' said Hugh. 'Administrative delays, that sort of thing; they happen all the time in big organisations.'

'Mr Chairman, is it true to say that this committee has a duty to look after the interests of the village hall and the community?' said Seth.

'Yes, that's true,' said Mike.

'Would it be in the interests of the village hall and the community if Alec Barton walked off the site with the job half done?' said Seth.

'No,' said Mike.

'Would it be in the proper interest of the village hall and the community if he finished the work?' said Seth.

'Yes, of course,' said Mike.

'Is it true that he won't get any more money whether we let him finish or not?' said Seth.

'Yes,' said Mike.

'I think we have an answer,' said Seth.

'I told you that,' said Old Mrs Stearns. 'You don't listen.'

'It's not very ethical,' said Mike. 'I don't like to be dishonest.'

'No one does,' said Seth. 'I'm never dishonest in my dealings, not unless it's absolutely convenient. Besides, we don't have to be over ethical, we're not Rotarians.'

'I suppose needs must,' said Mike.

'Mr Chairman, what would you like me to put in the minutes?' said Dave, secretary to the Village Hall Committee. 'Something like:

The committee agreed to defraud the contractor by letting him complete the work on the village hall, in the full knowledge that we can't pay him?'

'We can't say that,' said Mike. 'It would be like admitting to some kind of group criminality.'

'It would be a conspiracy,' said Dave. He spoke with authority, as his sister-in-law had a cousin whose daughter was a shorthand typist in a solicitors' office.

'I wish we'd never held this meeting,' said Mike.

'That's the answer,' said Seth. 'The letter from the National Lottery, which Dave has lost, stays lost, and this meeting never took place. There's no fraud, no dishonesty and we're still waiting for the money to come through.'

'Brilliant,' said Dave.

NINETEEN

Fiona and Alec stand for president-nominee

'It's Miss Smarty Pants,' said Susan.

'For me?' said Andrew.

'Well, it wouldn't be for me, would it?' Susan threw her head back and feigned putting two fingers down her throat, as she left the room.

'I thought that I'd let you know that there are two candidates for president-elect,' said Claire.

'And they are?'

'Fiona and Alec Barton.'

'Alec Barton?'

'Yes.'

'I thought that George wasn't going to nominate him.'

'He didn't.'

'Who did?'

'Kye.'

'Did he indeed?'

'You know what that means?' said Claire.

'What do you mean?'

'None of the men will vote for Fiona,' said Claire.

'There are some who won't vote for Alec Barton,' said Andrew.

Claire said, 'My best guess is that Fiona will get no more than two or three votes, and Alec will get a few more than that, with a lot of spoilt ballot papers.'

'You think he'll win?' said Andrew.

'Don't you?'

'I agree that the men won't want Fiona,' said Andrew, 'she makes too many waves.'

'So, it's Alec Barton, drunk or sober,' said Claire.

'At least he hasn't been drunk at any Rotary meetings since he's been a member.'

'So, you're happy to leave matters there?' said Claire.

'There's nothing I can do about it,' said Andrew.

'What about George?'

'He is adamant that he won't stand.'

'He might need some persuasion,' said Claire.

'Like what?'

'You could nominate him,' said Claire.

'I'd be happy to.'

'But what?'

Andrew said, 'I can't nominate him without his consent.'

'That's what the by-laws say,' said Claire.

'That's it then, isn't it?' said Andrew.

'Is it?' said Claire.

'Isn't it?'

Claire said, 'Just send me an email nominating George.'

'Don't you think he might notice that his name is on the ballot paper?'

'You'll just have to persuade him that he agreed to it,' said Claire.

'That's ridiculous. How am I supposed to do that?' said Andrew.

'Just do it.'

'Have you read Machiavelli's *The Prince*?' said Andrew.

'I wrote it.'

Susan came in as the call ended. 'Is Miss Smarty Pants annoying you, Andrew? That's my job.'

'I prefer peace and tranquillity.'

'That's as rare as peace the world over,' said Susan.

Andrew went into the study and switched on his computer.

TWENTY

Alec completes the village hall refurbishment

Although Alec did not know it, the conversation between Andrew and Claire would scupper his chance of becoming president. But he had a further problem.

'Mike? It's Alec. It's all done.'

'That's good.'

'Can you meet me here?'

'Where?'

'The village hall, where do you think?' said Alec.

'I thought you meant the Spotted Cow.'

'We might go there after.'

Not long after that brief conversation, Mike arrived at the village hall.

'What do you think?'

'It's a brilliant job, Alec.'

'And within budget, plus the cost of the repairs to the roof after the heavy rain.'

'Yes.'

'There's one final detail.'

'It looks good to me.'

'You owe me £25,000.'

'Yes, we're just waiting for the money to come through from the National Lottery.'

'I'm not interested in the National Lottery,' said Alec. 'I want my money now.'

'Alec, I swear I haven't got it.'

'I will meet you here one week today and I shall drive over in a JCB.'

'Why is that, Alec?'

'If by some remote chance you haven't got my cheque, I shall stove in the side of this fine village hall.'

'You wouldn't do that, would you?'

'That's fair, isn't it?' said Alec.

'Yes, Alec.'

'We've got a deal then?'

'Well…'

'We've got a deal, right?'

'Yes, Alec. But suppose the money hasn't come through, by then?'

'It better. I'm not a patient man.'

'What if your Rotary club gave the village hall committee a grant?' said Mike.

'I wouldn't count on it.'

'Would it be worth the village hall committee applying?'

'I'd rather stove in the side of your village hall,' said Alec.

'It would be another iron in the fire.'

'You can apply to the club secretary, if you like. I'll email her address.'

'Thank you, Alec.'

'You'd better make it sound good,' said Alec. 'I don't think they usually give grants for village hall projects and not for £25,000. One more thing, don't mention my name.'

*

Two days later Claire received an email requesting a grant from the club to assist with refurbishment of the Upton village hall. It described the work in detail without mentioning that the refurbishment had already been completed. The application was timely because Claire was drawing up a list of grant applications for club council to consider.

A few days later, club council met at Andrew's house. Claire was first to arrive, as usual. After they had settled and Andrew had made sure everyone had a glass of wine or fruit juice, he began the meeting. 'Apologies for absence.'

'I've received an apology from George,' said Claire. 'Erica rang to say that he was not feeling very well.'

'That's not like George, but we wish him well,' said Andrew.

'May I sign the minutes of the last meeting as a correct record?'

'Agreed.'

Andrew said, 'We've got some money in the charity account, that we can allocate. We've received some applications and there are of course the charities we usually support. Claire has made up a schedule.'

'The spreadsheet I sent out with the agenda has all the information we need,' said Claire.

'What about the amounts set against the names?' said Andrew.

'I have listed our favourite charities and the specific applications we have received and allocated a provisional sum against each. There is not a sum of money allocated against every name.'

'I'm not sure that I would support all these,' said Phillip.

'These are my suggestions to aid discussion,' said Claire.

'The water and sanitation project in Uganda is now a commitment,' said Paul.

'Yes, I think we must agree that,' said Andrew. 'We had an interesting talk on the details of the project from Robert Chapman from the other club.'

'I think we can all agree that water and sanitation are essential in the modern world,' said Dominic. 'It really is a good project for the club to get behind.'

'It does take a good chunk of our budget for the allocation of charity monies,' said Mark.

Phillip said, 'This lad who's going to Thailand next summer. I don't know the family, but I suspect that they're a middle-class family, who will pay whatever they have to for his trip. I am not sure that we should support this. In my view the money would be better spent on a children's group like young carers, where there is genuine need.'

'I wouldn't accept that,' said Ernie. 'This sort of adventure is character building and we should encourage it.'

'I see we have an application from the Upton village hall committee for help with the refurbishment work,' said Andrew.

'I haven't suggested a grant for them,' said Claire.

'It would be better if they look to their own fundraising to pay for this,' said Mark.

The debate continued for some time, then Andrew brought matters to a close. 'We've had a good discussion on this and I think we have come up with a reasonable allocation of the charity monies we can allocate at the moment. I'm going to put this on the agenda for the next business meeting, so that we can arrive at a club decision. Is everyone happy with that?'

'Agreed.'

Andrew said, 'Let's move on to preparation for the special general meeting next week. Phillip will move up to become our new president on 1st July next year, which is not many months away now. Dominic…'

'I really don't know how I'm going to be next year,' said Dominic. 'It's not just the prostate cancer itself, but the treatments.'

'But you'll continue for the time being?' said Andrew.

'I'll continue for as long as I can,' said Dominic.

'If you have to withdraw at some point, we'll deal with it when it happens,' said Andrew.

'If it happens after 1st July next year, it'll be me not you who'll have to deal with it,' said Phillip.

'It could be your first test as president,' said Mark.

'I believe that we are likely to have a ballot for president-nominee, Claire,' said Andrew.

'I've received nominations for Fiona, Alec Barton and George.'

'That's a surprise, but it makes an interesting field,' said Andrew.

'I thought that George was adamant that he wouldn't stand,' said Mark.

'I didn't know that Alec Barton fancied his chances,' said Paul. 'He simply hasn't had the experience and he wouldn't be right for us.'

'He's a bit of a dark character,' said Andrew. 'Maybe another time, but not now.'

'I never really thought that Fiona would put herself forward,' said Mark.

'I don't think she really expects to win,' said Claire. 'She knows that you lot would never vote for her, even if she were standing against the devil incarnate.'

'I thought she was the devil incarnate,' said Ernie, with a chuckle.

'Some might think that she's standing against the devil incarnate,' said Paul.

'I'm sure you don't mean George,' said Claire.

'I think you know who I mean,' said Paul.

At that moment, Susan came in with dishes of steaming hot cottage pie, topped with cheese and baked to a golden brown. There was crusty bread and plenty of butter. 'That looks gorgeous,' said Claire, and everyone agreed. Andrew topped up their glasses and club council took a well-deserved break for an enjoyable supper. When they had finished, Susan returned to collect the empty bowls and they resumed their deliberations.

'You remember that reporter, Georgina, who gave poor old George all that trouble?' said Claire.

'George certainly will,' said Paul.

'She's Fiona's niece,' said Claire.

'How do you know?' said Paul.

'Fiona told me,' said Claire. 'It's not a secret.'

'She certainly seems to take after Fiona,' said Andrew.

Claire said, 'According to Fiona, Georgina has very strong feminist views. From her early teenage years, she would berate anyone who dared to refer to her as a girl.'

'I still think of you as a girl, Claire,' said Andrew. He reddened, and immediately regretted what he had said.

Claire let that comment pass. She gave a wry smile and continued with her anecdote. 'She insisted that she was a woman and adopted the *Ms* form of address.'

'The correct form of address for a girl or an unmarried woman is *Miss*,' said Frank.

Claire continued, 'If she received a letter addressed to *Miss Georgina Archer*, she would mark it not known at this address.'

'What do you mean?' said Paul.

'She expected to be addressed as *Ms*. Lots of women do these days,' said Claire. 'There's a story that on one occasion, someone asked Georgina's mother if she, that's Georgina's mother, had children. Georgina's mother said, "Yes, three, a boy, a girl and a woman." Everyone laughed. 'That's a true story, not a joke.'

'I still find it hard to believe that George changed his mind about standing,' said Ernie. 'Did you persuade him, Andrew?'

'You mean did I nominate him?'

'Did you?' said Ernie.

'You don't need to know that,' said Claire. 'There are three valid nominations and the club will decide at the SGM. There is no need to mention George's nomination to anyone. They'll find out soon enough.'

The discussion continued for a little longer and then Andrew said, 'I'm going to close the meeting now and I shall see you all at the SGM in a few days' time.'

Members said their goodbyes and walked out into the hall to pick up their coats.

'Claire, don't go for a moment,' said Andrew and they both sat down again.

At that moment, Susan came into the room and saw that Claire was still there. 'Oh, I thought everyone had gone.'

'I've asked Claire to remain for a few minutes. We've got some further business to discuss that doesn't involve anyone else,' said Andrew.

Susan gave Andrew a withering look and said, 'I'm going to watch television in the other room.'

'She's not quite herself at the moment,' said Andrew.

'You should have said, we could have moved council somewhere else.'

'I asked you to stay for a moment because I wanted to talk about George.'

'I thought you might.'

'What are we going to do?' said Andrew. 'I've nominated him as president-nominee without his consent.'

'It was a stroke of luck that he wasn't able to make it this evening,' said Claire.

'Suppose he'd been here, what could we have done?' said Andrew.

'I wouldn't have revealed that he'd been nominated.'

'Members would have insisted that you name all the nominees,' said Andrew.

'I only ever tell you what you need to know,' said Claire.

Andrew said, 'When you hand out the ballot papers at the SGM, George will see his name on them, and I don't think he will be very pleased. He's bound to insist that his name be deleted before the ballot takes place. If that happens, we'll have a straight fight between Fiona and Alec Barton and Alec is bound to win.'

'We need to ensure that he doesn't find out until it's too late for him to withdraw,' said Claire.

'There's nothing to stop him withdrawing at any time.'

'Would he really resign as president-nominee, if he found that he'd been elected by the club and it's printed in black and white in the minutes of the meeting?'

'How could he be elected without knowing?' said Andrew.

Claire said, 'He could be kidnapped by aliens just before the meeting, have his mind wiped, then released after he's been elected.'

'That's a brilliant idea, Claire,' said Andrew.

'I wasn't being serious.'

'No, of course not.'

'But I have had an interesting thought,' said Claire.

'Good, what is it?'

'I need to think it through, first,' said Claire.

'I'll leave it to you, as usual.'

As soon as Susan heard Claire close the front door behind her, she appeared. 'Was that a nice little tête-à-tête with Miss Smarty Pants?'

'I don't know what you mean,' said Andrew.

'I think you do.'

'I don't speak French.'

TWENTY-ONE

The morning after the special general meeting, the shenanigans at which are described in Chapter 3

The deception at the special general meeting had produced the surprise election of George as president-nominee, a surprise that he had yet to discover. The following morning, he and Erica were having coffee. The weather was autumnal: wet and cold, and a dreariness seeped in through the very walls of the house. The phone rang and Erica answered. 'Hello, Susan…' Erica picked up her coffee cup and went into another room.

This could take a long time, thought George, as he picked up his empty cup and went into the kitchen in search of more coffee. He returned and thumbed through an old magazine, with no great interest. The post landed on the mat and the flap of the letterbox dropped back into its resting position with a crash. He walked out into the hall to pick up a few catalogues and sundry advertising material. There was nothing of interest, so he went back to his coffee.

Erica returned. 'Was that the postman?'

'Yes.'

'Anything interesting?'

'No.'

'I'm expecting a letter from an old school friend, Sylvia,' said Erica. 'You remember her, don't you?'

'She and her husband went to Hong Kong, didn't they?' said George.

'No.'

'Singapore?'

'Bury St Edmunds.'

'I knew it was something like that,' said George.

'I've just been talking to Susan.'

'I know.'

'How would you know that?'

'You said, "Hello, Susan".'

They were silent for a few moments and Erica said, 'It's very bold of you, George. I thought you were adamant you wouldn't do it again.'

'Was I?'

'It won't be for a couple of years, I suppose,' said Erica.

'It could be sooner.'

'You must have given it some thought?' said Erica.

'I think of nothing else.'

'You enjoyed it last time, didn't you?'

'Yes, it was wonderful,' said George.

'I'm not sure that you said that at the time.'

'I got some brochures a couple of weeks ago,' said George.

'A bit of guidance on how to go about it?'

'It's a long way to travel.'

'Last time you had to go on a course,' said Erica.

'It's no different to going anywhere else. It's just a lot farther.'

'Well, congratulations anyway.'

'Well, nothing's settled,' said George. 'We've hardly discussed it.'

'I thought it was settled last night.'

'I was at the SGM last night,' said George.

'It's entirely your decision. I won't stand in your way.'

'I was hoping you'd come with me,' said George.

'Come with you?' said Erica.

'Well, you did last time.'

'Metaphorically speaking?'

'I haven't spoken about metaphors since I left school.'

'Yes, we'll go on a metaphorical journey,' said Erica, 'if that's how you like to think of it.'

'Last time we went to New Zealand, we went to a couple of Rotary meetings,' said George.

'I would be happy not to go to any Rotary meetings if we ever go again,' said Erica.

'It was a good experience, but we don't have to.'

'George, I've got things to do; I can't sit here talking all morning about Rotary.' Erica picked up the coffee cups to take to the kitchen. 'I promised Imogen I'd take her some more of the frozen rhubarb. Would you go and find some in the chest freezer, as you don't seem to have anything else to do?'

'Yes, of course.'

'Anyway, congratulations,' said Erica.

'What do you mean?'

The phone rang again. 'Hello Frank,' said George.

'I just thought I'd give you a quick ring.'

'Miserable weather.'

'What exactly happened to Alec Barton last night?' said Frank.

'He was beaten up in the car park, as far as I know.'

'That chap who wanted him to move his car must have been a huge brute.'

'Everyone meets his Waterloo,' said George.

'He was pretty angry with you.'

'I'll keep out of his way from now on,' said George.

'President-nominee was important to him,' said Frank.

'Yes, he told me in no uncertain terms, but he got Kye to nominate him in the end.'

'Anyway, congratulations, George.'

'Everyone keeps saying that to me. I don't know why.'

'It's best for the club.'

Frank rang off and George was left puzzling why he had called at all: congratulations?

*

There was not much joy in the Barton household that morning. Alec struggled downstairs at about eight o'clock. He had showered and the dried blood and dirt from the car park of the White Horse had washed away. He had dark bruising around his eyes and his lip was swollen, but his nose did not seem to be broken. He had brushed his hair, which was still damp and flat on his head. Alec Barton looked human again.

'Alec, what happened last night?' said Karen.

'I was cheated by George Woodgate.'

'Why were you in such a state when you came home last night?' said Karen. 'You only went to a Rotary meeting.'

'He refused to nominate me, because he was planning to get himself nominated, the sly, deceitful bastard,' said Alec.

'That jacket's ruined.'

'I'll get even with him.'

'Did someone attack you?' said Karen.

'I could kill him.'

'You look a lot better this morning.'

'I think I will kill him.'

'Was it important to be president?'

'Of course, it was bloody important.'

'Can you have another go?'

'I would have won if he hadn't screwed it up for me.'

'How's that?'

'There were two of us, Fiona and me.'

'You don't like her, do you?'

'They would never have let her win.'

'What about the other women in the club?'

'As soon as he got himself nominated, it was all over. Bastard.'

'I've got to go to work, Alec. You sit quietly until you feel better.'

'I'm going to terrorise Mike Haker and extract some money from him,' said Alec.

*

A little later that same morning, George, with no particular plans for the day, decided to see if Oliver was about. As he reached the lane, he thought that he could see some activity in the Greens' garden. 'Oliver, I thought I could see someone. How are you both?'

'We're well, what about you and Erica?'

'We're both well.'

'It's good that we're all well.'

'Even Humphrey's well,' said George.

'Who?'

'The dog.'

'I trust all's well in your Rotary club.'

'We had our SGM last night.'

'SGM? What's that?'

'Special general meeting. We have one every year at this time.'

'Most organisations have an AGM.'

'We have an AGM as well.'

'I should have known.'

'In April,' said George, puzzled by Ollie's sudden interest in Rotary.

'On the first?' said Ollie.

'The date varies. You really must come along to a meeting some time.' George was oblivious to the mockery in Ollie's question.

'Twenty years, remember?'

'I could be dead then.'

'Aren't you feeling well, after all?'

'Never felt better.'

'Imogen sends her thanks for the rhubarb.'

'We grow tons of the stuff. We even have to freeze it.'

'So I've noticed.'

'Oh, well, must get on.'

'Congratulations, by the way,' said Ollie, as he turned and walked away.

Oliver went inside. 'He's asked me again to go to a bloody Rotary meeting.'

'Don't let it trouble you,' said Imogen.

'And more rhubarb.'

'It's very thoughtful.'

'He probably feeds the stuff to that dopey bloody dog of his,' said Ollie.

'I don't think so.'

'I hate rhubarb, I hate Rotary, and I doubt that custard improves either.'

TWENTY-TWO

Alec draws a bead on George

The week after the special general meeting, the Rotary Club of Debenham met to consider the recommendations of club council on the allocation of charity monies. This would involve some discussion and division, but council had evaluated the applications and made recommendations, to make the process easier.

George opened the door of the White Horse gingerly, and went in. He was not anxious to be confronted by Alec Barton, after their last encounter, but he could not avoid him entirely in a small club like Debenham. George saw him at the other side of the bar. He was talking in a group and seemed to be the centre of attention. His injuries were healing well and he looked much the same as he always looked. He had noticed George enter the bar and scowled menacingly.

Andrew, who was not part of that discussion, said, 'Hello George, a pint of Ghost Ship?'

'He's the centre of attention after his travails of last week,' said George.

'It was quite an entrance,' said Andrew. 'Does he often get into fights?'

'I don't think he goes looking for them, not these days.'

'You'd think he was too old for fighting.'

'I don't think he's ever walked away from a fight in his life,' said George.

'I shouldn't think so.'

'By the way, I had a call from Bertie Covell,' said George. 'The first shoot is this Saturday. You'll come?'

'Yes, of course.'

'I'll pick you up at around eight thirty,' said George.

'Rotarians, dinner is served,' said Bill.

They all walked through to their room and Bill started bringing out plates of pan-fried chicken with a red spicy sauce.

After dinner, Andrew said, 'We'll have a short break, so you may recharge your glasses.'

George didn't move until he saw Alec Barton go into the bar. 'A drink, Andrew?'

'Just a half of Ghost Ship, George.'

George waited until he saw Alec return before venturing out.

'Let's make a start, shall we?' said Andrew.

'About time,' said Kye.

'Apologies for absence?' said Andrew.

'There's an apology from Peter,' said Claire.

'May I sign the minutes of the last meeting as a correct record?' said Andrew.

'Agreed.'

'I didn't get a copy of the minutes,' said George.

'Here's a copy, George,' said Claire. 'I don't know why you didn't receive a copy.' She forgave herself the small white lie.

'The next item is allocation of charity money,' said Andrew.

George read through the minutes of the SGM until he reached the item on the election of president-nominee. 'Mr President, there's a glaring error in the minutes of the SGM,' said George.

'Members will have the report that I sent out with the agenda,' said Claire, ignoring George's complaint.

'The minutes have been signed as a correct record, Mr President,' said Kye, 'and George is recorded as being present.'

'It says that I was elected president-nominee,' said George. 'That's nonsense. I refused to allow my name to go forward.'

'Once the minutes have been signed as a correct record, that's final,' said Andrew. 'They would stand up in any court of law. I've heard you say that before.'

'Some of us have lost Claire's report, or didn't print it,' said Kye.

'I have some spares if you need one, or are you just attention seeking as usual?' said Claire.

'These minutes, Mr President,' said George. 'They really cannot stand…'

Alec Barton was puzzled by this exchange; he scowled and said nothing.

'Mr President-nominee – that's you, George – you were too busy taking a phone call from your lady friend at the time,' said Kye.

'What do you know about that?' said George indignantly.

'She was the secretary from the double-glazing company,' said Kye. 'She wanted to make sure that you had her details in case you needed any double glazing.'

'Don't be ridiculous,' said George.

'She wanted you to take down her particulars,' said Kye.

'George, Kye, perhaps we can move on now,' said Andrew. 'We can talk about the minutes later.'

'Don't let him get out of it,' said Kye.

'You will see from the report that council has spent some time on this already and we've suggested how the available money might be allocated,' said Andrew.

'So, we needn't bother then?' said Kye.

'You're always bother, Kye,' said Fiona.

Kye replied, 'Not as much as you.'

'Shall we get on?' said Andrew. 'Claire, would you like to introduce the report?'

Claire said, 'The report in front of you is essentially a table with the names of various bodies that we usually support and others who have applied to us for the first time. It also contains the allocations club council have suggested.'

'We can read,' said Kye.

'Oh, you've remembered your reading glasses this evening,' said Claire.

'I'm wearing them,' said Kye. 'Can't you see?'

'The second table lists those that we don't consider merit any further consideration,' said Claire.

'I really do not believe that we should spend money we've raised from the public to send the children of middle-class families on gap-year jaunts,' said Phillip. Not surprisingly, he was making the same argument that he had made at club council.

'You're referring to the lad who's planning to go to Thailand?' said Andrew.

'His trip isn't dependent on Rotary,' said Phillip. 'It's not a good use of resources.'

'I simply cannot agree with Phillip,' said Ernie. 'We should encourage our young people. This sort of thing is character building. The experience can make the difference between him getting a job and someone else getting it.'

'What about the children of poorer families?' said Phillip. 'They can never get the chance. We should double the amount for this young carers' group. These children give up so much to care for a disabled family member and they can never get it back, in terms of their education and life chances.'

'We should give more to the Air Ambulance,' said Frank. 'They save the lives of injured people who would otherwise probably die at the site of a road accident or some other accident.'

The debate continued and the club was moving gradually towards a consensus on the allocation of charity monies, as members argued the merits of their own particular favourites. Alec Barton, who had sat quietly during the debate, made an intervention. 'We should concentrate all our efforts on local causes. The public, the people who donate to our various fundraising activities, get tired of overseas spending. They might support ShelterBox when there is a disaster and they see those awful images on television, but they are not too concerned about sanitation and water projects in Africa.'

'International aid is essential,' said Paul. 'It helps to lift people in developing countries out of poverty and helps them to lead safer and healthier lives.'

'It helps to develop good government and helps with diplomatic relations between countries,' said George.

'Good government?' said Alec. 'Do you know which continent receives most foreign aid? It's Africa, and how many African countries are proper democracies, with free and fair elections, the rule of law, and human rights? Most of them are ruled by despots, who've killed thousands of people in bloody coups. When they get into power, they syphon off millions through corruption, to lead lives of luxury, while their people starve.'

'Overseas aid goes on infrastructure, such as roads and bridges,' said George. 'It's also spent on health, which includes water and sanitation, like our Uganda project. And think of the polio project that we in Rotary contribute towards.'

'The Government contributes 0.7% of our gross national income, to foreign aid,' said Alec. 'That means that out of every hundred pounds, seventy pence go overseas.

We should be spending most of that money at home and we should spend our Rotary charity money locally.'

'Foreign aid has the potential to save millions of lives around the world,' said Fiona. 'People who live in abject poverty.'

'It's about health, education, infrastructure and humanitarian disasters,' said Paul. 'It takes huge amounts of money from the rich countries of the world to make a difference.'

'I've looked into this,' said Alec. 'In the most recent figures I've seen, the UK gave over £13 billion in aid, to achieve the 0.7% commitment. Of the G7 countries, only the UK and Germany gave at this level. It's about a tenth of our spending on health and more than we spend on police. We need to pull back.'

The debate was becoming rather heated. Andrew said, 'Alec has made some interesting points, but the Government's commitment on overseas aid has now been written into law, so there's not much point in us discussing it in the context of our charity monies.'

'That may be so, Mr President,' said Alec. 'All the more reason to pull out of the Uganda project and let them take it from the billions the Government squanders every year.'

'That is an outrageous suggestion,' said Fiona. 'This is a very good project and we should give it our full support. What would Alec like to squander our charity monies on?'

'We should support the project to refurbish the Upton village hall, for a start,' said Alec. 'The village hall is very old and it desperately needs refurbishment. Most villages around here have modern community centres, that can be used for many kinds of activities for the benefit of the local community. If you asked them whether a water and sanitation project in Uganda would be a better use of resources than their hall, I can tell you what the answer would be. There's no Government £13 billion slush fund to help them out.'

The debate became more and more acrimonious and eventually Andrew drew matters to a close. 'We've had a lively debate on the allocation of charity monies this evening. Do we agree the list before us, subject to the changes we agreed this evening?'

'Agreed.'

'Apart from Alec, we're all agreed,' said Andrew. 'You don't want a formal vote on this, do you, Alec?'

'There wouldn't be much point, would there?' said Alec.

*

The next day, George said, 'I think I might invite Ollie to the shoot on Saturday.'

'It's short notice, isn't it?' said Erica.

'How long does he need?'

'A week would be more appropriate.'

'If he's got something better to do, he won't come, will he?' said George.

'Is Andrew going?'

'I'll try to catch him when I'm in the garden.'

'Perhaps it's one of his running days.'

'I spoke to Andrew.'

'Is he going?'

'I'm picking him up at half past eight.'

Later that day, George saw Ollie in his garden and walked over to have a chat. 'Hello Ollie, I trust you're well?'

'I'm fine, George, how are you and Erica, and the dog?'

'We're well.'

'It must be the rhubarb.'

Rhubarb? thought George. *I'm sure he's not right in the head.* 'We've got our first shoot on Saturday.'

'Pheasants?'

'Yes and a few partridges, even the odd duck if it's foolish enough to fly over. I've hung up my gun, so to speak.'

'You used to shoot?'

'I just do a spot of beating, now.'

'How much do they pay you for that?'

'The chaps from the village are the real beaters. Some of us just follow the shoot and wave a stick as we go.'

'Sort of second division beaters?'

'I started the shoot many years ago with a chap called Bertie Covell. He's an old friend of mine, an army man. He runs it now. I've left the syndicate.'

'The syndicate?'

'The guns who pay for it.'

'So, you don't pay?'

'I usually go with Andrew, a Rotary colleague.'

'It's not a Rotary shoot?'

'It's a good day out in the fresh air and we stop for lunch and a pint of Adnams at the Huntsman.'

'Who shoots there?'

'It used to be mainly city types.'

'But not anymore?'

'A few, but most go to the big commercial shoots.'

'Who does shoot there now?'

'It's mainly local farmers these days.'

'What about the harvest?'

'That's over well before the shooting season.'

'I don't know anything about shooting.'

'Some of the old farmers, semi-retired, shoot several times a week during the season.'

'There must be lots of shoots in Suffolk.'

'Would you like to come along?'

'It's definitely not Rotary?'

'I'll pick you up at a quarter past eight,' said George. 'It's wellington boots and an old coat, field jacket, wax jacket, whatever you've got, nothing too smart.'

'I'll raid the wardrobe.'

'And a cap.'

'In case of rain?'

'Exactly.'

On the day of the shoot, George rose early, trying not to wake Erica. He went downstairs, made some breakfast and fed Humphrey. Erica appeared before he could take her a cup of tea in bed. He had never perfected the art of silent creeping. Soon, he and Humphrey were out the door and in the car. He drove across the lane and stopped outside The Old Forge. Ollie appeared almost immediately, and they were off to pick up Andrew.

'You've brought the dog.'

'He finds it quite tiring these days.'

'He's getting old?'

'He enjoys it.'

'You're wearing a tie.'

'It's traditional.'

'Do they all wear ties?'

'No.'

'You used to shoot, yourself?'

'I used to shoot. Never shot myself.'

'But you gave up?'

'I've still got a shotgun licence.'

'And a gun?'

'In a secure gun cabinet.'

'You keep it locked?'

'I still have it serviced every year.'

'I suppose the law on shotguns is strict.'

Soon they were at Andrew's. He got into the car and they drove off.

It was cold and the ground was still wet from the overnight rain.

'I don't think we've seen the last of the rain,' said Andrew.

They took a turn off the road onto a narrow muddy track for about a mile and then re-joined the road. Another few minutes and they arrived at old Tom's farm. They got out and donned jackets, caps and wellington boots.

'You've brought walking boots rather than wellingtons,' said George.

'I thought wellingtons would be uncomfortable to wear all day,' said Ollie. 'And I haven't got any.'

'Let's hope it's not too wet,' said Andrew.

Land Rovers and other vehicles began to arrive, and everyone stood chatting. At nine o'clock, Colonel Bertie

Covell, the shoot captain, arrived in a Land Rover. He got out and exchanged greetings. 'Gather round, everyone…'

As the colonel was speaking, another vehicle drew up and out got Alec Barton. He joined the assembled guns and beaters in a semicircle in front of the colonel.

'We've got Edward Foster joining us today. You've shot here before, Edward, haven't you?'

'Yes, Colonel. It was the season before last.'

'We've also got Alec Barton. It's your first time here, I believe?'

'Yes, Colonel.'

George looked at Andrew. 'Well, there's a surprise.'

The Colonel continued, 'We're shooting ten today and moving up three. Nothing on the ground for safety reasons. You're live as soon as you reach your peg. The horn will sound once to signal the end of each drive and twice at the end of the shoot.'

George had known Bertie since their Cambridge days. He came from a military family and his career path had been determined from an early age. However, he left the army mid-career to go into a business venture with other friends. They had invited George to join, but he was not convinced that it was a viable project, or entirely lawful. Bertie always brought to George's mind the satirical Major-General song about the well-educated officers of Victorian times:

I am the very model of a modern Major-General
I've information vegetable, animal, and mineral,

I know the kings of England, and I quote the fights historical
From Marathon to Waterloo, in order categorical
I'm very well acquainted, too...

Bertie came to the end of his briefing. 'Any questions? No, good, let's move off.'

The colonel and some of the guns climbed into Land Rovers, the remaining guns and the beaters got into the tractor-drawn trailer. After a few minutes, a voice said, 'All the guns out here.' A little farther, and the trailer stopped again to let everyone else out.

'Ollie, choose a stick from the back of the trailer as you get out,' said George.

There was an expanse of open ground in front of the beaters, with a large patch of maize ahead. It was beginning to rain again. The ground ahead was covered in tall, thickly tangled vegetation and went down into a dip then rose sharply. Ollie said, 'Bloody hell, the water's come over the top of my left boot.'

'Everyone else is wearing wellingtons,' said George. 'They're not for decoration, you know.'

They reached the beginning of the maize and Martin, who organised the beaters, said, 'Hold on the right, you're too far ahead.' The line adjusted. The maize was above head height and Ollie soon found that he was lost in a cold wet jungle, out of sight of everyone. The leaves of the maize dripped water onto his jacket, up the sleeve of his beating arm; it ran inside the upturned collar of his coat, down his coat onto his trousers, which were soon wet through from the knees down.

Ollie could hear the squawking of pheasants as they were disturbed and rose into the air. Then gunshots rang out and pheasants dropped to the ground, some spinning as they fell. The pickers-up were busy with their dogs and soon all the birds had been gathered up. The horn sounded once, and the drive was over.

Back in the trailer, which also served as a game cart, two of the beaters started to tie the birds into braces – a cock and a hen in each – and hang them on the hooks above them. The tractor started up and they moved off to the next drive. There was a loud shout from one of the beaters, 'Look out!' and three deer darted out of the cover, panicked by the activity. Ollie looked up to see one of the deer, moments before it ran into him, knocking him flat. There was momentary concern as he struggled to his feet.

'Are you all right, Ollie?' said Andrew.

'Yes, I think so. Just a bit winded.' The line of beaters reformed and moved on.

They completed four drives before lunch, then drove back to the farm. George unlocked the car and they put their wellingtons and outer garments in the boot and drove to the Huntsman. There was a log fire burning brightly inside the crowded pub; it was warm and comfortable after the cold of the field. Erica and Susan had arranged to join them for lunch and they had brought Imogen. George saw them and waved. He enquired across the bar whether they needed any more drinks by an awkward drinking motion, which made them laugh. Andrew managed to find his way through the throng of bodies to the bar and said, 'George, Ollie, what are you going to have?'

'A pint of Ghost Ship, Andrew.'

'What about you, Ollie?'

'I'll have the same, please.'

Andrew passed the drinks back to the other two, and paid. They each took a gulp and moved through the crowd to join the ladies.

'Ollie, you look wet through,' said Imogen.

'I've got wet feet and trousers, and I'm all wet around the neck and up my sleeves,' said Ollie. 'And a deer flattened me. Apart from that, I'm fine.'

'Waterproof trousers and wellington boots are useful in the wet,' said Andrew.

'I've worked that out,' said Ollie.

'It's also best to get out of the way of a charging deer,' said George.

They all laughed, and Ollie was momentarily crestfallen. Bertie and his wife came over to talk to George and his party. 'George, how are you? Did you hear about my right and a left?'

'Several of the guns mentioned it,' said George, 'but no one actually saw it.'

Bertie roared with laughter and moved off to talk to another group.

A long table had been set out for the shooting party and their guests. A waitress ladled hot soup into bowls and members of the party passed them around. There were thick slices of ham, crusty bread, butter and cheese. They finished with coffee and port.

'The worst part comes next,' said Andrew.

'What's that?' said Ollie.

'Going back out into the cold.'

In the car, George said, 'Alec Barton kept his distance.'

'He did nod an acknowledgement, but that was all,' said Andrew.

'I tried not to notice,' said George.

'Is he a friend of yours?' said Ollie.

'He's a fellow Rotarian,' said Andrew.

'But not a friend?'

'I wasn't expecting to see him here,' said George.

'Where were all the other beaters at lunchtime?' said Ollie.

'They bring sandwiches and flasks of tea and eat in one of the barns,' said Andrew.

'They prefer to save their beating money,' said George, 'but they're the real beaters. We just follow the shoot.'

The wintery sun had disappeared behind a layer of cloud, as they pulled on their outer garments. After another couple of drives, the light was beginning to fade and they started the final drive of the day. The beaters moved through a thickly wooded area, and dogs ran back and forth, as their owners sent them into the thickets to flush out any birds. The guns were waiting in a field beyond the cover. When disturbed, the pheasants flapped furiously and squawked loudly as they rose into the sky, towards the guns. The air was filled with smoke and the sound of gunshots. The dogs of the pickers-up scampered about collecting the birds as they fell. The beaters were not able to hold a straight line in the cover and emerged in ones and two into the field where the guns and the pickers-up were standing a short distance in front of them. As George came out, he saw Alec Barton standing directly opposite. Alec Barton lifted his gun and pointed it into the air, as though to take another shot at a pheasant, then slowly let it down and drew a bead on George. The horn sounded twice and it was the end of the shoot.

'What's the matter, George?' said Andrew. 'You look as though you've seen a ghost.'

They tossed their things into the boot, including a brace of pheasants each. George said little on the way home, but Andrew chatted to Ollie about life in London and his new quieter life in the Suffolk countryside.

'I'm not sure what Imogen is going to do with the pheasants,' said Ollie.

'It's best to casserole them,' said Andrew. 'They have almost no fat on them, so they're not easy to roast.'

'I don't think she's ever prepared a pheasant.'

'That's your job.'

'I'm not sure I could do that,' said Ollie.

Andrew said, 'Nonsense, you watched them being blasted out of the sky all day. You should be able to prepare them.'

'I suppose so,' said Ollie.

'Let them hang for three or four days,' said Andrew. 'Then pinch up some of the skin and tear it. It comes off easily.'

'You don't pluck them?'

Andrew said, 'Cut off the head, and the wings, then the lower part of the legs. Draw the sinews with pliers. Then you remove the guts.'

'That's the bit I don't much fancy.'

'Good job you didn't live a hundred years ago.'

They dropped off Andrew and on the last part of the journey home, Oliver found it difficult to engage George in any conversation. He was deep in thought.

TWENTY-THREE

As someday it may happen that a victim must be found.
I've got a little list – I've got a little list

'Hello, yes,' said Claire, as she picked up the phone.

'It's Mike Haker, chairman of the Upton village hall committee. I've got your email about our grant.'

'I'm afraid you're not going to get a grant, Mr Haker,' said Claire.

'Why not?'

'The Rotary Club of Debenham has limited funds to distribute to charitable causes and the club wasn't able to help your organisation.'

'Are you saying that if you had more money to give away, you would have helped us?'

'No, I'm not saying that.'

'What are you saying?'

Claire said, 'I am saying that we considered your application and we decided not to give you a grant.'

'There must be a reason.'

'The club acted with reason, but doesn't give reasons.'

'That doesn't make sense.'

'Sense or not, your organisation is getting neither a grant nor reasons,' said Claire.

'Alec Barton's going to be disappointed,' said Mike.

'Do you know him?'

'He's probably going to kill me.'

'You've had dealings with him?' said Claire.

'He must have told your lot that he did the work on the village hall,' said Mike.

'The refurbishment?'

'A thousand or so from Rotary would have kept him quiet for a while.'

'You owe him money?' said Claire.

'About £25,000.'

'How come?'

'He doesn't know.'

'Know what?' said Claire.

Mike blurted out, 'I told him we're still waiting for the lottery money.'

'You've been refused?' said Claire.

'What can I do?'

'He probably will kill you,' said Claire.

Claire mulled over her phone conversation. It answered one question that had puzzled her and other members of the club. Alec Barton's great interest in the Upton village hall had nothing to do with philanthropy and everything to do with self-interest. She thought the president should know.

The phone rang in the Parker residence.

'Hello, Susan, is—'

'I'll get him.'

She thrust the phone at Andrew. 'Miss Smarty Pants for you.'

'Hello, Claire.'

'I've had a very interesting phone conversation with Mike Haker.'

'Who?'

Claire said, 'Alec Barton acted with a complete lack of integrity over the charity monies the club allocated at the last meeting.'

'In what way?'

'Mike Haker owes him money.'

'Who is Mike Haker?'

'The Upton village hall committee chairman,' said Claire.

'I'm sure Alec Barton is quite successful at extracting money from the recalcitrant,' said Andrew.

'He could kill him.'

'He might only maim him,' said Andrew, 'but what's it got to do with the club?'

Claire said, 'It looks like Alec Barton supported the village hall application, because the money would have gone straight to him, in part settlement of the debt.'

'I don't like the sound of that,' said Andrew.

'We turned down the village hall application, so he didn't gain from his actions,' said Claire.

'That's not really the point though, is it?' said Andrew.

'Do you want me to call a meeting of club council?' said Claire.

'No,' said Andrew, 'let's see what members think at the next meeting. That's what we did when George got into that spot of bother.'

'Will you tell him?'

'I'll put him on notice,' said Andrew.

The next club meeting was a speaker meeting. Members gathered in the bar of the White Horse. George walked in and immediately felt Alec Barton's glare fall on him from across the bar. At least he wasn't looking down the barrel of a 12-bore shotgun.

'George, let me get you a drink,' said Frank.

'A pint of Ghost Ship, thank you.'

'Coming up,' said Bill.

Frank said, 'I really don't know why that man is so angry with you, George.'

'He turned up at the shoot on Saturday.'

'Was that a surprise?'

'He drew a bead on me,' said George.

'What? Have you told the police?'

'I don't think anyone else saw.'

'It might be wise.'

'I haven't even told Erica.'

'Rotarians, dinner is served,' said Bill.

Andrew said, 'Good evening, members. This evening we're pleased to welcome Dunstan Donaldson, the coxswain of our nearest lifeboat station, who is going to give us a talk on the work of the lifeboat and some of the rescue missions they have undertaken. There's also another matter that I shall take after our guest has left us. Just some boring Rotary business, Dunstan, that we wouldn't wish to burden you with.'

Dunstan nodded. That was a relief.

Bill brought in plates of roast pork with crackling from the carvery. Dishes of crispy roast potatoes and green beans arrived next, followed by apple sauce and a rich gravy. Bread and butter pudding would follow, then coffee.

When all had been cleared away, Andrew said, 'We'll take a short break now and you may recharge your glasses. When we resume, I shall pass over to Dunstan.'

After a few minutes, members began to resume their places. Kye, in his role as sergeant at arms, was taking particular notice of stragglers, who would later face a financial penalty of fifty pence for this and every misdemeanour.

Andrew said, 'We're all here. I think I saw Kye write down some names, but we'll find out later. I'm now going to hand over to Dunstan Donaldson, who is the coxswain of the lifeboat station. Over to you, Dunstan.'

'Thank you and good evening,' said Dunstan. 'The Royal National Lifeboat Institution, to give it its full name, saves lives around our coasts and we've been doing so since 1824, when we were founded. We are a charity...' Dunstan went on to talk about the boats at his own lifeboat station, some of the characters who had been there over the years and some of the rescues they had undertaken. He then showed a short video of the crew in action. 'I hope you found that interesting and I shall be pleased to take any questions.'

There were lots of questions, to which Dunstan gave fulsome answers. After many years of giving talks on the work of the lifeboat station, he was rarely taken by surprise.

Andrew said, 'Dunstan, on behalf of the Rotary Club of Debenham, I wish to thank you for a very interesting and entertaining talk this evening.' Members applauded, and Dunstan had finished another speaking engagement.

When Dunstan had left the room, Andrew said, 'There's another matter that concerns Alec and the allocation of charity monies at our last meeting. I have spoken to Alec, and he said that he wishes to make a statement on the issues of concern.'

Alec said, 'Thank you, Mr President. I was surprised when you told me about the concerns of some members about my support for the Upton village hall application. You've now given me the opportunity to make a statement to allay members' concerns on the matter, but I am at a loss to know how to begin. I explained fully at the time, my belief that the Government should reconsider its commitment to spend so much money on overseas aid, and instead, to focus on meeting need at home. I went on to suggest that we, as a club, should support this application as a local community project, and if necessary, because of the limited funds we have, withdraw our support for the water and sanitation project in Uganda. The club decided not to take up my suggestion and that, so far as I was concerned, was that. I accepted the decision of the majority. Now you say that I should not have supported the village hall project. Conflict of interest, you say. But I say this; why shouldn't I support what I believe in? As to the matters alleged against me, they are vague and insubstantial. I stand before you charged with something. You believe me to be tainted with some kind of guilt, but, Mr President, I do not know what I am charged with. You have entangled me in a Kafkaesque web of intrigue, insinuation and trickery.' He paused for a moment and looked into the eyes of those around him, and then concluded, 'Mr President, now is the time for those who brief against me to make their arguments and prove their case. I will therefore give way to my detractors, but I reserve the right of reply.'

Alec Barton was controlled and deliberate in his delivery. He wore a dark suit, an immaculate white shirt with double cuffs and a sober blue-striped tie. His usually wild hair was smoothed down. Despite his calmness, he was in the mindset of a New York trial lawyer, a bruiser, who was waiting to tear into the opponents and rip them apart as soon as proceedings began. He knew he was on trial. He had few friends and many enemies.

'Very well,' said Andrew, 'I'll summarise the concerns to which I referred.'

Frank whispered to George, 'He really is an extraordinary chap. He's clever and articulate, but that might not be enough.'

George whispered a reply, 'Never underestimate Alec Barton. He's intelligent, well read and knowledgeable, but he can still speak the language of the men on the building site.'

'Well read?' said Frank.

'Have you read Kafka?'

Andrew said, 'The matter of concern in Alec's behaviour is this. He argued strenuously for a grant for the Upton village hall committee, but omitted to declare that he had a conflict of interest. This arose because he had carried out the work of refurbishment at the village hall and if the club had made a grant, that money would have gone straight into his pocket.'

George had been outraged at Alec Barton's behaviour, when Andrew had mentioned the matter to him. He felt compelled to speak out, although he felt keenly Alec Barton's antipathy towards him. 'Mr President, I do feel some concern in this matter. As Rotarians we are obliged to act with integrity and high ethical standards in our personal and professional lives. Alec Barton did not say that he had a clear financial interest in the village hall committee getting a grant. He represented his support in the guise of a concern about too much charity money and other aid going abroad, whereas his real purpose was to persuade the club to give a grant to an organisation that would pay the money straight into his own pocket. What he should have done is declared his interest in the matter and recused himself.'

Alec said, 'Mr President, George has impugned my views on charity money and international aid. It is my sincerely held view, that for this country to give seventy pence of every hundred pounds our economy creates, in international aid, is far too generous, when there are so many needs at home. The same applies when we as a club are allocating monies from our charity account. This is not some wild, far right view, but a perfectly proper opinion that's shared by many mainstream politicians.'

Is he dishonest or is he really taking a legitimate position? thought George.

When a felon's not engaged in his employment
Or maturing his felonious little plans
His capacity for innocent enjoyment
Is just as great as any honest man's.

'The international aid target is now a legal requirement, but it's got nothing to do with the allocation of charity monies,' said Fiona.

'It's about integrity as a Rotarian,' said Frank. 'What was in Alec's mind when he was arguing for the village hall? He was speaking as a member of this club and his focus should have been the best interests of the club. Instead, he was thinking of himself and putting that money into his own pocket.'

'Mr President, how could he possibly know what I was thinking?' said Alec. 'He's not a mind reader. I believe in what I was saying.'

'It's not just a matter of what was in his mind at the time, it's also about perception,' said George. 'A Rotarian should not put himself in a position where anyone would reasonably assume that he is acting wrongly.'

Alec came back strongly. 'Has anyone stopped for a moment to consider what's actually involved here? The club never gave the village hall committee a ha'penny, but if we had it would have been a few hundred pounds at most. The village hall committee still owe me about £25,000 for the work I did. They are the real villains in all this. They assured me that they would be getting a lottery grant and they keep telling me that it'll be here soon, but it never arrives. A few hundred pounds is nothing and this whole business amounts to naught. It's what lawyers call *de minimis*, not worth considering. It's a paltry, petty, piddling, piddly, piffling much ado about nothing.'

'Monetary worth is not germane to the matter,' said George. 'It's about other values, Rotary values and personal integrity. A conflict of interest arises when a member of this club has a personal interest that's in conflict with his duty as a member. Alec's duty was to assist in evaluating the competing claims for charity monies, but he had a personal financial interest in the village hall committee receiving a grant, because any money would go into his pocket. That got in the way of his duty as a Rotarian and a member of this club.'

'His issues with the village hall committee over the refurbishment work is not our concern,' said Fiona, 'nor is it his concern when carrying out his duty as a Rotarian. If they owe him money, and we have no reason to doubt this, he must take up the matter with them in the proper way.'

George said, 'Many members expressed support for particular charities that they consider to be more worthy of support than others. That's perfectly proper, but when a member has a personal interest, he should declare it and take no further part. The monetary value is of no consequence. It's a matter of principle, which is unshakeable.'

The debate went on until members had exhausted their argument and were beginning to repeat themselves. The loudness of the debate as members talked over one another became too much for George. He was now feeling extremely anxious and sat wringing his hands; his stomach churned relentlessly.

Andrew said, 'I think members have said all they want to say this evening. Alec, I should give you the final word.'

'I've nothing to add,' said Alec.

As the meeting ended, the atmosphere was sombre, all anger and emotion strangled and suppressed. Many members had not spoken because of their distaste for conflict. Those who had, did so through a sense of obligation, a duty which took them beyond their personal comfort zones. Even Kye had kept quiet. He had no qualms about unsettling members with his humour, but he did not care to express strong opinions on more serious matters.

'It's late and we've had a very full evening,' said Andrew. 'I'm going to close the meeting now and we'll leave the fiddle and the sergeant at arms. Before I do, I'd like to remind everyone that next week is a scatter, so we won't be meeting here at the White Horse. That means you should attend a meeting of another club and not take the evening off to watch television. Will you now please rise.' He paused for a few moments then said, 'Rotary and peace the world over.'

'Rotary and peace the world over.'

*

The next morning, Andrew was sitting quietly at home, mulling over the previous evening's meeting. The phone rang and he answered before Susan could get there.

'You moved quickly enough when you thought it was Miss so efficient, clever and bloody nice, Smarty Pants.' Susan looked straight at Andrew, now in conversation on the phone. As she caught his eye, she threw back her head in dramatic fashion, feigned putting two fingers down her throat and flounced out of the room. In other circumstances, Andrew would have been amused, but Miss Smarty Pants continued to be the unwitting cause of much tension in the Parker household, to the exclusion of all levity.

'Here, this evening?' said Andrew.

'Tomorrow's Friday and no one wants to meet on a Friday evening and you didn't want to leave it until next week,' said Claire.

'It's just that Susan might—'

'Tell Susan not to worry about supper, I'll bring something I can heat up when I get there.'

'I'll have a word with Susan. I'm sure she...'

Susan had come back into the room. *Whatever it was, don't be too sure.* The call ended.

'Have you got something to ask me?' said Susan.

'No, that is, well yes.'

Susan was standing square in front of Andrew, with her hands on her hips. 'Well?'

'It must be coffee time. I'll put the kettle on,' said Andrew.

'You want to have club council here?'

'Yes, how did you know?'

'One day next week?' said Susan.

'Not exactly.'

'So exactly when?'

'I've just been speaking to Claire,' said Andrew, weakly.

'Yes, I know. You put on that silly voice,' said Susan.

'What silly voice?'

Susan said, 'Well, you can't be talking about a meeting of club council this week, because today is Thursday and you never meet on Fridays, and you wouldn't have the nerve to say this evening.'

'Let's have coffee.'

'Let's have the truth.'

'Thursday evening, that's this week,' said Andrew.

'Do you really think that I can just knock up a hot supper for your Rotary friends at the drop of a hat?' said Susan.

'No, there's no need,' said Andrew.

'And why is that?' said Susan.

'Claire said that she'll—'

'Miss Smarty Pants, you always have to do what she says.'

'She's being really helpful…'

'Arranging a meeting in my house for this evening?' said Susan.

'Claire said that she'll bring something to heat up for supper when she gets here,' said Andrew.

'In my kitchen?' said Susan. 'Over my dead body. I will never allow that woman in my kitchen in any circumstances whatsoever. Is that clear?'

'What shall I tell her?'

'Don't tempt me.'

'I've got to do something.'

Susan said, 'I've got a block of cheddar in the back of the fridge that's got a bit of mould on it. I was going to throw it away, but I can make up some cheese sandwiches with stale bread and keep them in the fridge, so they'll be nice and cold.'

'Well…'

'It's what you deserve.'

'Probably.'

'Certainly.'

He knows I'll whip up a hot and tasty supper, thought Susan, *no matter what, but I'll let him squirm for a while, as a punishment.*

*

In the evening, with the punishment over, Andrew was ready to receive the members of club council. Claire was first to arrive. A few minutes later, George, Phillip, Mark and Ernie began to arrive. Paul and Frank arrived shortly after.

Andrew poured drinks for everyone and then said, 'Let's make a start. Apologies for absence?'

'There's an apology from Dominic, he's not feeling very well,' said Claire.

'Minutes of the last meeting, may I sign them as a correct record?'

'Agreed.'

'We know why we're here this evening,' said Andrew.

'We have to make a difficult decision,' said George.

'Yes, we do, but I don't want to go over all the arguments of last evening,' said Andrew.

'I suppose I should say something first,' said George. 'He was an old school friend of mine and I brought him into the club, so I feel a sense of responsibility for what's happened.'

'Yes,' said Claire, 'and it was in the face of considerable opposition.'

'Fiona didn't have much to say, which was surprising,' said Phillip.

Andrew said, 'The matter before us is this: did his action amount to a conflict of interest and was that conflict of interest sufficiently serious for us now to consider suspending him from the club?'

'I wouldn't be too sorry to see him leave,' said Claire, 'and in retrospect our decision to admit him to the club in the first place now appears to have been unwise. However, I shall try to remain objective.'

'In Government, civil servants have to follow a code of conduct,' said Ernie. 'So do ministers. They have their own. Civil servants generally do as they should, because they have a sense of responsibility.'

'Ministers do as they like, I suppose?' said Phillip.

Ernie said, 'If they're found out doing something, they shouldn't, like putting their hands in the till, so to speak, giving preferential treatment to a crony in conflict with their ministerial responsibilities or caught with their trousers down...'

'We get the picture, Ernie,' said Claire.

'Well, their friends and cronies brief against everyone else to throw up a thick smoke screen,' said Ernie. 'Obfuscation and robust denial usually work.'

'But not always?' said Mark.

'That depends on whether the prime minister has been waiting for the chance to get rid of the guilty minister,' said Ernie.

At that point, Susan came in with bowls of chicken curry and rice, with mango chutney and naan bread.

'Thank you, Susan, that smells heavenly,' said Claire.

Susan smiled and passed around the bowls.

'I've got plenty of beer if you prefer it, or white wine,' said Andrew.

There was a short interruption while they decided what to drink and settled down to eat. When they had finished Claire started to clear the bowls to take to the kitchen.

'Just leave them on the side, thank you, Claire,' said Andrew. 'I don't suppose Susan will want you to invade the kitchen when it's in a mess.'

Susan emerged. 'There's nothing wrong with the kitchen.' *But I don't want her in there.*

'I was talking to a chap on the shoot the other day,' said George. 'He's on the District Council. Do you know, every meeting, several councillors declare some interest or other in the business before the committee? It's usually something piffling and of no consequence, but no one wants to be accused of taking part in a debate when they have an interest in the matter, no matter how small. In fact, it's a criminal offence for a councillor not to declare an interest in a matter before the council or a committee.'

'So, Alec Barton could go to gaol?' said Mark.

'If we were a local authority, he would probably have committed a criminal offence,' said George. 'However, we're not, so there's no question of criminality here, but it gives us a useful yardstick against which to measure his behaviour.'

'There is no real doubt that we are considering a conflict of interest,' said Andrew, 'but what troubles me is that, in the event, he gained nothing from it.'

'Also, the maximum gain he could have made was only a few hundred pounds,' said Mark.

'The sad thing is that he believes that he's done nothing wrong,' said Claire, 'and in the world in which he operates, most people would say the same.'

'I'm beginning to lean towards a rap on the knuckles,' said Phillip.

'That's the wrong way to look at it,' said George. 'When in Rome…'

'Meaning what?' said Andrew.

'He's a Rotarian and he should act in accordance with Rotary ideals,' said George. 'We don't need to enquire too closely what he does when he's on a building site.'

'Do you really think that all Rotarians act in accordance with Rotary ideals?' said Phillip.

'I doubt it,' said George, 'but they should.'

'Well, there you are,' said Phillip. 'We've made it clear to him that what he did is not acceptable. Let's leave it there.'

George said, 'I would admit to being conservative in my views, but the plain fact is that there was a conflict of interest. The amount at stake is completely irrelevant. It's about principles, old-fashioned and stuffy though that might sound.'

'It's too easy to see the world in terms of moral absolutes,' said Phillip. 'We should consider the matter on its merits and accept that it was pretty trivial.'

'I'm not sure that I can agree that the amount is trivial,' said George. 'As a small club, we usually deal in hundreds of pounds not thousands, leaving aside Rotary International global grants and that sort of thing.'

'Suppose a man poaches a pheasant to feed his starving children,' said Phillip. 'Is his action automatically wrong, because we think of theft as wrong, or is there something else at play? The victim of the theft will hardly miss the pheasant because he has many more on his land, but the man who stole it has achieved a good outcome by feeding his family.'

'I don't accept that argument,' said George. 'In my view, theft is intrinsically wrong. There may be mitigating circumstances, but that doesn't alter the principle.'

'What would you do if you lived in the eighteen-hundreds, and your children were starving, and you were completely destitute?' said Phillip. 'I know what I would do. I would poach the pheasant.'

'What I would or would not do in those extreme circumstances, is not germane to the issue,' said George. 'Theft is intrinsically wrong and so is acting when you have a conflict of interest.'

'We can't sit here debating moral absolutism all evening,' said Andrew. 'We're going to have to make a decision. Do we all accept that there was a clear conflict of interest?'

'There's no doubt about that,' said Mark.

'There is a view that it was a trivial matter and that we should take no further action against Alec Barton,' said Andrew. 'I don't want to put this to a vote. It would be more satisfactory if we could reach a consensus that we're all comfortable with.'

'I'm unshakeable in my opinion that a conflict of interest is not a matter of degree,' said George, 'it's an absolute. Either it is a conflict of interest or it isn't, and in this case, it definitely is a conflict of interest.'

'I did push George on this, but, on balance, I am persuaded by his argument,' said Phillip.

'I agree,' said Claire.

'Mark, Ernie?'

'I agree,' said Mark.

'I agree,' said Ernie, 'but a government minister would just laugh at it.'

'We'll have to suspend him, but for how long?' said Andrew.

George had argued persuasively for swift and stern justice and other members had deferred to his view, to find against the accused. Now punishment must follow.

Defer, defer,
To the Lord High Executioner!
Defer, defer,
To the noble Lord, to the noble Lord,
To the Lord High Executioner!

'Execution,' said George and all eyes went to him. 'That is… execution of a suspension – sixty days.' The words and music were still running around in his head.

'That's two months,' said Phillip.

'It depends on whether we want him back,' said Claire.

'Shall we say sixty days?' said Andrew.

'You really don't want him back,' said Claire.

'Agreed.'

'We should write to him formally rather than do it by email,' said Andrew.

'I'll draft a letter for your signature, Andrew,' said the ever-efficient Claire.

The next morning, an email from Claire popped up on Andrew's computer. Attached to it was a draft letter to Alec Barton stating that club council had decided to suspend his membership for sixty days and setting out the reasons. Andrew printed it and went into the sitting room to read it carefully.

'Something interesting?' said Susan.

'It's a draft letter to Alec Barton about his suspension from the club. Claire has just emailed it…'

'Don't tell me that Miss Smarty Pants has made a hash of it.'

'I just think that I'd like to soften the tone a little.'

'Will you sign it as president?' said Susan.

'To tell you the truth, I feel slightly uncomfortable about it.'

'It's a bit late for that.'

'I'll put it aside and look at it again later,' said Andrew. 'Next week, I'll be going to Rotary on Monday.'

'Not Wednesday?'

'It's a scatter.'

'Where are you going?'

'Phillip and I are going to meet up with Jasper Hartley.'

'Wasn't he married to that horsey woman?' said Susan.

'He lives just outside Norwich now. We're going to meet halfway.'

'Where's everyone else going?'

'George and Frank are going to the Old Mill House, and Claire might go with them.'

'Where's that?'

'Near the old post mill at Saxstead Green,' said Andrew.

'Which club meets at the Old Mill House?'

'They do a jolly good carvery.'

Saturday morning's post would bring some disturbing news. Amongst the catalogues and holiday brochures was a small white envelope addressed in black ink in a tidy hand to A M Parker Esq. Andrew walked into the sitting room, took up the paperknife and carefully slit open the envelope. He pulled out a single sheet of crisp, white paper and unfolded it. 'It's from Dominic.'

'Dominic from Rotary?'

'He's resigned, forthwith.'

'His health?'

'Health reasons and the effects of his treatment,' said Andrew.

'Poor man.'

'I'll write to him.'

'You should.'

TWENTY-FOUR

Two down

It was a cold and wet Monday morning and there was a keen wind in the north.

'I wouldn't be surprised if that rain turns to sleet or snow,' said George. 'It's cold enough.'

'Are you sure you want to go out in this weather?' said Erica.

'It's my morning walk,' said George. 'What's different about this morning?'

The farmers had been harvesting sugar beet, and the mud on the road was inches thick. The stacked beet formed a giant Toblerone along the edge of the fields, awaiting delivery to the sugar beet factory. The factory in Bury St Edmunds turns the two million tonnes of beet local farmers produce into more than 300,000 tonnes of sugar every year. Now the rain was getting heavier and the wind was whipping it hard into George's face. The ditches had overflowed their banks onto the road to form large muddy puddles, which, in places, had joined together to cover the entire road surface. George took a footpath into a field. The ground was waterlogged and did its upmost to suck the boots from his feet and the strength from his legs. Still, the rain lashed into his face, reached up his sleeves and down his collar, but George leaned into the wind and pressed on relentlessly. Nothing would deter him from completing his morning walk. Eventually, he began to make for the warmth of home, with the wind and the rain at his back.

'It must be time for coffee,' said George, as soon as he got through the door of the house.

'It won't be long,' said Erica.

'The sugar beet harvest is in full swing.'

'You managed to drag home the evidence.'

'What do you mean?'

'You're treading mud everywhere.'

George said, 'Ollie couldn't believe how British Sugar is the only producer and that they set the price, tell farmers when they can accept the beet and pretty much control everything. Ollie likened it to a command economy.'

The post dropped onto the mat by the front door and the flap of the letterbox fell back into place.

'Anything interesting in the post?'

'No.'

That Monday was a long and tedious day. In the evening, George and Erica settled to watch some television. At ten o'clock they watched the *BBC News* followed by *Look*

East. Just before the end of the programme, the presenter said, 'We can bring you some breaking news that has just come in. There is a report of a serious accident on the A140, involving an articulated lorry and several cars. The emergency services are at the scene and the fire brigade have brought in heavy lifting gear. The road is blocked in both directions and motorists are advised to avoid the area. We understand that there is at least one fatality, but we have no further details.'

'How awful so close to Christmas,' said Erica.

'Looks as though Andrew and Phillip are going to have a late night.'

'What time would they have left?'

'It's dreadful conditions for driving.'

'They might have got through before it happened.'

The wind blew the rain hard against the windows and howled down the chimneys. It rattled garden furniture and triggered security lights on and off. It blew over flowerpots and hurled them across the patio, scraping and banging against hard surfaces. Sleep would not come easily this night. Eventually, through exhaustion, they slept.

The phone rang. George was in a deep slumber that he struggled to shake off. Erica, immediately alert, answered.

'Hello, yes… who is it? I can't hear you.' Erica was listening hard, the concentration etched into her face.

'What's going on?' said George.

'Shush. Is there anything we can do?'

It must be serious. Women always say that in a crisis.

'Good night… yes and you too… yes… yes. Take care.'

'Who was it?'

'George, the accident we heard about just before bedtime...'

'Not Andrew and Phillip?'

'That was Susan's sister...'

'What's happened?'

'She sounded terribly upset and wasn't making much sense,' said Erica.

'What did she say?'

'She's with Susan.'

'At the hospital?'

'Several people have been taken to hospital, three are serious,' said Erica.

'And Andrew and Phillip?'

'Serious.'

*

'George, I need your advice.'

It was Tuesday morning and Claire was on the phone.

'Is there any more information?' said George.

'I can't reach Susan or her sister,' said Claire. 'All calls go to voicemail, but I got through to the hospital.'

'And?'

'It's bad news, George,' said Claire. 'They lost Phillip early this morning. Andrew is in a critical condition.'

'But stable?'

'Yes, I think so.'

'We should tell members the dreadful news,' said George.

'I've drafted an email. That's what I wanted to talk to you about.'

'I don't think they'll want to go on a scatter,' said George.

'Shall I cancel the scatter and arrange to meet tomorrow, Wednesday, as usual?' said Claire.

'Yes, I think we should do that.'

'I won't tell everyone.'

'What do you mean?' said George.

'Alec Barton.'

'No, of course not,' said George, 'he's suspended.'

'There's another matter,' said Claire. 'I've prepared a letter for Andrew's signature.'

'Can't you sign it as club secretary?' said George.

'No. I'll bring it tomorrow.'

'Who was on the phone?' said Erica.

'They lost Phillip early this morning.'

'Oh no. And Andrew?'

'Critical.'

*

By the time Claire's email hit their computer screens, most members had made the connection between the crash on the A140 and their president and president-elect. All thoughts of a jolly jaunt to another club that week were forgotten. It was a sad and chastened group of Rotarians who arrived in ones and twos at the White Horse the next evening. They bought their drinks and exchanged what information they had on the tragic events of Monday evening.

George arrived and Claire greeted him. 'This is dreadful, George. I just don't know what to say.'

'Chin up. It's all you can do at the moment,' said George.
'You'll chair the meeting this evening, of course.'

'Yes, I suppose so.'

'You are president-nominee.'

'I'm still not sure about all that,' said George.

'It's written in the stars.'

'And in the minutes, so it seems.'

'You can question the stars...' said Claire.

'But, evidently, not the minutes?' said George.

'You've said it yourself on many an occasion,' said Claire. 'Once the minutes of a meeting have been signed, there's not a court in the land that will overturn them.'

George did not care to hear his own sage advice used against him.

Bill said, 'We're ready for you, if you'd like to go through, Claire.'

They went through to their meeting room and Bill began serving dinner: gammon and pineapple, with chips. Claire sat next to George and passed him the letter addressed to Alec Barton for his signature. 'This is the letter we spoke about.'

George read it slowly. 'It's a bit strong for you, Claire.'

'I've already toned it down at Andrew's request.'

'It's the sort of direct unambiguous language that I would have used,' said George.

'It's the suspension of his membership of this club for sixty days. You can't avoid putting that bit in.'

'Quite right,' said George, as he signed the letter and initialled a copy for Claire's records. He passed back all the copies.

'I'll drop this through his letterbox this evening,' said Claire.

'Is that wise?'

'I'll leave the engine running.'

George said, 'Claire tells me that I've got to chair the meeting, as I am president-nominee.'

'Hear, hear,' said Kye.

'I thought in the circumstances that, as immediate past president, I might have been called upon,' said Frank, 'but I'm happy that George should go ahead.'

They ate silently. When they had finished Bill cleared away.

'We'll have a short break and then we'll start our meeting.'

There was a scraping of chairs on the old wooden floor of the White Horse, which resonated around the room in the silence. Members moved to the bar without the usual buzz of conversation.

'May I get you another drink, George?' said Frank.

'Half of Ghost Ship, Frank.'

Members soon returned to their seats, ready for the meeting and dreading what was to come.

George addressed the meeting. 'As you know, we should all be going on a scatter this week, but in the very difficult circumstances in which we find ourselves, I thought that we should stay here, on our home turf instead, to try to make some sense of what's happening. We have no speaker and there is no business to deal with. In other circumstances I would call this a fellowship evening, but I'm not sure that's quite right this evening.'

'I think it's perfectly proper to stay here this evening,' said Frank. 'Have you got any further information?'

George said, 'Claire has been acting as a point of contact for the club and I shall ask her to update us in a moment, but first, I have some other bad news, although not of the same magnitude. Dominic has formally submitted his resignation from the club.'

'Is it the prostate problem?' said Fiona.

'He cites that and the treatment,' said George. 'He just doesn't feel up to it at the moment.'

'We should send him our best wishes,' said Paul.

'I believe that Andrew has written to him on behalf of the club,' said George. 'I'll hand over to Claire now to bring us up to date.'

Claire said, 'As I mentioned in my email, Phillip passed away in the early hours of this morning. I did speak briefly to a relative. Mary is distraught, as you might imagine.'

'What about Andrew?' said Fiona.

'I did eventually make contact with Susan's sister. Andrew was having surgery today. The prospects for a full recovery were reasonably good, but I'm still waiting to hear further.'

'All this has left us in a parlous state, as a club,' said Ernie. 'Andrew isn't likely to be back for some time, and Phillip...' His voice trailed away. 'We need to have an acting president from now to the end of the Rotary year or until Andrew is back.'

'I have never set my sight on becoming president for a second time,' said George. 'I've done it once and I'm content to leave it to others, but we are in difficult times.'

'As the immediate past president, I'm prepared to make myself available, if called into service,' said Frank.

'We have two candidates to take on the role of president for a temporary period, and I would be happy with either,' said Mark.

'We have one candidate who is on the way up, and one who is on the way down, and the one who is on the way up, has already been up and down,' said Kye.

'Thank you for that stunning analysis, Kye,' said Paul.

'And the one who is on the way down wants it, and the one on the way up and who has already—'

'That's not very helpful, Kye,' said Claire. Kye's attempt at humour did nothing to lift members' spirits.

'I think we should have a vote,' said Claire. 'If you give me a minute, I'll tear up some sheets of paper into pieces to serve as ballot papers.'

'Perhaps Fiona can help, she's good at tearing up paper in the middle of a meeting,' said Kye, 'except she tears very slowly.'

'Why don't you just shut up, Kye,' said Frank.

'You're always playing the clown,' said Fiona.

'At least I won't be eaten by the circus lions.'

Fiona said, 'I really shouldn't ask, but why is that, Kye? Why won't you be eaten by the circus lions?'

'Clowns taste funny.'

When Claire had finished tearing the paper into ballot paper-size pieces, she began to pass them around. 'I don't think George should preside over the vote, as he is one of the candidates. May I suggest that Mark and I, as club officers, take charge?'

'Agreed.'

'Have we got the power to take this action this evening?' said Roger. 'It's not a business meeting.'

'Yes, the club can act at any meeting,' said Claire. 'Besides, everyone who should be here is here.'

'Claire, the last time we had an election you were in a terrible hurry,' said Kye.

'You have before you a blank piece of paper,' said Claire, ignoring Kye's observation. 'Please print either George or Frank on the paper, fold it in half and hand it to me. I shall count the votes with Mark.'

Claire collected up the papers and put them on the table in front of Mark. Together they opened up the papers and put them in two piles; one for George and one for Frank. As members watched, they could see that one pile was rising faster than the other.

They counted each pile and when they were satisfied, Mark said, 'There are six votes for Frank and eleven for George. I declare that George is elected acting president until Andrew returns or the end of the Rotary year, whichever is the sooner.'

'Congratulations, George,' said Claire and others added their own congratulations.

'I must say that I had no aspiration to be president again,' said George, 'and in a larger club, I never would.'

Kye said, 'Perhaps I might remind Acting President George, that some are born great, some achieve greatness, and some have greatness thrust upon them.'

'It was a comedy, I believe, Mr President,' said Fiona.

Claire's mobile phone rang. She answered immediately

and walked to the door. 'Hello, yes…' She disappeared.

'This could be news of Andrew,' said Paul.

'Mr Acting President, you could be the shortest serving acting president ever,' said Kye.

A few minutes later, Claire entered the room, shut the door and leant back against it, her face ashen. The conversations stopped and all eyes were on her. She blurted out, 'Andrew is dead.'

TWENTY-FIVE

In the country everyone has a shotgun

'You're back early,' said Erica.

'Yes, I am,' said George.

'Has something happened?'

'Andrew died this evening.'

'Oh no, poor Susan.' Tears began to form in Erica's eyes, and she tried to blink them away.

'We still don't have a clear idea of what happened on Monday evening,' said George.

'It hardly matters now.'

'I really didn't want to be acting president.'

Erica said, 'I'm not sure whether I should try to ring Susan.'

George poured a generous measure of Talisker.

'Will you pour me a small one, please,' said Erica.

They sat quietly for a few minutes absorbing the enormity of what had occurred. George said, 'Do you know that rural roads are supposedly more dangerous than urban roads?'

'Why's that?'

'Narrow lanes, dips, blind bends, rabbits, deer and other distractions,' said George.

'That hardly seems relevant. It happened on the A140, which is pretty straight, and the speed limit is fifty.'

'It's more likely that the dreadful weather was a major factor,' said George. 'We just don't know.'

Meanwhile, Alec Barton picked up the envelope that had dropped onto his doormat. He opened the front door and looked out. The rain lashed against the windows out of a coal-black sky, driven by an unforgiving and relentless wind. As he peered out, he saw the rear lights of a small car disappear into the blackness. He pushed the door shut against the full force of the swirling wind and ripped open the envelope. He took out the letter inside and read. He blinked to focus his eyes on the paper in his hand. He had been drinking heavily.

He read aloud: 'Dear Mr Barton… conflict of interest… standards of behaviour… careful consideration… suspended for sixty days… yours sincerely George *bloody* Woodgate.' He screwed the letter into a ball and threw it into the general direction of the fire. 'The duplicitous, double dealing, deceitful, fucking bastard.'

Karen flinched. She was always on edge when he had been drinking. He was already angry about the Upton village hall. 'Try not to upset yourself, Alec. It won't help.'

'Upset? I'm bloody furious with Haker and Woodgate. I really need the money Haker owes me and now Woodgate's trying to destroy my reputation. I've had enough.' He put on his coat and gathered up his keys. He unlocked the gun cabinet. He took out his shotgun and picked up a box of cartridges. He grabbed a handful, loaded his shotgun, and stuffed the rest of them into his pockets.

'Please don't go out, Alec.' Karen flattened herself against the door, her arms outstretched. 'Alec, please, please, don't go.'

'Get out of the way.'

She felt desperate and looked at him imploringly. 'You'll only make things worse.'

'Get out of the fucking way, will you?' He raised his shotgun and smashed the stock into her face with all his might. There was a sickening crunch. She crumpled into a lifeless heap of bloody tissue and splintered bone, and he was gone; out into the dark of the night.

He drove erratically and at speed along a narrow lane towards Upton to a fateful encounter with Mike Haker. Headlights appeared. He braked hard and slithered almost to a stop as he bumped up onto the bank. There was a bang and a scraping of metal as he passed the oncoming vehicle. His side mirror disappeared and he accelerated into the inky blackness. Then there were street lights and a street sign announced Upton. He slowed. His passion and wild fury had contracted into a controlled madness. He knew that Mike Haker lived on an estate on the edge of the village. He drove slowly looking for Harper Avenue. He had driven past. He braked hard, crunched the gearbox into reverse, and pulled on the steering wheel to make the turn. He could not remember the house number, but he would recognise the house. It stood on a corner plot.

*

On the outskirts of Debenham, not five miles distant, George and Erica sipped their whisky in silence. Erica had turned on the television to provide a distraction. They sat and stared at the screen showing an old Cary Grant film, but neither paid attention. Outside the rain was still beating down. Humphrey raised his head and got up from his comfortable position in front of the fire. Something had alerted him.

'Look, headlights. It's a bit late for visitors,' said George.

'Who on earth could it be at this time?'

George went to the door. Humphrey was already there. He thought of the letter to Alec Barton, under his signature. He opened the door warily, just enough to peer out. He could feel his heart thumping as the car came to a halt. The driver switched off the headlights and all was in darkness. The car door slammed shut and heavy footsteps crunched on the gravel. George turned off the light in the hall, as a figure approached the house. He stared hard through the rain and he could just make out a shadow-like figure. Thoughts of Alec Barton drawing a bead on him, flashed through his mind. He slammed the front door shut.

'George, what's happening?' said Erica.

'Turn off all the lights,' said George.

Erica, panicked by the urgency in George's voice, did as she was told. The figure outside came closer, triggering the security lights by the front door. The doorbell rang.

*

Back in the White Horse, Bill was calling time. It had been a long and difficult evening and he had felt the drama as keenly as the members of the Rotary Club of Debenham. He remembered some words that Andrew had used. *To lose one Rotarian may be regarded as a misfortune; to lose two looks like carelessness.* The words had stuck with him, except it wasn't Rotarian, but something else. He couldn't remember what.

'There won't be anyone left at this rate,' said Marlene.

Bill said, 'It's a bad business and no mistaking it.'

'Poor Phillip and Andrew and their wives and families.'

'Poor old Dominic, too.'

'I really wonder if the club will fold,' said Marlene.

'They've been going for years,' said Bill, 'and they've been part of our lives since we've been here.'

'We've seen some good Christmas dinners and other Rotary celebrations over the years,' said Marlene, 'with just about enough sober Rotary wives to get them all home. What would men do without their wives?'

Bill said, 'Do you remember that story that Kye told one Christmas dinner, about the time he went into Ipswich Hospital for something or other and they kept moving him from ward to ward?'

Marlene said, 'Yes, he ended up in a ward with a side room just off it. And the patient in the side room was in police custody. There were a couple of policemen with him day and night, working a rota.'

'The way Kye tells it is that they were doing a crossword late one evening to pass the time and they got stuck on the clue about who lives at 1600 Pennsylvania Avenue,' said Bill.

Marlene picked up the story, 'And Kye was trying to get to sleep, so he put on his best American accent and said in a loud voice, "My president." And it all went very quiet.'

Bill said, 'The funniest part was in the morning when he woke up. He opened his eyes and saw this very attractive policewoman standing at the end of his bed. He said that he thought that Rotary had sent him a strippagram to cheer him up.'

'Fiona really went for him when he told that story,' said Marlene. 'I didn't dare say that I've done strippagrams for friends, in the past.'

'You were always the thespian,' said Bill.

'And the French tart.'

They laughed and then a silence fell upon them, as the events of the evening flooded back. Marlene said, 'They won't give up, will they?'

'No, of course not. They're Rotarians.'

*

The doorbell rang. Not the long aggressive ring of an angry Alec Barton, which George was dreading, but a short feminine ring. George opened the door.

'Good evening, sir. Mr Woodgate, is it?'

'You'd better come in.'

'Who is it?' said Erica from the sitting room.

'It's the police.'

'They had better come in.'

'Just one.'

The small figure of PC Jodie May crossed the threshold and stood dripping on the door mat. She removed her cap to reveal a head of closely cropped flaxen hair. 'Sir.' She saw Erica approaching. 'And madam. We've had reports of a firearms incident in Upton.'

'Upton?' said Erica. 'How does that affect us?'

'We believe the suspect is known to you, sir.'

'Who is it?' said George.

'Are you a member of the Rotary Club of Debenham, sir?'

'Yes, he's acting president, actually,' said Erica.

'Is that correct, sir?'

'Yes.'

'Do you know a man called Alec Barton?' said Jodie.

'The letter,' said George.

'What letter?' said Jodie.

'The club suspended him for sixty days, and I signed the letter as acting president,' said George.

'Do Rotarians usually resort to firearms when suspended, sir?'

'No, of course not,' said George, 'but why Upton?'

'Has anyone been hurt?' said Erica.

'No,' said Jodie, who was not going to impart any more information than necessary.

'What, he missed the target?' said George.

'The house was empty at the time,' said Jodie.

'You think he might come here?' said George.

'What do you think, sir?'

'Where is he now?' said Erica.

'No arrests have been made, madam.'

'So, Alec Barton is on the rampage with a shotgun,' said George.

'I never mentioned a shotgun, sir.'

'What if he does come here?' said Erica.

'I'll arrest him.'

What, all five feet one and seven stone of you? thought Erica.

'He's a strongly built man,' said George.

'He'll come quietly when I've got the cuffs on him, sir.'

'Oh, good,' said Erica.

Jodie's police radio came to life. 'Yes, Sergeant, I'm here now… what, now? I'm on my way.'

'Well, it's all quiet here, sir, and I've been called away. If there's a problem, just ring 999.'

The front door shut and George and Erica stood looking at each other. 'So, let me get this right,' said Erica, 'if an angry and tooled up Alec Barton kicks the door in tonight, we call 999?'

'I don't think we can go to bed with that in prospect,' said George, as he eyed his gun cabinet.

*

'He's suffered a dreadful shock and he's been badly injured by flying glass and other debris,' said Doctor Alice

Newsom, who was halfway through her shift in charge of Accident and Emergency this evening. 'He's also lost quite a lot of blood and we had to reattach his left ear.'

'But he is going to be all right?' said Erica. 'Isn't he?'

'He won't be able to hear you for some time.'

'All that blood…'

'His injuries aren't life threatening,' said Dr Newsom, 'and I would expect him to make a full recovery in time.'

'He never hears me at the best of times,' said Erica.

'We'll keep him in hospital for now, just to make sure.'

'I don't really know what happened,' said Erica. 'There was a man with a shotgun. All of a sudden there was this massive explosion, which blew in the sitting room window. The police asked me a lot of questions, but I couldn't focus properly on what they were saying.'

'The police said a shotgun had been discharged, but we couldn't find any gunshot pellets when we examined Mr Woodgate,' said Doctor Newsom.

'I hope they've got him by now.'

'He's had a very lucky escape.'

*

Erica and George's brother, Arthur, collected George from hospital a few days later and they went to Arthur's home in Felixstowe. Arrangements were already in progress for George and Erica to go to Perth, Australia, to stay with their son, Nigel, and his family. Two weeks after the events of that fateful night, they were on the plane.

TWENTY-SIX

Christmas and the New Year bring little cheer

Without a leader, the Rotary Club of Debenham was struggling. They met on the next Wednesday for a subdued Rotary Christmas Dinner, with their wives and husbands.

'I really missed doing the Father Christmas visit around Debenham and the other villages,' said Fiona.

'I painted the sleigh earlier this year,' said Roger, who kept the sleigh in a barn on his farm. 'And I've also got a new sound system for the Christmas carols.'

'The excitement and the looks of sheer joy on the faces of the very small children was so heart-warming,' said Claire. 'And people are so generous with our collection. Local children's charities are going to lose out on their usual donation this year.'

'And I was so disappointed not being Father Christmas again this year,' said Kye, with sadness in his eyes.

'I must admit that Kye is a good Father Christmas,' said Fiona. 'He's funny, completely uninhibited and he's very good at engaging with small children.'

'The parents are so pleased to see the looks of sheer delight on the faces of the children,' said Frances. 'That's why they're always so generous with donations.'

*

There was the customary two-week break over the holiday period before members met again on the Wednesday after New Year. Bill had made steak and ale pie, which he served with mashed potato, Brussel sprouts and carrots. He knew that it was a favourite with many of the members.

'I think we should ask Frank to be acting president until George gets back,' said Claire.

There was a chorus of, 'Agreed,' and no dissenting voices.

Frank took up the empty president's chair and looked around the room to make eye contact with members. He spoke slowly, with exaggerated solemnity. 'I've spoken privately to Paul, Mark, Claire, and one or two other members about the future of this club and whether indeed it has a future. Although it pains me to say so, they were all very downbeat.'

'Mr President,' said Paul, 'we are at a very low ebb. Our membership has been decimated, our leadership team has gone and we don't know if, or when, George will return. I feel an air of despondency hanging over us all.'

'Things have changed,' said Fiona. 'I could easily have stayed at home and watched television this evening. I've never felt like that before.'

'I come to Rotary for the fellowship and the good time we have, or did have,' said Roger. 'We don't bring each other much joy at the moment.'

'It's the middle of winter and going out in the evening on narrow country roads in snow and ice and treacherous driving conditions…' said Frank.

'Or rain or fog, in the pitch black, it's not a pleasure,' said Jeremy.

Frank said, 'How do we go about it if we do decide to close the club, Claire?'

'The correct term is the dissolution of the club…'

'As in the dissolution of the monasteries?' said Kye.

Claire continued, 'We give the charity monies to the charities we support, and the proceeds of club assets are shared amongst the members.'

'Not the Crown?' said Kye.

Claire said, 'We have to convene an extraordinary general meeting to pass a resolution to dissolve the club. It requires just a simple majority.'

'Need everyone be there?' said Frank.

'It's a simple majority of those who are present and entitled to vote,' said Claire.

'Who wouldn't be entitled to vote?' said Frank.

'An honorary member wouldn't be able to vote, or a member who has been suspended,' said Claire.

'They can't vote on anything anyway,' said Paul.

'Not less than twenty-eight days after the extraordinary

general meeting, we would have to hold a second extraordinary general meeting to confirm the resolution,' said Claire.

'By a simple majority of those present?' said Frank.

'No,' said Claire. 'This time, there must be a two-thirds majority of those present and at least half of the membership must attend the meeting.'

'What if it's one less?' said Kye.

'In that case, the resolution from the previous meeting could not be confirmed and it would fall,' said Claire.

Frank said, 'I am getting the impression that most members would wish to start the process of dissolving the club.'

'It looks as though the process is designed to give plenty of thinking time,' said Paul, 'so that no club should dissolve itself in a moment of pique.'

'Regardless of what the club does, I am going to resign forthwith,' said Mark. 'I've just had enough and I don't want to sit through the slow death that we have to go through to dissolve the club, spread out over a month or more.'

'We've reached a natural end,' said Fiona.

'If we carry on, we'll need another treasurer,' said Kye. 'That could be a problem.'

'Let's have an extraordinary general meeting next week,' said Fiona.

'Agreed.'

TWENTY-SEVEN

The end

The following Wednesday, members gathered again in the bar of the White Horse, each clutching a single sheet of paper; the agenda for the extraordinary general meeting, with a resolution in formal language for the club to pass. They drank in near silence and then trooped in to dinner. Bill was serving roast beef and Yorkshire pudding, to raise spirits and stiffen backbones. He was about to lose good customers and friends. Some, who lived in villages some distance away, he might not see again.

After dinner, Frank said, 'I don't think this is going to take long, so unless anyone particularly wants to take our customary break, I intend to crack on with the formal business.'

The consensus was to carry on. Frank said, 'You all

have the agenda, and you know what we have to do. Who would like to open the batting?'

'Let's just do it, Frank,' said Fiona.

Frank said, 'If no one wishes to say anything, perhaps someone would care to move the words on this piece of paper.'

'I so move, Mr President,' said Fiona.

'I'll second it, Mr President,' said Paul.

'All in favour, please raise your hands,' said Frank.

All hands went up. 'That's carried unanimously,' said Frank. 'We'll meet again in four weeks' time to confirm the resolution. We'll now go straight to the final toast.' Members stood slowly. 'Rotary and peace the world over.'

'Rotary and peace the world over.'

'Except in Debenham,' said Kye. 'That's the shortest meeting ever.'

The members now had four weeks to reflect on the wisdom of their decision. It was not yet written in stone but needed only confirmation at the second extraordinary general meeting. Dominic's resignation, because of his prostate cancer, was a blow, but not entirely unexpected. Now Mark had resigned. He had had enough, and he had no desire to bear witness to the drawn-out, bureaucratic and excruciating demise of the club, his club, and probably the end of his career as a Rotarian. George had gone to Australia and Andrew and Phillip had gone for ever.

Four weeks later, the twenty-eight days required by the by-laws, members gathered in the White Horse. It was the most forlorn and chastened meeting of Rotarians imaginable. Bill served dinner; no one would remember what they ate that evening.

'We'll make a start,' said Frank for the last time. 'There are no apologies for absence, except George who's recuperating.'

'Mark's not here,' said Kye.

'He's resigned,' said Claire.

'Do you agree the minutes of the extraordinary general meeting?' said Frank.

'Agreed.'

'The next item is to consider and confirm the resolution to dissolve the club passed at the last meeting,' said Frank. 'Does anyone wish to say anything, before we go to a formal vote?'

'Haven't we already done that by agreeing the minutes?' said Frances.

'No,' said Claire. 'The vote we have just taken was to confirm the accuracy of the minutes of the last meeting. What we need to do now is to confirm the resolution we passed at the meeting, to meet the requirements of the by-laws.'

'I'm not sure I understand that, but I'll let it pass,' said Frances.

There was silence for a moment, then Frank said, 'Would anyone care to move that we confirm the resolution of the last meeting?' No one responded. 'Anyone?'

'If we don't confirm the resolution, it falls,' said Claire.

'Actually, I'm having second thoughts,' said Fiona. 'The past four weeks have been the longest I have ever been without attending a meeting, since I first joined this club and that's a long time ago. And I missed it. I have to admit to missing Kye and his stupid quips, witticisms and one-liners, even though they sometimes made me cross.'

'That's a beautiful thing to say, Fiona,' said Kye. 'Which jokes didn't you like?'

'I'm having second thoughts too,' said Paul.

'I'm not,' said Peter, 'and I move we confirm the resolution from the last meeting.'

'I'll second it,' said Roger.

'Does anyone wish to say anything else?' said Frank. There was silence. 'In that case, all those in favour, please raise your hands.'

There were fifteen members present and entitled to vote and a two-thirds majority was required. Hands raised slowly, some members looking around to see what others were doing, before committing themselves.

Frank began to count. 'That's nine in favour. Those against, please raise your hands.' Hands went up and Frank counted. 'I can see five hands.'

'That's five votes, Frank,' said Fiona, 'just declare the result.'

'Are you abstaining, Frances?'

'I tried to vote for the resolution, but Fiona was holding my arm.'

Frank said, 'Is that true, Fiona? This is a serious matter and we must have the vote recorded correctly. I'm going to take the vote again, because I'm not satisfied.'

'On a point of order, Mr Acting President, you have a result and you must declare it now,' said Fiona.

'I'm not satisfied and I'm taking the vote again,' said Frank. 'All in favour of the motion. That means everyone who wishes to dissolve the club.'

Again, the hands went up and Frank counted nine hands. He looked at Fiona and Frances, who seemed to be arm wrestling. 'Fiona, please.' The distraction enabled Frances to wrench her arm free and she raised it. 'That's ten hands,' said Frank. 'And against.' Five hands went up.

'That's ten votes for the motion and five against. I declare the motion carried by the special two-thirds majority required under the by-laws,' said Frank.

Members looked at one another, as if to ask: what have we done?

'We'll now have the final, final toast,' said Frank. 'Rotary and peace the world over.'

There was an incoherent response, then a stunned silence. Were these really the final words ever to be uttered by the members of the Rotary Club of Debenham, as it dissolved into oblivion?

TWENTY-EIGHT

The renaissance

In Perth, George was making a rapid recovery; his wounds had healed, his hearing was returning and his sanity restored. The sun was a golden blaze in an azure sky, and George's naturally pale complexion was a lobster pink, as he relaxed under a large canopy, with a glass of beer. Nigel, in contrast, was tanned and fit. He was cooking lunch on the barbecue and Erica and Olivia, Nigel's wife, were playing with the grandsons, Leo and Charlie, aged four and six. George realised that they were Australians now. He felt a tinge of sadness, as he watched the boys running and laughing, and jumping in and out of the paddling pool. It was now more than two years since they had emigrated and this was the first time that he and Erica had seen them since then. George drained his glass and settled back in his garden chair.

'Let me get you another beer, Dad,' said Nigel.

'I'll get it,' said Olivia, 'while you serve the barbecue.'

'I'm beginning to get a taste for this Australian beer, under an Australian sun,' said George. 'Mind you, I couldn't imagine drinking beer this cold in an English winter. It has to be Ghost Ship at home.'

After lunch, George said, 'Do you mind if I try to get my emails, Nigel? I just want to see what's happening at the club.'

'Yes, of course, Dad, if you feel up to it. Just put in your email address and you should get straight into your emails.'

George started trawling through his emails, clothing catalogues, from every online retailer he had ever used and many more. As he deleted the dross, up popped one headed "Extraordinary General Meeting", and there were others with the same title. He started reading and was shocked by what he saw on the monitor in front of him. He focussed his attention on the last communication, to which was attached the minutes of the second meeting about the dissolution of the club. He read: *Resolved... majority of two-thirds... as required... By-Law 12... the resolution to dissolve the club... be confirmed... the Rotary Club of Debenham be dissolved... from the date of the surrender of the club's charter.*

'Good Lord,' said George, 'they're dissolving the club.'

'What is it, Dad?'

'We'll see about that. We're going home, Nigel.'

'Well hold on, Dad,' said Nigel. 'I need to check with Uncle Arthur that the work on the house has been completed and he'll probably need to ring your neighbour, Ollie. We'll have to book your flights…'

'What on earth's going on?' said Erica.

A few days later, with the arrangements made and all impediments removed, George and Erica were homeward bound.

*

After touching down at Heathrow and going through the usual procedures, their driver was waiting with a board which said "George Woodgate". Their journey around the M25 and beyond seemed interminable. It was dark and cold after the sunshine to which they had become accustomed, and George was feeling very anxious. 'How much longer?' he shouted to the driver, like a small child.

'We won't be long now,' came the reply. 'We're just about to leave the A14 and turn up the A140 Norwich Road.'

The mention of the A140 did little to relieve George's anxiety. As soon as they arrived home and the cases were in the hall, George picked up the phone. There was no answer, so he left a message and waited impatiently. 'She must be home by now,' said George.

'Claire's unlikely to ring at ten o'clock at night,' said Erica, the voice of reason, as ever.

At nine o'clock the next morning, not a minute before, nor a minute later, the phone rang. 'Hello, Claire.'

'How did you know it was me, George?'

'Who else could it be? Everyone else thinks I'm in Australia.'

'Are you fully recovered, George?' said Claire.

'Yes, I'm fine,' said George. 'Now these two extraordinary general meetings...'

'And how's Erica?' said Claire. 'It must have been a difficult time for her too.'

'She's very well,' said George. 'Now these resolutions...'

'When did you both get home?' said Claire. 'No one was expecting you.'

'Claire, will you just listen to me?'

'What is it, George?'

'Claire, I want you to call a meeting.'

'A meeting, what sort of a meeting?' said Claire.

'A meeting of the club, what else?'

Claire said, 'It's all over, George. There won't be any more meetings, ever. Dissolved means dissolved; it's final, it really is the end. The Rotary Club of Debenham no longer exists and there are no members to call to a meeting.'

'Not quite. They may think it's all over, but it's not yet,' said George.

'What do you mean?'

'You haven't surrendered our charter yet, have you?' said George.

'I've got a letter addressed to the district governor and the club's charter in a large envelope that I'm going to hand to the postman when he gets here,' said Claire.

'What time?'

'He'll be here any minute... that's him now, I've really got to go, George.'

'No, don't do that. Wait, just wait and listen to me.'

'I'm going to miss him. I've really got to go,' said Claire.

'Claire, just listen to me, will you? Claire, Claire…'

Erica, who had heard George's raised voice, came into the room to see what was happening. She took the phone from George. 'Hello, is that Claire? I'm so sorry that George was shouting…'

'I've got to go, Erica. I've got to catch the postman.' The phone went dead.

'That's odd,' said Erica, 'she rang off, something about the postman.'

George grabbed the phone and rang Claire's number. He listened impatiently, as the phone rang for an eternity and then he was directed to voicemail. He threw it down. 'That really is it, then. It really is all over. I've been shot at, blown up, exiled to the colonies like a criminal. I've raced halfway across the world like Phileas Fogg to save the club and I'm two minutes too late. I just can't believe it.' He felt utterly dejected and now his head was beginning to throb, louder and louder, and his anxiety increased, until he could no longer bear it.

The phone rang and Erica answered. 'Hello, Claire… not at all… It's Claire for you.'

Claire said, 'George, are you sure you're feeling all right? You sounded rather strange when we spoke a few minutes ago. What do you want?'

'The envelope with our charter,' said George. 'I suppose you've just given it to the postman.'

'You made me miss the postman, George. I promised to post it today.' It was Claire's first failure as a Rotarian.

'That's good news,' said George, as a sudden rush of adrenalin lifted his spirits and his headache and anxiety melted away.

'Why?' said Claire.

'The surrender of our charter is the final step in the dissolution of the club, isn't it?'

'Well, yes, technically, but everyone knows what we're doing, including the district governor.'

'I don't give a damn about the district governor,' said George, in a statement little short of treason.

Claire said, 'I have to send the charter to the district governor. He sends it to RIBI and RIBI sends it to Rotary International in America.'

'Dare I ask what Rotary International in America do?' said George.

'They terminate us.'

'What?'

'The Americans can be dramatic,' said Claire.

'But we haven't been terminated yet?' said George.

'No.'

'We've got to move fast. Call a meeting for Wednesday.'

'I'm not sure about that,' said Claire.

'And tell Bill we want roast beef and Yorkshire pudding,' said George.

'Is that important?'

'Imperative.'

'What shall I say?' said Claire.

'Just this: "I see you stand like greyhounds in the slips,
Straining upon the start. The game's afoot:
Follow your spirit, and upon this charge
Cry 'God for Harry, England, and Saint George!'"'

'Gosh!' said Claire.

'Tell 'em George is back!'

This book is printed on paper from sustainable sources managed under the Forest Stewardship Council (FSC) scheme.

It has been printed in the UK to reduce transportation miles and their impact upon the environment.

For every new title that Matador publishes, we plant a tree to offset CO_2, partnering with the More Trees scheme.

For more about how Matador offsets its environmental impact, see www.troubador.co.uk/about/